# The Ragged

# Edge

## *The Battle Fought Within*

A Novel Based on a True Story

*T. C. Thomas*

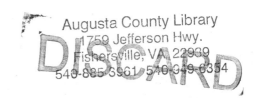

1133



Library of Congress Control Number 2006940587
ISBN No. 978- 0-9760923-3-9 Softcover

Second Revision Third Printing 2009



This is a work of fiction. Names, characters, places and incidents either are the product of the author's imagination or are used fictitiously, and any resemblance to any actual persons, living or dead, events, or locales is entirely coincidental. Though fiction, events are based on a true story.

Published in the United States by Thomas Publishing Company

**What readers are saying about this book.**

"The character, Cary, was awesome! I was *so* into the story, and what a beautiful ending. I started reading the book on Saturday morning, couldn't put it down, and finished it on Sunday."-----Sharon Hargrave

*"I couldn't put it down!* Finished it in two days. I wished there was more, didn't want it to end....waiting for his next book."------Della Harrison

"Watching Cary making decisions from a broken marriage kept me going from an adventure to a *new* future."-----M. J. Roeder

"The story goes from one exceptional experience to another with breathless speed. I was reluctant to finish reading the book because the stories are so well crafted it was hard to *"put a stop"* to it."-----Jerrell Sober

"I started it on Friday and finished it on Sunday. *I couldn't put it down!* It was the *most inspiring* novel I've ever read! The book portrays a great lesson to all of us. To always get back up after falling, and push forward."------Christina Wolfe.

"I was so inspired with the book I bought five more for my family who said it was so interesting they couldn't put it down until they finished it. They described it as "awesome and wonderful." -----Hazel Butler

"I normally haven't the time to read books, but picked up The Ragged Edge and went to the garage and the time found me. I couldn't put it down!" ----Kenneth Parker Jr.

The Story

Various circumstances have caused Cary to teeter on the ragged edge of schizophrenia. His childhood was one, losing his business because of his embezzling partner was another, and finally his wife files for divorce telling him he needs to see a psychiatrist.

His suffering was becoming unbearable, and as the last resort when he was afraid of losing it, he turns to prayer for help from the Almighty.

And then it happened. A young unknown girl comes to him and commences to disappear in front of his eyes. As she returns to normal with a white, bright aura surrounding her head she points to his dining room window and said, "I was pulled her from a light that emanated from that window."

This was the same window where Cary had said his nightly prayers for the last two months.

"What does it feel like when you make yourself invisible," Cary asked.

"Illumination, like being filled with light," she answered.

**This is the first time this true phenomenal event has ever been published, and surely be treasured by all who have wondered of the effects of prayer, and perplexed at the responses they may have received, or not received to their own prayers.**

Therefore I say unto you, what things soever ye desire, when ye pray, believe that ye receive them, and ye shall have them.

St. Mark 11: 24

For Dixie, Katharine, and Barton

In consideration of Love and Affection

## Contents

# Chapter One

## Break Up!

Cary had a problem, but hell he thought, he's always had problems. Everyone has problems. Problems were things you worked on and tried to resolve. Cary normally resolved his daily problems while maintaining a state of equanimity and had almost completed seven years of marriage that were the happiest of his life. He was a one-woman man and was married to the kind of wife that a man would die for. His only problem, he thought, was his work that seemed a mad, never ending merry-go-round. Little did he imagine in his wildest dreams that by the end of this day, this problem would dissolve his world into a state of nothingness.

"You love your job *more* than me, you're a workaholic!" she screamed.

"I work hard for both of us," he countered, "the cost of living is high! We'll never have *anything* unless I work overtime."

Scarlett was furiously pacing the dining room floor in her tight blue jeans, shaking her head and swishing her long red hair around her freckled nose. She abruptly turned and was right up in his face as far as her tiptoes and five foot something could reach. Her eyes glared up at him as she poked his chest with her forefinger to make a point. A deep furrow creased her brow, her blue eyes narrowed, and he knew it was coming. "That's *bull!* You've done it for *you—not me!* You're *sick,* you've got a problem, you're always working, gone, working I guess, well . . . I *can't* take it anymore!"

"Done it for *me?* This new house is for *both* of us!" he answered spreading his dark sun tanned arms.

"Yes, a big *empty* house—you *don't* know," she said weeping. "You don't *know* how many nights I've waited here, fixing your dinner, and watching it turn cold, waiting for you to come home and finally going to bed alone. All the time thinking, hoping, well . . . seven years is enough, I'm weary of waiting . . . hoping, *tired* of being alone."

J*esus!* I've had to work overtime just to get the down payment. That's the only reason—it's *not* going to be forever!"

"*Not forever*? You've been doing it ever *since* we've married—and it's not *just* for this house—you've done it for *that business*! You're obsessed with it—you love it *more than me!*"

Cary couldn't believe his red-headed woman's words.

She had never complained of this before and he didn't know what to say and wondered what brought this on all of a sudden. "You're cute as hell when you're mad, Red" he said hoping her anger would blow over. She turned away with tears flowing and he hated himself for kidding.

Sobbing now, she softly said, "Cary . . . I *only wanted* the *simple* things in life . . . like being *loved* and you spending time with me, but you're always *working*. This has gone on for all seven years of our marriage—since I was seventeen. You're not going to change." She stared at the floor and her shoulders drooped, *"I don't think you can* . . . it's dumb for me to go on, my mind is made up—I'm leaving!" She took a breath, leveled her eyes at him and spoke in measured tones. "You know . . . you need to look into a mirror and admit the problems you have. You need to see a shrink—a psychiatrist, before you destroy everything in your life, but I *don't* believe you have the guts to do it . . . goodbye—it's over!" Cary's wife of seven years, Scarlett Williams, packed some clothes, made some calls, and was out of the house an hour later.

He knew he couldn't stop her when her mind was made up. He wandered around the empty rooms till the memories drove him out. Several days passed before he realized she *really* wasn't coming back and several more before he figured out what she was saying . . . he had put his work ahead of his wife. For seven years he'd spent more time at work than with her, and evidently had neglected her something terrible.

*What can I do* he thought . . . and then remembered her reprimand: "You need to see a shrink but don't have the guts to do it." Well damn it to hell, he thought, *I'll show her.* He reached for the phone book and flipped through the yellow pages for some time until it dawned on him that he couldn't find a psychiatrist because he couldn't spell it. His insides were churning as he flipped through the pages. He thought she appreciated him working so many hours of overtime. Workaholic did she say? *My God!* Is that wrong? Is *that* a sickness? She's leaving me for that? That's the *last* thing I thought I'd be accused of, hell, I'll never understand women. I was doing it f*or* us—*not* me! I was working for *our* future, not mine, but evidently she doesn't see it that way. She doesn't feel like she's the most important thing in my life. She *is,* but I guess I haven't shown it—and she doesn't feel it.

Cary made up his mind, right then and there, that he was going to be man enough to change his ways and win her back. He vowed to do anything it took. He loved her *more* than life and he knew he couldn't live without her. *Don't* think I have the guts, huh, *I'll show her*; I'll take her advice and *prove* I'm man enough to see a psychiatrist. Damn it to hell, I'll show her. They say it's a wise man that's not afraid of seeking help when he realizes the need for it. Well, if he ever needed help—now was that time and now was the time to act. He would do it even though some would label him crazy just for going. *Oh God . . . what would people think? How would they perceive me if they knew I was seeing a shrink?* What have I *thought of others* who were doing the same? What would Scarlett *really* think? Would she write me off because my condition had deteriorated to the point that I needed help? Would the stigma follow me the rest of my life? Well . . . I don't think I have a choice . . . it's the *only chance* I have to win her back and that's the *only* thing that's important. Cary made the decision; he would do it if he could find the damn phone number. After he went through the "D's" looking for doctors, he was referred to physicians, where he finally found a shrink's phone number. After much haggling with the receptionist to convince her that yes, he was over eighteen and that *yes*, it *was* a matter of life and death; she agreed to make an emergency appointment the very next morning.

He never imagined seeing a shrink could really be necessary but he was going to prove he had the guts to go. Entering the doctor's office he was pleased the room didn't smell of anything medical, but more like his living room, except for the flower arrangements that reminded him of a funeral parlor. The doctor asked him all kinds of questions, gave him several strange tests, and after three meetings, the doctor said his conclusion was that he was on the verge, on the path, of becoming a paranoid schizophrenic. That statement slammed Cary like a baseball bat. *Damn,* could Scarlett *be right again?* That I've got problems . . . *and didn't even know it*?

"What's this schizo stuff about anyhow, Doc?"

The doctor gave Cary a bemused look and then explained. "The definitions are diverse. It's like a loss of perception of the realities of life, a distortion of actuality. It's incorrectly deciphering the environment, thus losing contact with it. You do not perceive reality correctly and thus don't react as a normal person would. Paranoid is—oh you've seen examples—the guy whose past girlfriends have cheated on him and now the thinks all women cheat. He irrationally accuses her of cheating on him when she was not. Another example is this: Suppose you come upon a life-threatening problem one day and you had to make a momentous decision of how to solve it. After giving it much serious thought, you finally come to a solid conclusion that it had to be solved in a certain way. Then the next day, you change your mind, and decide to handle the situation in a manner that is absolutely opposite . . ."

"Heck, Scarlett does that all the time!" Cary interrupted. Rolling his eyes, the doctor continued and explained that being paranoid is worrying excessively about some minor problem and not understanding it correctly. Hell, Cary thought, he *knew* many people who did that! Even so, he took the doctor's findings to heart, thinking *damn,* there must be many crazy people out there.

"Cary," the doctor reiterated his point again, "you have a distortion of the reality of life. You must simply face reality, look yourself in the mirror, be honest and true to yourself, admit your faults and begin working to correct them. Admit your wrong thinking, face up to these facts, determine what conditions caused them and then work to overcome them. If something is really bothering you, recognize it, be man enough to admit to it, and then *do* something about it. Don't just let it hang!"

The doctor sighed and moved his stool to confront Cary face to face and looked into the brown eyes of this man with dark complexion. In sincerity, he tried once again. "Cary, understand this . . . you may, as many people have, come to this state of mind by experiences you encountered while growing up. For many people a plethora of their problems can be traced to their childhood. Now listen to me carefully—you *must* go back and review your life in detail from your very first memories and take note of all the experiences that have caused you pain. Write them down if necessary, then acknowledge them, and ask yourself how you reacted. Did you confront the pain and its source and then resolve it? Or did you keep it inside, festering? If you didn't deal with it *then,* these infections will always boil up in the future, overflow, and God knows what trouble they'll bring. You have to face your demons and resolve them, and when you accomplish this, you could be on your way to living a normal life. Just recognizing and acknowledging these incidents will, in many cases, solve the problem. Be man enough to look yourself in a mirror, as hard as it may be, identify your problems, the incidents that caused you pain and heartache, and admit to yourself that these things bothered you. You *must* face these problems, you *must* admit to yourself that they tortured you, and then you must try to resolve them. You must make peace with yourself, Cary."

Cary listened, but winced, "I don't know Doc . . . I don't know . . . I think that would be painful."

"It is," the doctor said, "but it's important to your well-being, hell, it *could be* your only way out."

"Men don't like to admit to such things," Cary said.

"Yes, that's true and the people who jumped off the San Francisco Bridge *also* didn't want to admit to the things that perturbed them *either*! The few that survived said they were sorry they jumped . . . you can only *imagine* what the others thought before they hit the water. Many other people didn't want to admit to these things either, and what did they do? They took the easy way out and shot themselves in the head. *Which* is the manliest thing to do? Who is taking the easy way out? Are you man enough to do what I've asked? Or would you rather walk the ragged edge of insanity? Have you *ever* heard of anyone referring to suicide as a respected act? Do you want to turn to alcohol? Who would respect a drunk? And who would *respect* a dead one at that? Do you think the world would stop if you were found stone dead drunk in a ditch beside the road? The world would scarcely notice another hopeless statistic. It takes more courage to do what I've laid out; I think my alternative is the better way—the *only* way to go. I'm telling you hard stuff Cary, but that's the way it is. You *best* take my advice to heart—seriously."

As he left the office, Cary realized this may be the most difficult nemesis he'd ever encountered, trying to overcome a problem that was not *even* tangible, but he knew he *had* to try. Maybe his thinking had been wrong all along, he thought it only natural for a man to act crazy sometimes, *just* to keep from going insane. But he thought it best to fight this paradoxical thing the Doc's way; he had never thought of suicide, much less considered it. Of course he had never lost a wife before either. However, he was determined to try, try *anything* that would get him and Red back together.

The next day he was standing in his empty house seriously contemplating his first move and thought himself silly, but then, he was desperate. He decided to take the doctor and Scarlett's advice literally. "You need to look into a mirror," Scarlett had said, and now the shrink was saying the same thing. He thought he would give it a try—the San Francisco Bridge was too far.

He glanced around to make sure no one was looking, lest anyone think him crazy. He took a deep breath, faced the large dining room mirror, and actually, physically, looked at himself and tried to identify what problems a man could have besides the only one he knew about—sex or more specifically, the lack thereof. He thought this dynamic drive propelling him relentlessly forward would surely be the cause of mental illness, but thank God, that didn't happen when he finally discovered girls had a similar problem. He didn't see much resemblance to his father who is of English descent except his angular face and his height of five feet ten. His mother was pure Russian and he could have easily passed for one. He saw a twenty-nine year old man with big, dark eyes, black crew cut hair, dark complexion, and a large-boned body of one hundred and seventy pounds. His skin was tan and smooth and his nose was okay he thought, but he winced at the sight of his protruding lower jaw. He had no complaints about his body as it had sustained him through many hard working jobs, a few fist fights, couple of motorcycle wrecks, and dozens of hard hitting football games.

Cary's outward signs of anxiety from childhood days had settled into a state of emotional intensity. At first he only noticed his physical defects, particular the protruding lower jaw, and honestly admitted that long ago he had come to hate the deformity. Was this an abnormal feeling? Had this made him schizophrenic? If so, was he obligated to do something about it? What *could* he do, correct it with *plastic surgery?* Sounds like that was what the doctor was sanctioning, maybe he should and made a note of it. He then reflected on every situation, every problem he had encountered in life that he could think of. After doing this, which took awhile, he had to admit he'd probably not always reacted in a rational way. He honestly admitted to himself, as hard as it was, every abnormal action that he could remember. It was a tough and humbling thing to do . . . and it was scary. It was probably the hardest problem he'd ever encountered and he knew it would take some time to correct it. He flopped down on his couch, exhausted and perplexed at the turn of events.

As Cary closed his eyes he remembered the one final piece of advice the doctor had given him concerning his marital situation: "Don't stalk her. You've made the first step to get help, and if she really loves you, she will stand behind you. She will know you are really trying to change your ways, and that's your *best* bet to get her back. She will remember her wedding vows, but stalking her is not going to work in your favor. Stay away from her until you've made some progress."

Still, Cary decided to go see Scarlett one final time, just to tell her he'd taken her advice and went to the doctor. He knocked on her apartment door late one Saturday evening where she was staying with his sister temporarily.

She barely cracked the door. "What do you want Cary?"

"Five minutes."

She opened the door and motioned him in. She sat down on one end of their simulated leather couch he'd left with her and crossed her arms and waited.

"I took your advice . . . I went to see the shrink."

"*And*?"

Cary sat on the other end of the couch, looking at the floor, trying to form his words. "He said I have some problems . . . said I was heading . . . said I was on the verge of becoming a . . . a paranoid schizophrenic." Scarlett rolled her eyes and heaved an I-knew-it sigh.

"*But he told me what to do*!" he turned to her readying his best explanation.

"What was that?"

"Well, he . . . he explained how I should decipher my problems and . . ."

"What problems did he say you have?"

"He said I had to figure them out for myself."

"Great!" she said studying her freshly painted nails, "that's just great."

"He said I had to analyze myself, discover my problems, you know, figure them out, dig them out, and admit that I had them. and then go about correcting them."

"Un huh," was her response as she gave him a condescending look. "Admitting to them will be your hardest job—and *you paid* him for that?"

He slowly edged towards her, looking for *anything*, but she winced away and he dropped to his knees at her lap. His dark eyes searched her face for any sign of hope. She stiffened and turned away but his face turned with hers. "And *I've* decided *to take* his advice." He lowered his head when her cold eyes stared him down but countered with "I'm *sorry* for every thing I've done, I *ask* for your forgiveness, I *do love you so*, I care about your thoughts, I worry about your worry. I've always wanted to give you peace . . . peace in your heart, peace in your mind. I've always wanted to make things right. *I want to grow old with you Scarlett*. I'm taking the Doc's advice."

Scarlett rose and opened the door, "Your five minutes are up." Cary awkwardly arose from his knees and lumbered towards the door . . . then paused to look at her. She avoided eye contact and said, "Leave, Cary, I've got to get ready, someone's coming—"

"*Who's* coming?"

"I've got a date."

"You've got a date!" you haven't wasted much time *have you*? He was furious and his heart was pounding as he walked out the door and the click of the lock was like a death knell. He was dumbstruck—this could not be the woman he'd married? The doctor was right, the only chance he had was to really change his ways. It was a long shot, but he had to do it, his life would be *wasted* without her. He made up his mind to comply with what the doctor ordered, but he wondered—would there be enough time?

As hard as it was, he started thinking back over his past, wondering how all this could have taken place. Cary and Scarlett lived in the Hampton Roads area of Virginia. They had married and moved here in 1960 and now the year was 1967. His business partner was fifty-seven and he twenty-two when he started working for him seven years ago in Richmond. He had graduated from high school, was attending college part-time when the two of them discussed marriage. It was readily apparent that Scarlett was adamant about tying the matrimony strings the week after her high school graduation, though she didn't give a rational reason. They made all the usual plans for a formal wedding in her family's church, but one week before the wedding her parents said, without explanation, they would not be attending the ceremony. This insult on top of Scarlett's finding out that her mother had read every letter she had received from Cary, had made her furious. Her parents didn't deny her permission to marry Cary, for they willfully signed a declaration that was necessary for her to marry because she was only seventeen. It was only after they ran off to South Carolina and got married that Cary began understanding only a part of the mystery of her childhood. She was diagnosed with polio in her pre teen years and there was something about her dad having some disease that affected his brain. Then, just weeks after they were married, he caught her sleepwalking in the middle of the night. She was walking from room to room talking to herself in extreme despair. He would gently, without waking her, guide her back to the bedroom, and the next morning she remembered nothing of it. A few nights later there was the nightmare in the middle of the night, she evidently thought Cary was, who knows, a monster or something, and attacked him like a wild tiger. Her body was taut with adrenaline pumping and she scratched him 'til he bled, and it was all he could do to contain her, telling her it was okay and finally calming her. She never said, may not have even known, or if she knew she didn't say what this was all about, and Cary never pressed the issue, but he felt something terrible was haunting her from her past. He was gentle with her and as the months passed, she recuperated, at least physically, but there was something wrong . . . but he wasn't sure what, and never did know.

Just prior to their marriage, Cary's company moved from Richmond to Hampton Roads, where business was booming, and he made the decision to go with the company as he needed a job and felt he could have a future with the small corporation. Unfortunately, there were no colleges nearby at this new location, so he never finished his schooling. Probably the biggest mistake he'd made, he thought, was working all those extra hours, holidays, nights and weekends to further his career. Now he wished he'd taken those hours and sought out a college and completing his education. Maybe that was a mistake, but they *both* wanted to get married and he had to earn a paycheck.

His partner noticed his dedication and hard work. He told Cary if the company's sales climbed to a certain level in the next two years, he would reward him with a half interest in the company. This may have been his undoing because such an incentive made him strive to work even harder. Three years later, with his many extra hours of work, weekends and nights, they reached this goal and he was rewarded with half ownership in the company. Cary had pushed the company to be the largest of its kind in the area. He was elated, but Scarlett wasn't as she hadn't seen any monetary rewards as yet. All she saw was that he worked too many nights and too many weekends. She felt he had neglected her while Cary thought she understood that he was doing it for their future.

He had left all his earnings, over and above his salary, in the company to help grow the business. It takes money to make money and this was the only way he knew how to build capital. Scarlett didn't seem to understand and it never occurred to him that this would affect their marriage. He later thought this was a tragic miscommunication at the least, or was there more that he didn't know? This would later give him many worries concerning what really did happen. Was there more to the story that he was unaware of? Did he do all that work for nothing? She *couldn't* have betrayed him, could she?

His partner started building houses on the side. Unfortunately though, the market slumped, interest rates jumped and his houses sat with no buyers. The interest on his unsold houses put him deep into debt. Only later, when his partner took his profits and went on a vacation to the Bahamas, Cary found a second set of books at the office. They revealed many large invoices that had gone unpaid; the money was gone and they were almost bankrupt. The books revealed his partner had *embezzled* funds from *their* company to pay the interest on the unsold houses. He was able to embezzle a large sum only because their largest vendor's account receivables bookkeeper had gotten sick for a period of time and overlooked how much their company was in arrears. This book keeper was a relative of the owners and they didn't want to replace her, but she was out longer than they expected and no one was watching the store. By the time she returned and noticed the discrepancy, a huge amount of money had been lost.

Later, Cary realized his partner had planned the whole thing; he'd put all of his assets in his wife's name and when this vendor came to collect, they realized he had not a dime they could touch. They gave up trying to collect the debt and wrote it off. It was a wonder they both didn't go to jail. Cary's name was not on the contract with this vendor and after much browbeating, they realized he was innocent of any wrongdoing and didn't press any charges. This vendor, a window manufacturer, retrieved the inventory, prohibited further shipments and that was it. Without this vendor, there was no way they could operate. The doors were closed and Cary was out of work, out of a future, and out of a wife. He felt betrayed by his partner, his wife, and his disillusionment was great.

And what was worse, his partner was now sixty-four and had previously, two years before, made an agreement with Cary. The agreement was that he would retire at age sixty-five, sell him the business, and Cary would buy out his interest with monthly payments. This would be his retirement and Cary's future. But there was no business! His actions ruined their reputation with other vendors, and on top of that, the entire area began to suffer an economic slump. It was all over, and the dream had become a nightmare. Cary's future business plans were destroyed as well as his partner's retirement because he lost the income that Cary would have paid him in future years. His partner's crime of embezzlement came back to hurt him in more ways than one. He destroyed the business and lost the future income he would have received from Cary.

Scarlett didn't understand the gravity of it all, and Cary soon spiraled into a deep depression. He was tired, weary, and his stomach was killing him. During this period, he told her something stupid, "I guess this is the end of us too." He thought everyone was letting him down, including her. She didn't appreciate the decision he'd made which was to work instead of going on to college. She didn't think about how hard he had worked and why. She didn't seem to realize he was doing it for *their* future. He felt her thoughts were on herself and wasn't looking at the big picture. Cary felt utterly abandoned yet ashamed for what he had said to Scarlett. He knew his work took him away from her, but he never expected it to last. It was not going to be a way of life. She never asked him once to reconcile, never said she would stand by his side, and turned her back on him when he needed her the most.

He felt like a complete failure and he was pushing thirty years of age. Nevertheless, Cary forged on with a stubborn will.

# Chapter Two

## Leaving . . . Looking Back

They sold their house. It was their first and was new when they bought it two years ago. Proudly standing on a large corner lot, the two-story colonial was surrounded by a dozen old pine trees in the neighborhood of Denbigh, Va. and lay only a half-mile from Cary's building supply business.

Cary left her the newer car and took his old 1960 Chevrolet convertible that had been garaged. He loved it more than anything except his wife and now it would have to suffice as his *only* love. He had maintained it with care and it was still in excellent shape. He paid all of the bills, made arrangements for Scarlett to move into an apartment, and made sure she was financially stable. She had found a good job in civil service two weeks before they physically separated. She met many new men at work and was dating a few weeks later. He couldn't hate her even though his insides were being eaten out. She had been a good wife and he still cared about her well-being.

Cary's sister lived in the area and Scarlett had her for moral support as they were close friends. He often wondered how much she was involved, if at all, in his wife's cold change of heart toward him. His sister may have sided with Scarlett instead of her own brother. He didn't know what had occurred between the two of them but he often wondered. He left her good-to-go but his heart was pounding as he told her goodbye. He had no business, no wife, and no job. To maintain his sanity, he tried not to picture her with another man. A few weeks later, he was served with official papers notifying him of the divorce proceedings in progress. He looked at the calendar . . . it was the very day of their seventh wedding anniversary, July 18, 1968. What a *present?* A *dagger* to the heart! He couldn't or wouldn't believe it was done on purpose. It just couldn't be, could it?

He couldn't stay here, this close to her—he had to get away. He had nothing to hold him, so he sold some of the products left over from his business, packed a few personal items and left her the rest. He paused in his driveway just before leaving, having just thought of something. He went back into the house and opened the closest door and there they were. She would have no use for his guns but he thought he might. He grabbed his 12-gauge pump shotgun that held seven big ones. The long black barrel still smelled of oil from the last time he had wiped it down and cleaned it. He took the shotgun, his 38 revolver, and his M-1 Garand rifle that had killed a few Nazis in WWII, took them and loaded them into the trunk of his car. He went back, found some more ammo, grabbed the books of

Thoreau and Dickinson, dropped them in a duffel bag, and threw them in the back seat of his Chevy. He put his rage and what was left of his sanity in the front seat and left.

He looked back one last time at the two-story house where he had spent the happiest days of his life. Now it loomed hollow, sad and forsaken, like the emptiness of his insides. Knowing he was leaving it for the last time, he slowly drove down the suburban street and glanced at the neighbors' houses. Children were laughing in the yards and husbands and wives paused in their leaf-raking to wave a friendly hand. He waved one back and forced a silent smile for the last time, smiling as though it was just another drive to work, only this time the drive would be accompanied with a heavy load of heartache—a burden he would become more acquainted with in years to come.

Without thinking, he started driving south; it was the only place he felt drawn to. It was early autumn and the night was warm as he pulled over and put the top down on his convertible. He opened a beer and felt some relief as he left I-64 and took a shortcut towards I-95 South. His heart was aching, but he felt a piercing comfort as he traveled towards the *only other place* that seemed like home, his birthplace, Florida. She was dating and he was leaving, *how* could she, *so soon*? Times had gotten hard but he never expected this. He could not imagine himself with another woman as it would feel like he was cheating, but evidently it didn't bother her. Scarlett's mind was already on another man, her vows meant nothing, and he was cast out and forgotten. He felt betrayed and naïve for having been unaware that circumstances had gotten so out of hand until it was too late. He didn't understand her and apparently she didn't understand him.

The evening shadows were growing longer as he left Virginia and began his long journey through the Carolinas. The skies were overcast and a light rain brushed across his face, disguising his tears. As he drove he began working on his project the doctor said was a necessity to reach normalcy. *Normal*, he thought. *Have* I ever been normal? *Is anybody? What* is normal? As he drove along with his eyes fixed on the highway, Cary began attempting to do what the shrink had recommended about analyzing his past. It would be *agonizing he knew . . .* but then he had promised himself. He would have never ever thought of doing such a painful thing until the doctor explained this was his only chance of reconciling with his wife. He *only prayed* the shrink knew what he was doing. He would attempt to accomplish it—*but* in the shortest time possible. He decided to start from his very first memory as a child and then come forward, trying to recall all significant events in his life, then decipher those events until he could understand the effects, if any, on his being.

After doing this, he planned to analyze his condition and

if it proved abnormal, he would lay out plans to correct the abnormality. To do *whatever* it took to get his wife back! So he began his journey, recalling in detail the bits and pieces of his life that the doc said could have been so traumatic that it caused him to lose the most precious thing in his life. He started to remember back to the beginning . . . .

He was born in O'Brien, Florida, a small town situated in the northwest corner of the state. At the age of five, he heard talk of the Great War that was in progress. They called it World War II and it bothered him that evidently there had been a World War I. He didn't know what war was all about and thought the grown-ups surely must understand these perplexing oddities in life. He thought he might too when he was older, but it never happened. As he matured, he never forgot the disheartening feeling when he realized that adults, seemingly, didn't understand any more than he did as a child. He found that becoming an adult doesn't necessarily give you enlightenment and realized that many adults were not more than children when it came to understanding the mysteries of life.

When he was seven they had to move and he had no doubt it was because of the war. They moved again almost every year for the next five years. He ended up going to five different elementary schools and three high schools, four in Florida and four in Virginia, where they finally settled in the city of Hopewell in 1948; a city that was born because of WWI. Some of his worst memories were going into these new schools in the middle of the school term and seeing the reactions of the class as though he was an alien from another world. His fourth grade teacher almost finished him off—at least that's what Cary thought after his parents had taken him to the doctor and got his prognosis. The doctor said Cary was having stomach and nerve problems and should be taken out of school for one year so as to recuperate. He said his nerves were shot, he had nervous twitches, tics and rapid blinking of his eyes. But "Blinky," as he was nicknamed for years to come, would have none of it and continued in school. By the time he'd entered his second high school, he had a tremendous feeling of being different, not belonging, and this feeling stayed with him for years to come.

He remembered it like yesterday when his fourth grade teacher, Mrs. McCaleb, pointed her finger at him and said, "Cary, read the first verse in the Bible out loud and clear. Stand up straight—face the class and quit mumbling!" And later, "Now explain to the class the meaning of that verse." When he couldn't, she would again aim that finger at him and he felt like the whole world had caved in on him. He hoped that at the age of nine his soul was not already lost and he would not spend eternity burning in hell. He stayed in school because he didn't want to fall back a grade and give the kids another reason to giggle and poke fun at him.

During this time he was awakened every morning at five a.m. by his mom and dad. Unknowingly, they woke him with their arguing that was in low, hushed, whispered tones. That was enough to worry him but when he heard them always arguing about money and paying bills, it made him more depressed. "Feeding the kids" came up so often it gave him a guilty feeling. This scenario went on for years. Money was so tight that his dad kept telling his two older brothers to quit school and find a job and help pay the family expenses. In later years he told all the kids, more than once, "I have fed, housed, and put you through school. When you graduate, I expect you to turn around, go to work, and take care of your mom and dad." He really didn't think Dad realized how this sounded, but said it more than once.

When thirteen, he was awakened around two in the morning. The house was glaring with lights and there was shouting, slamming doors, and finally someone said, "*Jim's been shot* and he's being taken to the hospital!" Jim was Cary's eighteen year old brother. They learned the details in bits and pieces, Jim had been shot in the chest accidentally, they thought, by one of his football teammates. It happened outside of a restaurant in downtown Hopewell as he sat in the rear of a friend's car. He had been rushed to the local hospital. Cary's mom and dad had taken off running, telling Cary and his siblings to stay at home. They got there just in time to see Jim as the emergency crew was leaving. The attendant and doctor came out, explained to them that Jim had been shot in the chest, was stabilized for the moment, but must be rushed to MCV Hospital immediately for further treatment.

They kept him for three weeks before sending him home. As he healed, Jim told us everything that happened. "Roy and I were in his car at the Libbys Doughnut parking lot and he was in the front seat and I sat in the back. We were debating some trivial matter when he pulled a gun and said, 'Well, I'll *end* this debate.' He pointed the gun, empty he thought, pointed it at my chest and shot me. I put up my arm to shield myself but the bullet only grazed my arm and went into my chest. What I mostly felt was the air being knocked out of me, as though I'd been hit hard by a linebacker. As they rushed me to the hospital, I tried lying down to keep the blood flowing to my head so I wouldn't lose consciousness. But Roy lost his way and I had to give him directions. Looking through the hazy, wet window I could see the ghoulishly blue sign that read Gould's Funeral Home. I thought I might be in there tomorrow."

Reaching the hospital they lifted him up ignoring his protests and then he passed out. As he regained consciousness sometime later, he sensed a sheet being pulled over him and heard the doctor say, "*This boy is dead.*" He tried to move but couldn't, finally it seemed an eternity, they evidently noticed a movement underneath the sheet and pulled it back, realized he was barely alive, and decided to rush him by emergency crew to the Medical College of Virginia. He started talking on the way over and they told him to stop and save his energy. He said he was not about to stop for fear they'd think he was dead again!

The doctors called for blood donors and realized the fellow that shot him had the proper type. He came into the hospital, walked half way down the long corridor, paused, turned, and left. Later when Jim heard this he murmured a prayer of forgiveness for him, then, in case he died. A nurse soon found another donor and gave him a transfusion. The doctors tried vainly to remove the bullet by couldn't because it was too close to his heart. They stitched him up and after carefully monitoring him for a couple of weeks, sent him home. They told him to recuperate, get his strength back, and then they would operate again to try and remove the bullet.

Jim went back to the same hospital three weeks later. They examined him for a long time and finally came to him with a consensus. Jim remembered the doctor telling him, "Jim, we're afraid we could kill you if we go in again . . . the bullet, it's only an inch from your heart, and after much study, we frankly think your best bet is to leave the .22 bullet in your chest. Chances are the bullet will probably never bother you again. Our decision is not to operate and leave the bullet in." Jim was soon to turn nineteen, and on this and future birthdays, we found we could never kid him again about getting older. He would just smile and say it was better than the alternative. He knew the bullet was still there because he could feel it move now and then. In years to come he said it was a constant reminder to put his priorities in order.

The next year Cary's two other brothers, Brad and Jay, joined the Air Force. Their dad had told Brad, "If you fail the tenth grade again next year—out you go!" Next year he did fail and Dad sent him packing and he joined the Air Force at age seventeen. The oldest brother, Jay, had just graduated from high school, found a good-paying job and was helping their mom and dad with their bills. He had been dating the same girl for about a year and had fallen in love with her. He asked this girl to marry him but she turned him down. This enraged him and he quit his job, dropped everything, and joined the Air Force too. He probably never realized the problem was not his, probably never knew the girl had personal problems she wouldn't share with him.

A few years later, Jay told his parents he wanted to marry a Catholic girl he had met in New York. His mom protested vehemently as it was strictly against her Protestant upbringing and strongest beliefs. Of course she was not happy that the girl was a Yankee but would never say so. The girl's Catholic mother held feelings that were just as adamant about her daughter not marrying a Protestant boy that was from a Southern blue-collar family. Why she categorized them that way was beyond Cary's understanding as the girl's father was a plumber, and as far as being a Southerner, my God, they were in Virginia now and that was a lot further north than Florida! The two were married, and both disowned their parents and severed their relationships with them forever. Cary never forgot his mother's face when she showed him the short note from Jay, her first born, which said in effect, as of this day I disown my family. Cary felt something inside of her began to die that day.

They learned later that Jay had become a first-rate jet pilot, graduated at the top of his class from the Officers Training School, served in the Korean War and become a member of the interceptor squad that protected the East Coast. He had two sons they had never seen. Cary had always looked up to Jay with admiration. He kept a picture of him outfitted in full jet pilot gear from an old military magazine. The picture and following article were used in recruitment activities as a personification of what it was to be the best jet pilot in the Air Force. Cary couldn't believe he would never see his oldest brother again. He never did, and his Mother was never able to convey to him how proud she was.

Cary knew things were bad and money was tight, so he worked from the age of eleven. He didn't make enough to give his earnings to his folks, but he did pay most of his expenses through high school. He had to lie about his age to get his first job—said he was twelve and began delivering papers.

He carried papers, delivered milk, and sometimes did both simultaneously. He arose at four a.m. in mid winter to deliver milk from his dad's truck. The odor of spilt milk in the truck didn't help his queasy stomach, and the situation worsened when the truck heater reached the milk and turned it sour. In addition, there was the nauseating smell of the haze that enveloped the city from the chemical and paper mills. The combination of these two made him sick to his stomach, but he finally figured out a solution. First thing every morning, before he got sick, he would stick his finger down his throat and throw up. Then he could make it through the rest of the morning. When he trudged into school at eight, barely awake, the teachers accused him of being up all night and doing heaven knows what. His older brother was supposed to help his dad on alternating days, but some mornings he wouldn't budge from his bed. On these days, Cary would call to his dad to hold up, that he was coming. He would then roll off his bed, fall to the floor and let the jolt jar him fully awake. He never did let his dad go alone.

During this time Cary realized that some of his paper

route money was missing from his dresser drawer where he kept it hidden. After a month of paying his bill and having nothing left over, he set a trap and discovered this same brother was stealing from him weekly. He raised hell and then tried to forgive him. Around the same time, Cary remembered complaining to his mother about how hard life was. He never forgot her response: "Cary, you don't know what hard times are yet—just wait until you're older." That response was not exactly inspirational, and he tried to brush it off, figuring Mom was having a bad day. Little did he realize, until later, the wisdom of her words.

By the end of his sophomore year, Cary had endured fist fights, smashing football games, and accidents from bicycles and motor scooters. His battered face had finally given way, and two of his top front teeth fell out. He was terrified to go to a dentist, but more terrified to show up at school and see the reactions of his classmates. With his two front teeth gone, he knew he had to do something. It was a very long dreaded walk to the tooth doctor. It took him an hour to walk the ten blocks, but he gutted it out. The dentist said he must have lacked calcium when he was born.

His top teeth were so deteriorated that he ended up having all of them pulled that summer and was fitted with an upper plate. He was okay until the next year when he discovered two more new teeth coming in and pushing down on his denture. They were pulled and finally he was all set for his junior year.

The next year he found himself between jobs for the first time, so he went out for the varsity basketball team. He had his denture knocked out a couple of times and quickly realized how his gum could be cut when receiving a blow to his mouth—another reason to avoid fighting he reasoned. He never made the first-string line up and never complained, but thought it partly was because he was not included in the in-crowd. He was never considered one of the boys and was never invited to join any of the fraternities. He reasoned it was because he was not a life-long member of the school and that his pride or independence wouldn't allow the demeaning acts the fraternities required. Anyhow, he couldn't distinguish himself if they wouldn't throw him the ball.

He was really proud he had made the team but didn't think it wise to tell his dad. He guessed he felt guilty for not working that one semester. Things went along okay until he came home unusually late one night from a varsity basketball game. They had played a game in a distant city and their bus didn't return until two a.m.

Unfortunately, his dad heard him sneaking in and gave him hell for staying out so late. "What could you be *doing* out there this time of night?" he had hollered. That was the closest his dad came to knowing he'd made the team. But his dad never knew, Cary never told him and he never came to see him play. Cary was no star on the squad but was proud just to have made the varsity team. It was years later when Don Lewis told him the story: "Cary, you remember the days in basketball practice when the coach would come out and shoot beside you and the other players?"

"Yeah, we use to shoot three-pointers from all around the court."

"Well, you may not know this, but the coach told us some time later, ""That Cary, he out shot me more times than not!'"

"Well, he was just the coach and he was an older man," said Cary.

"Old man? Maybe to you! When you're seventeen, you think everybody over twenty-five is old. He was twenty-nine then and was the best shot on his college team!"

Cary just smiled and said, "Too bad he couldn't get the other players to throw me the ball. I guess I could have been better, but I was a little nervous back then."

"You weren't so nervous," Don remembered, "when you made those twenty-five free throws in a row."

The senior year in high school was his best only because it was his last. He was ridiculed many times because of his upper plate and his jutting lower jaw that made it hard to talk clearly. Sometimes when he was depressed, he questioned God's ability in forming mankind in His own image.

All this was nothing compared to the hurt he received when his teacher made him read out loud for the class. When the class clown was asked to answer a question concerning what Cary had read, the guy said, "I don't know 'cause he couldn't understand a word Cary said." The whole class blew up with laughter, and everybody thought it was funny but Cary. He felt like the deformed chicken in the midst of others who would circle and peck a little here and a little there, torturing him slowly because he was different. Many of these kids were chickens in more ways than one. They were cowardly, sadistic, and usually ran in packs. Abusing someone who was already hurting was beyond Cary's comprehension. Life so far had made him a genuine non-conformist.

His homeroom teacher recognized him one evening as he was coming home from delivering papers and stopped to give him a ride home. She said, "You'd better get home and get yourself ready for the senior prom tonight!" He didn't bother telling her he wouldn't be going for he had no proper clothes, no proper face, and no date. In his condition, it wasn't difficult getting a girl's attention, but obtaining a date from her was something else when her mind was overwhelmed with his blinking eyes, nervous neck twitches, and stumbling incoherent speech. It had been awhile since he had even tried and so far he hadn't decided which was worse, being alone or being denied. So far denial was winning out. It was at this time that Cary started to *hate himself*, and vowed that someday he would *compensate* for all of this.

Cary would remain in this state for another year until, when out of the blue, his angel would appear. This girl would give him the happiest seven years of his life, and even though he would eventually lose her, she may have, in the long run, saved his life, for through her, he realized what happiness was.

He flunked some courses but made them up in summer school and graduated high school only one year late. Many students were crying as they walked to get their diplomas, their tears resulting from having to leave years of fond memories behind. Cary's tears were tears of joy because he didn't have to come back. He had had a recurring dream at least once a year that lasted into adulthood. The dream, more like a nightmare, was that he had failed his senior year and had to return and attend his senior year all over again. He was laughed at for failing and being older than the other seniors.

He thought times were tough, but he saw families and other kids that he thought had suffered more than he. For instance, he knew a boy down the street who lived with alcoholic parents. On top of that, he had seven brothers sleeping with him in one bedroom while Cary only had three. Now that he looked back, evidently these years affected him more than he realized.

He loved his parents and was sure they loved him too. He thought he was okay, surely not perfect, but acceptable. His parents never mentioned the idea of him going to college. A few years later he heard they had insisted, and paid for his only sister's college education. She was the only girl and the only child out of six siblings to obtain a college degree. He was happy for her.

Cary went from bicycles to motor scooters and then to motorcycles. He rode incessantly all over town as if something were chasing him. Every cop in town knew him and wondered why he was always going in such a hurry. The motorcycle changed his life—if he had to pick between his obsessions, only music would be a close competitor. He was a kid of sixteen out to see the world with only the income from a paper route. The dollars in his pocket were enough to keep the gas tank full and take him to as many places as his young body could stand. In the summertime he was seen riding with jeans, a tee shirt and that was about all—no helmet, no shoes, free as a breeze as he cruised many miles of country roads. The engine between his legs was powerful, and he felt a complete sense of freedom as he and his beloved bike roamed the countryside in their nightly excursions. If he ever ran into trouble, whether it was a cop attempting to write him up for speeding or someone with road rage trying to run him off the road, he simply went off the highway and slipped away between trees where cars couldn't fit. The summer nights were like heaven as he traveled many unknown roads for the first time.

There was the night a pretty country girl waved him down, he'd learned early how the throbbing Harley engine and the freedom of the road affected girls. In years to come he thought it was the *only* thing he understood about them. He stopped; she jumped on behind him and held him tight as they blasted away into the night with her hair streaming in the wind. He never forgot her trying to restrain her firm breasts from his back as he braked hard to let her off. Nevertheless, never thinking he'd done it on purpose, she showed her appreciation with an unexpected kiss on the lips, and he never forgot how well endowed she was, or the sweetness of her lips. His greatest pleasure, beside this, was gliding through country roads at night when the moon was full and the smell of honeysuckle wafted in the air. This freedom, this independence, would remain with Cary and would have an influence on many decisions later in life. His parents were very busy working and didn't worry too much about Cary as he didn't pester them for money and didn't cause them trouble. They just asked to be informed when he would be away overnight. He always did until he ran off to Florida at age eighteen.

When Cary was seventeen, he graduated to the automobile that developed into a long-term relationship. He purchased his first Fifty Ford coupe with the money he had saved from his paper route. The car became his sanctuary and his best friend. It would take him anywhere he wanted to go. He could sleep in the back seat, and unlike a motorcycle, it would protect him from the wintry weather plus his car had a radio that his motorcycle didn't.

His car was always waiting for him and never deserted him; it was his best and truest friend. It was an unusual love affair with a mechanical entity, but the girls and the auto did have things in common. They were both classy, painted up, had beautiful curves and were always ready to travel. The boys loved their cars; they were their first thought in the morning and their last thought at night. They washed them, waxed them, and pampered them with a passion that their girlfriends could only envy.

He and his neighborhood buddies would gather and talk shop. Their cars didn't intimidate them as girls did, and they were their comfort and companions. Oh, they had their girlfriends, but it seemed they were temperamental beings that could get upset about the slightest thing. When this happened and they stalked off in a huff, their cars were always there, waiting for them.

They trusted their cars even thought they had their

problems, but they understood them better than girls. When their cars broke down, at least they had a manual on how to fix them, instructions that didn't come with girls. They would spend hours repairing them, talking to them, and when they cursed them, at least the cars sat silently and never argued back. Their cars never hurt them, never made fun of them and never betrayed them. They became sentimental over their cars and it was always sad to see one die, whether it was from old age or a tragic accident. This love affair with their cars was possibly a unique thing, for many reasons, at this time in the history of the automobile. For many of these boys in the fifties, this love affair never ended. If there were a betrayal, the boys were the guilty ones. They were the ones that deserted their old cars for newer fancier ones, and as time went by, many of them returned, searching for their first true love. In later life, the ones that could afford it found them, restored them, and tried to mend their broken romance. They would lie in the back seat, close their eyes, and remember beautiful memories. Ahh, they thought . . . if only back seats could talk.

The boys talked cars, engines, horsepower, handling, gear ratios, camshafts, and so forth. They worked on their own cars because they couldn't afford to pay the garage mechanic. They replaced rear axles, transmissions, water pumps, and removed and replaced engines.

On summer nights when the moon was full, they would

go to the old deserted racetrack in Dinwiddie County and race their cars in single file and make bets to see who could circle it the fastest. After tearing down fences on the third and fourth corners and running from the law frequently called, they were finally persuaded to stay away from the track or risk the dire consequences of facing old Judge Binford. After this, they settled for racing around old Jandl's farm field when he was out of town.

They loved the stock car races and went many times to the local dirt tracks. As kids, they didn't have the money to buy tickets and mostly viewed the races from outside the track. One of their favorite places was the third corner of the old half-mile dirt speedway at the local track at the Petersburg fairgrounds.

They would climb high onto the limbs of the closest tree to the track. The boys would laugh as they moved behind the tree trunks to dodge the dirt and mud spewing from the cars as they spun around the third turn. It was fascinating to watch each car desperately trying to take the turns as fast as possible without flying off the racetrack. The fastest time in which you could circle the track was "ten-tenths" and the slowest was "one-tenth." Traveling the track at ten-tenths was down right dumb or as one driver said, you'd be flirting with disaster. It was commonly referred to pushing the ten-tenths as *the ragged edge.* The group went to a race one night and watched it from the pits, the area inside of the track, and watched many drivers pushing the safety limit. Two drivers were racing down the back stretch, side by side, fighting for the inside position for the third turn where it was a necessity to make the turn without sliding off the track. Neither driver would back off, and the driver who lost the inside position was going too fast, lost control, and flew right off the track, flipping end over end.

Luckily, no one was hurt and after the race the two had a confrontation. The one who made the turn asked the other why he was driving stupid, asking him why he didn't give and back off. The other replied with a punch to the face; but before they could fight any further, they were separated and we heard the one who flipped shout. "Damn you! I thought you would chicken out . . . me, hell—I don't really give a damn! I have nothing left to lose!"

Cary had never forgotten this, for somehow it rang a bell within him. Some of the drivers were half-drunk when they raced, a few were decent men while others seemed driven—driven by some unseen force to drive with wild abandonment for unknown reasons as though they had nothing left to lose. They seemed obsessed with a tortured desperation to win the race at all costs.

Cary and his friends seemed to have a driving force to succeed, to overcome and to win. They had won some and lost some, but they always *expected* to win, after all, they lived in a time that was unique, a time that was rare, for it was a time when the whole population of their hometown, ten thousand of them, were caught up in a state of jubilation as they filled the stadium each week and watched the awesome accomplishments of their high school football team. The team won 35 straight games and held the Group AAA state record for consecutive games won. Some of the boys had never seen their team lose throughout their high school years. Two of the co-captains had never lost a game while in high school, and still a greater accomplishment should be noted. The football team should not have even qualified for the Triple A status because the whole student body only numbered a little over five hundred students while most schools that played in this top division had students that numbered in the thousands.

The Hopewell High Blue Devils went undefeated and won the state football championship in 1949, 1950, and 1951. Their undefeated streak started in 1948 and ended in 1952 when they lost for the first time in four years. Their will had finally been broken. Cary witnessed this heart-breaking loss and he couldn't withhold the tears that flooded down his face.

As he looked about the Hopewell fans, he realized it was the first time he'd ever seen so many grown men cry; their tears fell like raindrops, but were shed without shame. As the team bus returned home from Granby, the sad, depressed faces of the boys couldn't believe their widening eyes when, at two a.m., it seemed the whole town was waiting in the parking lot and applauding them. The huge crowd was clapping their hands and the applause was deafening. The team was astonished at first until they realized they had nothing to be ashamed of, but sat transfixed in wonderment at the continuing applause. The crowd was thanking them for far more than just one game. They clapped for their courage; they cheered for their toughness and continued applauding for many things the young boys wouldn't understand until they were older. In the hearts of all, there is a yearning to overcome, to test your will, to reach down, and with every fiber of your being, strive to reach your full potential, and to win your ultimate goal. Many of the fans had not accomplished such, but for the past four years, they could bear witness that it could be done. They cheered, they shouted, and it was all done with reverence. The winning team had given the adults pause from their suffering and balm to their healing. The team had given them memories—they proved that a small school, with small enrollments from a little town, could overcome and defeat larger schools, and do it continuously for three and a half years.

It was a fascinating thing to watch the intricate plays designed by the coaches and executed to perfection by the team. One such play was calculated for the sheer quickness of the boys. For instance the offensive lineman didn't waste their time just blocking one would-be tackler—they quickly knocked the first man they encountered off balance and continued on and did the same to others. By the time they recovered the speedy running back was through the gap and gone.

Most of all the townspeople thanked the team for giving them hope, a wondrous gift that would stay with them a lifetime, and reward them every day. The team awoke from their stupor and began clapping too in support of their fans.

There were fascinating bits and pieces of memories that Cary remembered. One of the greatest games the Devils ever played was the tremendous comeback the team displayed to defeat their rival, Petersburg, who had them down 18 to 0 at halftime. Their will would not be broken as they held them scoreless in the second half and won the game 26 to 18. Another ferocious battle, more like a war, was the time Petersburg was seemingly out to maim the running backs; evidently their only game plan. He watched the courageous running of Johnny Dean as he carried the ball relentlessly on every play and eventually across the goal as time was running out. Though hurting, he withstood the fierce onslaught of every defensive linebacker who keyed on him on every down. The team's will had not been broken and their win was not denied.

There were so many other great players, too numerous to mention, but not to be forgotten. Cary remembered the pride he felt when their team played an away game, playing at the opposition's field on a frosty, fall night. He watched the intimidation creep upon the faces of the opponent's fans as they watched the ever-increasing Hopewell crowd invade their stadium, more fans than their own team could muster. The whole population of Hopewell would be sitting across from them by the time the game had started. Then they were astonished as they watched the Hopewell majorettes come prancing out, leading a booming band. The majorettes were the prettiest and sexiest in the state and strutted their stuff with so much confidence that it only brought fear of what was to come next. The beauty of the majorettes would be their last enjoyment of the night. In later years when the good ol' boys rehashed the great games of Hopewell, they never forgot to include their fascination with the beauty of these girls, Tamara, Sophie and Julie.

Such were the times for these boys as they left their childhood days. They went forth with confidence, hope, and an attitude that any obstacle could be overcome. The competitiveness they retained would help them in years to come more so than they realized at the time. Time went by slowly in these days, and little did they know that these slow days would be their last, but their accomplishments would last a lifetime.

Cary was now leaving the Carolinas, and it came to him that he had identified some of his problems, but he wondered how can you overcome these invisible problems? He admitted he had suffered some, but he thought there were others whom had suffered more. He had his first glimpse of what caused so much pain and suffering in the world. If his problems had caused the destruction of his marriage, he could only comprehend the failure of others who suffered greater than he. The doctor had given him some insight of what caused people to go insane and commit vicious crimes. There were the physical assaults that hurt, but worst were the crimes of the mind and heart of those people whose actions were aimed to destroy the very essence of another person's being. These premeditated thoughts could be cold-heartedly delivered by word or action and their effects could be more devastating then any physical blow. Their target was the very marrow that held the intended victim together and their purpose was to slice the spirit, defile the mind, and obliterate hope—the last defense before the fall. The chance of survival of these intended targets depended on the recipient's reservoir of resistance. The taking away of a person's hope is the cruelest crime of all. A person can endure everything else but when hope is demolished, the spirit dies . . . and the soul is left languishing in despair. These cuts, the deepest of them all, leave scars that remain a lifetime. When in this condition, one could only pray, for there is nothing left. He realized there were walking time bombs out there and who knows who will get hurt when they reach the breaking point. The slightest thing could touch them off and they would vent their outrage amongst those surrounding them. Unfortunately, these were usually their closest friends and family members, the people who loved them most of all. He now understood the saying and the words of the song: “You always hurt the ones you love, the ones you really shouldn’t hurt at all.”

Tears welled up in Cary’s eyes; he could barely see the road ahead and pulled his car off the highway. It was so hard for him to realize he’d let these invisible things affect him. But evidently these problems had affected Scarlett and now himself. He felt he now understood what the doctor was telling him. He had identified his problems and there they were: His jutting lower jaw—his mangled speech—his introverted personality—his childhood poverty, probably the cause of his workaholic ways. He guessed he had identified the enemy . . . and it was *himself!* He thought maybe the doctor was on to something, and now all he had to do . . . was to *do* something about it. Easy to say but hard to do . . . but at least he had identified his enemy.

# Chapter Three

## Heading South

It was midnight when he ran out of gas just south of Brunswick, Georgia. It was too late to do anything about it, so he crawled into the back seat of his Chevy and spent the night. Luckily, he was in the South now and the fall weather was warm. The next morning he started walking back to where he remembered passing an old Esso gas station sign. He looked around him as the bright morning sun shone in his face. This part of the I-95 was in the eastern part of the Okefenokee Swamp. It was a desolate place that somehow reminded him of his birthplace. There were no trees, just marshy swamp grass on both sides of the built-up highway. There were seagulls swirling around him, and the air smelled of salt, reminding him that he wasn't far from the Atlantic Ocean. As he walked the lonely highway, he realized there was not a live soul to be seen and the uninhabited area gave Cary a sense of foreboding. Very few cars had passed him by the time he exited the off ramp two hours later and finally reached the old gas station located another two miles from the interstate.

He was too proud or too stubborn to thumb for a ride, preferring to punish himself for being so stupid for running out of gas. He guessed this was one of his hang-ups the shrink was talking about, one of his problems he should be working on. There was no activity at the station, and it dawned on him that it was Sunday and the place was closed down. There were no cars, no movement, except the scattering of leaves when the wind blew, and he hoped the place hadn't been shut down for good. What could go wrong next he wondered as he sat dejectedly on an ancient bench. Then a man appeared from behind the station and startled him when he spoke.

"Son, we're closed," he shouted and then, realizing he had frightened the boy, explained he lived behind the station. The premises looked little used, and Cary realized the station was like many, whose business was sharply curtailed after the Interstate was built and their business was by-passed. He was dressed in brown work clothes and had thinning gray hair. He was an older man Cary thought, and probably someone's grandpa.

"I ran out of gas, my car is miles down the road—anyway you can help me?" Cary pleaded. The man paused and looked him over for a second.

"Where you from boy?"

Cary thought before he spoke thinking the old man could be a grouchy red-neck who hated Yankees. Realizing his car tags couldn't be seen from here he answered. "My folks are from Pelham Georgia," he offered.

"Oh," he said as he grinned. "Georgia cracker huh? I've got a grandson over in Macon," he said with interest while rubbing his chin. "Haven't seen 'em in two years though."

"Yeah I'll get you some gas," he said turning toward the station door and reaching for his keys. "I'll have to turn the pumps on first, and you'll have to pay me for a two-gallon can for the gas." He gave Cary the gas and waved off his many gestures of thankfulness. "Take care of yourself son," he said with his hands resting on his hips watching Cary disappear down the road. Cary walked all the way back to the car, put the gas in, and hoped it would start before the battery ran down. It did, and he gave a sigh of relief as he left this God-forsaken place.

Nostalgia flowed over him as he finally entered Florida on Sunday afternoon. He drove straight on the interstate till he reached a suburb south of Jacksonville. He had a strong urge to see his dad's mom though he didn't know why. His grandma lived in a hamlet named Brandon, fifteen miles south of Jacksonville, spread along the St. John's River. She lived here now by herself, next door to his dad's brother. She was eighty-four and still in good health. He hadn't seen her in seven years since he came down on his honeymoon and introduced her to his new bride.

He pulled up in the deep white sandy lane and parked. As always, he was thrilled when reentering the state of his birth. Grandma's one-story house was built on a concrete slab. This, he was told, was to keep the termites in Florida from eating the wood foundation. The land was flat with mostly tall pine trees surrounding and giving shade to her white clinker-built house. He emerged from his car, stepped on the hot sand and remembered walking barefoot on it as a child. He couldn't walk barefoot on it in early summer, but by mid-summer, when the bottoms of his feet had gotten tough, he could walk on the hot sand without burning his feet. Shoot, by then, he could even bend briars and stickers with the bottoms of those leather-like bare feet.

Grandma was sweeping the pine needles from her front sandy yard as he approached her. They didn't have grass to mow that he remembered so they swept clean the sandy yard. It seemed most of Florida was covered with sand, which Cary interpreted as meaning that the area had been under water at one time. The homes with pretty grass yards were usually found in higher-income neighborhoods, but the families he knew couldn't afford to have good topsoil brought in. The huge old live oak tree in the front yard didn't look as big as he remembered, but it was still covered with hanging Spanish moss, nearly touching the ground.

"Hi Grandma," he shouted. "Sweeping your yard? We

mow our lawns in Virginia."

"How's that?" She turned and squinted in his direction, "Is that you Cary?"

"Yes ma'am," he reassured her.

She looked him up and down and spoke. "You've gained weight and grown a foot since I last seen you." She leaned her broom against a gate and ambled towards him, wiping her hands on the ever-ready apron she wore around her waist. Her flowered dress reached her ankles. She still looked round but tough and still had her silver hair, tinged with orange, bundled on top of her head.

"What are you doing here?" She looked at the empty car almost knowing the answer before she asked. "You by yourself . . . where's your wife? You in some kind of trouble?"

"Just come to see you," he assured her.

"Hmm, doubt that," she said. Grandma was always direct, straight to the point and sometimes to a fault. He grinned and mumbled something about just facing reality and trying to adjust to this crazy world.

"Sounds like you've been talking to a shrink." She was so blunt it hurt. After telling her about his divorce, he thought an onslaught would be forthcoming for breaking his marriage vows regarding the consequences of hell and a reiteration of just how hot hell really was. It was almost unheard of anyone getting divorced in their clan and it was scandalous. He had spent summers with her and she was tough. She went to bed at dusk, arose at daybreak, and expected the same from him. If he didn't, he had to face her demeaning glare. "That's the way God intended it, you can't work in the dark," she would say. And when you stayed with Grandma, she expected you to work. It seemed her favorite saying was idleness is the devil's workshop. She was not mean, just disciplined, his family said, but it was only years later that Cary understood the difference. Grandma never had any electricity until she was sixty. It was available but she didn't see any necessity for it. She was still using her kerosene lamps the last time he was here.

He remembered many years ago when she had her first contact with a telephone. She was alone, in her oldest son's house next door when the phone rang. It rang and rang till she couldn't stand it anymore. She finally picked it up and said "nobody home" and hung up. "Damn contraption," she said, "I'm not gonna talk to a machine."

She always slept with a .22 pistol underneath her pillow and a flashlight beside her bed. About three years ago she awoke in the middle of the night and got the two of them confused. She thought she had heard some commotion and got up to look around. She took her right hand and pushed the pistol into her left hand to turn on the light. She shot a .22 bullet straight through her hand. They said it was one of the few times they had ever heard her cuss. She was probably cursing her old age for doing such a stupid thing. She was wise and had a world of knowledge, whether it was cooking collards or how to handle a coiled rattlesnake. He never attempted to know or understand the hardships she must have endured, but he knew there had been many.

She gently took him aside and they talked of many things. She finally told him something he never knew. Sometime later he figured she told him this information on purpose, thinking it would help him . . . and it did. "You know, Cary, I was really worried about you as you were being born. I was there at the time you know. You heard the story about your sister drowning?" She motioned him out of the hot sun to her small shaded front porch and looked at him earnestly.

"Yes, I remembered the story my Mother told me. My sister was one year old . . .it was on her first birthday; she had just taken her first steps and fell off our back stoop and into a full rain barrel. They didn't think she could have crawled there, but must have stood up and walked. My Dad had seen her first but thought she was a doll and didn't come running 'til my mother screamed. By then it was too late . . . her first steps were her last."

"That's just the way it happened," Grandma said. "What

you may not know was your mother was carrying you at the time and you were five months along. Your mother was hysterical . . . we did everything we *could* to save the baby, but finally there was no doubt in anyone's mind that she was dead—except your mother's. She had given your dad three boys, and this was the first girl. Your mother knew how much your dad wanted a girl, and she couldn't admit she had lost her. Grandma looked at the ground, "Your Mother's eyes glanced at each of us . . . *pleading* for help . . .  and then upwards as if petitioning the Almighty for a miracle.  It almost killed her—and you.

"She frantically insisted your dad take her and the baby forty miles to the nearest hospital. Before your mother left, I grabbed her by the shoulders, shook her and said, 'Peggy, this child is gone, don't forget about the one you're carrying.' I think this was the first time she'd thought about you. As she ran towards the car I told her once more, 'Peggy, please be careful with the medication they'll try to give you, to sedate you.' Nevertheless, she had your dad carry them to the hospital. She rode all the way, hysterical, with your dead sister on her stomach . . . lying on top of you. When she finally came back with the hard reality that the baby girl was dead, she stayed in a deep depression until you were born."

"So . . . you were there when I was born?" Cary said studying the floor.

"Yes I was."

"Was I okay?"

Grandma raised her head, looked at him, and said as gently as she could. "Cary . . . you had nervous twitches and . . . and your eyes were blinking. I don't think your dad was overjoyed you being a boy. It was a depressing household for months to come and you were probably somewhat neglected. And of course after you, your mom did give your dad a girl and she was his pride and joy."

"So that's why they called me 'Blinky' in school. That's why I've always been so nervous—I'll be damned! I am damned! Why *didn't* they tell me? It would've *helped* if they'd of told me . . . if I had 'uh known."

# Chapter Four

## Old Home Town

He heartily thanked Grandma for all she'd told him, said goodbye and left. He headed west from Jacksonville, drove down Route 10 for an hour and finally turned onto a secondary road leading to Lake City and from there to his birthplace. It was another hour's drive and it gave him time to think. His mind raced as he thought that maybe he had more problems than he realized. This inner exploration was getting more complicated than he imagined. He was not so sure the shrink knew what he was getting him into by having him delve into his past and he wasn't sure it was going to work.

He entered Suwannee County and drove down the dusty back roads to his birthplace O'Brien, Florida. He still had the top down on his Chevy and he took in the nostalgic feeling he always felt when returning to his birthplace. The warm autumn wind blew his black hair around as he lit a cigarette. He smelled the honeysuckle vines that grew wild among the weeds lining the miles of tired-looking farm fences. He turned onto a sandy road and had to slow his speed. The huge live oak trees lined the road on both sides with limbs extending over the road, touching each other, and making a tunnel for as far as he could see. The Spanish moss hanging down was almost touching his car.

He reminisced about all the times he'd walked these roads as a shoeless kid and catching a ride home on the back of some farmer's pickup truck after watching an outdoor movie. He laughed as he remembered a time when he was six years old and still walking barefoot everywhere including school. One night after watching a movie he and his three older brothers were walking the two-mile sandy lane that led to their home. There was no moon in the pitch black sky and you couldn't see your hand in front of your face. The older, more civilized boys had been wearing shoes for two years or more. They had walked ahead of him and he soon heard them fussing. They were lost, unable to find the lane that turned towards home. Cary knew because his bare feet told him where the large oak tree was that stood only twenty yards from the turnoff. He could tell because the sandy road was warm, even at night, where there were no shade trees, but when the sand turned cool to his feet he knew he had come to the huge oak tree. He remembered his brothers cringing when he explained to Mom and Dad how he had led them home.

As he entered the small town, he noticed the changes. When he was a child, there were three gas stations, now there was only one. There were two grocery stores, now one, and they had torn down the old train depot and taken up the railroad tracks. The old wooden stores on the sandy main street were empty now, some leaning, faded and weed infested, but they held together with pride and stubbornness. Cary was thankful they were still here; glad because they reminded of pleasant boyhood memories of scrambling in and out of each. He stepped on the porch of old Ford's now-closed grocery store. The wood planks had weeds growing up between them and brushed his dusty boots as he walked across the creaking floor. He looked through the window and saw the old wood stove that was still there when he was a child.

He drove past the old wooden Methodist Church that he had attended every Sunday morning. It still stood but its two segregated front doors were now boarded up. He looked at the grassy lot beside the church, remembered it being covered with long tables of food and surrounded with laughing faces. He drove around the church to his childhood elementary school where he had attended the first and second grades. The two-story brick building was now gone. He left his car and wandered around the empty grounds, realizing it was all long gone now, like his dreams, faded into oblivion.

It's very seldom an adult goes back to his childhood home and finds it smaller now than before. One explanation was that the county supervisors didn't want changes. They particularly loved the old Suwannee River that encircled half the county. The county was named Suwannee because the area contained more miles of the river than any other. It originated from the Okefenokee Swamp just south of Waycross and west of Savannah, Georgia. Slowly flowing south, it meandered half way around Suwannee County, finally drifting on its one-way journey into the Gulf of Mexico in the adjacent county.

To Cary, Suwannee County had a laidback atmosphere; everything seemed to move slowly, there was no hurry and no one got excited about anything. Something Cary had not been used to since he moved from this place. It relaxed his nerves and he'd wished many times that they'd never moved. There were mostly farmers that worked from sun up to sun down. The rest were the ordinary people you see everywhere: county employees, teachers, utility workers and a smattering of government employees, mostly farm related.

Suwannee County was located in northwest Florida and had four seasons, though not as distinct as those in Virginia. The majority of northerners who decided to make Florida their home moved further south where the weather stayed warm all year round. Whether they were retirees or people looking for jobs, they bypassed this area because there were few jobs and cold winters. About the only connection most of these people had with

Suwannee County was the State's song, "Old Folks At Home." There's a memorial down the road by the river dedicated to Stephen Foster, the author of the song.

The county had changed little in the last twenty-nine years he had known it. It was mostly cold in winter, lasting from late December to March with some freezing temperatures. When the first day of spring came it quickly turned to summer and stayed hot until late fall, which brought some cooler temperatures but mostly a smell in the air that carried a tang of autumn. It was ghostly quiet and dark except when the moon was out, shining through the moss-covered oak trees. The moon shone brightly on the white sand except when the wind blew and the tired oak limbs covered with their dress of silver moss swayed eerily in the night, leaving ghostly shadows flickering on the ground. These nights often gave Cary a creepy feeling. Even so, he loved to walk, preferably barefooted, on these warm nights when the moonlight lit up his path.

He had always felt the Suwannee River brought some of the ghostly atmosphere from its swampy source. Cary used to think the murky, slow-moving waters were draining the swamp dry. Later he realized the river's dark color was mostly derived from the marshland vegetation and the majority of the river was actually spring water that boiled up from the many natural springs found along its journey. He would swim in the river during the day but at night the river, to this day, gave him a foreboding feeling. He knew the black waters contained moccasins and alligators, and the banks were inhabited by rattlesnakes.

The county supervisors couldn't bear to see industry move in and change the homeland they had so much affection for. For this reason, they never encouraged development. He would have agreed right along with them if he'd been in their place. Where else and who else could enjoy the nostalgic euphoria of coming back many years later to their birthplace and seeing their old swimming hole unchanged from childhood? Cary had enjoyed every acre of this place before his family left to go north, looking for jobs after the Great War ended as many families did back in the forties and fifties.

He visited the old town cemetery where many of his relatives were buried. In the past he had always come here first for some unknown reason when he visited his hometown. He had never come here and seen the cemetery in disarray. It was always well maintained with obvious loving care by unseen souls. He strolled past the magnolia trees that seemed to be perpetually blooming and paused to savor their fragrance. Some things never change, he thought. There was a scattering of palm trees that must have been transplanted because they were not indigenous to this area.

He meandered among the sandy graves, picking wild flowers as he strolled, memories flooding over him as he paused beside each headstone of someone he remembered. Among his relatives buried here were his dad's father, two of his uncles and their wives, his one-year old sister, and many other distant relatives. He paused at his sister's grave and looked at the childlike stone statue of a sad angel weeping. Time had left her leaning, partly molded and one hand broken. He was there until the sun set, and the long shadows were quickly replaced by low dark clouds that loomed above and smelled deeply of rain. Childhood thoughts inundated Cary and he paid no attention to the weather. His heart was overrun with painful memories and he couldn't withhold the tears that flooded down his face. He sighed and leaned back wearily on his hot dusty Chevy as he dropped flower petals one by one, and watched them flutter hopelessly among his departed loved ones. He had never felt so all alone.

## The Invention

## Chapter 5

He spun the tires and slid sideways as he exited the cemetery, heading to his brother's home. He lived in the adjacent county only miles down the road and across the Suwannee River at Branford. As he crossed this bridge the rain was coming down so hard he could barely see the old sign above his head, with musical parentheses, that boldly read, "Way Down Upon the Suwannee River." Cary had not been to Jim's home in ten years but remembered where he lived and thought he could find it okay. The area looked unchanged since the last time he was here, not a new business to be seen and no new houses. Momentarily he would pass an old Gulf gas station that had a faded sign proclaiming wrecker service and car repairs. There was a scattering of porches with attached wood frame houses that, more times than not, contained a swing with a social security recipient idling his time away. It was a desolate looking area he was passing as he slowed and looked through the pouring rain for Jim's driveway. Dixie County indeed looked, as Jim had told him, like the poorest county in the state of Florida. He finally came to his sandy lane and turned in. Cary bounced down the road and wondered why in the heck Jim had moved to this God-forsaken swampy looking area that seemed cut off from the world.

Jim was very secretive about his affairs and we never knew what he was really involved in. The family had always thought him a little on the fanatical side but of course they never told him that. Jim, since a teenager, always seemed to be working on some great invention. One was a still that would transform the moonshine business. Then there was the auto tire, imbedded with metal, which would last twice as long as the one now being used. The last invention they heard him mention was a great automotive engine that would, of all things, mostly run off of water and triple the gas mileage for the family car. These momentous invention ideas soon faded into oblivion. Cary snaked around several dusty curves and then the road sloped downwards. He thought surely he must be below sea level, but as he approached Jim's place, the road jutted upwards towards a narrow hilltop just as he came to his driveway.

Jim's home was still located on top of this hill where he remembered it, overlooking the river. He parked at the end of his sandy driveway, exited his car, and began walking towards Jim's mobile home. It was dark and quiet now and the rain had stopped just as quickly as it had begun. Low storm clouds hovered above, bringing darkness sooner than normal. Jim's home was here in the county miles from the closest town. There was not a house to be seen, just a forest of huge live oak trees with tremendous branches stretching out horizontally and soaked with Spanish moss. The undergrowth was thick and green and everything was wet and smelled of rain. The deep sandy ruts made it difficult to walk and he wished he were barefoot. The only sounds were blackbirds squawking and gliding in the dim moonlight that was just emerging from the misty fog over Jim's home. To a stranger, the place would seem eerie, but to Cary it had the warm nostalgic feeling of home.

"Jim, you here?" he hollered as he headed down his lane, not having thought to call before he came. After a moment he saw a large double-barreled shotgun, shimmering in the light of the moon, advancing in his direction. A bearded man followed the shotgun with a cap pulled low over his face. The gun was pointed straight at him and he froze . . . then, calmly spoke, "Jim, it's just your brother Cary—don't shoot!"

"Cary who?" a gruff voice growled.

"Me, your brother Cary!" he replied, afraid to move and quelling the urge to run. The gun came closer and then Jim appeared with his ghostly shadow following as he questioned who this intruder was.

"Is that you Cary?" he asked, his eyes squinting at him in the darkness.

"Yeah, put that gun down."

Jim lowered the gun and said, “Well . . . I’ll be damned, I didn’t recognize you there in the shadows.” Jim came over with a big smile and hugged his brother. “Man, I didn’t recognize you, why didn’t you call? You gave me a scare! Let me look at you. You’re still taller than me and looking lean and mean.” Glancing at his car said, “You still have the old Chevy.”

“Yeah, my old white convertible, had it a long time, couldn’t part with it.”

Jim walked towards Cary’s car and looked it over. “Still got the dual exhaust and the fender skirts I see . . . and the car still looks good. Is it fast?”

“It is,” Cary said, drying his face with his sleeve, “got the big V-8 with a three-quarter cam.”

“Well, we’ll haf’ta see,” Jim said, pointing to his old sixty-one Ford, “this one goes pretty good too; maybe I’ll race you around the pond later. What’cha doing down here? You didn’t call.”

With a sigh of relief, Cary said, “It’s a long story, get me a beer and I’ll tell you all about it. Damn, I’d forgotten how ghostly quiet it was down here.”

“It only seems quiet ’cause you’ve been away so long.” Jim leaned his shotgun against the trailer, stepped inside, and came out with two beers. The pair sat down and popped open their cans at a picnic bench overlooking the river that now was enveloped with darkness. The harvest moon was rising above the trees and lit up the steamy mist coming off the river as it always does after a rain storm. The only sounds Cary heard were the rhythmic chirping of the crickets and the deep croaks of the bullfrogs.

Cary was surprised at his brother's initial reaction and curiously looked him over. Jim was five years older than he, about thirty-four, and he hadn't seen him in five years since he had visited Virginia. Jim returned to Florida over a dozen years ago as he'd always been homesick for his birthplace. He'd grown a beard and was wearing a tan mechanic's jump suit. His black hair jutted outwards from his cap seemingly screaming for a haircut.

He appeared unusually nervous. Cary remembered him as always being calm and under control but now his demeanor was very unusual. He sensed something wasn't right and thought back about his past. He remembered Jim running off to Florida after he caught his best friend in bed with his wife who later had a child that was probably not Jim's. This best friend was never seen again, and his name was never mentioned in Jim's presence. They had known then that something bad was going to happen, or maybe already had. He never forgot the night Jim found them. Cary was awoken after midnight in his fourth-story apartment located in the Fan district of downtown Richmond. As he wondered what woke him, he heard a slow moan, and then opened his door. Jim was slouching towards the floor with one hand still clinging to his door knob. Cary dragged him into his room and onto his bed. He mumbled what happened and pleaded for Cary to hit him hard and knock him out. They both were aware of the doctor's warning after he had been shot three years previously: "You must remain calm in all situations or there may be dire consequences from the bullet still sitting next to your heart." While Cary was debating whether to call the emergency crew or hit him as hard as he could, Jim passed out. Later Cary wondered how he had gotten there since the downstairs door was locked. After investigating, he realized Jim had gone to the apartment building next door and actually jumped from the top floor of that building to his, then somehow slid inside his floor from an unlocked window.

Jim physically survived that night, but we were never sure what happened to the rest of him. His life had drastically changed in just three short years. At eighteen he was a handsome boy, had a beautiful girlfriend, and was a star running back on his undefeated high school football team. He was enrolled in the scientific course at school and desperately sought a college football scholarship. After that he anxiously awaited the fulfillment of his biggest dream of all: his marriage to his lifelong sweetheart. Life's turn of events changed all that. When he was shot, the scholarship was lost. He did marry but three years later his wife betrayed their trust with an act of adultery. After all this he was just dead in the water. As the years went by, Jim became more embittered, and seemed to live life with reckless abandonment. These events had filled him to the brink and imbedded him with utter contempt. He was soaked with hatred and anger and he couldn't help but let it show. He had never learned to find a safe way to expend this God-awful, pent-up misery, and eventually it permeated outwards. Cary thought he'd heard the definition of this before, could have been from his shrink, maybe.

Cary finished his beer, told Jim about the divorce and everything that had happened. They were quiet for awhile until Jim finally showed his remorse.

"Damn, I'm really sorry Cary, those women are hard to handle . . . I know by experience, but I'm sure glad you're down here and I hope you can stay awhile."

"Yeah, sure, I don't have any plans. As a matter of fact, I don't have anything, nothing . . . zippo. Hell, if you've got it—I'll ride it! Right now I'm broke and all I've got is a little money for gas and a few cans of beans that may last me a couple of weeks. I'm sorry about not calling, but hell, I didn't even know I was coming . . .'til I got here. Tell me Jim, how you been? You okay, what's with the shotgun and all? You scared me!"

"I've had my problems too. You stay with me awhile and I'll fill you in. They sat outside underneath the moonlight, and Jim put a pot of coffee on his campfire. As Cary watched the coffee percolate, he thought of how Jim's life and his had things in common. Both had lost the two things most precious to them. They both had lost them in Virginia and now both were back here at their birthplace. *Must be a brother thing,* he thought. He wondered if he would end up like Jim . . . alone. They reminisced about the past and brought each other up to date since their last meeting. Jim did more outside cooking than inside, mostly coffee and beans and sometimes fried fish from a morning fishing trip down the river.

"What's with this weather?" Cary asked. "I almost drowned as I left the O'Brien Cemetery."

"Well, didn't you hear? We got us a hurricane banging around in the Gulf. It's the beginning of hurricane season and this is the first. We're getting rain from those bands coming off that storm and we'll get more tonight. My lake is already rising."

"No, I didn't hear" said Cary. "I haven't paid much attention to the weather."

"Cary," Jim said somberly, "I've got worries down here."

"What kind of worries?"

"Well, its *good* troubles maybe, it's about my invention, you know the one I mentioned to you years ago."

"Yeah . . . I remember the auto engine you were working on. Hell, you've been working on that for ages, hoping it'd get high gas mileage. I figured you'd given up on it by now."

"Oh no," Jim said as he adjusted the perking coffee pot away from the now crackling hot fire, "I never gave up on it."

"Well, tell me about it," Cary drawled with a sigh of disinterest as he leaned back. He'd heard these ramblings before.

Jim sat up, his eyes were twinkling and he seemed ready to burst with some great secret he couldn't contain any longer. He glanced around and then said with an emerging toothy smile, "Cary, I did it, *I did it!"*

"Yeah . . . did what?" Cary asked.

Jim paused and poured them both a cup of coffee. He sat his down to cool and took out two big cigars and handed Cary one. Cary knew not to rush him, he felt that in his own good time, Jim would reveal some profound revelation to him, some daydream that was only a reality in Jim's mind.

"Cary, you know I've been accused of being paranoid."

"Yeah, I'll admit to that. I've probably accused you of that myself." He didn't tell him the psychiatrist had discovered a more serious condition of himself.

"Well, I'm going to tell you something, but it's terribly important that you know the significance of it. I haven't told anyone and I have a hard time trusting anyone with this information." He looked straight at Cary for a long time and finally said. "Can I trust you? I'm *serious,* damn it! You could endanger both of our lives if you reveal what I'm going to tell you."

Cary realized that Jim was serious as hell but he still was unconvinced as he sat up and took a sip of his coffee. "Jim, look . . . we're brothers, and we've been through a lot together. Tell me . . . let me help you. You can sure as hell trust me."

"Okay, but promise you'll follow my instructions regarding this information. It's awfully important. Damn, I'm glad you're here—I need someone I can trust . . . I really do."

Cary put out his hand and shook Jim's while looking him straight in the eye and said, "I promise."

Jim relaxed for a moment, sipped his coffee and took a long drag from his cigar. His dark eyes narrowed and he glanced around suspiciously as if to be sure Cary had come alone. He leaned forward towards Cary and whispered, *"I finished the engine invention . . .* I took a test drive. I drove from here to Jacksonville and back on *less* than two gallons of gas."

*"Good God!"* Cary jumped up. He swirled around thinking, "Damn, that must be roughly, uh, uh, must be at least a 200 mile trip!"

"Two hundred and ten," Jim replied, finally smiling.

"That's unbelievable Jim, you're pulling my leg—are you

*sure*?"

"It's true, believe me!"

Cary was up now, dancing all around and shouting, "You're rich Jim—*you're rich!"*

Jim was motioning to him with his arms while whispering. *"Calm* down, calm down, it's not that easy."

Cary sat down with his spirit dropping . . . afraid he'd been duped again by Jim's weird manifestations. He remembered him working on an engine innovation for as long as he could remember. It was hard for his folks to take him seriously anymore because he always had a reason, an excuse they thought, for not succeeding in completing said project. The last excuse he remembered him saying was that he couldn't afford to build a garage.

So now Cary was ready for another disappointment. He hadn't forgotten that for many years Jim had a habit of telling outlandish stories to anyone who would listen. He did this for some reason the family had never fathomed, unless it was for some neurotic need or twisted pleasure. Cary felt Jim's actions revealed a case of paranoia by his seemingly strong need for recognition, coupled with delusions of grandeur. In the course of some of his diatribes, he would embellish every incident in never-ending loquacity, and skew every detail with ambiguities.

The last story was about a large rock he had uncovered in

his small lake. He swore he had justifiable reasons to think it was the remains of a comet and had sent a portion to Florida State University to verify his theory. With a smile he said it could be very valuable, but we never heard of any reply from the university. Later, we noticed many similar rocks at entranceways to the small towns in the area, but he would never admit he was pulling our leg. And he hated being found wrong . . . wrong about anything and on top of that, he hated to lose at anything. He would argue you unceasingly and if he thought he might be losing the argument, he would change the subject, and hoped you would soon forget about it. It seemed a mortal sin to him to ever be caught wrong about anything. We finally got used to it and would just smile and let it drop. So now Cary was ready for another of his neurotic daydreams and finally asked, "What's not easy, Jim?"

Jim was still calm as he leaned back with an air of confidence while puffing on his cigar and finally answered: "The engine worked fine, oh, it will need some refinements to make it marketable, but that's not a problem. The most important thing is I have proven my concept was valid, and my idea was sound. But now that I've proven it," he said with a perplexed grin, "I don't really know what to do next, and *that's* what worries me."

Yeah, Cary thought, Jim was dumbfounded that now it appeared he may have *actually* accomplished something. "What do you mean you don't know what to do next?" Cary said as his brief excitement plummeted.

"Well, it's been so long in coming, I never really gave a thought to what to do when it finally happened. I thought that part would be easy."

"Get it patented," Cary blurted.

"No," Jim was shaking his head, "call me paranoid, but I don't trust the system. Someone there could steal it. We are talking about millions . . . *maybe billions* of dollars here." He was up now and pacing between the live oaks and talking with his hands waving in the air just beneath the hanging moss.

Cary noticed that Jim was still in shape and still had the rugged body and cat-like movements that had won him the game ball after his team had won the high school football championship. Jim turned and faced him on the other side of the blazing campfire that now lit up his face. Cary could still see the scar just beneath his bottom lip where a football cleat had torn a jagged hole and knocked out some teeth in the Petersburg game. He remembered the heated argument on the sidelines whether he was to get stitches or return to the game. They were down by three, time was running out, and what was more important? Jim winced as though he was carefully choosing his words and spoke. "Don't you see why I was hesitant to tell you? This much money could make ordinary people do strange things, much less the oil companies that'll lose billions if this system was put on the road." He turned and looked at Cary. "The oil companies you know . . . they could be after our heads."

Cary didn't know what to think and was getting angry. He jumped up while trying to control his temper. "Damn it Jim, I've just lost my wife, my business—*my whole world!* I don't know where my next meal is coming from. Don't bullshit me now—I'm in no mood for it!"

Jim was taken aback by Cary's reaction; he paused, giving Cary time to settle down, picked up a piece of wood, stoked the fire and calmly spoke. "Listen . . . I know some of my past stories were, maybe . . . a little exaggerated, but this is the *truth* I'm telling you now."

"Well, I'm sorry, but this time you'll just have to prove it before I'll believe it. I can't stand any more disappointments; I've had all I can handle. I can't live on daydreams."

Jim was undaunted by Cary's remarks and his enthusiasm continued. "Cary, can't you see? If you let this out, I would have vultures out here tearing the place apart and our lives wouldn't be worth two cents."

Cary, trying to calm himself, decided as usual to give him the benefit of the doubt, but only this time, he would *have* to prove what he was saying. He nodded in agreement and said, "Okay, don't worry, I promise, I'll keep my mouth shut. But Jim, there must be someone we could trust . . . ”

“Yeah, who? I’ve racked my brain. You see we’ve got two problems, we could go to someone, maybe someone we could sell the system to, but then they’d have to see it operate before they’d purchase it. We would then be exposed with no patent, no protection and if they were the wrong kind of people they could possibly try to steal it. I don’t have the funds to manufacture it myself—all I can do is try to sell it, particularly if I thought my life was on the line. No one’s going to touch it ’til they turn over the money first. That’s where it stands at the moment. I’ve also got a problem,” he pointed down towards his garage close to the pond. “I’ve installed the engine in the old Fifty Ford and there it sits—and it makes me nervous. My only chance is to sell it because I’m really afraid the gas companies wouldn’t allow it on the market. I honestly think, researching the past inventions of this sort, there have been others similar to mine that may have been bought off by the oil companies and the inventions never made it to market. We’ll just have to take it easy and figure this thing out.”

“You think your invention may already been patented?” Cary questioned.

“Oh no, I’ve researched the patents and this invention has definitely not been registered.”

“But,” Cary said still doubtful, “but how are you going to

sell it if you don't let anyone touch it? I mean, they're not going to take your *word* the engine will travel a hundred miles on one gallon of gas."

"Yeah . . . I've given that a lot of thought and here's what I've come up with. We'll prove the engine by showing them a test run," said Jim. "Yes, that's how we'll prove it. We'll demonstrate it—we'll *prove* it that way."

Cary still had doubts about the authenticity of the invention. He thought of all the other schemes and inventions Jim had tried to complete but never finished. This time, before he got his hopes up, he would like to be sure that Jim was really on to something. He turned to Jim and looked him straight in the eye and said, "Would you demonstrate the gas mileage for me tomorrow? I mean Jim—I've gotta see this for myself!"

A big grin crossed Jim's face as he looked at Cary. "Ah, you think I could be pulling your leg, huh?" He looked down and knocked some ashes off his cigar. "Well, I can't blame you for being skeptical, after all, it is a massive story I'm telling you."

"Yeah, and you know it wouldn't be the first," Cary said without smiling.

Jim looked at Cary with a mock hurt look on his face and said with a confident smile, "I'll be glad to give you a private demonstration first thing tomorrow morning!" Cary thought to himself, I'm no mechanic and the only way I'd be convinced the engine could travel a hundred miles on a gallon of gas would be *to see it* with my own eyes.

The fall night was still warm; the full moon shone down through the massive oak limbs and left huge shadows on the white sandy ground. The two country boys were huddled around the dwindling bonfire, dreaming and scheming into the night. Both were alone, broke and out of work, but for the moment, in their minds they were rich and had momentous decisions to consider and meditate upon. This was deep stuff for these swamp boys—what to do with an invention that could affect the economics of the whole world and could make them rich beyond their dreams. Having problems were nothing new to them, they had become a way of life.

"Have some beans?" one said.

"Thanks, but when we get our millions..."

"Billions," the other corrected.

"Have you got a beer left?"

"Yeah, and one can of beans."

"Well, this may be better than picking cotton."

"Sure better than cropping tobacco."

"I think the first thing I'll do is give my ex wife a million just to flaunt it in her face," Cary said. They both chuckled. Hell, Cary barely knew what a million dollars was, much less a billion. He'd never had a reason to count that high.

"You still jogging every morning, Jim?"

"I'll race you to the paper box at daybreak!"

"Oh, man . . ."

They went to bed and were asleep as the moon disappeared and the rain began pouring down in torrents. Daybreak came and they sprung out of bed when a loud gust of wind rocked the trailer. Jim was looking out the window towards his pond, "Oh god, Cary, the pond is flooding—the hurricane must of turned towards us—the water has surrounded my garage and my car is in there. It must have poured all night! We've gotta get it out uh there. *Hurry!* We have to move the car before the engine is ruined!" Cary pulled some clothes on and was behind Jim as he reached the garage and unlocked the door. The water was up to their knees, the winds were howling, and the oak limbs were swaying. "I can't drive it and we can't push it through this water, we've got to pull it out with my truck." Grab that chain off the wall and hook it to the car while I go and start my truck." Cary sunk to his knees as the water lapped around his face. Without being able to see, he wrapped the chain around the front axle of the Fifty Ford. "Cary!" Jim shouted from the top of the hill, "I can't get close enough!"

Cary struggled up the hill and made his way past Jim and opened his trunk and retrieved a thirty-foot chain.

"Here, add this chain to yours and I think it'll reach."

They did this and Jim started pulling the Ford out of the garage, but only got it about twenty feet when his tires started spinning as the rising water was making the Fifty Ford too heavy to pull.

"Hold on Jim," Cary said as he trudged back through the rising water to his Chevy, backed it up and attached another chain from his car to Jim's truck. "Alright, Jim let's pull together." They were on high ground but the garage and the old Ford were much lower and closer to the pond that had now risen another foot. Cary's car had just enough power, added to Jim's truck, to slowly pull the Fifty Ford up the hill to safety. They finally got the car completely out of the water and to high ground before the engine got wet. The wind was still raging, and the spits of rain pelted their face as they made it back to the mobile home that sat under the massive oak trees.

"Whew, damn—thank God you were here Cary, you saved the day, that pond sure came up fast."

"You think it'll get to your trailer?"

Jim shook his head no, "It's never got this high before; we're okay. And after the rain stops, the pond will go down just as fast as it came up. I'm more concerned about a limb coming through the roof than anything else."

"If one of those massive oak limbs falls on us, we'll be tomorrow's news," said Cary.

Jim smiled, "Naaw, those trees are some tough sons-abitches; the other trees would go before the oaks."

"How close was the hurricane to us?"

"Its going past us was the last thing I heard last night, but they did say it could veer a little towards the east. It's not a big-time hurricane, but damn, it sure brought some rain," he said as he peered through the window. "I think the worst is over." They both took a deep breath for the first time and laughed when realizing how soaked they were. "Come on," said Jim, "let's dry off and get a change of clothing and I'll put on some coffee."

"That sounds good—all this work before breakfast. Heck of a way to welcome your brother... you been flooded before?"

"This is only the second time in fifteen years. The county said this wouldn't happen again, since they'd put in larger drainage culverts. But this is Dixie County and their thinking doesn't always pan out. We're used to hurricanes down here but you never know where they're gonna hit."

"Damn, thanks for helping me Cary," Jim said as they huddled over their coffee. "You may have saved us a million dollars."

"Lucky I was here, huh?"

"Yes and maybe I can reimburse you if you can help me sell this thing." The boys stayed inside the trailer and watched the hurricane forecast. The newsmen said it would be out of the area the next day and they were relieved that the most damage was only from the water it brought. They went out the next morning to check everything. The pond water around the garage was already descending and the lane to the highway had two low spots that still held some water, but otherwise there were no problems.

After coffee, they both hovered over Jim's engine as he checked it over for the test run. Jim only explained the basics to his brother. "You see this small motor, it's a Swirling Engine, that's been around for decades but no one has found a feasible way, an economical way, to generate the power to run it. That's what I have accomplished but I won't expound on that for now. I did have to utilize several batteries you see there and the Swirling Engine in return recharges the batteries. Before the batteries can run down, I've devised a system that will recharge the batteries. When brakes are applied, this energy is rerouted to the batteries and keeps them recharged. They're marine batteries and can stand recharging for longer periods of time. Now these batteries combined with smaller amounts of gas are what power the Swirling engine. The real secret is the great amount of energy the Swirling engine produces."

He went into some more detail until they both realized Cary was lost. All he could do was to take Jim's word for it and that was difficult knowing his past history. Jim finished the work needed, checked the engine over and by evening had it ready for the test run. Jim looked at the garage that still held some water and said, "We'd be smart to wait another day for all this water to go down." Jim went to his other garage high on the hill, opened the door and took two fishing poles from the back wall and they spent the rest of the day fishing.

The next morning they got ready for the test run. Cary asked whether Jim could verify that only two gallons of gas would be put in the gas tank. "Yes, I'll let you do it," said Jim. He showed Cary the gas gauge that was setting on empty.

"Yeah, but the gas tank could still have some gas in it," Cary doubted.

"Start the engine and let it run until it stops, until it runs out of gas." Cary started the engine and sure enough it sputtered to a stop after a few minutes. "Now get that can of gas out of the garage and verify how much gas it contains." Cary lifted the can, looked it over and agreed it was a regular two-gallon can full of gas. "Now you pour the two gallons of gas in the old Ford." Cary carefully poured the two gallons in and they jumped in the old Ford and took off for a trip to Jacksonville. Cary received a cramp in his neck after continuously leaning over trying to see if the gas gauge ever moved. They returned home some four hours later. Jim had Cary check the gas gauge and he could see that it was sitting on empty as the car continued to run. It was now just running on fumes and Jim let it run until it sputtered to a stop a few minutes later. Cary was satisfied the engine had made the trip on two gallons of gas and had also confirmed the Jacksonville round trip mileage was a little over two hundred miles. He was transfixed and had a difficult time admitting what had just occurred. He couldn't help wondering whether Jim pulled some elaborate hoax. If he had, he sure went to a lot of trouble. He was astonished as he considered the implications of what Jim had accomplished and still had other questions.

"Jim, are there any other problems? Cary asked thinking this was all too good to be true.

"As I said there may be some modifications necessary, but nothing I can't handle. You see, the engine is not powered by batteries and as you witnessed, the engine powered the car just as normally as any other." Cary couldn't think of anything else to question, and could only think of the ramifications this engine would render throughout the world market.

Jim looked at Cary and waited for a sign of long awaited recognition, but Cary's mouth was open with disbelief. It slowly dawned on him that Jim appeared to have finally pulled off something remarkable and all he could do was mumble, "I'll be damned." He didn't notice it but Jim was gushing with pride as . . . finally, a family member had witnessed first-hand that he, Jim Williams, had finally completed a long talked about dream. Cary glanced up and noticed Jim's expression and said respectfully

"Congratulations, Jim Williams. Seems you've invented something valuable here, how valuable . . . I can't imagine."

Cary was still puzzled as to how Jim had accomplished such an engineering feat with only the help of a couple of falling down garages and a few mechanical tools around. He was still having problems believing everything he had just experienced knowing Jim's history of fabrications. Had he been out here in the backwoods too long? Had his mind gone astray? He kept waiting for Jim to say, "April Fool" but he had checked and it wasn't April the first. On the other hand he had to concede that maybe Jim had the intelligence to invent such a thing. After all, he remembered him making straight A's while taking the scientific course all through high school and his head was always stuck in some scientific magazine. He was no dummy and it was true he'd been working on this invention since high school days. He scratched his head and finally spoke, "Jim, now that you've proven the gas mileage test, you might as well tell me the rest."

"What rest?"

"I'm not stupid Jim you couldn't have put that invention together in that dilapidated garage there."

Jim looked at Cary for a long time and shook his head. "Cary, you *are* a hard man to convince, aren't you?

"It just *seems* too good to be true, and I'm tired of disappointments—that's all."

"Well, it goes against my grain, but now that you have agreed to be my partner, and since you have as much to lose as I do . . . I guess I can tell you. I'll show you something that no one's ever seen but me. Come, follow me."

Cary followed Jim to the highest part of the hill on his property. They walked to his old two-car wooden garage where Jim opened the garage door and there sat his fourteen-foot fishing boat.

"This is it?" Cary asked scratching his head as Jim walked to the back where it appeared to be just an old wooden garage wall with fishing poles hanging on it. As Cary watched in amazement Jim moved his hand to an area hidden behind a workbench, and lo and behold, the back wall went up and over, fishing poles and all. The wall was actually a garage door camouflaged as the back wall of the garage. They walked in and Cary couldn't believe his eyes when Jim flipped a switch and the interior lit up in blazing light. After they were inside, Jim hit another button and down went the door.

"So this is where you did it!" Cary shouted as Jim grinned. The room was huge, larger than a four-car garage and it was spotless. The floor was white smooth concrete and the walls were solid cedar. There were intricate machines and tools of every kind in immaculate condition and carefully positioned around the room. There were sturdy tables surrounding the workshop topped with metal lathes, drills and various types of equipment that Cary had never seen. The walls were precisely adorned with smaller tools. They were positioned by size, side by side, from the most minuscule to the largest. Cary slowly strolled around the worktables; his fingers carefully brushing the tools. "This is a mechanic's dream," he said. Further along Cary noticed Jim's music collection. There were various tapes ranging from Beethoven to the Blues, and high on the wall, was his treasured game ball. He realized he was seeing a part of Jim he'd never known. "You rascal," Cary said, "I *knew* it—I knew damn well you couldn't have completed that project in that old garage outside."

"Well, no one has figured it out but you," said Jim.

"Yeah, but I wouldn't have either until I saw what you had accomplished." They walked out and closed the door and Cary walked around the outside and shook his head. "It's all underground, under that hill." He was still puzzled, still doubtful. "Now where did you get all that machinery in there Jim? It's *gotta* be worth over a hundred thousand dollars! You didn't steal it, *did you*?"

Jim was grinning and shaking his head sideways. "That's a long story, but I'll tell you the short of it. There was a retired old German widower who lived down the road a piece. He was very knowledgeable in many areas; he was a superb machinist and had his own business up north until he retired here a few years ago. He brought his equipment with him and set up a shop for his only son to start a business of his own. His son eventually got messed up on drugs and ran off. I befriended him and we became close friends as he was a frustrated inventor himself. Actually, some knowledge I garnered from him helped me complete the invention. Old age caught up with him, he fell seriously ill, his son never returned, and I was the only one that cared for him. I was at his bedside when he died. A few weeks later I received a legal paper signed by him giving me legal ownership of all his machinery. I could never have accomplished what I did without his knowledge and his machinery."

Now things were falling into place and Cary's doubts diminished as he muttered, "That's some story Jim . . . you've got a hell of an operation here."

"Yeah," said Jim, "took me years . . . it's been a long haul and now you see why I was so cautious in telling you about it. Cary, you coming down here was . . . was like a special co-incidence to me. I needed someone to trust and after you arrived, it dawned on me that you were just the one to help me. It just seemed like the right thing to do. It's come to me that I can't handle this situation alone any more. I'm taking a chance on you and hope you won't let me down. You're not crazy or anything or you?"

Cary thought about that and grinned, “No, I don’t think so.”

They had just walked away from the garage when they heard a truck pull into Jim’s sandy driveway. They dropped their conversation and walked to meet the visitor. It as a man Jim knew.

“Hey, Jim!” the man hollered as the two were walking away from the garage.

“Hi Jack,” Jim said. “This is my brother, Cary, down from the North.” Jack glanced at Cary and nodded but his attention was on another matter. Jack was a big man who was a native of the county. He was one of the good ole boys who drove a beat up pick-up truck that usually included the doghouse for his coonhounds in back and rifles hanging on racks behind the truck seats. He chewed on his tobacco and between spits, chatted with Jim about everything from coon hunting to butchering hogs. His long hair was stringy and greasy looking as it stuck out behind his matching John Deere cap. He knew all there was to know about living in Dixie County and he displayed this knowledge each and every morning over cups of coffee at the local McDonald’s where the locals hung out. These local boys didn’t let much work interfere with their everyday plans.

“Jim, how’s it going boy, what cha been up to?”

“Nothing much Jack, same old stuff, trying to get this car

running." He pointed to his 61 Ford. It turned out Jack was an auto mechanic in Old Town seven miles down the road.

"Seen you last week," Jack said, "heading east on route 10, honked my horn, but guess you didn't see me. Where were you going, got friends up there?"

Jim was steadily thinking; he knew if Jack had seen him, he also saw what car he was driving and it wasn't the one he normally drove. He answered, "No, just checking some junkyards looking for a carburetor for this car over here," still diverting his attention towards the 61 Ford he usually drove.

"Oh yeah," Jack said, "I'd stopped to get gas at Fast Eddie's and he mentioned you had just stopped in. Eddie was laughing, said you must of have been broke 'cause you only bought one gallon of gas in that old 50 Ford of yours." He looked around and asked, "Where is it anyhow?"

"I've stuck it in the garage there, gotta check the transmission, it's making a strange noise," Jim motioned Jack away from the nearly dry garage and to the 61 Ford that needed carburetor work and said, "Well being out of work, money doesn't go far, you know, times are tough," Jim laughed.

They talked about the carburetor for awhile until Jack seemed to lose interest, said he had to go and drove off. The two looked at each other and Jim was shaking his head. "Damn it, that guy being a mechanic, always wants to know what I'm up to." He looked straight at Cary and said, "See what I mean—see what I mean! It's a wonder he didn't ask to see the old car locked in the garage. This is making me nervous."

"Think we ought to hide it somewhere else," Cary said.

"I don't know," Jim said shaking his head.

In the evening they went fishing in the lake behind Jim's house. They wrestled with their dilemma while not catching any fish. Cary finally came up with an idea.

"Jim, didn't some of the locals know you were experimenting with some kind of engine, ten years ago, when I was down here? Hadn't you mentioned it before? Couldn't that be why Jack comes poking around here? I know you must have mentioned it to some of your buddies—now didn't you?"

"Yeah, I guess so," Jim said admittedly, "but that was before I thought the thing would really work."

Cary jumped up, "That's the answer, that's the answer!"

"What do you mean?"

"Well, go on telling them it's gonna work, but the secret is—make it so outlandish that they will think you are paranoid and you can get them laughing behind your back. They won't take you seriously. I know that may hurt your ego—but I'll bet you it will work! They will laugh it off and then seriously forget about it. Think about it! They'll call you old paranoid deadhead Jim! Then that will give us time to come up with a solution, an answer . . . of how to go about this whole thing." Cary grinned and said, "It'll be a natural for you, after all . . . you are a little paranoid you know."

Jim did think about it, thought about being called paranoid and didn't like it one damn bit. It took him a day to overcome this and it was finally the next day before he agreed. "Cary, I hate to do it, *hate people calling me* paranoid, but I think you are right. I really think it'll work."

"Jim, I know it may be hard for you to do this, but *these* are hard times . . . and sometimes we *gotta* do hard things."

Jim was nodding his head in agreement. "We'll do it, it'll work . . . and I'll have some fun with it," said Jim. "I'll fabricate some far-out stories of why my sure-fire invention will work and I'll have then just shaking their heads." He was chuckling now as though seeing himself doing it. "They will call me old paranoid Jim . . . I can do it. Maybe I'll invite them out to see it. They won't know what they are looking at anyhow. I'll even ask them to invest in it . . . I'll tell them I only need a hundred thousand to get it up and running. That'll run them off for sure."

They laughed and both agreed to the scheme. Cary thought it would be a natural for Jim as he was somewhat paranoid anyhow. "Jim, I think I'll go back up to Virginia, get a job, and start looking for anyone interested in the invention. Maybe scout around and find someone with money in their pockets."

"There's not much money around here," Jim said "Dixie County is the poorest county in the state of Florida. Now Cary, let me make this clear, if we pull this off there will be money galore for both of us. I've invented the engine but I'm gonna need a lot of help from you to sell it. My job will be protecting the engine and I want to stay inconspicuous as hell. I need you to be my spokesman, my go-between; I want you to be my contact man for any negotiations with the oil companies or anyone else who may want to buy it."

"I do need a job. This may pay pretty well, huh?"

"It'll be better than minimum wage, I'll guarantee you that."

Cary grinned and said, "I can live with that. I'm your man and I'm ready to start."

"Okay, it's a deal. Check around, you can look for investors first, and if that doesn't work out, you can feel the oil companies out. But be careful and don't tell them too much and certainly not who or where I am. I don't want any surprises down here. Now listen, I've got several more months of work on this engine before we can put it up for comment. There are some refinements I've got to make, so that'll give you time to do what we've talked about. Okay?"

They spent their last evening fishing in the river and

having an idle conversation about everything in general and nothing in particular. Cary realized this was the first time he had committed himself to any project with Jim since earlier days when he discovered they had different priorities in life.

After staying with Jim two weeks, Cary knew he had to go back to Virginia and find work. Jobs in Dixie or the bordering Suwannee County were hard to come by. They both agreed they might be billionaires to-be but for now they had to find work to raise some finances to further their project. They also had minor problems such as buying food and paying rent.

The next morning the boys had their usual coffee and paper at the local Hardees and then Cary told Jim goodbye. He entered Suwannee County and stopped by his favorite spot as he always did before leaving his home place. The spot was the Little River Springs where he first went swimming as a boy. Because the river often flooded, Cary always slowed as he came to the last curve before reaching the springs, but today the river was low and he was able to park close to the edge of the high bank overlooking the springs.

The springs were located adjacent to the body of the Suwannee River into which they emptied their never-ceasing flow of water. The live oak trees that surrounded the springs devoured thousands of gallons of water per day that was necessary for their survival. The long strands of Spanish moss were hanging down, almost touching the water. Nostalgia rolled over Cary as he watched the silver moss glistening from the reflection of the sun as it shone on the rippling waters. As he sat in his car, hands around his steering wheel and staring at the springs, he considered the situation he had found himself in. He thought of Jim and wondered of his stability. Cary was trying to help himself psychologically, but he knew Jim would go crazy if he even mentioned the word. Talk about festering inside . . . Jim was full of it. Cary knew he couldn't help him, hell, he could barely help himself.

He emerged from his car and sat on the bank overlooking the huge spring. It was large, big enough to swallow a car, and the water flowed swiftly just above the solid rock underneath. He had learned to swim here above this boil as the ever-bubbling water kept him afloat.

He gazed at the old live oak tree that had stood there since he could remember. He remembered swinging and dropping into the spring from a rope they had attached to a now-dead limb. The old tree still had faded markings where they had kept track of the many divers that had never emerged from their excursions deep inside those underwater caverns. Someone was still making these marks and noticed the latest count was 110. The divers would wear their wetsuits with oxygen tanks strapped to their backs and enter the large opening. They would go down and explore the underwater caves that stretched for miles. It was said that many lost their way in the labyrinthine cavernous channels and died when the tanks were exhausted. Later, to avoid getting lost, they would attach a rope at the opening and carry the long rope with them so as to follow it back. Still, after this, the rope was evidently never long enough, and many were still lost as they tried to find their way back. They were fascinated with the underwater caverns that stretched for miles in this and other surrounding counties. Cary often wondered what they had found below that pushed them to risk their lives with repeated dives. He could only hope that he and Jim wouldn't run out of rope.

As Cary meandered around the springs he noticed that nature and time, not man, had altered the area and for that he was thankful. He left for Virginia with a heavy heart but soon his spirits rose when he glanced at the headline of his morning paper: Gas prices up again—five cents!

# Chapter Six

## Going Back . . .

## Starting Over

As he drove north to Virginia, old, hurtful memories enveloped his being again. It dawned on him that his heartache had subsided the last few days and realized why. With all the excitement of Jim's invention taking place, he had forgotten to hurt, but now the pain was returning. Cary felt he had discovered a great secret: if he could stay really busy, completely involved—no—*totally obsessed* in a project such as Jim's, the anticipation would keep the pain away. This seemed, he thought, a plausible way to ease the aching, or at least not thinking about it, which could be the same thing. He surmised it was because you couldn't hold two thoughts at the same time, and he grinned at the wisdom of it all. By his way of thinking it certainly seemed smarter than getting bombed out of your mind with drink or drugs.

Returning to Hopewell, Va. where he had spent most of his adult life, Cary knew he had to get busy and find some work because he still had to make a living. He arrived back at his folk's place two days later. Dad was working in the cemetery where he had been the manager for the past fourteen years. "Cary," his father called when he saw his son emerging from his car, "good to see you, heard you took a trip to Florida. Find any work down there?" Cary told him there were no jobs available where he had gone. "Well I may have something for you, I'm turning sixty-five next year, and I've decided to retire from this job and devote all my time to my tax business. I'm going to take my Social Security while it's still available. Look, I've offered this job to Brad; you know he's just retiring from the Air Force. If he doesn't want it, I'll offer it to you."

"Well, I sure need a job, but I guess Brad does too," Cary replied.

"I offered it to your brother first . . . well, because he's a little more settled than you."

This hurt, but Cary didn't show it. "Okay, thanks Dad, let me know then." Dad didn't think much of divorced people, particular his own son and he didn't bother hiding it. Cary obtained a room in a Hopewell boarding house and idled his time away lounging on the home's large front porch. He found himself with three older retired men and all of them loquacious with their conversation. The men were having rather heated conversations about the origins of old Hopewell when Cary joined the conversation.

"I didn't enjoy growing up here myself," he said, "seems people are so different . . .

"Why yes, they are different—that doesn't make them bad though," said Jeb Smith, a man 'bout eighty. "Son, you'd have to know the history of the place to understand."

"Yeah," Mack said removing his pipe, "you would've had to been here in 1915 when the town started."

"What was so special in 1915," Cary asked from his seat on the steps where he had retreated leaving the chairs for the older men. To his amazement, the men's expressions lit up, and they all answered his question in unison.

"*What* was so special?" they replied. The men glanced at each other as though wondering who would talk first. They relaxed back into their rocking chairs as it seemed each one was readying a story. Big Jake, the guy with the glasses turned to Cary. "There was no town here in 1914," he said as he spread his arms "just a few farms and a scattering of people. This whole area where we are sitting was nothing but a cornfield. The little village of City Point was here and the old Eppes plantation but that was about all."

"And a year later they were over 40 thousand people here," another added.

"*Do what?*" Cary asked with amazement, "you ole codgers pulling my leg?"

"You see Cary," said Jeb, "World War I broke out in the latter part of 1914 and England and France urged the Dupont Company to come to their aid with munitions."

"Why Dupont?

"Because Dupont was already in the process of making dynamite and is was fairly easy to change their operations to manufacture guncotton, an essential element for making munitions," Jeb explained. "Huge contracts for guncotton came in from France, England and the Russian government."

"Dupont owned land here?" Cary asked.

"Yeah," answered Mack, "they bought 1800 acres for around $20 an acre from the Eppes people."

"This required a work force of 30,000 people," Jeb said, "and they erected seven housing villages."

"Where did they get 30,000 people from?" Cary asked perplexed.

"Dupont sent multilingual employment officers to New York to meet the immigrant ships as they docked. The offer of a job, housing, and a ticket to the Dupont factory sounded like an answered prayer to these people. These recruiters worked faster then the construction crews, and many new arrivals lived in dormitories, and had to share their beds. Some lived in tents and some in the open. Rooming houses operated on three 8-hour shifts, and even old boats were converted to rooming houses."

"Yeah," Big Jake said grinning, "one was the Magic City Hotel that was two stories high. It was a fine place; had verandas on each side and an observation deck on top. Had a dining room that served 40 men at a time, had a barber shop and a shoe shine stand. There were orderlies that kept the rooms neat and clean. Rooms were $10.00 a week and that included laundry. Water was pumped from a spring on shore and the food was good."

"Yeah, but it was not so good otherwise," added Jeb, "overcrowded conditions led to irritations and some pitched battles in the housing camps, and just like a western town—many people carried pistols. Consequently, a raucous town sprung up almost overnight. Where, a few months before, corn had been grown, there were so-called streets lined with shanties, sheds, tents, lean-tos and other nondescript affairs in which business of every description flourished. Many were called squatters. Tin, tar paper, packing boxes and canvas were used. Seemingly, every language under the sun was spoken by members of the thirty-five different nationalities counted at one time. Native born had difficulty in making out names on business houses and, indeed, pronouncing the names of their neighbors."

"And that's when all hell broke lose," Mack injected. "It was a perfect situation to draw in every scoundrel for miles around. Money was floating everywhere. Prohibition started during this time and lasted almost twenty years. Illegal liquor selling, gambling and prostitution soon became rampant. There were floating brothels, one was named "Bo Peep" and it floated up and down the James River. There was one saloon or more on every block and shootings and murders became commonplace. There was no police force, only a few Prince George County authorities that were completely overwhelmed."

The three old men were laughing now as though they were enjoying old memories. "After prohibition set in," Jeb continued, "the Mapp Act permitted each person to have one quart of liquor a month shipped to him from out of state. And didn't you know for a time, the local post office was the busiest in the nation."

"Yes, and we had another distinction," Mack said laughing, "bootlegging became a leading industry."

"What happened next?" asked Cary?"

"On Dec. 9, 1915, a fire broke out and burnt down most of the village and some brick buildings. Of course the worry through out the day was the fear of the Dupont plant catching on fire. An explosion there would have obliterated everything for a mile around, but it was not affected, and the plant had the men back to work the next day. The fire smoldered for days as guardsman with bayonets on their rifles patrolled the area to prevent looting."

It was well past dark and the men were getting tired, retreated to their rooms chuckling, and telling Cary there was plenty more to be told. Jeb winked at him and said, if he could stand it, maybe they would tell him the good stuff another night. Cary stayed late on the porch wondering and grinning if he was the descendant of any of these squatters. After all, his mother was Russian, and she did come over here when she was thirteen and . . . that would be around that time. He had never heard the details of how his home had been born. Little did he know that there was much more that he would probably never be told?

It was just the next Sunday evening when Cary received a phone call. "Cary," his Dad said, "I talked to Brad last night and he's already decided he doesn't want the job. He said he wasn't into burying people. By the way, you don't have any inhibitions working in a graveyard do you? You know it's not for everybody?"

"I've been involved in worse things," said Cary.

"Yes, maybe you have . . . but I'm going to recommend you for the job anyhow. By the way, I may need you to help me in the tax business too. The business has been growing steadily and it's getting to be a little too much for one person. If you want some extra income, study up on the current tax regulations, okay?"

"Ok, Dad, I'll help if I can." Cary had always been interested in his Dad's income tax preparation business and had stayed familiar with the tax laws. He had been filing his own taxes, and many of his acquaintances. Extra income would be nice but he was more concerned that it would keep his mind occupied. A few days later, Cary met with the cemetery board to garner their approval.

Everything went okay until a local lawyer rose up and said he had a question concerning Cary. The presiding president asked Cary to step outdoors for a minute. He did and thought, damn, *they must have heard about my divorce too*. Ten minutes later they summoned him back and said they had approved him for the job. Cary was not overjoyed with the terms they offered but reluctantly accepted the meager paying job. Cary knew he had descended to a low point in his career and felt like an alcoholic who had hit rock bottom. He felt he had dropped from the top of the mountain to the bottom of the grave, and knew that starting over wouldn't be easy, but money was not his top priority at the moment. It had been for the last seven years, while running the largest business of its kind in the Tidewater area. Seven years wasted with only the results of a failed business, a deserting wife, and a throbbing heart. He cheered up when he remembered that this was only temporary until he hopefully could sell Jim's invention.

Later, the president told Cary that the lawyer thought he was the Williams that had been caught for operating an illegal still some time back. After some discussion, it was clear that he was not the guilty one. Little did they know what he knew; it was his brother in Florida they were talking about, and who now was into inventions of a different kind. Under the circumstances, Cary thought now was probably not a good time to ask for investments for Jim's project. Not for a brother that some remembered as being involved in moon-shining. Cary had a starting point, a job and a house furnished by his new employer, a big empty house located in the middle of the cemetery. The board were civil in their conversations with him, but it was evident they didn't regard him as an equal in their elitist world. He was just the son of a farmer and a divorced one at that. Well, that farmer owned a hundred acres when he was born and he was proud of that farmer, his Dad.

He realized he didn't fit in with their crowd; he hadn't graduated from the proper schools, hadn't joined the right civic groups, and didn't possess enough vanity to elbow his way into the proper social circles. Cary didn't knock those who navigated that route, but it wasn't for him. He didn't like the way the game was played because it reminded him too much of the fraternities of younger days. The cost of acceptance to join the elitist crowd was too high, and he couldn't bring himself to play the in-crowd game. His artificial smile would have given him away sooner or later anyhow. The pretentiousness necessary was not his style and right or wrong, he was his own man, and would listen to all, but would follow no one. His feeling was: it's not how high you have risen in life, but how far you've come from where you started. He disdainfully but respectfully overlooked their attitude and just told himself that hell; maybe he'd buy the cemetery one day.

Cary told Dad he could do this job, but he began to worry that it may be somewhat depressing because of what he was going through. But it was so different and there was so much to learn that it kept his mind occupied, and that was the important thing. His job requirements were many: he was responsible for meeting the relatives of the deceased and making funeral arrangements. It was his job to locate, mark off and dig the graves, place the vaults, and lower the caskets. Besides that, he had to erect the headstones, maintain the grounds, and keep the records. He thought it might be interesting being involved with the mourners of the deceased as he already felt a kinship with people who had lost loved ones. He felt he could identify with them.

The hardest part was meeting people who had just lost their spouse or their child. If the deceased were elderly and had died of natural causes, death was not so hard to take. But then you had people who were murdered, people who were killed in horrible auto crashes, and worse, there were the children. You had suicides; you had kids who died of drug overdoses and some who had burned to death. You lowered these caskets, these human beings into the ground as their loved ones looked on. Sometimes as you were doing this, you had a strange feeling the relatives of the deceased viewed you as somehow being sinisterly involved in the tragedy. They wanted someone to blame and there you were and how dare you put them in the ground and cover them up with dirt? Somehow, you were supposed to distance your feelings, as the funeral directors seemed to do, but seldom could Cary do that. He could always imagine the deceased being his mother, father, brother, wife or child. He had empathy for them all.

One fall day Cary was standing beside the bell tower awaiting a funeral service. Quiet sobs were coming from the solemn mourners as they followed the preacher, the funeral director, and their loved one's casket from the hearse. They moved quietly, zombie-like through the cemetery grounds. He waited beside the burial plot where he had double-checked the lowering device. It was the day before Thanksgiving, and a gentle breeze sent golden-brown leaves fluttering to the ground. It had been cold and rainy earlier, but today it had turned warm and the skies were dark and swirling winds threatened rain. He could feel the dampness in the air and the foreboding sense of winter coming on.

The preacher was a slow-drawling Carolinian who led the procession towards the gravesite. As he started the service and began speaking, Cary could tell that he, unlike Mark Anthony, was the type who only extolled the good deeds of the deceased and omitted the bad. The sobs were uncontrollable now, louder, and Cary could tell this group was going to be more emotional than most. As the preacher finished describing the positives while omitting the negatives of the recently departed soul, a man standing behind the mourners started shaking his head in evident disagreement. Cary heard him mumble, "I knew it, I just knew he was gonna do that."

The service was almost finished when he heard a commotion and then a woman screaming, "I can't stand it, I can't stand it anymore!" It wasn't the man, but rather a young woman, evidently a relative, sitting in the front row who now jumped up and continued screaming. She kept shrieking, and a man sitting behind her stood up and attempted to comfort her. He grabbed her shoulders, but she squirmed away. He then shook her, but it did no good and finally in desperation to quiet her, he slapped her lightly on the cheek to bring her to her senses. She drew back and slapped him back hard, almost knocking him to the ground. She kept shouting, "It shouldn't have happened! It shouldn't have happened!" Before anyone could do anything further, she ran off sobbing and hid behind the bell tower. Cary and the others looked at each other, and their eyes said just let her be. He motioned to the preacher to continue and though, w*hat have I got myself into?*

After the mourners left and they were closing the grave, Cary turned to the funeral director and asked. "What did this man die of Bob?"

"Auto accident," he replied.

"Kinda' young, wasn't he?"

"Yeah, just twenty-nine."

"Oh, God, that's my age! Damn, *what* happened?"

"When they called us to the scene, we noted several things. It happened at two in the morning, there was little traffic, it was on a wide divided highway, the road was straight and the weather was clear. It hadn't been raining, there was no fog and no other car was involved. It was a one-car accident, he was alone, and there were no signs of alcohol. He slammed head-on into a concrete pillar that supported an overpass.

The policemen said no tires had blown out and saw no defects in the roadway. The officers told us they have seen other accidents of this sort; accidents with fatalities where absolutely no evidence of any cause was found. He added that all of these types of accidents had one thing in common; the driver was always the lone occupant. He said that off the record, the policeman called them, 'suicide-on-purpose accidents.'"

Cary's mouth popped open, "You mean they think these people committed suicide?"

Bob just shrugged, "Your guess is as good as mine."

The day after the funeral Cary was attempting to do some record keeping at the cemetery office, but could not get yesterday's scene at the grave off his mind. He kept thinking about the outburst of the woman, the estranged wife it turned out to be, over losing her loved one at such a young age.

The job kept his mind occupied till he went home. He lived in the house alone and that was tough. He slept on the couch every night . . . he couldn't go near the empty bedroom. The evenings and nights at home were unbearable and he couldn't wait for another days work. Sometimes his job was hard on the senses, but nothing compared to going home to an empty house that sat in the middle of a cemetery and thinking of what his wife may be doing. He was beginning to live in a rage right when he was trying to attain normalcy.

# Chapter Seven

## "I want to come back . . . don' t worry, we' ve got time."

The next morning was Sunday, a few weeks before Christmas, and Cary was sitting on his front porch, basking in the warm sun as it neared high noon. Months had gone by since his wife had left him, and he was trying hard to adjust and accept it. Just then, a car pulled into the driveway. It was the car he left with his wife, a red Chevy convertible. They both loved Chevrolet convertibles, and that's all they had owned since they had married. The door opened and out came his wife. She didn't venture past the driver's door when she saw Cary sitting on the porch. He stood up and opened the screen door, and they looked at each other silently for a few minutes. Her auburn hair was pushed up the way he liked it, and she was wearing a green blouse with black slacks. He could tell she was not coming any closer.

*"I want to come back to you Cary," she said.*

He thought he would fall over. He had been working hard to get over her and now this. He couldn't speak. He didn't know what to say.

Finally realizing this she said, "I know you're in shock, and its okay. You don't need to say anything now look, think about it and call me or . . . I'll call you." She turned her head sideways and curiously said, "*Don't worry, we've got time.*" His mouth was open, but no words would come. He tried hard to read her face. Was there a softening; was there a hint of a smile? She returned to her car and drove off. Wonderment came over him. He tried hard to be happy, but mostly just felt puzzled. She said he was in shock, she had been dating another man for six months, said we were through—*what did she expect?* She had driven from her apartment to here, a forty-minute drive, to tell him she wanted to come back. She had not even questioned his normalcy project. Did she even care? The rest of the day was spent in a daze. He finally went to bed after much thinking and trying to figure out her actions. *Could it be*, he thought, *that she only had an argument with her boyfriend?* He tossed and turned the whole night. Cary thought he would never understand women.

He worked the next day and thought of every possible explanation. Finally, he had to take her at her word; he couldn't do otherwise. She wanted to come back. Against his better judgment, he started making plans; his hopes were sky high. His heart had stopped its painful aching for the first time in six months. He was elated . . . he *knew* he couldn't live without her.

She had worked for the civil service at the Fort Eustis army base but had now transferred to Langley. Cary quickly thought of the two military posts here in the area. He knew it was possible for her to transfer here. The next two weeks were spent contacting personnel in the two army bases nearby. They both assured him she could get transferred and it was done quite often. They did say sometimes it took awhile, but Scarlett said "we've got time." He worked with nothing on his mind but Scarlett and how he could visualize them getting back together. They were both working now, and he was sure she wouldn't mind transferring here. Maybe the doctor's strategy was right about leaving her alone and not stalking her. Maybe she *had* reconsidered her wedding vows, he thought.

Cary spent several nights carefully composing a letter to Scarlett. He told her how happy he was, explained the details about the job transfer, apologized for the hurtful things he had done, asked for her forgiveness, and said he wanted to reconcile too. He said the doctor had given him some insight concerning his problems and explained the remedial actions necessary to remedy them. He promised her it would never happen again. He told her that now he realized what a precious thing they had, and he didn't want to lose it. He thought contacting her by mail might be the best thing he could do. He could never say in person all the things he could put in a letter. He sealed the letter and began the long walk to the post office thinking if he was doing the right thing. Scarlett was a good girl . . . she had been a perfect wife. He thought of the doctor's advice, figure out your problems, face them, and overcome them. Well, he had identified his problems, but honestly, that was about all. He hadn't corrected them, and didn't even know if he could or how long it would take. But he knew that until he cleansed himself, he could never be whole, and would be no different than before. Besides, deep down where the demons live, he had a problem even the psychiatrist's hadn't discovered, and he hadn't really admitted it to himself. But the truth was that he hated himself, and was punishing his being for all of his failures. Punishing himself by walking away from the greatest, happiness he had ever known. If he ever felt he was losing it, this was the time.

Entering the post office, he stopped in the hallway, and glanced at the mail slot and then the trash can. His wife was special he thought, and deserved better than him. His eyes filled with tears, he sighed, moaned, and slowly tore the letter into little pieces, and threw them in the waste basket. It was like tearing up his heart, and throwing it away. He made this decision but the rage still burned, and the struggle between his mind and his heart continued.

Though he conceded he had lost her, he still felt a terrible need for closure and reached for the phone several times in the next two weeks but didn't make the call. Finally, realizing he just wanted to do the right thing, and since she had made the first move he now felt it was his place to contact her. Maybe she was sitting home, alone, waiting for his phone call.

The next Friday, he gathered the courage to call her around nine in the evening. The phone rang a dozen times, but there was no answer. The next night he called again about the same time. Nothing! This was driving him crazy, so the next Friday evening he drove to her apartment and arrived about eight. Her car was there, so he walked to her apartment and knocked on the door. There was no answer, the apartment was empty, and his mind was swirling.

He walked to the convenience store, bought a six pack of beer and went back and waited in his car that was parked a few doors away from her apartment. Finally, about midnight and three beers later, a car pulled up, and a couple emerged. It was Scarlett and a man he recognized—it was the same man she'd been dating before! They were laughing and holding hands as they walked towards her apartment. They went in and he could see them talking to each other, smiling, and then Scarlett came to the window. Her eyes glanced to the right and then to the left. *Was she looking for him?* Then she snapped the blinds shut.

He stumbled out of his car and went to the apartment door. He stood there, trembling, his hand raised to knock. He could now hear them talking and laughing. He sat on the steps that led to the apartment, trying to think clearly though his heart was pounding. He couldn't help but overhear their conversation through the walls. He listened to them; there were little shrieks of laughter and then long pauses of nothing. He must have sat there for an hour, trembling, shaking, with tears flowing. She was not sitting alone waiting for him, and there was no evidence that she was missing him. He was afraid it was over, and he was afraid of what he might do if he didn't leave. He only thought, *How could she, how could she?* She made a promise—"Don't worry, we've got time." He left in a rage. It was good he hadn't brought his gun.

As he drove home, he tried to figure her out. *Was she vulnerable? Was there some defect in her character he didn't understand?* Was she so afraid of being alone, that she was reaching out desperately . . . for anyone? She had dated this guy for six months, and then came back and said she wanted to reconcile. If she loved him, how could she still be seeing this other man? Maybe they did only have an argument. His hopes dropped to his knees. Maybe she hadn't thought of her *wedding vows, maybe she really didn't take them seriously after all. Hell, he had boyhood friends who took their Huckleberry Finn and Tom Sawyer vows more seriously than that!*

Cary couldn't take it anymore; he had to have some

answers. He made up his mind he was going to see the man she was dating. He drove to Newport News the next Thursday night. He felt he would be home, probably not dating her on this night. Scarlett had told him in a past conversation what the man's name was. He had looked up his address and then it hit him. *Oh God!* He had forgotten this was the *same* man that Scarlett had called him about just before he'd moved out of town. She had asked him to come and remove him from her apartment for some unknown reason. He had ended up in a fight with him, had tried to throw the guy out of her window. *Oh well*, he thought, *that was six months ago,* I'm here now and this situation calls for hard decisions. All he can do is slam the door in my face *or* take a swing at me. He pulled into the parking lot where Gary Johnson had a first-floor apartment. A light was on and Cary hoped he was alone. He drew a breath, composed himself, and knocked on his door.

"Gary Johnson?"

"Yes."

"I'm Cary Williams, Scarlett's husband. I really need to talk to you. Can I come in for a few minutes?"

Gary looked at Cary for a minute without answering. Cary knew he had to be deciding whether to slam the door or not, remembering the last encounter they had. Cary took two steps back and raised his hands in a non-threatening way. "Listen,"

Cary said, “please, I’m not here to fight, but man, just give me five minutes and then I’ll be gone. I . . . I just need some answers.” The situation was tense because they had never met formally, and all they knew of each other was whatever Scarlett had disclosed.

Cary was hurting and Gary could tell. After an embarrassing moment, Gary said, “The last time I saw you, which was also the first time—you jumped me. You sure you’re not looking for a fight over Scarlett and me?” “No, no, no. I apologize for coming over without notice . . . hell I apologize for coming over period, but . . . well—I just couldn’t help it.” Gary’s discomfort eased a bit as he thought he might have questions, too, regarding the separated husband of the girl he was in love with. He opened wide the door and ushered Cary in.

He extended his hand, smiled condescendingly, and said, “You’re the first man I’ve fought with before being introduced. I’m Gary Johnson.”

Cary, slightly embarrassed, shook his hand and attempted a smile. He didn’t bother telling him that it had been Scarlett’s idea to throw him out of the apartment.

“Come on in, looks like it’s going to rain.” He moved some paper work off his couch and waved his hand towards the seat. “Been doing some catch up work for my job,” he said. “Can I fix you a drink?”

"Yeah, thanks, I could use one." Cary said.

Gary finally grinned in an effort to defuse the situation. "I think we both could use one." He went to the kitchen and came back with a bourbon and coke for both of then and they sat down. Cary thought he seemed like a decent enough person. Still, the tension could have been cut with a knife.

"Gary, I know this is awkward, but I have to have some answers. I know you've been dating Scarlett for about six months, and I have stayed away from the both of you. I've tried not to make an ass of myself." Then, thinking of their fight. "Well . . . not again anyhow. You don't have to answer, and you don't even have to talk to me. Particularly since our last encounter . . . but do you mind telling me what's going on between the two of you? I mean, are the two of you on—or *off?*"

Cary could tell Gary was a little tense but for some reason it looked like he was going to talk to him. His outward demeanor was calm, but Cary was sure his insides were churning.

"I'll tell you Cary," he took a swallow of his bourbon, took a deep breath and said, "Scarlett and I were getting serious after just a few months of dating and finally marriage came up. I tried to avoid the subject, but she was insistent on an answer, and I finally had to tell her the truth. The truth of why I'd never married and didn't plan on it." Cary could tell he was approaching a subject that was very painful, and he listened quietly.

"I . . . I told her that I had committed an awful deed when I was seventeen." He paused and Cary let him take his time. "I told her that I had accidentally dropped my baby sister whom I was holding. She fell on her head . . . it *hurt* her terrible . . . it *damaged* her brain, she was, and *still is,* brain-damaged. I vowed I would take care of her the rest of my life. I was not going to let *anyone* come before her care. I guess I couldn't bear the idea of getting married and being happy when it was *my* fault that my sister would *never be*." He was trembling now as he was telling Scarlett's husband such a deep personal story that concerned all of them.

"Anyhow, Scarlett broke it off with me . . . but I couldn't stay away, and that's why she called you to throw me out." Cary was beginning to see the picture. His opinion of Scarlett dropped when he realized how desperate she was to get married. He was shocked that she cared enough about Gary to *want* to marry him but now was going to drop him because he refused to marry her because of this obligation. *God*, Cary thought, he had more compassion for Gary than his wife, and she *supposedly* loved him. Gary said no more, and Cary suddenly got up to leave. He felt he had gotten the answer he was looking for, and he couldn't stand anymore.

"I'm sorry about your sister," Cary said but that was all he could say realizing what was coming next . . . and said it before Gary had a chance. “You’ve *changed* your mind about not getting married, *haven’t you*?” Gary’s face was blank. Cary wanted to tell him that was the right decision, that he *shouldn’t* let the incident ruin his life, but *hell*, he thought; *his decision could be ruining my life*. He wanted to congratulate him, but he couldn’t because he was talking about marrying his *wife.* So instead Cary thanked him for seeing him, and told him good night and thanks for the drink, and left. He wanted to wish him good luck, but he couldn’t do it. How could he, when he wanted to wish him the worst? He was glad he had come; he had gotten some answers and his five minutes were up. Cary walked into the rain and controlled his rage and carefully drove home as the cold rain had turned into an icy snow. Evidently, he thought, Scarlett didn’t believe in the part of the marriage vow that said you promise to love someone in good times as well as bad.

Months passed and it was the first day in May when she called and reached him at the hospital. Somehow she found out he was having an operation at the Memorial Hospital. He was taking the action the doctor had recommended—admit your problem, face it, and correct it. He was taking action and working on himself, or in this case, having the surgeon do it. It was fairly serious; the surgeon went inside his mouth and cut out a half inch from his lower jawbone on both sides. It was a corrective procedure to line up his lower jaw with his upper. It was more corrective to his heart than it was to his face. Maybe it would correct his marriage. He had always hated the way his jaw looked and the way it affected his speech.

She called just after he was wheeled back into his room after surgery. He was still dopey, and his whole lower jaw was wrapped tight with bandages.

"Cary, this is Scarlett, how are you?"

He was shocked to hear her voice and mumbled a reply to her, which she couldn't understand. He guessed she figured the operation wasn't successful because he didn't talk any more clearly than before. He guessed it was good she didn't understand what he said, for it was probably not exactly normal. What he said was, "I'm working on one of my problems: I'm taking remedial measures to get myself back to normal, but it's too soon to tell the outcome."

She realized he wasn't all together, so she said a few words of consolation and then goodbye. That was it. She never called back to see if the operation helped him in any way. Later he realized she wasn't calling about his operation at all.

She did call one more time some weeks later, but did not inquire about his operation. Her voice was very weak, and she sounded disoriented. They made small talk, and he could sense something was amiss. He told her he was heading her way in his boat and asked if she would meet him where the two rivers met. He mentioned a place and time, but she only stumbled in her talk and mumbled something that he interpreted as saying okay. She then said goodbye and hung up. He headed to the location to meet her, but his outboard motor malfunctioned, and he got there twenty minutes late. He waited an hour, but she never showed up.

It was to be months later when he talked with a friend of his that worked with her, and was told she was married a week after that incident. It slowly dawned on him like a sledgehammer. She had called only to say she was getting *married,* but didn't have the guts to say it. And the guy she married wasn't Gary; she married a man she hardly knew. And the girl he thought Scarlett was—*wasn't*. The pedestal he had placed her on had collapsed. She was not a stand-by-your-man girl, as Cary had thought; she *didn't* stand by him, a man she had been married to for seven years. She *did not* stand by him when he lost his business and was seeking mental help. And now she *did not* stand by Gary, a man she professed to love yet wouldn't stand by him when he needed psychological help. Her true nature turned out to be a fair-weather friend—not a girl for all seasons.

Cary vowed that someday there was going to be some payback. He knew he should leave retribution in God's hands, but for now there was no feeling of forgiveness, just an uncontrollable feeling of rage. She didn't have the guts, the *decency,* to meet him face to face and explain what the hell happened. She couldn't even say it over the phone—it was like she was still keeping him on the line—just in case! It appeared to be a situation of complete *deception—a downright betrayal.* Cary felt like he had been played for a fool, and his only thought was to gather his guns.

He threw himself into work and put in seventy and sometimes eighty hours per week. The months went by as he got up at five and worked till eight p.m. six, seven days a week. He worked with a passion; it was the only way he could keep his mind off her. Sometimes he drank too much and went a little crazy. He made up his mind one Friday night—*the hell with everything.* I'm going out on the town *and let myself go, damn the torpedoes! Let it all hang out. Why* can't I go out and find somebody, too? He started with several drinks of Early Times, cleaned up from work, dressed up and took off to Richmond for a big night. He was back at home at ten p.m.

He couldn't do it, couldn't do it to himself. He had his own moral standards to live up to, his own code of ethics; he had to answer to himself and his God if nobody else. Or maybe he just had too much pride to lower himself and he still had a promise to keep. A promise to keep to whom . . . nobody! Well, the promise was just to him from now on, because no one else cared. The hurt wouldn't stop, and his heart kept pounding. He made a promise to himself that night. He promised himself that before his life was over, he would see Scarlett face to face, and have her admit to what she had done. This promise allowed him to ease the pain for the moment, believing he would get an answer in the future. You might say it was like Scarlet in the movie saying, "I can't think about it now, I'll think about it tomorrow." Today he had to manage the job of living.

He controlled his drinking, and didn't let it interfere with his work. He met several women in conjunction with his work. He never asked any of them out, but now and then one of them would ask him out, and he would go. One thing led to another, and he found himself actually dating some of them. After all, he was only human. And then there was sex, that overpowering force he figured God must have given to man to insure that human kind would continue. But following their separation, Cary's interest was dormant concerning the opposite sex even though it was very obvious Scarlett was evaluating every male that passed her way. The girls he came in contact were varied, but he only had intimate relations with a select few. They were decent women, but unfortunately, most of them were suffering from breakups just as he was. The escapades he was involved in would have been ludicrous if they were not so sad. Simply put, he was kicked out of bed before daybreak more than once by recently abused women who couldn't bear their disgraceful act being discovered by the morning sun. That disgraceful act was not sex itself, but the fact that they had just loved a man, and so passionately, while presently having utter contempt of their very being.

After dating several girls in the ensuing months, one of them shocked him with the truth she was able to discern. Her name was Darlene; she was neat, intelligent, and Cary really liked her. They had been happily dating for several months. but Cary had never made a commitment to her and finally she had come to a decision. They had just come from a movie, and he had driven her home. She made them a drink while Cary was watching a football game on TV. She handed Cary his drink, walked over, turned the TV off, and came to Cary with tears running down her cheeks. Cary saw the tears, and at first thought she was thinking of giving herself to him with no love in return.

"You still crying over that movie?" he asked.

"No, not the movie—crying over *you!"*

"Over *me*?"

"Yes, over you, Cary . . . I've decided to *stop* seeing you! I've just turned twenty-six years old, and my time is running out. You know I'm crazy about you, and I think you feel the same towards me, but you've got a problem. You've never *gotten over your first wife,* and I *don't* think you *ever* will!" That slammed Cary like a brick. It was the first time anyone had deciphered his secret that he barely admitted he had. He slowly walked over to her window and stared into the darkness. He knew she was right.

"*Oh God, I didn't know it showed* . . . I'm sorry Darlene." God . . . *what* am I doing, Cary thought. He turned to her, guided her to the sofa, took her hands in his, and knelt between her knees, and tried to speak, but couldn't.

"It's okay," she said. "I don't think you meant to mislead me. I don't even know if you realized it."

"But how . . . how did you know? I've never even admitted it to myself, but . . . inside I know . . . I know it's the truth. It just never occurred to me that this scenario would take place."

"I've been around the block a few times Cary; I've seen other men with . . ."

*"Baggage?"* Cary interrupted.

"Well, I wouldn't be that crass . . . ."

Cary staggered up with shoulders drooping; he felt bewildered as he stared at the beautiful girl he would see no more. "Baggage, that's me . . . and I don't know how . . . how to rid myself of it. I've tried everything but nothing seems to work. You are wise to recognize it Darlene; I wouldn't wish it on anyone."

This same scenario continued; he met many neat, attractive, intelligent women, but he could never return their affections. He lost many opportunities to start a new life. Scarlett's memory haunted him and wouldn't let go. He was afraid normalcy was going to be hard to come by. It hadn't dawned on his conscious mind 'til now that this attitude, this mental irregularity . . . had destroyed relationships before, and now was likely to continue in the future. The thought never occurred to him until now just how awful it was to love someone when they couldn't return that love. That was a game he would never consciously play and was not playing with Darlene. This was a deadly game he had seen both sexes engage in the past. He despised all that participated and wanted no part of it.

Cary's jaw surgery had healed, but it was awhile before the swelling had finally disappeared. After his final check-up, the doctor declared the operation a success but emphasized that fistfights should be avoided. He went and *faced* the mirror *once again* and looked at his jaw. It was okay, and for the first time in his life he felt his looks were normal. His speech wasn't perfect, but he could live with it. One normalcy objective had been achieved and overcome, and he was working on the second one. Because of his jutting jaw and the fact that his imperfect speech drew attention to it, he had never been able to speak in public. He had never overcome the fear of addressing an audience and making a presentation. He knew he had to overcome this fear in order to advance in life. He had to rid himself of his introverted personality. This was his next objective.

Cary stopped dating; he couldn't bear to hurt any more women like Darlene. In the ensuing months, he spent his nights walking the streets of Richmond alone while contemplating his future. After severing his relationship with Darlene, a woman called him and said she and her husband were close friends of Darlene and would like to discuss the situation concerning her. He debated with himself about going, but then relented, and went out with them to dinner as they had asked.

As they sat at their country club he couldn't believe the words the woman was saying, "Cary, you may not love Darlene now, but you could marry her, and it would come in time. My husband here, *I didn't love him either when we married*, but it slowly came as time went by." Cary couldn't believe the words he was hearing, that a complete stranger could tell him such an intimate thing and in *front* of her husband. It was unbelievable to Cary that anyone could marry someone they didn't love. He told them he was sorry, but he couldn't bring himself to do such a thing. He didn't bother explaining the baggage thing but later wished he had.

And then he thought of Scarlett, *is that what she did? Was she so desperate that she would marry someone she didn't love?* It was hard to believe such a thing, but it dawned on him that it appeared to be true. Cary realized how little he understood women. Because of their femininity, the so-called weaker sex, did they have a different set of values than men? Were we supposed to give them more leeway to break the laws of virtue and morality? He went back to the streets of Richmond and spent many lonely nights walking, wondering, and pondering his ignorance.

This only lasted for awhile; he couldn't live without human contact, especially the female kind. He tried a different tactic to solve this problem and got himself involved with girls that he felt had a similar inclination, relationships where he felt no one would get hurt. He met Jane at an acquaintance's office party, and both were attracted to each other, though it may have only been physical on Cary's side. He felt that was okay, as he didn't think Jane was looking for a serious relationship. But after dating her several times he realized it was a big mistake, especially after he chidingly pinned a nickname on her, a habit he had done with other girls. It was all in jest but evidently not funny to her. His nickname for her was "Crazy Jane," a name borrowed from some forgotten song. He began referring to her by that name before he realized she was under the care of a psychiatrist, and a crazy one at that.

"*You don't respect me do you*?" Jane asked.

"I have no reason not to respect you," Cary said.

"Just because I told you I've been going to see a

psychiatrist—*you think I'm crazy, don't you?"*

"I think it's a wise person who understands the need for help and a courageous one who goes forth and actually does it." She was getting hysterical.

"You're making fun of me aren't you? All you want from me is sex, isn't it? *Isn't* it? *That's all you want*!" She didn't let him answer, which he thought was probably just as well. "You've *never* taken me out in public—and you've never introduced me to your parents *either*! What's the matter—you think I'm not good enough? I am human you know." Those words struck a chord within Cary and he thought about his own problems.

"You are human Jane, and God loves you. Would you like to meet my folks tomorrow?" She agreed with a broad smile. The next day, just before lunch, they were at Cary's parents' home sitting on his mother's couch. Jane was dressed as though she was entering Joe's Place Dance Hall on Saturday night instead of Monday noon on wash day at his mom's house. Her skimpy outfit was over-accessorized with dangling earrings, eight gold bracelets, four-inch heels, and perfume that was a little too much. Cary's mother came out from the kitchen where she had been taking her morning wash out of the dryer. "Mom, I'd like you to meet Jane, a friend of mine."

"Why, it's nice to meet you Jane. You look lovely today." His mother glanced at Jane and though a world of information concerning her was revealed instantaneously, she never paused as she smilingly discussed the weather and other mundane matters of the day. His mother never judged another person. He was grateful she was the only one home because his father would not have been so discreet.

It would be some time before Cary broke the ties with this girl, and it was not pretty when it happened. It was an experience he didn't need, and one he could barely handle. He felt he had met head-on what the shrink had warned him about: the cumulative effect of ignoring one's mental irregularities. Or as the doctor so succinctly stated, "You'll find one hot-bed, hell-of-a-mess on your hands." Jane embarrassed him at work, destroyed the relationships with the next two girls he dated, and finally, drinking vodka straight from the bottle, she rammed her jealous arm through his living room window, which resulted in blood spewing everywhere. Cary, with help from his female companion, held her down, put a tourniquet around her arm, threw her in his car and rushed her to the hospital.

He sat in the waiting room, splattered with her blood, and listened to her constant ranting as they stitched her up, screaming about what that vile man in the next room had done to her. The sad thing was, they all believed her. He now understood why people discreetly crossed the street and gave wide berth to those known to have mental problems. Crazy Jane was her name and crazy was her game.

It was back to the streets again, and by this time, Cary had walked every damn street in the entire city of Richmond and vowed he would avoid the opposite sex as long as he could stand it.

# Chapter Eight

## *The Ragged Edge...*

Cary had finished work on Friday and was tired and weary as he sipped his coffee the next morning on his front porch. He was glad no one died, and he had no graves to dig as he picked up the ringing phone.

"Cary, this is Scarlett. We've got some problems with the house we sold. Can you meet me at the lawyer's office this evening so we can straighten this out? The buyer has defaulted on his house payments and the bank is looking to us for the payments."

He agreed to meet her an hour later. As he entered the lobby, she was waiting there with her new husband. This was the first time he had met him and understandably, didn't like him. *Hell,* he thought, *how could you be objective about the home-wrecker that destroyed their reconciliation?* He was a mousey-looking little fellow who Cary had heard was divorced soon after his first wife had realized what a controlling character she'd been stuck with. Someone said he held a job with the Civil Service. He looked the type who'd memorized the SOP and seriously followed it line by line and expected his co-workers to do the same or face dire consequences. It was clear to him that Scarlett's taste in the opposite sex had radically changed from men to boys.

Looking him up and down, Cary said, "Look what the dogs dragged in! You traded me for this? You must have taken the first thing that came along. Was this the best you could do?"

Her husband's face quickly turned from pallid white to rosy red. He clenched his fists, gritted his teeth and sneered at Cary. "Listen, Mr. Smart-ass," he blurted, "I'll . . . I'll have the Illuminati after you—yeah, that's what I'll do—they'll take care of you."

Scarlett jumped in between them, and with both arms spread wide, separated both with a straight arm like a football running back. Her husband shrunk back in obvious relief while Cary was grinning and thinking. Thinking how the fool had just indicted himself, divulging secrets of the Masonic group which, he even knew, was a no-no.

It was all Scarlett could do to keep them from throwing blows. "Just settle down— both of you!" she said trembling as she turned to Cary while still holding her arms out, and trying to calm herself. "The lawyer said . . . said that the man who took over the payments on the house has defaulted, and you and I are obligated. We have to make up the back payments, or the bank will take the house back. If you want the house, say so, and if you don't, we'll take care of it." He remembered when they sold it; they had just let the buyer assume the loan never thinking he would default, and the house would come back to them. "The title is still in both our names, and I want to know if you want it," she said.

Cary looked at the strange little guy with the weird mustache curled cutely at both ends and tried hard not to laugh. Now he knew the truth for sure, and it was a sad feeling realizing that Scarlet had gotten so desperate. "I have no use for anything down here! You can have the house and the sweat equity in it."

"Well," she said, "that's what I thought and if you don't want it, we'll make the back payments and we'll take it." Good *God*," Cary thought, *he's got my wife, now he's going to take our house*. "If you'll sign the release here," she said, "we'll take care of it." His blood was boiling but he signed the paper and walked out. Left her with her sidekick, the weird little fellow he'd heard was the manipulative type, a controller of all in his little world, the Napoleon of his time and surely a great legend in his own mind, and by now, Scarlett's too. Diminutive guys like him fell into a peculiar group to hide their insecurities. They probably never had a real job, lived off the taxpayers, never met a payroll in their life, and couldn't fight their way out of a paper bag if they had to.

Her husband must have wet himself, Cary thought, when he discovered the Masonic group. He probably joined the group knowing, with his extensive memorizing background from his government job, he could, after years of rehearsing, obtain the lofty status of Grand Worshipful Master. Now he had the old, horrific, ancient, fifteenth century menacing history of this group to intimidate his enemies. And the depths of his degradation could be much lower, being the Grand Worshipful Master of the Hampton Roads area, he admitted the Illuminati existed, admitted they were connected to the Mason's, and, by his threat, he was probably a member also. This was degrading as its worst, and Cary hoped for Scarlett's sake, he was only a dupe, and didn't realize what he was doing. Scarlett may not know the depths of his involvement because the Illuminati's reported reputation is one of utmost secrecy, and they are not *even permitted* to reveal these disgusting secrets to their wives. Some say their deceptive goal is, to not only take over America, but the whole world. Was this dumb cluck a part of it, or was he just plain evil himself? Probably another reason his first wife divorced him. He will laugh, and tell Scarlett this stuff is just a wild, crazy conspiracy, related by a bitter, ex-husband, but, inside, he knows the Illuminati will not.

The man's twisted ego must have bellowed wide and high

that now, he'd have a group to fight his battles for him. He was probably an embarrassment to the current Masonic group who, in majority, were reputable people who could see right through him. But debauched people like him loved to find weak people they could brainwash with their sick ego-driven pomposity, and they usually picked the weaker sex. These were usually women whom they could easily control and spout off their commands of when, where, and how they should go relieve themselves. Cary could see him now, standing on tip-toes in elevated shoes directing traffic for her, pointing the way, expertly and in detail, to the nearest toilet.

He was greatly admired, but only by himself, and those he could control. Those who didn't realize he was only a shadow of a man. Well, he had already crossed Cary, and it would only be a matter of time before Cary would spit some Beechnut in his eye, give God a day off, and do a little controlling of his own. This fool had duped Scarlett, and realizing that, Cary's feeling of reverence for his ex-wife's character had just dropped to a new low, and it saddened him.

With heart pounding and mind raging, Cary jumped into his Chevy. He stomped the gas pedal, his big V-8 roared to life, and he left the place with tires squealing and leaves swirling. This Route 5, from Williamsburg to Richmond, was a smooth, winding, asphalt road. The state kept the road in perfect condition because of the many tax dollars the tourists brought in as they traveled this scenic highway. Cary had installed sway bars on the rear of the car for better traction. He flew past a car full of black teenagers, and the rear view mirror reflected their fascination as they were smiling, waving, and honking their horn at him as he went out of sight. He was flying now and taking each curve at near ten-tenths speed. The beautiful road was enticing to him, and he kept pushing the gas pedal down, listening to the roar of the engine that throbbed like his aching heart. This winding road was challenging, and a feeling of exhilaration swept through Cary. It was like a beautiful raceway, this smooth asphalt pavement with miles of repeating curves coming at him. The smell of early autumn was in the air, and it was a titillating feeling as he streamed through the winding road, and listened to his squealing tires as they barely held his car to the pavement. The trees were flying by his open cockpit in a constant blur and his hair was streaming backwards. It crossed his mind how he could stop this suffering in just one moment. One flick of the wrist—one turn of the wheel—one huge tree . . . .

He was trying to keep his mind on the highway but couldn't keep Scarlett out of his head. One curve to the left was sharper than his speed could take, and he lost traction. He nudged his wheel to the left and tapped his brakes. His car's rear end broke loose—the car was now sliding sideways down the right side of the road. The front and left rear wheels were on the roadway, but the right rear wheel was spinning, vainly trying for traction as it spun just off the pavement. The car slid, seemingly in slow motion, as he turned his front wheels to the right in the direction of his slide trying to keep the car under control.

And then he lost it—the car slowly spun all the way around until Cary was facing back the way he had come but in the other lane. His car was now skidding straight backwards and he quickly turned his wheels parallel to the highway. He glanced in his rear mirror for oncoming cars—and slammed on his brakes. Before the car stopped, he had already shoved the gear into low and slammed the gas petal down—his rear wheels spun, squealed, caught traction—and his car was flying as he blew past the teenagers coming back towards him. Their mouths were open with wonderment as he passed them by at ninety miles an hour. There faces reflected a bewildered look as if they couldn't comprehend how he could have turned around so fast.

He smiled at their astonishment and thought he was driving well, streaming through the turns smooth as glass, and as fast as they could be taken. He was again taking the turns at ten-tenths speed, and a surge of exhilaration swept over him as he felt he and the car were one. It was an overwhelming feeling of euphoria and emotional release. He marveled at the feeling 'til he realized he was heading back *towards* his ex-wife. That's when he pushed the pedal to the metal a little too hard, and that's when tears filled his eyes.

He took one hand off the wheel to wipe his eyes an then it happened. The ragged edge had caught up with him. He took the next curve too fast, slid off the road and blasted *head-on into a telephone pole*. He had made a mistake; it was probably a pot hole or a bit of unseen gravel or . . . *Scarlett*! The right front of his car caught the pole, and threw the car violently to the left, the left rear side skidded into a ditch and bounced up and caught a tree, and his driver's side door flung open, and sent him flying out of the car. His body fell downward into a valley of grass, just missing the pavement. He landed back first on the damp grass, tumbled over several times and finally slithered to a stop on his back only inches away from the base of a huge pine tree. He was knocked out . . . he was down . . . and this time he was out!

When he came to, he found himself staring at the heavens and lying in a damp, grassy field downhill some twenty yards from his flaming car that was lying uphill underneath a broken telephone pole with sparkling wires dangling on top. Two guys were standing over him and one was pushing something into his mouth.

*"Hey, man, you okay?"* one was asking. Cary took felt all over his chest and didn't feel any broken bones. He glanced around and realized, luckily, that his journey had stopped just

before his head had rammed the tree. Feeling his wet head, he realized it wasn't blood, but just due from the grass and he felt back with relief.

"Yeah . . . I think so," he said.

*"A cop* is pulling up! Chew on those mints in case you were drinking!" Cary chewed on the tablets, and thought how considerate they were. The cop walked towards him and hovered over his head.

"Cary, is that you?" Cary recognized him; he was Buddy Lovelady, a former high school classmate. "Are you okay?" Buddy asked.

Still feeling over his body, Cary said, "I'm okay, I guess . . . I don't feel any bones sticking . . ."

"*Was* anybody in the car with you?" he shouted pointing to the burning car. The heat from the fire was getting intense.

"No, I was by myself."

"Well, we've got to move you away from that car—it could explode." The men didn't think he had a choice, so the cop and the two Carolina boys grabbed him by the shoulders and dragged him backwards away from the blazing car. The two guys told the policeman they were traveling from Carolina and had witnessed the crash. They said it appeared some car had run him off the road—he hit the light pole and the wires came down just ah popping, and landed on his car and started burning it up. Cary winked to them in appreciation.

"Well, I don't smell any alcohol, so I guess you weren't drinking," Buddy said. He took Cary to the hospital and told the attendants to check him out and left. Cary was there for an hour before they took him in for x-rays. They found no broken bones and sent him back to the waiting room. Finally, two hours later, Buddy came back and Cary pleaded with him to take him home. He said he could only take him as far as the turn off to his house because of regulations. Cary's back ached as he got in the police car, he felt as though a hundred bones were vibrating throughout his back.

He could hardly walk when Buddy dropped him off along the highway. He looked around and found himself close to a girl's house that he had once dated. He slowly hobbled towards the house and knocked on her door. The girl looked at his condition and was afraid to let him in. "You look like you've been in a fight . . . *and* have you been drinking?" she asked.

"No," he replied, "I've been in an auto accident; I'm just trying to get home." She wouldn't come out, but she sent her boyfriend to take him home. After arriving, he checked himself over and wondered why he wasn't hurt worse. He took off his shirt and saw the whole back was stained green. Luckily, he had missed the pavement, he thought. The only bruise he had was between his thighs where a beer bottle had sat. *Thank goodness it didn't break,* he thought. The bruise must have occurred when his legs slammed against the door as he was thrown from the car.

The whole experienced had overcome Cary and he fell to his knees and gave thanks to the Almighty as he had never done before. The realization of what just occurred swept through his mind and his body shuttered as tears fell. The many accidents he had witnessed up close flashed across his mind: the broken, twisted bodies, some thrown through windshields, others soaked in blood, flesh torn, and strewn across the car.

He thought of the survivors, some mangled for life, many living a lifetime of regret, others wishing they had died, and here he was without a scratch. "God," he moaned as his body quivered, "thank you Lord! I don't know why you saved me . . . but you *must* have a *reason.* Oh Lord, I *promise—I vow today,* I'll try to reconstruct my pitiful self and use my remaining days helping others." As Cary lay on the carpeted floor he felt he had found a reason to live. Instead of feeling so useless, he realized if he could help others, maybe he wouldn't be worthless. The idea of caring for others, Cary thought, could be powerful. The thought made him smile.

Cary finally stumbled his feet, and checked his body over in detail. The only thing missing from him was his bottom denture. He thanked the Almighty again.

The next day he went back to the accident site, and was

looking for his denture, when an acquaintance came by and questioned what he was doing. Cary said he was looking for a hubcap he had lost. Sometimes he told white lies. He never did find his denture, and so it was back to the dentist.

The policeman wrote him up a summons, and Cary had to go to court and explain to the judge what had happened. He described the wreck in pitiful detail including what he had just found out a day before---- his auto insurance elapsed with his last car payment that was paid a month before the wreck. The judge just shook his head after hearing his testimony, and dismissed the case. but insisted he attend driving school. Over his objections that he knew how to drive he attended the class one week later.

The room was full of drivers similar to him. The instructor, Mr. Eddie Blanks, was a former wrestler and a bull of a man. He bore down on the reckless drivers. "First thing you do before driving is: you *don't* drink alcohol—you *fasten* your seat belt, and you *lock* your door!"

"Excuse me," Cary said, raising his hand, interrupting him.

"*What!*" He bellowed.

"I just had an accident, and if I was wearing my seat belt and had my door locked, I couldn't have escaped my burning car . . . and if I hadn't of drank couple of drinks I would surely have broken some bones as I tumbled through the woods . . . and . . .

"*Shut up and sit down*!" The instructor yelled. The class bellowed with laughter. *Oh God*, Cary thought, I've started off on the wrong foot. The instructor didn't take kindly to him the rest of the course.

Cary went the next Saturday to look at his beloved Chevy and see how badly it was damaged. It was worse than he thought. It was burned up completely from the electric line that fell on the car when it broke the utility pole in half. The car had slammed the telephone pole hard, the windshield was shattered, and pieces were scattered everywhere. The steering wheel was pushed up towards the windshield, and was turned sideways, pointing towards the driver's door. It was totaled. It was not as bad as losing his wife, but he felt he had lost his best friend. He now realized how his wife had felt when she realized her cat, her only companion, was crazy and she had to get rid of it. Damn, he thought, maybe that's *why* she got rid of me! It was the first time this memory had crossed his mind, and it was bothersome.

It was funny now that Cary thought back; she left me because she thought I was crazy, and made me get her a cat to replace me. I paid $35 for that inbred Persian cat, and weeks later she called me back. "Come pick up this crazy cat—he belongs with you." He had not been able to replace his first love, and now he didn't know whether he could replace his last love. And the damnedest thing about it, his first lost caused him to lose his second love, and now there was no love left at all. He felt even more alone now. Hell, he was alone.

This gave Cary a sobering thought concerning what had happened to cause the accident. He didn't have a blow out, and no other car was involved regardless of what the good ol' Carolina boys had said, God bless 'em. He remembered what the funeral home director, and the policeman had told him about the cause of some auto accidents. He remembered thinking it interesting, and he had researched some. The experts said that they thought some auto accident fatalities were suicides-on-purpose accidents. They said there were too many accidents that happened with no possible explanation for the cause. Maybe something in the subconscious led these people to kill themselves *accidentally on purpose*. He did remember seeing that telephone pole; he did remember looking at it. The more he thought . . . the more he didn't want to think. Do people hurt so deeply that they could actually end it all this way . . . is it possible for the subconscious to take over? Was he losing it? It was a scary subject, and he didn't want to think about it. He'd think about it tomorrow. Then another statistic crossed his mind. There were more suicides each year than there were homicides, and these suicides-on-purpose were not even counted as suicides.

# Chapter Nine

## A Spiritual Journey...

Though his body ached all over Cary was back working at the cemetery the next day. It was a beautiful summer morning, he found himself strolling through the newest cemetery section, The Garden of Time, one he'd laid out several years before. As he walked among the graves, it occurred to him that an unusual amount of young children had been interred in this garden. He decided to go back to the office and do some research. He wrote down the name, age, and cause of death of each child buried in that section since its inception.

To his astonishment, seventy per cent of the people buried in that particular garden were young children, and most had died a tragic death. This garden was no different than the three other gardens in the cemetery, and it was not designated particularly for children. When the parents came out to pick a gravesite for their children, Cary had no reason to lead them to that garden as the prices were all the same. He was fascinated and could see no reason for all those children to be buried there. His only conclusion was there was something spiritual going on. He wondered whether God was gathering the children together for some reason.

One child was a nine-year old girl who had committed suicide and left a note. When the mother ordered her child's memorial she inscribed a phrase she overheard her six-year-old son mumble as he watched his sister's grave being covered with dirt. The verse read: "I know that all of Becky's hopes and dreams are not lost in that grave with her."

Another boy, a seventeen-year-old high school graduate, was exuberantly celebrating his liberation from school at a lake when he died in a diving accident. Cary shook his head thinking, what a waste of all that education. Another was an eight-year-old boy who died after a long battle with leukemia. When Cary asked the mother her child's birth date for the headstone she was ordering, she said he was about thirty-five. Cary knew she was not talking about his physical age. He looked at the young parents, and couldn't fathom the depths of their suffering, as they watched their only son slowly die, willing to pay any price, but knowing there was nothing they could do.

There were many teenagers killed in auto crashes, and he realized those that died of drug overdoses were not interred in this garden. Did God have a reason for this, Cary wondered, to keep these apart? There were two teenagers who were murdered by other teenagers.

Then there was one mother whose sixteen-year old son

died in a car accident, and she buried him in the fall. There were several snowstorms that coming winter, and Cary saw the boy's father visit the grave *every* day for the next six months. He overtly drove his four-wheel pick-up truck through deep snowdrifts seemingly oblivious to them. His mind, his wife said, seemed totally immersed in a world she couldn't decipher, a nemesis she couldn't understand. Six months of heartache was all this man could take, he died, and was buried by his only son.

Cary met with his wife later when she came to pick out a marker for his grave. She opened up to Cary as others had done after burying a loved one.

"For the last six months, I've watched my husband grieve himself to death. I've heard of people dying of a broken heart, but it's the first time I've witnessed such. And I was not able to help, I . . . I *tried* but I was helpless because my being was just as shattered as his." She stared into nothingness and quietly spoke. "He grieved himself to death . . . the angels took him up from toil and carried him to God." She then bluntly said, "When I join them, I'm going to kick both of their butts for leaving me so unnecessarily alone." This attractive lady, still young herself, had lost her whole world, unexpectedly, in just six months. Cary was surprised when she described these events with lines of Emily Dickinson.

The lady scarcely noticed when Cary quoted another line.

"The sweeping up the heart and putting love away—" and she joined in without realizing it and they both finished the verse in unison, "we shall not want to use again until eternity." She gave Cary a bemused glance that a mere man would know lines of poetry.

She laughed a broken laugh and said, "Can you imagine anything worse, my husband grieving himself to death over our son, especially so young? I mean—both of them, my son was only sixteen and my husband thirty-eight."

Cary started to speak choosing his words carefully, he never dared presume the extent of another's suffering, and realizing this lady had just lost everything she had lived for, said "I'm sure he was having a hard time finding closure."

"Yes, I suppose he did," she replied. "But I'm the one still living, *what about my closure?* Hell, they were the only reason I got up in the morning, now . . . it makes no difference."

"Do you think the old saying is true of what they say about time healing?" Cary asked.

"Aww—that's bull!" she said. "Who *knows* if time will heal?" Cary thought to himself but couldn't bear saying it out loud, m*y wife is still living and I have no closure*. It was the first time he compared the suffering of those who were divorced, and still living, to those who lost a loved one through death. Her loved ones were dead and buried, and whether her closure would come or not, Cary wasn't sure, but at least she didn't have to contend with the memory that her husband was in bed with another woman each and every night.

His wound was still bleeding, and his hurt was ongoing. Cary wondered what she would have thought if he had asked, but of course he didn't.

Cary thought this wife and mother was special as many other women were. No one knows or quantifies the momentous attributes of these women. Many would think the gracious deeds they do for their families are insignificant or small because they seem like little things. The various unselfish actions they do to comfort their husbands in a thousand ways that a man never fully comprehends, or understands until their loving ways are no longer available. Then, when they are gone and too late to recognize their contributions, the men realize the awesome favors they acquired and wonder at the beauty of it. It was sad that some men would never enjoy such from their wives, and would live their lives out, without realizing what they were missing. It was just as distressing for the wife, that there were men who did entertain same, but shown no appreciation.

Then there was this twenty-year-old single girl who was found drowned in her car in the river. The policeman who got there first said that it appeared she came down the hill at City Point and drove straight into the James River. "You know the hill," he said, "the old brick-paved road by the Eppe's plantation in City Point that led to the river? The road curved at the bottom of the hill but there was no evidence, no tire marks that showed she tried to make the curve. They may rule it an accident but I know it was suicide."

"Why are you so sure?" Cary asked.

"I found her purse sitting on the riverbank where she must have sat previously while contemplating her actions. There were pictures of a young man carefully strewn about. You could tell they were placed there and had not fallen out of the car. Furthermore she had left a poem; here, I still have it in my wallet." The policeman pulled a folded paper from his wallet and showed it to Cary.

"I'll probably give it to the family," the policeman said, "but, they were so torn up that I thought I'd wait until the appropriate time . . . if there is an appropriate time."

They buried her next to her twenty-three year old brother who had died a few months earlier of cancer. Her dad attended the funeral, and when he took his hat off, it was evident he was taking chemotherapy.

There were many more, but it was too hard to think about them. Cary thought walking through the cemetery would alleviate his pain, but it didn't. He only felt the suffering was over for those amongst him while his torture was ongoing. He remembered again the statistic: there are more suicides each year than homicides. That was sad, he thought, and crossed his mind that it was unfortunate these homicides couldn't have happened to those who wanted to die, and not to the ones that were murdered and surely wanted to live. At least there would be fewer deaths altogether.

Cary had now witnessed many interments at the cemetery, and had talked with many of the aggrieved, left behind and alone with only their grief and memories to keep them company. Some were casual conversations, but many were of a deeply personal nature. These people would open their hearts more to him than those closer to them. He didn't know why . . . maybe they regarded him as a guardian overseeing their loved ones twenty-four hours a day. He only hoped he helped, in some small way, to alleviate their pain, but if nothing else, he listened patiently. This was heavy stuff for his mind and heart to absorb, and only time would tell if this would help, or hurt in finding his own closure.

Cary had not had any training in grief counseling, except experience, but he could understand the need for a dose of it. As far as closure was concerned, a healing to their suffering, Cary was not so sure they all attained it, or at least not equally. From what he had witnessed, it appeared that some might have lived with a deeper love commitment than others. He wouldn't judge, but he thought that maybe some couples took their marriage vows more seriously than others. And for these, the best conclusion he could come to was that their closure may only come with death, and if not, they were saddled with an emptiness for the rest of their lives: a piece of themselves dead, a hole in the heart, never to be replaced. For these, he hoped they were older when this came upon them and their suffering would be for a shorter period of time. God help the younger ones that had a longer period of misery. *Missing in action*, he thought, *life is like a silent war and just as deadly. Some of us die, some of us survive, some of us are walking wounded, and God help those whose bleeding never stops.*

# Chapter Ten

## And the Truth Could Set You Free

The next morning Cary was finishing his coffee when he read an article in the paper that really depressed him. A twenty-two-year old girl tried to commit suicide by driving her car of the Lee Bridge high above the James River in downtown Richmond. A witness said she slammed her car head-on into the side of the bridge with the expectancy, he guessed, of going through it and down to the river below. She was not successful, so she backed her car up and rammed the railing again. After ramming the barrier a third time and still failing to get her car through, she exited her car and in frustration, jumped.

Rescue workers were summoned, but they felt sure the girl must be dead. As they reached her location in the river they were astonished at what they found. She was standing up in knee-high water, seemingly kicking it in despair. Physically she appeared to have only superficial wounds, but by the dazed look on her face, one could not decipher the damage to her being. Imagine her frustrations when realizing that even killing herself was just another failure she had with the problems of living. They couldn't fathom the depths of her despair realizing she must have felt she couldn't *even* kill herself properly. She desperately had wanted to die, leaping a hundred feet into the rocky low-level river where few jumpers rarely survived. Cary couldn't imagine the state of her mind now and couldn't comprehend the problems the future held for her damaged being.

Cary needed help. He thought long and hard and decided to seek out some churches or maybe some pastors. There should be some answers somewhere. His mother had always said the answers were found in the spiritual world.

He never doubted the existence of God, but now he was having a problem obtaining blind faith unless he understood the scripture he was reading. Maybe that was what was wrong with him after all the hurtful things he had encountered. To take just *anyone's* word for the truth was hard. Maybe that was Emily's concern when she wrote: Faith is a fine invention for gentlemen that see, but microscopes are prudent in an emergency. What *good is Bible study*, he thought, *if one time a minister describes a scripture one way and the next day another interprets it differently?* For instance, he couldn't get past the beginning of the Bible, much less the rest.

He couldn't get a straight answer about what really took place between Adam and Eve and the Serpent. Late one evening while reading the Bible and debating whether to go to church or contact some pastor, he heard a knock on his door. He opened the door and there stood a couple. The man said he was the pastor of a new church, and he and his wife were going around inviting people to attend.

Another coincidence? He couldn't believe it. If they had come five minutes sooner or five minutes later, he wouldn't have been stunned, but *now*—the very moment he was thinking about church and had the Bible open in his hand! *Maybe it's a sign,* he thought, and debated whether to let them in.

They saw the Bible in his hand, and Cary said, "You've caught me red-handed," and motioned them in. They introduced themselves as Jake and Pam Oliver. "I'll tell you up front," Cary said seriously, "I haven't had much luck with preachers in the past. I've been going to church since I was little, but I don't think I've learned very much. Heck, I can't even understand the first Book of the Bible Genesis, much less the rest."

Jake and Pam looked suspiciously at him and glanced at each other with a knowing glance they'd found a soul that needed saving.

The pastor gave Cary a look he'd seen before, and he knew it was coming, "Have you been saved?"

"I've been asked that question a hundred times and I still don't like it," Cary said with irritation. "Why do all the preachers ask that; is it a marketing technique you were taught in seminary school? Were you taught this in the same schools that now are teaching that Jesus will come before the great tribulation? I've answered that question in every way in the past. I've answered it, 'yes' and 'no' and 'I don't know.' The preachers always said they could save my soul and lead me to salvation in the future, but none could explain how to stop my hurting while I'm living."

Jake ignored this remark and tried another tactic, "Well let us try to help you? What do you not understand about the book of Genesis?"

"Plenty," he replied, pointing to the Bible—"I can't get past what happened in the Garden of Eden, much less the rest. It's hard to believe that Eve eating a green apple could've been such a great sin. For instance, let's start at the beginning. Who was the father of Cain?"

"Adam," Jake replied.

"Here it says the Serpent beguiled Eve," Cary pointed out.

"Serpent beguiled Eve? What's that got to do with the father of Cain?" asked Jake. "The serpent beguiling Eve meant he influenced her."

"Well, I guess that's where we have a disagreement—the meaning of that word—*beguiled,*" Cary answered.

"How so?" asked Jake.

"Well it's my understanding the Bible was originally written in Hebrew and Greek." They nodded in agreement but still wondered what he was getting at. "Well," Cary added, "beguiled, in the Hebrew translation, means *wholly seduced.*"

"We never interpreted it that way," said Jake. "I think beguiled was a spiritual meaning, not physical."

"Well, that's not what Christ thought," Cary answered

"How's that?"

"Well over here," he turned to the New Testament, "in a sentence or two of John 8 verse 37, Christ was speaking to those who were seeking to kill him: 'Why do you not understand my speech even because you can not hear my word, ye are of your father, the Devil and the lust of your father ye will do. He was a murderer from the beginning.'"

Jake and Pam looked at each other, and Jake said, "We don't understand it that way, and I'm not sure that proves anything."

"I see," Cary replied. "Well, another verse names Cain the son of Lucifer is in First John, verse 12: 'That we should love one another not as Cain whom *was* of that wicked one and slew his brother.' Could it be that some of us are descendants of Satan? Could I be a descendant of Satan? Does that explain the wickedness in the world? Could that be my problem?"

Pam seemed to be genuinely interested in what Cary was saying, but Jake was defensive in a nice way. "You may be taking things out of context, but I'll look into it. Besides, Cain and Able were twins, how could Adam be the father of one and Satan the father of the other?"

His wife looked at him and explained. “It is possible, there can be two water bags and she could have been carrying two babies by two different fathers. There are records of this happening even today.”

“Well,” Jake said, “I didn’t know that. Well, we don’t have our Bible with us, but let us go and research your point of view, and we’ll get back to you.”

“While you are looking into it,” Cary said and turned to another page, “I’ll give you a couple more verses. In Revelation 2 verse 9, it says, quote,” ‘He knows thy works and tribulations and poverty but thou art rich and I know the blasphemy of them that say they are Jews and are not but are the synagogue of Satan.’ And besides that, nowhere in Adam’s genealogy is the name Cain found anywhere in the scripture.”

Jake looked at him earnestly and said, “We were not taught that interpretation in seminary.”

“Well,” Cary said grinning, “I haven’t been taught anything, it’s all *Greek* to me.” Jake caught the pun and smiled for the first time since they had been talking.

Jake shook Cary’s hand and said, “I really hope the Lord will hear your prayers, come to you, talk with you, and help you overcome your suffering.”

“Well,” Cary said, “I know many preachers have said God has talked to them but so far, I haven’t heard from Him.”

"Maybe you haven't been praying hard enough," said Pam, annoyed, but trying to be helpful.

"Maybe not," said Cary as they turned to leave.

"You've given us much to think about," said Jake as he opened the door for his wife. "Keep seeking the truth and the truth will set you free."

Cary thought they were nice and after they closed the door, and left he responded silently. *"Yes, I believe the truth could set you free, but therein lays the problem."*

# Chapter Eleven

## The Billion Dollar Invention

The next week Cary came home from work and checked his messages. There was only one from Jim cut off in mid sentence. Cary was afraid something was wrong. Some time had passed since Cary had returned from Florida, but he had stayed in touch with Jim. In past conversations, Jim said he had almost finished the final details of the engine and would soon give Cary the green flag to start pushing the sale. Cary had talked to several possible investors but had received no positive responses and had relayed this to Jim. Cary dialed Jim's number and waited . . . but there was no answer. Cary warmed his microwave dinner and tried to waste time watching TV, but couldn't get his mind off his brother. Finally, at eleven p.m., he called Jim again, but still there was no answer. He finally drifted off to sleep . . . . Five in the morning the phone rang.

"Cary, it's me." Jim's excited voice rang out. "Something's going on, someone broke into my garage and house!"

"What happened, what'd they do?"

"They haven't touched anything as far as I can tell. I think I interrupted them when I came home. Look, it scared the hell out of me. I took it, you know, *the car,* and drove off. I'm keeping it with me. Listen; tell me—who all have you talked to about the engine? You haven't mentioned to anyone where I live, have you?"

Cary was now wide awake and thinking, "No, I've told no one."

"Well," Jim said, "think, have you ever talked to anyone who might have known me?"

Cary took a deep breath and tried to remember. "I've talked to three oil companies, but mentioned no details and was just trying to feel them out. Heck, no one would take me serious, said they would need proof before they would talk money. I did talk to several wealthy business owners but never mentioned your name."

"Did any of them ever know me?" Jim asked.

Cary thought and said, "Well there was one guy, Buddy Jones, who you knew many moons ago. I learned that he'd become wealthy, some said a millionaire, but again I didn't mention your name. But I did mention the engine"

"Oh hell." Jim said, "That could be it. We used to race stock cars many years ago, and I discussed the engine with him then. Our relationship soured when I found out he was involved with drugs. I also mentioned coming back to Florida with him back then. He's now a millionaire, huh . . . well he probably made it selling drugs. I don't know if it was him, but he could have figured it out, and I wouldn't put anything past him, particularly since he's got money behind him. He's not a nice guy. Anyhow, I think we've found something, and I'll be on the lookout for him just in case. Cary, be very, very careful. Listen, I've got to run, I'll call you soon."

Jim hung up and Cary fumbled around and made some coffee. He sat down and tried to think. *If Jim has left his home, where's he going and what is he going to do?* Cary couldn't go to work; he paced the floor the rest of the morning trying to think things out. Finally that evening, he was sitting on the front porch when he noticed a dark sedan driving unusually slow past his house. It appeared as though the occupants were looking for an address. They drove slowly through the adjacent cemetery and finally parked beside his house. Two well-dressed men emerged and began walking towards him. Cary couldn't imagine who the hell these people were coming here so late. They knocked on the screen door of the porch and Cary slowly opened it. Two men in business suits stared straight at him.

"Mr. Cary Williams?" one of them asked.

Cary looked at them and wondered whether it was the police, the IRS or someone from his past concerning his failed business. “Who wants to know?” he asked.

They gave their names and said they were with the EPA. They flipped out IDs but it was too dark for Cary to read them. “We just have a couple of questions; it will only take a few minutes. Can we come in?” Cary waved then to a seat on the front porch. He didn’t want strangers in his house.

“The EPA?” Cary asked. “Questions about what?” They sat down and one of them brought out some papers and looked through them.

“Our job involves tracking down possible hazardous materials.” Cary could only think of chemicals he used at the cemetery for weed killing or maybe pesticides.

“Yeah, well, what does that have to do with me?”

Looking at one particular paper the agent said, “We see where some type of fertilizer and carbon were delivered to this address under your name a few months ago. We just wanted to know what this was used for.” Cary remembered Jim had ordered several items over the years for his engine in Cary’s name and address. Cary never questioned it; he just thought Jim was paranoid about something.

“Fertilizer! What it is used for?” he asked frowning. “It’s for growing grass, what else?”

“Well,” the dark suit replied, “why did you have it sent in your name and not the cemetery’s?”

"Well, everybody at the cemetery is dead," said Cary, not smiling, "and I am the only one alive to accept delivery. What difference does it make?"

They both looked at him not smiling, the agent holding the paper asked.

"How about this carbon you received?"

Cary knew Jim had ordered this for his engine and said, "That was a mistake. I thought that was a chemical that could be used for breaking up hard clay."

"Well, what did you do with it; we don't see where you returned it?"

"I couldn't use it—it didn't cost much and I laid it aside. It's probably still around here somewhere, I don't know. By the way, what is all this? Fertilizer and carbon isn't hazardous that I know of."

Well, it could be, just depends on how you use it."

"Use it like how?" Cary questioned.

"Like a bomb, like explosives," they answered. Cary didn't realize until later that they were not lying.

"Well, everyone in the cemetery is dead . . . it can't hurt them, can it?"

The men folded their papers, stood up to leave, and with serious looks on their faces asked, "Do you mind if we looked around the place?"

“Sure,” Cary said, not knowing if they were on the level or not, “help yourself.” They walked through each room in the house and then outside and inspected the contents of the cemetery garage. They appeared to be satisfied.

“Thanks Mr. Williams, we appreciate your cooperation.” They walked to their car, and before they drove off, Cary quickly looked at their license plate through binoculars. They were not driving a government car.

At midnight Cary was sitting on his front porch underneath a half moon. He couldn’t sleep and was wondering what he’d gotten himself into. The phone rang and Cary ran to get it.

“Cary, it’s Jim, how you doing?”

“I’m not sure.” He told Jim all about the EPA guys. They talked for awhile, and both thought the visit was suspicious.

“Damn Cary, I’m afraid someone is on to us . . . we had better make some plans to cover our tails. This phone could be tapped, so from now on, we’ve gotta be extremely careful. I’m in the area and will meet you exactly in one hour at Square’s house. Don’t mention the directions, just tell me if you know where I’m talking about and hang up. Don’t be followed!”

“I know the directions and I’ll be there. Goodbye.” Cary got his keys and jumped in the old Chevy he had just bought. He finally had found another similar to the one he had totaled.

# Chapter Twelve

## Strategy

### *Press On*

Summer had cooled into fall when Cary left Hopewell and headed towards Square's house where he remembered him living just outside of Petersburg. Five minutes later he was traveling through the old town remembering how Jim and Square were always obsessively discussing the Civil War. As he looked at the few downtown buildings that had survived the Yankee's bombing from Violet Hill, he passed the old City Hall Tower. So the story goes, General Grant had ordered his cannons not to destroy this building that housed the old clock. The city still maintained this clock to this day and Cary's watch agreed. He remembered Jim and Square debating about every aspect of various battles in minute detail in heated arguments, as hot as the small kerosene stove around which they huddled.  They both owned many relics, a sword engraved 1862 and a rifle from the same time period, while others had been lost in poker games. They had several letters, still in their original envelopes from soldiers writing home, talking mostly of hunger. He remembered Jim telling him the old town had never recovered from the Civil War. Many deteriorating and decaying buildings confirmed that. Still, there were many elaborate porches and grand, tall windows that testified of past elegance. Cary could still the soldiers lingering upon these huge, covered porches.

After leaving town, he soon turned and drove up a winding dirt road that led to the old ram shackled house that sat on a small hill. Cary had first come here with Jim some ten years ago and had met his close buddy, Square. An elderly, eccentric man owned these nine acres, a pond, and five identical two bedroom houses that he rented cheap with the understanding that the inhabitants would help maintain the place. But the whole area looked desolate as though no one had lifted a finger in years. The holes in the road were deeper, wider now and downright dangerous. You actually had to swerve right and left to avoid them or you might lose your car forever. The row of houses leaned lop-sided as maybe the foundations were giving way. Screen doors were dangling from their hinges, and paint was peeling off the walls. The pond out front looked smaller than before or maybe just appeared that way because the surrounding uncut weeds had spread and grown taller. The place looked like a hide out to Cary and probably a foretelling of the characters that resided there. Ten years later he saw nothing that had received any loving attention. Once Cary had asked Jim about these people, but Jim just glared and only said, "Don't ask—everybody is hiding out from something."

Cary parked his car beside Jim's Fifty Ford and saw Jim motioning him over to a shelter of some sort. The refuge had no sides, the sagging tin roof was supported by four round, rusting metal poles, and the area was large enough to park four cars inside. A falling down unused brick barbeque sat at one end, and the whole area was enveloped by tall weeds except a narrow path where footprints had prevented their growth. It looked like a pavilion area that was never finished—a place where good intentions were probably defeated by kegs of beer.

Jim was grinning when he said, "We've got a hell of a mess here don't we?" For a minute Cary thought he was talking about the surroundings. They sat down on some old wooden benches and Jim handed Cary a cold Budweiser. "Cary, I don't think those guys were from the EPA. I think they went through the house and garage looking for any iota of evidence concerning the whereabouts of the engine and me."

He changed the subject and pointed to the old Fifty Ford coupe he was driving with the special engine. "Well, I've got the bugs out and it's running good. Guess what? I drove it from Florida to Virginia on six gallons of gas! Pretty good, huh? It ran okay and I didn't have any problems. It was the first time I'd ever driven it that far and I picked a hell of a time to do it worrying about watching my back and all." His demeanor then turned serious. "Cary this whole thing is getting dangerous, are you still with me? It may be a scary ride before it's over."

Cary took a long swallow of beer and thought for a moment. He remembered Jim and how different they were. Cary had been working steadily the last ten years trying to improve himself both socially and economically while Jim seemed more intent on tempting the law. Cary had been trying to learn and get ahead in life, at least until the bottom fell out, whereas Jim gave the impression that he knew everything he'd ever need to know.

Jim had been flirting with the law on more than one occasion in times past. Personally, Cary didn't think he'd ever recovered since the police was able to catch his hopped up Forty Ford. Now he seemed possessed with a vindictive motive to seek redemption. Another time he was caught operating an illegal still. He was not doing anything wrong he'd told the cops, the still was just another invention he was trying to improve, but this explanation didn't fly with the law.

On the other hand hauling whiskey had been prevalent here since the twenty's when, at one time, it was Hopewell's leading industry. Men were explaining they were self-employed painters, but their trucks filled with painting tools never moved. When asked to explain their hopped up cars, they said they were building race cars, but none ever raced. They filed their taxes washing their liquor hauling income by saying it was self-employed earnings. Some said from painting, others from carpentry jobs, and others said it was from odd jobs. Odd jobs alright—whiskey hauling! Another time Jim was convicted of counterfeiting twenty-dollar bills and spent a short time in prison, an invention that had gone wrong in more ways than one. Cary never forgot the two men that came looking for him one day. It turned out they were agents with the Secret Service and had tapped his phone. They wanted to see the special camera he'd bought when he was trying to break into the printing business. They told him, after checking it out, it could be used for counterfeiting and that was the reason for their visit. A fact Jim probably knew but didn't bother informing Cary.

He never forgot the night when his brother asked him for a meeting at the Holiday Inn in Chester. Cary was parked beside the motel at the appointed time when he watched his brother pull in few parking spaces down. Suddenly police seemed to emerge from everywhere and surrounded Jim's car. A forty-five pistol was pointed at Jim's head.

"Freeze!" the cop yelled. "Don't move a muscle!" They had gotten to his car before he could take it out of drive. Jim's foot was still on the brake pedal, as indicated by the rear brake lights.

"Okay, okay," Cary heard Jim say without turning his head or moving his hand from the wheel. "But the car's still in gear," he told them.

"Move and you're dead," the cop ordered. Cary didn't know who was the most frightened, Jim or the cops. He figured it was the cops as they seemed close to panic in their decision of what to do next. Jim finally calmed then down by explaining that he, or they, had to cut the motor. They seemed afraid to reach across Jim to turn the motor off and didn't trust Jim to do it. The passenger door was locked; they couldn't get in that way. Jim was afraid of moving for fear of getting shot. The situation was comical but no one was laughing. Finally, in desperation or stupidity, another cop with a gun in one hand pointing towards Jim, took the back of his Billy club with his other hand, and smashed open the passenger door window, reached in and turned the key off.

After they arrested him, Jim again justified the counterfeiting as a soon-to-be noble endeavor. Cary remembered going to court with him and while sitting in the back row, to his horror, heard the judge tell Jim, "I am going to find you guilty, but I don't think you could have financed this project alone since you have no visible means of income. I have no proof, but I think your brother was involved too." Cary was relieved that the judge didn't know he'd given him the old offset printer which he probably used to print the money plus the fact he probably used his camera for the same reason. It didn't occur to him that maybe Jim had been using him for his own gain. As he grew older he realized their differences and they moved in opposite directions.

Then after Jim got shot and almost died, everyone had empathy for him. Cary had always prided himself on his reputation and had tried to improve his lot by working hard and honestly. He also remembered that before his divorce, Jim did too. He thought about this engine situation, but he couldn't think of anything illegal about it, dangerous maybe, but not illegal. And now after losing his wife, his business and his home, he really didn't have anything to lose except his values. He would not prostitute them and he was not going to commit any crimes. Finally, he looked at Jim and responded, "Yeah, I have thought about it, and I'm ready for the ride."

"Whew, I'm glad you said that. I just wanted to make sure cause I'm gonna need all the help I can get. I think it's time to put something in writing between the two of us. This is what I've got in mind; my past is a little shady while yours is clean. I've got to protect the engine, and I still need you to be the front man. You will do all the negotiations with the oil companies or whoever else would want to buy the invention. You have become more extroverted while I'm not, and you've been involved with business dealings, lawyers, and so forth. I do trust you, well, as much as I can trust anybody. You handle your part and I'll take care of mine. For this I'm willing to offer you half of whatever you can sell the invention for. I'm willing to put it in writing, so that no matter what happens, you'll be protected. Does that sound okay to you?"

"Hell yes!" Cary said without thinking.

"Okay, I've been thinking up a plan of action on my drive up here. You've got to stay distanced from me and you must not tell anyone about the whereabouts of the engine or me. That way you can do some things that I can't without divulging my whereabouts. You have got to be my go-between! I'll have my hands full just taking care of the engine. Please understand why I'm so adamant about protecting the engine—it's simply because I don't have it patented. If someone stole the engine they could claim it as their own. That's why I've got to stay hidden—you understand?"

"Yes."

"I don't think we have a choice of what we have to do," said Jim. "We haven't been able to raise the money to develop and market the engine. I don't think we could ever do it anyhow; the oil companies are too powerful. I think we'll have to sell it to the highest bidder, and you'll have to be the negotiator. Now I want you to contact me secretly and I'll give you instructions of how to go about it. We gotta be careful, as I said; your phone could be tapped. I've spent a whole day writing down directions for you. Here is a list on this paper, take them with you, study them, remember them and then burn the paper. Call me paranoid if you want, but for now, in this position, I'm glad that I am. I also have written down instructions for you to follow concerning your negotiations with the oil companies. I think they will offer us billions, but that is not the important thing. The important thing now—is to get what we can and escape out of this situation alive." Cary thought this was the first time he'd ever felt paranoid was good.

"Jim, shouldn't I contact the automobile manufactures, too?"

"No, I've have plenty of reasons why I don't think they can compete with the oil companies. Just forget the auto companies for now. Besides, we've got another problem. This billionaire-to-be is broke—anyway you can raise some cash? Things are heating up and we're gonna need some funds to operate on. We're *too close* to run out of money now!"

Cary studied the barbeque pit for awhile and finally made up his mind. "The only thing I can think of . . . is, while I've still got my job and good credit I could go to the bank and borrow all the money I can. But then I'll have to quit my job to be able to carry out these plans. I'll be putting myself out on a limb, but I guess it's worth the chance."

“Good” Jim said. “I think that would be a good investment on your part and hopefully it will carry us ’til we can make the sale.”

“Jim, are you sure there’s no one we can ask for help?”

“No, we have too much to lose to ask anybody for help, there’s nobody I trust—we’ll just have to trust each other . . . cause that’s all we’ve got. There will be more than enough money for both of us, so I don’t think we’ll double cross each other. That seems hard but it’s realistic.” It was the first time Cary realized that *even he* was not immune to Jim’s suspicions. Cary reasoned that Jim felt if his own wife, the closest of all relationships, could betray him, then why would a brother be above suspicion? He also remembered this was not the first time Jim had asked him to raise funds for a lost cause. He pondered the decision he had made; he was doing something that went against his grain. He knew he was putting himself into jeopardy, going out on a limb, and he hoped the limb wouldn’t break.

Cary looked at Jim and thought about Scarlett. “I have no one I can trust either, at least not in these circumstances. Jim, I won’t do anything without your say so.”

“Good. Now go and study that list and stay in touch with me as I’ve directed.” These events took his mind off Scarlett temporarily, and for that he was glad, but it was not exactly what he’d had in mind.

# Chapter Thirteen

## The Test Run

Cary woke up, stretched and looked out the window. It was a bright, sunny day and he thought this was a good time to start a whole new chapter in his life. He was glad, glad to have his mind filled with exciting plans that may solve his money worries for the rest of his life. He made his coffee, read the morning paper. and set out for the local bank. He haggled with the bank for a half-hour before realizing they weren't going to lend him a dime, something about past work history and not having been long enough at his new job.

He walked across the street to the Ezy Loan Company and gave them a long story of divorce, losing his business, and starting a new job. They didn't much care. He was working and should be able to make the payments, and if he didn't, they would garnish his wages. Besides, they were going to stick him with thirty percent interest. The most they would give him was seven thousand dollars. Cary could not care less about the high interest under the circumstances. He signed the papers, and the agent counted him out seven thousand dollars and gave him a big smile and a slap on the back as though he was his best friend.

Cary went to the cemetery and notified his boss that he

was quitting. They pleaded with him not to go before someone could be found to replace him. After all, they needed someone to dig the graves and handle the interments. People were not going to wait to die until they had a gravedigger. Cary thought they had a point but he was anxious to leave, and the only person around with any experience was his part time helper, Curt Flowers. The cemetery had hired Curt to help Cary when he found himself preparing multiple funerals. Cary considered recommending him for the job but had doubts about his ability.

He had known Curt for about a year and had let him live above the cemetery garage. He was intelligent in some matters but ignorant in others. He realized he had some problems after finding him early one Monday morning sunk tail first into a five gallon empty bucket on the concrete garage floor midst three lawn mowers. He was dazed, hung over from the weekend, and in very much distress. Cary looked up and saw a gaping hole in the ceiling and realized he had just fallen twelve feet from his make shift apartment. The only thing separating him from the cement floor was the five gallon can that was about five inches tall. Curt's knees were now level with his head as he squirmed around trying to exhume his rear end from the dilapidated container when he noticed Cary's bewildered look, and tried to explain his predicament with his know-it-all German intelligence."Didn't . . . didn't even hit the floor," he groaned. Luckily, Curt didn't break any bones, but could barely move for two weeks, and Cary had to dig the graves alone for the next three weeks.

After this Cary found him an apartment in Hopewell and helped him move in, but ever since then he seemed to forget to pay his rent and utilities. He finally discovered Curt's problem when he asked him about his past. He was in his forties now, but when he was twenty-one he had had a terrible auto accident. A city bus had run over his car with him inside and almost killed him. He was rushed to the hospital where the surgeons placed a metal plate over the hole found in his skull. Afterwards he seemed to function normally in most situations. Still, Cary thought his problems were deeper than that.

He could never forget the two auto accidents Curt had been involved in while working at the cemetery; both had taken place in the first few months of winter. Curt didn't have a car to get back and forth to work so Cary found one for him and helped him buy it, not realizing until later that this was a mistake. One morning after a night of freezing rain, Curt was trudging down the road in front of Cary's house at the cemetery. Cary saw Curt but not his car and wondered what was going on. Curt was trying to walk down the highway but kept falling on the frozen pavement. He would take two steps and then fall, two more steps and fall again. Curt's eyes were wide and his unshaven face was filled with frustration. He yelled "Whoaaa", as his legs flew up and he landed on his backside.

Cary got to him and helped him to his feet and realized he'd been drinking the night before. "Curt—what the hell are you doing, where are you going?"

Curt's bug eyes were looking down at his feet as they started sliding outwards. "I'm . . . trying . . . trying to go get to my car, gotta get it out the woods. I, uh . . . I spun it out last night on old Jandl's curve—be right back!" He trudged on down the frozen roadway, taking two steps and falling, two steps and falling. It wasn't two months later when the same scenario occurred at the same place.

"What happened this time Curt? Where you going with the backhoe?" Curt turned to him with wide glassy eyes; he was hung-over and was pumping his fist up and down like someone who had forgotten something.

He was shaking his head in disbelief and said, "It's that *same* old damn curve again Cary, I can't . . . just *can't* seem to get the hang of it; be right back; gonna pull 'er out with the backhoe this time." He had missed the curve again and had plowed into the woods, narrowly missing several trees. But he was learning from his mistakes, Cary thought, and hoped he'd learn before he killed himself.

Curt told him later that he came down this side road last night to avoid the cops after spending Saturday downtown drinking beer. Cary just shook his head, wondering why he was driving the four miles here last night instead of going home. He learned later that he had simply forgotten where he lived, which was only blocks from where he did his drinking. After this, Cary was sure of his doubts, but decided, reluctantly, to recommend him for the job anyway. He didn't want to be the one that held him back from improving his lot. The cemetery hired Curt, and he was tickled with the job, didn't complain about the pay and was grateful to Cary. He thought it odd when Curt told him, "I could care less about money, and if I ever had any, it wouldn't change me a bit!" Before leaving, Cary told Curt to contact him if he ever needed to. Cary was anxious to get back to his project, but drove away with a feeling of foreboding concerning Curt. Before going home, Cary contacted Curt's landlord and his next door neighbor, Mack, and gave his phone number just in case.

For the next seven days Cary studied Jim's instructions and then burned them. He rented the old home place downtown, paid three months in advance, and drove to the designated place Jim had specified to receive his messages. Jim met him at the 21st street dock overlooking the Appomattox River right after dark. "Thanks for the money," Jim told him. "I hope it's the best investment you've ever made."

"I've taken all my winnings and risked them on one pitch and toss." said Cary.

"How's that?"

"Just an old saying,"

"You always did like your literature didn't you?

"Words to live by," said Cary.

"Okay, I think it's time for you to begin negotiating with the oil companies, Cary. Now the biggest problem I see is that they are gonna want to see it, inspect it, and who knows, maybe want to steal it. We can't take that chance so we've got to be careful. I don't feel like I can trust them or anybody for that matter. We've got too much to lose; it's too big of a deal. Tell them we would prove the gas mileage by doing a test run. I'm willing to do that if necessary and then we'll go from there. So go ahead and start with the oil companies and let me know."

Cary left and the next morning he drove to a local gas station. Gotta'start somewhere he thought. He got a phone number from the attendant for their home office in Dallas. Cary thanked him and drove home and called the home office.

When someone finally answered, Cary said, "I want to talk to the department that would be interested in a high- mileage gasoline engine."

"Hold on." Finally a voice came back.

"Engineering division, Thompson speaking."

"Mr. Thompson, I represent a group that has invented a high-mileage gasoline engine and was wondering if anyone there would be interested in talking to me."

"What kind of engine?"

"Well, I don't want to go into details over the phone but I'll just say our test drive proved our car got 100 miles to a gallon of gas."

"Well," Thompson said, "no disrespect, but we get odd-ball calls like this quite often and we would not be interested. Thanks anyway." Cary hung up and called information and got the numbers of two more oil companies. He talked to both and more or less got the same treatment. They were not interested. He contacted Jim as he was directed and met him later the same day.

"Yeah, well, I kinda' figured that might happen," said Jim. "They think they know all the answers and can't believe it's possible to achieve what we've done. Well, I have a back-up plan for this situation. You find a reputable reporter and contact him; you might look through the auto magazines to find one. Try to find anyone familiar with the Swirling engine, if possible. Convince him to take a test run with us."

"Will do," said Cary and headed home again.

He spent the next day in the local library and wrote down every phone number he could find for reporters or columnists who wrote for auto magazines. After another day, and many long-distance phone calls, he finally found two that had connections to a Swirling engine. He called them but could only leave messages saying he had developed a high-mileage gasoline engine that involves a Swirling engine.

He waited by the phone for two days and finally on the third day he received a call from one of them.

"Yes, I'm returning a call concerning your engine, my name is Jackson Boyle and I'm with *Auto World* magazine."

"Yes," Cary answered. "Listen, without going into details, I have a car that will travel 100 miles on a gallon of gas. I've talked to several oil companies and they've shown no interest. I would like to find a reporter to ride with me, to verify and publish the results. Maybe then I can obtain some attention."

"You've spoken a mouth full. Are you sure you know what you're talking about? How about you bringing the engine to me and let some mechanics check it out? Let us take it apart and verify that the engine is what you say it is."

"There are reasons I can't do that at this time," replied Cary. "A person only has to take a ride with me to verify the MPG. You can verify the empty tank, you can put the one gallon of gas in and we will travel the 100 miles."

"You say a Swirling engine is involved?"

"Yes."

"Well . . . I've have been interested in the engine for years. I always thought it had possibilities . . . ." He paused and Cary waited. He finally made up his mind. "All right, I'll do it;

maybe it will be an interesting article for my magazine if nothing else."

"I'll carry you from Richmond, Virginia to Washington D C on one gallon of gas."

"I can get away next week if you are ready."

"Thanks, we've got a deal," said Cary. "I'll call you tomorrow and we'll iron out the details." Cary hung up and hollered. "We're moving on!"

He contacted Jim at a special number and told him the deal was set. Jim was glad but was already worrying what could go wrong. "Cary . . . we're putting ourselves out for comment, and it's a little scary. I'll map out some stipulations tonight and I'll meet at the river tomorrow at ten, and I'll draw them out for you."

Just as Cary hung up he heard a knock on the door, and slowly walked towards it wondering who now? He was dressed up in a three-piece suit but Cary still recognized him. He was wide and thick reminding him of a baseball umpire.

"Buddy Jones, how the heck you doing? You ready to invest?"

"Hi Cary, thought I would stop by, got to thinking 'bout that investment you were talking about. You want to tell me more about it? I came across some funds that I may want to invest." Cary decided to go along with the plan he and Jim discussed in

Florida. This guy knows Jim and lying to him just wouldn't fly.

"Well, Buddy, it's my brother Jim, you remember him. He claims if he had the funds, he could purchase the right equipment and could complete an engine innovation that would get high gas mileage."

"Yeah, he said that ten years ago," Buddy drawled. "I wouldn't invest then and won't now on just *talk.* Has he got any proof that it works?"

"Not exactly," said Cary, "but he said he could do it if he had the money."

Half disgusted now, Buddy stared at the ground and said, "Yeah, how much money?"

"He's talking about a hundred thousand or two."

Buddy laughed and turned to leave. "Where's he at now, anyhow?"

"Still in Florida." Buddy shrugged his shoulders and left. Cary thought his lack of interest was probably for the best, remembering he could have been the one who broke into Jim's place. After talking to Jim, he didn't trust him anyhow.

After meeting with Jim the next day he called Jackson back. "We don't want any publicity just yet, so will you promise to keep this trip a secret until we finish the trip?

"Okay," Jackson said, "I've told no one."

"A couple things more, we would like to make the trip

and then put away the engine before it's publicized. We also would like to keep the name of the driver anonymous. You may ask the driver any questions, but he will only divulge a limited amount of knowledge concerning the engine. I want you to only use my name and number as the contact person."

"Okay, that seems reasonable."

"We can meet you tomorrow morning at ten. Cary gave him the exact location off I-95 just south of Richmond.

"I will be there." Jackson agreed to ride to Washington D C where he would be let off after verifying the gas mileage. Jim said he was all set, and Cary agreed to follow them. The mileage to D C was a little over one hundred miles.

The next morning Cary met Jackson behind a Holiday Inn and introduced Jim as Bob. The fifty Ford coupe was idling and Jackson checked the gas gauge. It was sitting on empty.

"Okay Jackson, you can take it from here—tell us how to proceed."

"What do you mean?"

"Well, if you are going to verify the gas mileage, you should be in charge from the git-go. You are free to check the car over as much as you like."

"Okay great," Jackson said with enthusiasm. He took off his coat and threw it in the back seat of the fifty Ford. "Okay if I drive the car to the gas station next door?" he asked. Jim nodded okay. Jackson first raised the hood and carefully inspected every item in and around the engine. Jim and Cary could tell he was mechanically inclined, and was very meticulous. He raised the car up on the lift and inspected the undercarriage. He lowered the car and went inside and pulled both front and back seats up and peered underneath. He checked the trunk and then the gas tank and traced the gas line all the way to the engine.

Finally he seemed satisfied. "Okay, I only see one gas tank, and those three extra batteries there." He recognized the small Swirling engine next to the V-8, but it wasn't big enough to hold any gas, and he didn't give another thought to the extra batteries. He paid the attendant and had Jim drive the car to the gas pumps. "Now keep the engine running until it runs out of gas," Jackson asked. It ran for two minutes and sputtered to a stop. "Now I will put one gallon of gas in the car." He carefully watched the pump and stopped it at one gallon. "Okay," he said. "I'm satisfied. Let's go." Just before leaving Jackson questioned Cary with a smile. "You'll be behind us in case we run out of gas, won't you?" Cary told him he had a two gallon can full of gas. He and Jim headed north on I-95 in the fifty Ford coupe with Cary following.

Nearing Washington, Jackson, for the fifth time, checked the gas gauge and shook his head in disbelief. He was still shaking his head as they entered the city limits. Jim drove straight to the White House and parked right in front. Jackson quickly figured the gas mileage—they had traveled one hundred and eight miles. The gas gauge was sitting on empty and the engine was still running. He got out with his camera and took several pictures of the car with only Cary appearing instead of Jim. Cary reached into the trunk of his car and brought out a can of gas. As he walked towards the coupe he motioned to Jackson with a grin. "Looks like you didn't need any more gas!" It was then the car ran out of petrol.

"Well you've convinced me! Jackson said still looking bewildered. I'll have the story in next month's publication of Auto World. *You'd* best get ready for some publicity." Cary poured the can of gas in the Ford; the two boys shook Jackson's hand, thanked him for verifying the ride, and all departed separately. Jim took the car to an undisclosed location and Cary headed home.

Jim and Cary waited anxiously for the magazine to be published. Finally, after two weeks, Cary received a copy of the Auto World in the mail. He rushed over to show Jim and they looked at it together. On the cover of the magazine, there it was—all in color, the picture of their car with Cary beside it grinning. The bold headline declared:

**Fifty Ford Drives from Richmond, Va. to Washington D C**

**on One Gallon of Gas.**

**Reputable automotive reporter, Jackson Boyle of Auto World, tells of the ride of his life as he personally verifies test run that breaks all records for MPH for a gasoline engine. Details of the invention were not disclosed by the spokesperson, Cary Williams, but his phone number is listed below . . .**

# Chapter Fourteen

## All Hell Breaks Loose...

"We've done it now Cary. You're in for a wild ride," said Jim. "I'm glad it's you and not me. I've never been good dealing with a lot of publicity. Heck, I've never had any, at least none that I'm proud of. It's in your hands now; we've been as careful as we know how so far, and you must continue being cautious. Good luck! "

Cary headed home and tried to gather himself for the upcoming publicity. The thought was just dawning on him what an *awesome* undertaking they had set in motion. He browsed amongst his books of inspiration. He remembered the words of James Dean, his favorite actor:

"Some people avoid greatness because they don't like the responsibility that comes with it."

His non-conformist hero, Thoreau, said: "How deep the ruts of tradition and conformity! I did not want to take a cabin passage, but rather to go before the mast and on the deck of the world, for there I could best see the moonlight amid the mountains. I do not wish to go below now."

"I did not wish to live what was not life, living is so dear;

nor when I came to die, discover I had not lived." Reading these passages usually helped to sustain him, but tonight Cary went to bed worried

Early the next morning the ringing of his phone woke him, and he stumbled to pick up the receiver.

"Mr. Williams, my name is Johnson with the *Daily Press,* what are your plans are for the engine?"

"What time is it?" Cary mumbled.

"Six a.m.," the voice answered.

"You woke me up," Cary yelled and hung up. It rang again immediately, and he took the phone off the hook. He pulled some jeans on, washed his face, and left the house for McDonald's to get his coffee. He hadn't finished his first cup when a man sat down across the aisle from him, ordered coffee, and opened his morning paper to the headlines.

"*Wow,*" the man said out loud, "some guy has invented an engine that gets 100 miles to a gallon. It says he drove it from Richmond, Virginia to Washington D C on one gallon of gas." A dozen people gathered around the man and his paper.

"*Really,*" one said, "that would be *great* because have you heard? Gas prices jumped up three cents a gallon yesterday." Cary was in the midst of a community conversation, but when he realized no one had connected him with the engine, he ordered breakfast and listened. News really travels fast, he thought.

“It’s about time someone came out with an invention to help the people,” the one with the paper said.

“Yes,” another chipped in, “gas prices are killing us.”

“Yeah, isn’t that *great*? He’s *shown* it to the world!”

An old retired farmer at his seat beside a large glass window spoke. “Don’t get your hopes up yet—when the powerful oil companies hear about it, they will probably buy it up, give him a billion dollars, hide it away, and that will be the last of it. You’ll never hear of it again.”

A collective “Oh nooooo” went up.

“They *wouldn’t* do that, would they?” another questioned.

“The old timer continued: “Well, you’ve heard about them in the past haven’t you? I’ve heard reports about high-mileage engine inventions before, and as soon as you get your hopes up, all of a sudden you hear nothing else about it. In my opinion that’s when the oil companies have stepped in and bought them out. I’ve always wondered why the media drops the mention of it. Maybe the oil companies bought them up too, you know, to keep it quiet. I’m sure it’s been done before.”

“Yes, but look how much this would help us and the economy,” another answered. “They wouldn’t be that greedy would they?”

The farmer further explained his philosophy: “Look how much money they would lose if our cars got that kind of mileage.

They would lose millions, maybe billions of dollars. It always comes down to the dollar. I still say, with all their money, they could buy him out, shelve the engine, and we'd never hear another word about it. The kid better watch his back."

"Well, let's *hope* this fellow wouldn't sell us out," the waitress said.

The farmer leaned back and sighed, "The oil companies are powerful and could be pretty mean when someone is messing with their money. You know, they could make him an offer he couldn't refuse, that is, if he wants to live. By the way, what company does he represent?"

"Well, there's no company name mentioned," the paper owner said, "just an individual's name and his picture. His name is Cary Williams and he's from Virginia. There's also his phone number—*hey,* he's got a local number—and that's *our* phone exchange!" The excited man looked all around, scanning the crowd and while his eyes were passing Cary he announced, "I'll be *damned,* he could be a regular fellow living here . . . right among us!" Cary turned away and pulled the brim of his cap down.

"Well, think of that . . ." several murmured.

"You mean they don't mention that some large corporation is involved . . ."

"*No sir*, just one individual name, no mention of him

representing any huge conglomerate."

"You mean, just an average guy like you and me?"

The man next to Cary turned to him and said, "Sounds like it, wouldn't that be nice, he could be some regular mechanic that came up with it. Heck, we could have a billionaire living right here, ha, ha, ha." Cary was getting uncomfortable. He finished his breakfast, paid his bill and left.

The waitress watching Cary leave said, "Hmmm, that boy doesn't seem too excited about it."

Another said, "He doesn't appear so, but maybe he's rich and the price of gas don't bother him."

*Damn*, Cary thought, walking to his car, *now I'm going to be the bad guy. A greedy guy selling out to the oil companies instead of making it available to the public. Damn, I would love to, but don't have a clue of how to go about it.*

Cary went and bought a new answering machine to replace his old one that was acting up. This was not the time to miss any calls. The phone was still ringing when he entered his front door, and he was surprised the word had gotten out so fast. He listened to it ring almost constantly and was glad he had connected the new machine. It would give him time to collect his thoughts before answering all those questions. Hell, he hadn't counted on this much publicity; he only thought the oil companies would be calling. He listened to the tape and deleted the messages that were not important. Most of the calls were from reporters trying to get a story. Some were from magazines and some just left their names and phone numbers.

One call was different—a woman left her name, number, and a message saying she was not a reporter or a crackpot, said she represented a firm interested in making the engine available to the public. She hoped he would consider her proposal before selling to the oil companies.

The call intrigued Cary so he dialed her number and said he was returning a call to Molly Anderson.

“Mr. Williams, this is Molly Anderson. I’m glad you called, and I hope you will give me the opportunity to discuss the matter.”

“I’ll tell you right off, Ms. Anderson, I would rather see this engine made available to the public.”

“I was hoping you would say that. You know if you sold it to the oil companies, they would only shelve it and the engine would never make it to market.”

“That’s a no-brainer,” he answered.

“I’m in New York. Can I fly down and talk to you?”

“I’ll call you back shortly,” Cary said and hung up.

Cary contacted Jim and reiterated the conversations at the restaurant and with Ms. Anderson. Told him there were no calls from the oil companies.

# Chapter Fifteen

## The First Offer

Cary called Ms. Anderson the next day, and she picked up the phone. "Good morning, Molly Anderson speaking, can I help you?"

"Ms. Anderson, Cary Williams here, is there any way possible you could meet me tomorrow?"

"Would you please call me Molly? I would appreciate it."

"Sure," Cary said. "Molly it is."

"Okay, let me see . . . uh yes, I can be in Richmond tomorrow afternoon." They chatted for awhile and worked out the details of their meeting. Cary asked and received all the pertinent information concerning her group and said goodbye. He called information and got several numbers for companies that she had connections with. He called them all, and she checked out to be who she said she was. Cary was relieved.

The next evening, he was sitting at the terminal overlooking the landing strip at Richmond International Airport. Molly said he could identify her by a bright red hat. He watched several large passenger jets pull in and unload their passengers, but none wore a red hat. Then he saw a small jet pull in He thought it might be a private business plane or maybe a celebrity.

He watched as only one person departed. The beautiful, expensive plane fascinated him, but not as much as the stunning young woman. He waited for others to depart but the woman was the only one, and then the doors of the plane shut. The young woman wore a well-tailored suit that fit snugly over a trim body, looked in her mid-twenties, and walked with an air of confidence in her high-heel shoes. Her dark hair was partly covered with a bright, red hat. *Oh,* Cary thought, *could that be her?* Cary watched as she neared the pick-up area, paused, and looked about her, evidently looking for someone. *Good lord, she's beautiful* he thought as he started walking towards her. He hoped the girl *is* Molly as he finally looked away to avoid her pretty eyes staring at him as though he could be one she was looking for. As he passed behind her, he turned to enjoy one final glimpse and as he did, she almost collided with him—she had turned towards him thinking he may be looking for her. She abruptly stopped to avoid running into Cary and her attaché case swung forward and bumped Cary in the knee.

"Oooh!" He said faking it somewhat.

"Oh! *I'm* sorry!" She said as she leaned down to retrieve the fallen case with one hand, while holding on to her red hat with the other. "Are you okay?"

Rubbing his knee he said, "I think I'll live." He was face to face with the most dazzling beauty he had ever seen. He stood there gawking, dumb struck for a moment.

"Would . . . would . . . you be Molly Anderson?" He finally stammered.

"That's me," she said with a smile and extended her hand. Cary was awestruck with her beauty as two large dark eyes now gazed at him. "You must be Cary Williams?"

"Uh . . . yes." He reached for her small case, "Can I help you with that?"

"Oh, no, it's small and I would just as soon hold on to it." Cary pulled his staring eyes away from her and tried to gather himself and think of something to say.

"That jet is some kind of plane! You kinda travel in style don't you?" She analyzed Cary for a moment and summed him up; he was not a sophisticated guy.

"Yes, well, my people wanted to get me down here as soon as possible and frankly, obtaining a passenger plane into Richmond was not so easy." Cary now wished he had worn some better clothes and had cleaned the car before he came. Whatever he had been expecting—it wasn't this. *What* could this sublime beauty know about car engines?

"Well, you've come South now among us country boys," he said, trying not to let his nervousness show. She could tell that he was not pretentious, and she liked that. Cary guided her to the parking lot and to his sixty Chevy convertible. He opened the door for her and said, “My limousine.” She smiled and took a seat, not knowing what year and make the car was. Cary went to the driver’s side and slid in beside her and her textured suit and tried not to stare at her. Her long hair was fine, almost black, and was topped with her little round red hat. She turned to him with a freckled nose and full lips surrounded by a cameo face of milky white skin. She had a noble nose with two dots for nostrils and dark eyes accentuated by butterfly eyelashes. Her soft beige business suit was tinged with a light bit of red to match her hat. He caught himself self-consciously looking at her and finally had to apologize, for he knew it had become obvious. “I’m sorry, I . . . I just wasn’t expecting a beautiful young lady,” he gushed. Molly knew how her looks affected men and quickly acted to diffuse the situation.

She blushed slightly and demurely said, “Well thank you, I’m glad I didn’t disappoint you. Is your unique engine in this car?”

“Uh, no . . . well, it’s damn special to me.” He was thinking of all the dollars and time he had spent on the second hand car he had bought. “But it might not be the one you are thinking about.”

“Well, the paper said the car was a . . . a 1950 Ford Coupe, right?”

“Yes, that’s correct; it’s about ten years older than this

car." He noticed she seemed disconcerted and added, "We do go first class." She laughed for the first time, revealing a pretty smile with unusually white teeth.

"Wanna go any place particular?" he asked.

"How about your place?"

"Okay, but it's nothing special," he said. Cary could tell he was probably in some high-class company. He tried not to be intimated, realizing that, after all, she was the one that flew in a private jet to see *him.* After a twenty-minute ride, they crossed the James River and entered the small factory town of Hopewell where Cary grew up. They pulled in front of his small one-story house that was similar to the others on the street. It was just a plain old one-story frame house, about fifty years old, where he had spent his childhood. The sun was fading as factory workers were returning home and kids were playing in the surrounding yards.

"What a beautiful little town," she said. "It very much reminds me of my home in Georgia."

"It's a small city, population 'bout ten thousand, mainly a factory town with blue-collar workers." Cary led her into his house.

"My father worked at an auto factory in Georgia, so it feels a little nostalgic to me," she replied. They sat down at the kitchen table and he offered a drink.

"All I've got is beer, bourbon and coffee."

"I would be happy with coffee."

"A coffee drinker too, huh? Coming right up," Cary said. "That's my specialty." He put on the coffee, and they both seemed to relax.

"That was pretty impressive, coming in a private jet."

"Well, I guess my people wanted to impress you and we are very anxious."

"Impress me?" Cary grinned. "Is that why your people sent a neat miss in a sleek jet instead of a middle-aged cigar-chomping male? Your company must have some pretty shrewd people in charge. I'm impressed already," he said, trying not to smile as he turned the heat down on the coffee.

Molly held a smug smile of her own as she responded. "You've caught on to us already, haven't you? Listen, I have my credentials in this case when you're ready to see them."

"Tell me," Cary said, "what do you have in mind?"

"First off," she said, "you know that you possess something of great value, and we know the oil companies will be pressing you to purchase the rights and shelve the invention. You know they wouldn't put it on the street, don't you?"

"Probably not."

"By the way, if you don't mind my asking, have any of them contacted you yet?"

"Not as yet."

"Good." She went on, "My first objective is to try to convince you to make this engine available to the public. Heaven knows, they could use the savings with the gas prices going up and all. Also, the economy would be greatly improved in various ways and would directly affect the people in a positive way. Just for one instance, we could get goods transported at a lower cost. That would mean lower prices to the consumers." She stressed the point, "For instance, say a company's fuel prices go up to deliver a side of beef. They would simply pass the additional cost on to the consumer. I mean . . . I could go on and on but you get the picture." Cary nodded.

"That seems like a pretty high ethical goal," he replied smiling, enjoying her Georgia accent.

"Well, we like to think our group has ethical and moral standards, and we wish to be an advocate for the people."

"What company did you say you worked for?"

"I represent a non-profit group whose goal is to do good in this world. I would say they are a spiritual bunch, an older group of people who have achieved much in their careers and now desire to give back to the people. They consist of people across America and other countries. Most of them are legitimate billionaires. The group's official name is *The People's Advocate*. They were formed about twenty years ago. I will leave you a packet of information concerning them. You can look it over, read their past accomplishments, and check out their references. To be frank, they can't match the oil company's money, but they're prepared to write you a check to purchase your invention outright, a check large enough that you could retire tomorrow if you wanted to."

The saleswoman in her continued, "Understand, selling to the oil companies will present you with problems. Number one, they will want to pay you underneath the table and have you sign an agreement that you would never disclose the transaction. They wouldn't want the public to know they committed such a greedy, unethical deed as denying this savings to the people. Then, number two, you would then have another problem, how would you spend the money? The IRS would be on your back asking where this money came from."

"Wow, you've done some research and covered about everything," Cary said. "And believe it or not, I've actually considered these aspects. You have confirmed some of my suspicions."

"You are wiser than I gave you credit for then." She replied. "But these subjects are really elementary and common sense."

"Do you think your group can accomplish this—getting the engine developed and on the market?"

"Well, we've debated it. Our people are willing to give it a shot if your price is not too high. We do have concerns about the oil companies, but if we buy your rights to the engine, there's not much they can do. Anyhow, you won't have to worry about that, we realize you want your money up front."

Cary thought about the situation and said, "Molly, all this sounds good, almost too good to be true."

"I know, I know, but please look through the documents, check the group out, give it some serious thought and get back with us." She heaved a sigh of relief. "Well, my foundation will be relived I was able to speak to you before the oil companies got to you."

"Why so?" Cary asked.

"Well, what I mean is, if you hadn't heard me out first, I may not have had a chance to converse with you. We were afraid that if they had gotten here first and waved a billion or two under your nose, you might have taken the money and run. Money can do funny things to a person you know, and they *will* be coming, so you might as well brace yourself." She looked pleadingly at Cary and tried again. "Will you check out our group and give us a serious consideration *before* you make a decision?"

"I will," Cary said, "I will."

"Now," Molly said, "let's put business aside and tell me about yourself. I would love to hear more about you and this amazing accomplishment. *How* in the world did you do it? My guess," she looked around her, "is you are not exactly wealthy. You must have accomplished it with a limited amount of funds, while these large research companies out there, with their vast resources, have been working for years trying to devise an engine that was more fuel efficient and haven't done it. How in the world could you, just an average guy and so *young*, come up with an invention like you have?"

Cary didn't like taking credit for something he didn't do, but now was not the time to clarify the subject. "The Wright brothers were not wealthy; maybe they just had a dogged determination. Maybe we believed in ourselves or maybe we just got lucky. We are amazed everything came together too. We certainly don't think it was any superior intellect we possessed. We may have stumbled upon the answer just months before someone else would have. Or maybe this has been discovered before and maybe the powers that be didn't want it on the market." Cary realized this was the first time he said "we," but then was glad he did after her reference to his young age.

"Do you *really* think that's happened." she asked.

"I've heard people say that but I have no proof. Who knows, I'm just thinking out loud. Heck, it's just common sense though, economically speaking. But one thing for sure, they don't have one like ours; least none recorded at the patent office."

“That’s interesting,” Molly said as she removed her hat, kicked off her heels and stretched her legs across a chair. “I really have no idea. I guess you’d better be careful; the oil companies surely will not want this invention on the market. They are powerful and, if I were you, I’d watch my back.”

“You can imagine I’m running scared, this situation is bigger than I realized, and that ringing phone has not stopped since yesterday. You can see I’ve taken the phone off the hook for now just so we could talk. This is something we’ve worked on for a dozen years, and yet I’m still astonished that it all came together at last. I’m actually paranoid worrying that something could go wrong.”

“That’s more reason,” she replied, “why you should make a decision as soon as possible.”

“Yeah, but I have to spend so much time checking people out. As much as you impress me, I can’t take the chance of trusting you by words alone. I will have to check you and your group out carefully. They say when something sounds too good to be true, it probably is, but damn, you are mighty convincing.” Cary was overwhelmed with her beauty and demeanor, and he was glad she was so friendly, but he was curious as hell about her and finally summed up the courage to ask. “By the way,” Cary couldn’t help himself and stammered, “are you . . . uh, are you married? I mean, if you don’t mind my asking.”

She blushed, laughed, and said "No, I'm not married; not attached at the moment." And then with a grin she said, "I've been waiting for a billionaire."

Cary couldn't tell whether she was serious or not. "Well," he said, "will you give me a billion?"

"Yes, Mr. Williams," she replied teasingly, standing up and holding one finger in his face, "that's our tentative offer, one billion—up front and legitimate for your invention. Then you can find a girl that is looking for a billionaire"

*"One billion! Are you kidding?"*

Molly was amused, "Yes, one billion," she said seriously.

Cary remembered Jim saying the invention could be worth this kind of money but now he actually had an offer for that, and he couldn't believe it. "That's a lot of money," he said.

"It doesn't take a mathematician to come up with that figure. Surely you must have figured that out . . . .The savings in gas, not only in the US, but throughout the world would be astronomical. And besides that, there are many other situations that would benefit financially."

Trying to act nonchalant, not wanting her to think he couldn't do math, he blurted, "Well, with a billion dollars and a girl like you, a man would be right contented, now wouldn't he?"

They both laughed and she asked, "Have you got a shot of bourbon to go with this coffee?" The comprehension of the situation was making both of them giddy. “I also heard you mention the word we but that doesn’t surprise me. I figured you must of had some help.”

He spiked both of their coffees with a shot of bourbon, and they talked on into the night as if they were old friends. Cary couldn’t help but like her, and she appeared to reciprocate, but he never forgot she was a salesperson. Around midnight he put her in his car and found a room for her at the Holiday Inn just outside of town.

As Cary was about to leave she said, “Here, take this briefcase, it’s for you.” Cary took it and promised he would be in touch with her in the near future. She smiled and said she would be anxiously anticipating his call and hoped it would be soon. Cary went home with the briefcase but was too excited to sleep. He opened a beer and tried to relax, but all he could think about was Molly, the beautiful girl he had spent the evening with. The billion dollar offer was nice but nothing compared to her. Molly was class in Cary’s eyes. She revealed it in her dress, her mannerisms, her demeanor, and all without a touch of vanity. *One billion, did she say?* He tossed and turned fitfully for awhile and finally drifted off to sleep.

The next day he contacted Jim and they decided to meet at Square’s house. He drove to Petersburg and then five miles further into the countryside. He turned in the driveway and again dodged the holes and crawled up to the hill as they called it. Cary thought it more of a retreat for the dysfunctional. This time Jim was cooking hot dogs over the outside, weed-riddled, falling-down barbecue pit.

"Have a dog, Cary?" asked Jim.

"No, I don't have much of an appetite." He informed Jim of his meeting with *The People's Advocate* group and their offer.

*"Man,* that's good news," he shouted as he looked as his burned hot dog. "Damn Cary, let's get us a lawyer and take the money, I'm getting tired of burnt hot dogs and pork and beans."

"I'm ready to take their offer," Cary said. "I sure like the idea that Molly's firm would put the engine on the market. Doesn't that mean something to you? Wouldn't you like to see your invention helping the people? Wouldn't that give you a lot of satisfaction? You know the oil companies would just shelve it, and it would be forgotten. All your work, in a sense would be lost; think about it."

Jim was silent for a long time and ate his hot dog before speaking. "Yeah, I sure would like to see it on the road . . . wouldn't that be something?"

"Yeah, and you would really feel good about it. You would have really made a contribution. Don't you think you could live with yourself a little better? If we sold to the oil people, we wouldn't be any better than they. It's not like you have to. We do have an alternative with Molly's company."

"Yeah, that's true. I suppose I never figured on there being a group like that. All along I was only thinking the oil companies had the funds to buy the engine and I was convinced they wouldn't offer it to the public because gas sales wd decline. Never though some firm would actually manufacture the motor and put it on the road." Cary slowly realized that Jim seemed hell-bent on selling to oil companies, and no one else. He wondered why.

# Chapter Sixteen

## The Oil Companies Come Calling

Cary awoke the next morning from a deep sleep, the first he could remember in years. Thinking about the billion dollar offer kept him smiling until the phone rang.

"Mr. Williams, this is Thompson calling. If you remember, you had called me about your engine invention a few weeks ago."

"Yes, Mr. Thompson, you said I was probably just an oddball and your company wouldn't be interested."

"Please forgive me, I apologize, but this is the situation. I'm no longer with the oil company. I'm now working for another group. Those oil companies are not interested in a high mileage engine; hell, they want cars to use more gas instead of less. Listen, I see you have proved your engine could perform as you stated. I'll tell you flat out, the group I'm with now would be interested in paying you a huge sum for the patent rights. Could I talk with you?'

"I would listen," Cary replied.

"I can fly down tomorrow; just give me a time and location." Cary told him he would be in front of the post office building in downtown Hopewell at four p.m. tomorrow evening.

"I'll be there," said Thompson and hung up. Cary had no idea how he would get here that fast. Cary contacted Jim and told him of Thompson's phone call, told him he said he was now with another company, and that he was going to meet with him tomorrow.

"Great," said Jim, "I don't care who he's with, long as his money's good, go ahead and hear him out." The next day Cary was sitting in front of the post office when a long black limousine pulled up. A door opened and a man gestured for him to get in. Mr. Thompson introduced himself and the car drove them to the Jordan Point Country Club. He escorted Cary into the main dining hall. They walked until they came to a table, where three distinguished looking executives warmly greeted Cary. Mr. Thompson introduced them as the President, Treasurer, and CEO of Global Enterprises.

"Mr. Williams, we thought this place would be as good as any to have a business talk. You belong to the club, Cary?"

"No, I couldn't afford to."

"Well, you'll be able to soon." Cary recognized some of the club members there, and they buzzed with murmurs about his important looking acquaintances. As the members drifted by they all spoke and nodded. Cary thought it was amusing.

"Mr. Williams, as the president of Global, I am ready today to offer you a sizeable amount of money for the rights to your invention. What do you say?"

"How sizeable?" he asked. They all laughed.

"You get right to the point, don't you? Well, I will too—how about two billion dollars today?"

Cary smiled, "That's a lot of money, and how would I spend it?" This caught them off guard and they stopped laughing.

"What do you mean?" the president asked.

"Well, how are you going to show the purchase? Would you give me a 1099 form that shows you purchased the invention? I mean I have to think of the tax implications here." They were silent for a minute, realizing Cary was leading into a touchy subject. It was evident that Cary was knowledgeable about the tax consequences. "You know," Cary said as serious as he could, "that two billion dollars after taxes would only leave a billion or so."

"Okay, Cary, we'll have to be up front with you; the money would have to be paid under the table. That's just the way it has to be."

"Yes, I kinda figured that, but if it's under the table, how am I going to spend the money without the IRS being all over me?" He thought of Molly and how she confirmed these suspicions.

"Oh," the president answered happily, "we can help you with that. We know several ways, for instance, an off shore account or a Swiss Bank would be one way. It's done all the time, that's the way business works." He was smiling now, thinking Cary would consider taking the money illegally. "Look at the bright side—you would have two billion instead of one if you did it our way."

"Well, that would be illegal wouldn't it?" They didn't answer. "Are you going to develop the invention the engine and make it available to the public?" Cary asked.

"Well, uh, we'd have to determine that down the road. You know, we'd have to do a feasible study and so forth and that depends . . ."

"I'm concerned about getting this engine to the public," Cary interrupted.

"Mr. Williams," the president said. You're rather a self-righteous kid here aren't you? Are you really going to thumb your nose at two billion dollars because of that? He was getting irritated now. His countenance turned to anger and his body quivered as he leaned towards Cary's face and without a smile, spoke.

"Look here, Mr. Williams, the treasurer here has got the

checkbook, our lawyer has the papers drawn up—we could complete the deal today, and you could walk out of this club with two billion dollars. All you have to do is sign this paper. Hell, you could buy this club with your petty cash. Now time is getting short, so tell us, are you going to take it or *not*?"

*These guys are trying to intimidate me*, Cary thought, *and it's working*. He didn't really know anything about this group of Thompson's. For all he knew, they could be con people or crooks and could be scheming to steal the invention. He'd heard horrid stories of legitimate, powerful corporations and the types of men that drove them, much less this group he'd never heard of. For the first time, Cary became fearful and was looking for an exit. Cary tried hard to calm himself, looked at the president and said, "Give me a few days . . . there are others involved, others I must consult with. I'll present your offer to them and get back to you." With that he got up to leave but after a few steps, he turned to them and said, "A wise old man told me once, if you go slow you won't have to back up. We will consider your offer and be in touch soon. Thanks for coming down. By the way, you can leave me here; I'll get a ride back." He glanced around the club and said, "This is a nice place, thought I would look around, may want to join some day . . . or maybe buy it."

The men just sat there, not believing that a young kid could thumb his nose at two billion dollars. Then they closed their mouths, and with disgusted looks all around, gathered their papers and huffed out. They had wanted a done deal—their way. As he watched the unhappy big boys leave, one of the club members who had been watching approached Cary. He was a guy Cary remembered from high school by the name of Smitty. Cary had noticed he had been eavesdropping on the conversation with the executives. He was an in-crowd type who hung around the club to let everybody know he had made it big in the pizza business.

"Hey Cary," he spoke, "couldn't help but overhear you. Did ya say you may want to *buy* this club?"

"Yeah, you heard right, but for now it will have to wait 'cause my business deal didn't go through." Smitty was watching the group leave and turned to Cary.

"Who were those big-wigs? Looks like some big shots to me, but by the looks on their faces, you're not getting any money from them."

"Those were the President, Treasurer, and CEO of Global Enterprises."

"You're kidding," he said with his jaw dropping. "Who are they and what did they want with you?"

"They wanted to give me two billion dollars." Smitty's demeanor changed to one of astonishment as he turned to Cary.

"Go on!" Smitty said, "tell me about it."

"Give me a ride home and I will." He readily agreed and led Cary to his car. Driving back to Hopewell Cary told him some details of what had just transpired. Cary was still shaking inside and soon regretted what he had disclosed. He knew it would spread all over town, but at the moment he didn't really give a damn. It was too much for Smitty and he felt Cary was pulling his leg. His arrogance returned, and he let him know it when he dropped him off.

"Keep dreaming bud," Smitty remarked.

"Have a nice evening," Cary replied. He remembered the in-crowd from high school. They had no self-confidence, and their top priority was mundane such as joining one of the fraternities, so as not to be labeled *different.* They routinely followed the footsteps of the popular people in the clubs, thus leaving them with no real self-identity. Most had never had an original thought and were followers, not leaders. When hard, important decisions had to be made, many monitored others and then followed suit with the majority. After high school, they questioned each other what college to attend, and not only that, they did the same concerning what subject they were to major in. They surely didn't want to make the grand mistake of trusting their own intuition with their future. They thought it obscene to have a different ambition and, heaven forbid, a desire to do something unique from one another. When they settled down in their jobs, they again joined one club or another and began a new ritual of you-scratch-my-back-and-I'll-scratch-yours. This just seemed a little unethical to Cary. He didn't pass judgment on these souls, but it wasn't his style. He'd never known their stripes to change, and he was sure many wondered later why they were unhappy. Cary had gone to five elementary schools and three high schools and had learned to rely on his own judgments and intuitions. He winged it on his own with the help of Henry David Thoreau.

Cary was wondering why Jim was adamant about not contacting the automobile manufactures. If they could put cars on the road obtaining double the gas mileage of their competitors, they would out sell them like crazy. Why had Jim only thought of the oil companies? And this guy Thompson, leaving the oil company and joining another group seemed odd. And who or what was Global Enterprises? Thompson wasn't interested in providing any details of this company's intention. There must be some reasoning behind this, but Cary couldn't figure it out.

# Chapter Seventeen

## Introspection

Cary poured over the contents of the briefcase that Molly Anderson left. He made several long-distance calls confirming the group that she represented. After reading all of the information, he came to the conclusion that these people could really be on the level. Overall, the members of this group were mostly elderly and had achieved wealth the old fashioned way—by working for it. They didn't come out and say so, but there seemed to be a spiritual aspect to their undertakings—as if they were nearing the end of their lives, they wanted to store up their treasures in heaven.

Listed in the information were case histories where they had helped people in various ways. Most cases involved aiding persons who were trying to help themselves. Several situations involved veterans who were physically, emotionally scarred, and crippled to various degrees. Many felt they were not appreciated and Cary contacted some of these. He asked them about The

Peoples Advocacy and they all responded in a positive way. They said they were greatly helped by these people. They were surviving and many of them flourishing in their careers. He also noticed something else he thought unusual; all of the people he contacted were involved in one manner or another in supporting others. They said it was their way of helping themselves. It was their way of coping with their own personal demons and finding peace and closure to their nightmares, physical, mental, and emotional.

There were divorces, auto accidents; and various dysfunctions. There were tragic scenarios that he read about in the newspapers that made him wonder how these people coped and were able to live normal, productive lives. Cary was touched by these and became introspective about his own suffering. *Could it be*, he thought, *could there be a solution, a healing to his own long time suffering? If these people could overcome their terrible ordeals, which were much worse than his his, could he too find a way to heal himself over Scarlett, a prescription to stop the hurting?*

Maybe it was more than her deserting him that hurt. Maybe he couldn't forgive his own guilt. He put Molly's information aside and pondered his current situation. Was it possible to end this nightmare of suffering that he thought would never end? Was Molly for real, and did he dare think she could be for him? Would this merry-go-round ever end?

And this group, The People's Advocacy, what drove them to help all these people? He had never heard of them before, but then there were many things unknown to him. He just shook his head, thinking they must be too good to be true. After seeing so much evil in the world, it was rewarding to hear about the good, and it brought him to his knees. This was becoming an obsession with him—this matter of good and evil. He wished he could understand where evil came from when good was clearly the way to live.

He went to bed early and slept through the night as his mind had found a little peace. The next day he gathered himself together, and with a foreboding feeling went to see Jim, and told him about the meeting with Global Enterprises and their offer of two billion.

"You mean they were gonna write you a check for two billion dollars on the spot?" Jim questioned.

"Yes."

"And you didn't *take it*?" Cary was shocked and taken aback that Jim was seriously angry.

"Jim," Cary said, looking down thinking, "I just couldn't believe anyone would give us two billion dollars. I just couldn't imagine it. I was afraid it was just a scam to turn over your rights to the invention."

"I told you," said Jim, "I told you it could be worth that kinda money. I've sat down and figured it; I've calculated how much money they would lose if this was put on the road. The figures are astounding."

Cary was shaking his head. "But you said you only wanted to sell to an oil company, and this group was not an oil company. They didn't offer any information about their intentions concerning the invention. I didn't trust myself or them to sign anything without your okay. Besides, hell, I had no idea they would write me a check for two billion on our first meeting. I don't think I would have signed their *damn* papers anyhow without a lawyer and besides, they wanted to *pay us under the table!*"

"Oh, my God," said Jim, scratching his head. "A check for two billion dollars, and I don't have twenty bucks in my pocket. I don't give a *damn* what they do with it, as long as their money is good. You mean they were *really* going to give you a check for two billion without verifying the engine?"

"That's what they said, but I didn't read the contract, and you know the devil is in the details. Hell, there's no telling what was in there—I'm not a lawyer. They could be crooks for all I know. They were some scary people; hell; they *could've* ambushed me before I got home. Could've killed me, took the check and tore it up. People have killed for a lot less than two billion. I'll admit I was scared. Besides, I've never heard of this group before. I don't know anything about them. Don't worry Jim, I told them I'd be in touch. The money is still there."

Jim seemed to be satisfied with Cary's explanation. "I guess you did the right thing Cary. You're right; we don't know a thing about this company . . . but *two billion* dollars?"

Cary then told Jim all the details concerning Molly's company that offered the lower bid. He explained all the information she had left in the briefcase and how he had researched and verified everything. Then, lastly, he told him about the people they had helped.

Jim listened but Cary was afraid he wasn't convinced to go with them. Jim was very distrustful of everyone and couldn't justify selling to this concern for one billion when Global would pay two. Cary wanted to go with Molly's company, but Jim sided with Global. Cary said money wasn't everything and Jim checked his wallet.

"Yeah . . . not everything, how much you got left anyhow?"

"I'm down to seven hundred."

"Yeah, I'm down too, only got six hundred left."

"We've got to do something pretty soon before we're broke," Cary said.

Jim was quiet for a long time and finally said, "Well, let's analyze the situation. None of the oil companies have shown any interest and now this never-heard-of Global—*hey,* you know what I think?" I bet you a hundred to one that this Thompson guy got all the oil boys together, pooled their resources, and plans to buy us out. That answers the question why none of the oil companies have shown any interest, and also that's why they still want to pay us under the table. Evidently they're still afraid they could be connected to the oil firms. I bet you anything they're all in this together with Thompson under this Global Enterprises name.

"Now why the auto companies have shown no interest, I don't know. They've certainly heard about it by now but maybe they're thinking it would be too costly considering the retooling and other massive changes that would be required. They may not think it is 'cost feasible' to invest two billion dollars. These auto makers may also realize the fight they'd have with big oil knowing they wouldn't want this engine on the road. Anyhow, my decision is to go with Global, but I know you would like to go with People's Advocacy."

Jim paused and thought about Cary. He had worked hard on this sale, and he knew how much he wanted to go with Molly's firm, and he thought it best to give them one more hearing, at least for Cary's sake. He didn't want to blow the whole thing with Cary getting upset and yes, he would like to be applauded, if possible, for bringing this invention to the people.

"Listen, I've been thinking about Molly's group. I'd sure like to be certain about them. How about you dropping in on them unannounced, and let's see for ourselves if they're really as they say. My concern is they're not auto manufacturers and I'm not convinced their intentions are to put this engine on the road. I know, I'm probably paranoid, but if you want to sell to them, you've gotta convince me."

"Personally, I don't think it's necessary," said Cary, "but I'll catch a plane tomorrow if you really want me to."

"I'd feel better if you did," said Jim.

Cary didn't argue because he wanted to see Molly again anyhow. He still couldn't figure why Jim was fixated on selling to the oil companies. He guessed he had his reasons though and after all, it was his ballgame.

As the plane was landing at Kennedy Airport the next day, Cary checked the address Molly had given him. He hailed a taxi and told the driver to take him to an address on West 42$^{nd}$ street. As they moved through the city, Cary smiled, thinking of Molly, but wondered of his explanation why he hadn't yet made a decision. But, he thought, he could use the old saying about going slow and not having to back up.

The driver pulled in front of a skyscraper and nodded towards the building Cary was looking for. He walked into the building, fascinated at everything he saw. The granite floors were silver-gray and the marble walls glistened with various colors. He took the elevator to the twenty-fifth floor, and when the doors opened he saw firm's name written on a bronze tablet beside a door. He entered a waiting room that was large enough to hold two of his houses.

It was empty of people. There was several dark, leather chairs arranged in front of red and black drapes that covered tall glass windows. Four tall granite vases matching the drapes, greeted visitors with fresh, multicolored flowers, from each corner of the room. Indirect lighting softly lit up the sculptured walls inlaid with intricate designs of various colors. A shapely receptionist entered the room clicking her high heels on the granite floors and echoing off the walls. She greeted him with an automatic smile.

"May I help you?"

"Is Molly Anderson available?"

"Do you have an appointment?"

"No."

"May I ask your name?"

"Cary Williams."

"Please have a seat and I'll see if she's available." Her smile disappeared as quickly as it was manufactured. Cary sat and waited in one of the leather chairs and surveyed the expensive surroundings. *Such is the atmosphere of billionaires,* he thought. Ten minutes went by and Cary was up and nervously checking his attire. He was wearing a lightweight tan corduroy suit with a brown tie over a pale, yellow shirt that contrasted with his dark, tanned face.

"Hi Cary," said Molly as she walked towards him smiling. "What a surprise, it's good to see you. Sorry I kept you waiting."

"Hi to you too." Look, I apologize for not calling before I came . . . I just had an urge to drop in."

"Well, I hope it's because you want to check us out,"

"Something like that," he added.

Cary was glad she wasn't upset. "Come on in and meet some people," she said waving her hand. "We were just having a meeting about your engine." He followed her through three more huge rooms. Dressed in a business suit she exuded confidence as she strolled. He lifted his dark eyes from her form as they entered what appeared to be a conference room. Around a long, walnut conference table, a dozen people sat in leather upholstered chairs. The walls were covered with oil paintings of distinguished-looking men and women.

"Members of the board, may I introduce Mr. Cary Williams. I believe you've all heard of him by now. He wanted to drop in and say hello." She introduced him to each person, and they smiled very graciously shaking his hand with a hint of admiration. They were seven men and five women of various nationalities. They were all dressed formally, and Cary was glad he had worn his only suit and tie. Some appeared to be over seventy and all looked distinguished.

"Cary, meet the members of the Board of Directors of The People's Advocate. You must have ESP because our meeting was primarily about you and your engine. Would you sit down and talk with us?"

"Sure," said Cary, giving them a smile, "but I'm just a Southern country boy and I'm probably out of my element."

A thin gentleman with white hair combed straight back and a neatly trimmed mustache arose from the head of the table straight across from him. He offered a cheerful greeting and said, "Mr. Williams, my name is Jeremy Jackson and by what we understand from Molly, you may very well be in your element in the near future."

"How's that?" asked Cary

"Well," he answered smiling, "it's possible you could soon be eligible to join this group if you so desired." The rest of the group clapped in agreement. Cary thanked them, nodding his head.

"Mr. Williams," he continued, "we were just discussing the many facets of getting your engine on the market if you decided to go with us. We were investigating costs and roadblocks we could encounter. We've asked our accountants to come up with financials of how soon we could recoup our investment. He's still figuring and hasn't gotten back to us. We've heard comments that it could take anywhere from months to years. Although recovering our investment is not our prime priority, it has to be considered since we are talking about laying out a huge sum of money. We realize the difficulties will be many, but the rewards of putting vehicles on the road that can travel a hundred miles to a gallon are phenomenal."

"We feel very confident to go forward with the project especially since gas prices have jumped ten cents a gallon in the last two months. The vastness of the value is mind boggling. To be honest with you, your value could be many times more than the one billion we offered. You were probably wise in delaying your decision. We are pleased you dropped in today and hope you will seriously consider selling us your rights. Please ask us any questions that you may have." The members turned their eyes on Cary and wondered about the young man who was soon to be a billionaire. Cary stood, smoothed his tie, and addressed them.

"Well, first let me thank you for being so candid concerning the value of the invention. As far as my delay in making a decision, a wise old man once told me, if you go slowly, you won't have to back up." The members smiled in amusement. "So far your organization is the only one that has approached me with the idea of making the engine available to the public. That is what I would like to do. I am not responsible for this invention alone as you might well have imagined. I have others to convince this is the way to go. They have a concern though—you are not in the auto building business as far as we know. We are very concerned how you are going to put the engine on the market." Cary paused and looked over them as they listened in rapt attention. "What's a few million dollars difference in the grand scheme of things? When I die, I'm sure a decision to make this available to the people would rest my soul a little easier."

The group gave him a gracious ovation. Jeremy Jackson rose to speak, "Let me answer your question concerning our capability of marketing the engine. If we have an engine that can generate twice the mileage, we can afford to go into the car-building business."

The formal proceedings ended and Cary mingled amongst the members and immensely enjoyed stories each shared concerning their activities. Many were very open and told the personal experiences that brought them to join this association. He was touched and overwhelmed by their experiences. As they were breaking up, Cary was surprised they didn't push him about his decision to sell, and mentioned this to Molly as she was escorting him out.

"Well," Molly said, "I guess they are leaving that up to me . . . that's what they are paying me for."

"Oh," Cary was surprised, "you mean you're not one of the members?"

"Oh no, I'm employed as project director for special assignments."

"You mean . . ."

"No," she laughed, "I'm not a billionaire, not even a millionaire, just a country girl from Georgia working for a living." She grabbed his arm, walked close to him and spoke with a mischievous grin. "*Why* did you think I told you I was waiting for a billionaire?"

Cary was surprised and said seriously, "I don't think you would marry a country boy just because he was a billionaire."

She turned, quizzically looked at him and seriously said, "No, I would not." And then again with a grin, "But then billions could make a girl lose her head."

"See . . ." Cary said while looking straight ahead, "I know you better than you think."

Waiting for the elevator she asked, "Do you have to fly back right away? Couldn't I show you around the town tonight?"

"Thanks for the offer. That's very considerate of you and

I appreciate it, but you don't have to spend the evening entertaining a business client. I'm sure you have a personal life." She was a little surprised at his response, but decided not to press the issue.

"Okay," she said, "but sometimes I *do* mix business with pleasure." He entered the elevator, turned and looked straight at her, and spoke before the door closed.

"You may not be a millionaire, but you look like one, and a beautiful one at that." He then winked and said "Good day."

After the doors closed she smiled a smile of bemusement, twirled around on her high heels and answered out loud, "*Thank you* . . . I believe I like you too."

On the plane ride home, Cary contemplated the day's events. He was happy the meeting had gone so well. He had studied their credentials, checked out their bank resources, and now had met the directors in person. They answered his question about manufacturing the engine. They were all real and the group still appeared to be on the level, and Molly had said they would pay the money up front. He wondered if this would satisfy Jim's concern, and he certainly didn't see anything wrong with Molly.

Cary's flight landed in Richmond, he departed, and drove home. It was almost midnight when he called Jim and related the day's events in detail.

"I'm sorry, but I'm still worried," said Jim. "It just seems too good to be true, and you know what they say about that. But, I'll consider selling to them, but now *listen* to me carefully, the devil is in the details, so get their proposal, and we'll look it over closely. After all, they have only the verification of our test run to prove the worth of the engine. They may not give that money up so easy without stipulations."

"What kind of stipulations?" asked Cary.

"*Oh hell*, I can imagine all kinds . . . like we would have to give the money back if the engine were too expensive to fabricate or something like that. There's no *telling* what they would stick in there. Listen, at this point I'd rather take much less money if the contract had *no* stipulations. I'll repeat myself—I would rather take much less money if the contract had no stipulations except that we guarantee to give them all the details concerning the engine. We guarantee we'll turn over everything they need to get the invention patented. We'll agree to all the above—as long as they have no legal ramifications of us giving the money back. Am I making myself absolutely clear?"

"I understand," said Cary, "absolutely!"

"Okay," said Jim, "go for it! Use your own judgment. I'm tired and there's no sense in putting it off." Cary hung up the phone and wondered whether Jim was losing it, and he wasn't so sure about himself.

# Chapter Eighteen

## Molly and Cary and . . . Stipulations

Cary picked up the phone the next day and dialed Molly's number.

"The People's Advocate, Molly speaking."

"Molly . . ."

"*Cary*! Oh Cary, I've been thinking about you all day. I've wanted to call you."

"Well, you sound excited about something."

"Excited about hearing from you!" she whispered.

"I'm glad to hear that."

"*Well, you should*! When am I going to see you?"

"I'm available."

"Well, how about I fly down there?"

"Okay, but could you bring me some money? I'm broke."

"How much you want—seriously?" she asked

"Enough to take you to dinner."

"I'll bring a blank check and some papers, and I can be down tomorrow evening by four, okay?"

"Okay, I'll pick you up at the airport, same place, same

time."

"We've got a date, I'll be there," she said and hung up.

Cary put the phone down and realized he was trembling, a feeling he'd thought would never have again. She had said that money could do funny things to a girl, and that worried him even more.

The next evening he met her at the airport. She hurried to him with a smile, and this time gave him an unexpected hug.

"Well," he said surprised, "I'm glad to see you too." This time she had a larger briefcase and was willing to let him carry it for her. As they walked towards his car, he felt the heavy weight of the case and with mock seriousness said, "Man, this thing is heavy, did you bring a billion in cash?" She rolled her eyes at him and shook her head no. "You must be ready to do some serious negotiations."

"I've brought what it takes—I'm armed and dangerous," she said without cracking a smile.

"Where to this time? he asked as they drove away from the airport.

"Why ask me—you're in the driver's seat, you're holding all the cards! Me, hell—I'm at your mercy."

"Well, now, I've *never* been in control of a woman before, so it may take me awhile to get the feel of things. Molly couldn't stand it anymore and broke up laughing.

She finally got control of herself and, trying not to smile, said, "Who the hell is doing the negotiations? You're not fooling anyone . . . *never* had control of a woman—bull! You're doing a pretty good job of it." She turned her body towards him in a confrontational manner, put her hand behind his neck, squeezed it hard and said seriously, "*Who* the hell are you *anyhow*, Cary Williams?"

"I've told you. . ."

"Yeah, I know, just an ole country boy," she mocked him, "just an ole country boy . . . trying to take a billion dollars off of me."

"Aww," he said, "it's not just the money..."

"It's *not just* the money! " she said and then stopped herself, turned towards him and gave him a serious look as his eyes stayed glued to the road. "Not *just* the money—what else you have in mind?"

"Nothing," he answered. He knew he had said the wrong thing. It took her back for a second and she removed her hand from his shoulder, straightened her skirt and leaned back properly in her seat.

"I think maybe we had better do our negotiations in a hotel."

Cary smiled while watching the road and said, "Just what I had in mind." She folded her arms and gave him a serious glance from her pretty brown eyes.

"You know what I meant—a hotel conference room instead of your house." Cary didn't say any more and quietly drove her out of town towards the James River. They were silent and kept their thoughts to themselves. They were traveling parallel to the river now, and Molly was watching with interest, not worrying about where he was taking her. Cary turned and slowly drove onto a narrow tree-lined road and then down a smooth asphalt pavement that carried them to the front of an elegant building that was aglow with light directed from the manicured lawns. He pulled into the parking lot of the James River Country Club and stopped. They exited the car and Cary escorted Molly down a brick sidewalk with a lighted view of the riverbank. As Cary watched Molly walk in front of him, he realized how fascinated he was with this woman. This evening she was dressed to kill and he hoped it wasn't his funeral. He could tell she had spent some time in front of the mirror enhancing the beauty she possessed. He couldn't take his eyes off her form: she was a bit over five foot, and maybe 115 pounds. She was gorgeous, he thought, and wondered why she wasn't married. She was indeed, as she said, armed and dangerous.

Couples passed them as they waited to be seated. Not a man missed a glance at her, and the women looked at her too, as they always do when confronting a woman more beautiful than themselves. Some secure women gave her a gracious smile while others glared at their husbands to see if they were staring. The gentlemen would take one look while others were quickly elbowed by their female companions. Part of Molly's allure was that she was not self-conscious or vain about her beauty, but was lady-like-embarrassed about the attention she always attracted.

She was a wisp of a woman with curves in all the right places. Her long dark hair spilled down around her white silk blouse that was decorated with a long necklace of several strands of colorful stones. *God help me*, Cary thought, *if she aims all of this ammunition in my direction.* Cary was seriously considering splitting his billion with her if . . .

"Oh, *my,* it's beautiful Cary," she said interrupting his daydream as the waitress escorted them across the carpeted floor into the lounge.

"I don't know about you," he said, "but with all your carrying-on—I need a drink."

"You'll probably drive me to drink!" she replied. Their table was beside glass windows overlooking the river.

"Oh, the briefcase—you did lock the car, didn't you?"

"Yes, but you said you didn't bring cash." She made a face and said it was the contract she was worried about.

"Now this is the kind of place I was *trying* to tell you to take me," she said, trying to cover herself, "not a motel—oh you know what I *meant*." The waiter brought their drinks, a gin and tonic for her and a bourbon and coke for him. Cary drank half of his down at once, took a deep breath, and looked at her. She had an air about her, he thought, as though she was a soul from a higher order of beings. She was dark, and he wondered if she was from further south than Georgia. He didn't know what nationality she was but she looked like a regal princess to him. Maybe one descended from aristocracy. She smiled, revealing white teeth that contrasted with her olive skin. She wore long dangling earrings that sparkled when she turned her head.

"Now," he said, "maybe I can put up with your negotiations; I'm sure I'm going to have a struggle on my hands."

*"I'm the one* worried about a fight," she said quietly.

"Yes, but I'm the one worrying about paying the bill here."

"You don't have to worry about that—you made it very clear to me when you asked me for this date that I had to buy . . . you made it perfectly clear, *bring* some money, and *on* our first date, *huh*!"

Cary was overwhelmed she called this a date and couldn't help smiling, "Yes, but there's no telling what your demands will be before you'll give me . . ."

It's simple," she said, "all you've got to do is sign some papers."

"Yeah, but I'll have to read all that damn small print."

She stirred her drink and looked up at him with serious eyes without smiling, "Cary, how can you be so, *so flippant* about this situation?"

"You mean about us?"

"Noooo, not *us—this* agreement, damn it! The one there in the car . . . in my briefcase."

Cary looked down, trying to form his words, clasped his hands together, rested them on the table, and raised his head to look her face to face and spoke.

"Well . . . you see . . . I've got a problem."

"Hell, I knew that. What else is new? What problem now?" Cary was still serious as he looked at her and continued.

"Because I enjoy your company so much, I'm afraid, afraid that after I sign those papers, you'll hightail it back to New York and I'll never see you again." Molly opened her mouth but no words would come. She was silent for a moment, then wiggled in her chair, turned her head sideways like a puppy, and stared at him as though trying to understand something she couldn't quite decipher. She narrowed her brown eyes at him until they were nothing more than narrow slits.

"You son-of-a-bitch, I can't tell whether you are serious or not!" Her eyes welled with tears and Cary wasn't sure why. *Could those tears possibly be for me*? Or did I only remind her of some painful memory. This couldn't be part of a sales routine, could it?

He reached for her hands and said, "I was serious about what I said." She squeezed his hand and cleared her throat and looked away. Cary wondered of her past which she had never mentioned. Wondered if she held old hurts and memories he knew nothing about.

Hoarsely she said . . . "I'm sorry . . . sorry I cussed you."

"Molly, I'm sorry too . . . I . . . guess I wanted to find out if you were serious too."

She showed a little smile and said, "Well, that's a hell of a way to do it." She gathered herself, dabbed her eyes, and finished her drink. She leaned back, crossed her legs and lit a cigarette. She inhaled the smoke and blew it upwards past her dark eyes that were intently looking at Cary's. "You know I'm on pins and needles awaiting your decision."

"As far as I'm concerned, I've decided to sell to your group," he said with no emotion.

Molly came alive and her eyes lit up, but then she spoke with controlled emotion, "Well . . . wow . . . thanks, that's a relief to know." She looked at him for the longest time, and he seemed the saddest man she'd ever known. She spoke slowly, "Cary, most of the people we've contracted for one reason or another in the past to pay millions, let alone a billion . . . well, by now they would be celebrating and jumping with joy. But, now you . . . you seem like you've lost your best friend—what's wrong?" Cary leaned back a little and winced, jarred that she'd so thoroughly diagnosed him. He managed a slight smile, sighed, leaned back, tried to change his attitude, and spoke.

"Money isn't everything," he said not believing he said the words. Then quickly added, "Oh, I'll have fun with the money; I plan to put it to good use."

"Yeah," she said, "doing what?"

"That's a deep subject."

"I'd love to know."

"You'd have to stick around awhile to find out."

"I plan to . . . if you'll let me."

*He was jolted.* He looked at her with sad eyes as she leaned over, lifted his chin with two sculptured fingers, and softly kissed him on the lips. "Will you?" She asked softly, looking into his eyes.

Cary's armor was shattered. *Could this gorgeous creature care for me?* he wondered. *Could this really be happening?* He was afraid his emotions were exposing him. He choked back the tears that wanted to come. He looked away from her into the now-dark window and tried to smile. He turned to her and said, "I would like that." Molly accepted that for what it was and it wasn't *yes.* But in her mind she felt he had a deeper problem and thought it best to let it go for now.

"Something is bothering you about our deal isn't it?" she asked.

"I'll tell you my problem with that. We are terribly concerned about the stipulations you may have in your contract."

"I've got the finished contract. Let's get it and look it over and go from there." Cary nodded his head okay.

He checked her into the adjoining hotel and retrieved the briefcase from the car. When he came back into the hotel room, Molly had tears in her eyes and she was shaking. "Molly! What's wrong?" She pointed to the television while turning her head away.

"Turn it off! *Turn it off*!" She screamed. Cary turned the TV off and came to her but she turned away, wiping her eyes. He looked at her with wonderment.

"What happened? *What's* wrong?" She quickly composed herself, turned to him, and now the fright had left her, and she was calm again.

"I'm fine, I'm okay. It was just a scary scene on TV. There was a man falling off a tower." She smiled and apologized. "I'm sorry; it just startled me for some reason."

"Well, you scared me, you sure you're okay now?"

She opened the case and smiled, "I'm okay, look, here's the agreement." Cary carefully scrutinized the document as

Molly acclimated herself to the room. She was a little disconcerted now because her feelings were mixed when final negotiations were discussed. “You want to tell me of your other offers?” she asked.

“I’ve been offered two billion from one company, probably an oil company, which I doubt would put the engine on the market.”

“My group has still authorized me to offer you one billion dollars. That would leave you quite a bundle after taxes. I can have it wired to your bank when we sign the papers at your lawyer’s office.” Cary ignored her and slowly read the entire contract and then looked at her.

“We’ve got some problems here.” he said.

“What problems?” she asked.

Cary underlined several conditions on the contract and turned to her. “Well, here’s a phrase that bothers me: “The payment of this contract will be held in escrow until the purchasers have had ample time for their engineers to fully tear down the engine and are completely satisfied the invention would be marketable.” Cary said he couldn’t live with that.

“What’s wrong with that?” Molly asked.

“That opens up a whole can of worms; it’s just way too vague.”

“If the engine is what you say it is, why are you worried?”

Cary just shook his head and realized what Jim was talking about.

"I'm sorry Molly, but I can't accept that. We have not had the engine patented and can not give access to it before payment because the idea could be stolen. It's as simple as that."

"Sounds like the can of worms could be in *your* minds. What's the matter, afraid we'll find something that's not worth one billion dollars? That 'not patented' business is a little hard to swallow; something smells to me." Cary had no response, and Molly looked at him realizing he was serious. She took the contract and put it back in her briefcase. "Well there's nothing more I can do but go back and tell the group what you said and see if they are willing to change it." She was dejected.

"I'm sorry Molly, but that's the way it is."

"I'm sorry too," she said now distinctly angry, "they were ready to wire you the one billion dollars in cash if the engine had been found acceptable. *One billion dollars*! And you are going to turn it down?" She took a check from her briefcase and stuck under Cary's nose. "We were going to *give* you this check for a $100,000 dollars *today* but I'm tearing it up." She ripped it into pieces.

Cary thought to himself, *yeah, Jim is turning it down, not me*, but Jim was adamant, and there was not one thing he could do about it. "Molly," he said, "we would be willing to take much less if you would delete that one sentence."

"Cary, that just doesn't make sense to me, patent or no patent. Sounds like you have something to hide or somebody's damn well paranoid." He came to her and tried to kiss her on the cheek but she turned away, still upset.

He turned to leave, smiled and said, "See, I knew you wouldn't put out that money so easily. I knew you were going be a tough negotiator."

"Hell," she said with a hollow laugh, "there was no negotiating! You *just turned down* one billion dollars over one simple sentence."

"That simple sentence could withhold the money indefinitely, and then I'm not sure we would ever get it. That sentence carried many ramifications." He headed towards the door, turned, and quietly said, "Let me know if your people change their minds and like I said, if it makes any difference, we would take less money if they would delete that one stipulation."

"Okay, I'll tell them and get back with you. But Cary, let me tell you one thing before you go, you may sell to the higher bidder, the oil companies, but I hope you think about what you are doing. If your engine is on the level, there may be larger ramifications you haven't thought of."

"Like what?" Cary asked, thinking this must be her final pitch. Molly started pacing the room and finally spoke.

"The big picture," she said. "Can't you see what your

engine would mean to your country? Besides the savings to the people, it could mean salvation for our nation!"

"How so?"

"Our country only produces a small fraction of the oil that we consume. We are dependent on foreign oil, and what I'm getting at is this. What if those Middle East countries where we get the majority of our oil from, what if one day they turn on us and hold us hostage for the oil? Who knows, one day they could even double their prices to over a hundred dollars a barrel, and your invention would double in value. You believe in the Bible don't you . . . that one day Armageddon would be the war between the East and the West? And where would they get their money to wage war—it would be from our own pockets."

*Good God*, Cary thought, *what a saleswoman!* Now she's going after my moral judgment . . . and a hundred dollars a barrel—she's crazy. It was a jolting reminder not to forget that she was just doing her job. While looking at her, he wondered if her feelings for him were all just a professional act. He thought he had the tendency to read people, but in the past he'd made some terrible misjudgments concerning women.

"Damn," he said, concealing his amusement, "I'm just trying to make a living, didn't want to mess with no world affairs. You think my decision could have such repercussions?"

"If your engine was on the market, it *most* certainly would make our country less dependent on foreign oil. It would lessen the stockpile of money to those Muslims if one day they decided to turn on us."

"Yeah, well, I'll keep that in mind," he said as he waved goodbye. "I guess that's something to think about. By the way, what time should I pick you up tomorrow?"

"Bout ten would be okay."

Cary left and did think about what she said, but he also thought the salesperson in her was reaching a bit far, but then again, it gave him much to contemplate. But it wasn't the invention or world affairs he was thinking about. It was Molly and how he may be deceiving himself, how he may be setting himself up for another heartbreak. *After all*, he wondered, *what could she see in him?* She was all class and he was just . . . just plain, he guessed. He had evidently attracted some women in the past and only remembered a couple of incidents that he thought were odd at the time. One girl had told him when they were breaking up: "It was your total air of confidence that attracted me." Another one's last words were, "Your obsessive energy intrigued me." He hadn't considered whether these were physical attractions or what. As far as looks was concerned, he only remembered his mom telling someone that his brother was the best-looking one in the bunch. He only thanked God that he had what he had.

He couldn't believe Molly would give herself to a man for mere money, and he dismissed the thought from his mind. Well, as neat as she was, he knew he would never have her on those conditions. Her actions, her feelings toward him, they seemed so genuine, but she lived in New York. She was beautiful, intelligent, and was exposed to thousands of men more attractive than he. How could she not be taken, and how could she still be available? Was there something in her past? Did she have some deep-seated problem? And what was that all about—her reaction to that TV scene? He went home, but he didn't sleep much. He returned the next morning and took her to the airport. They tried idle conversation but it seemed everything was said last night. He watched as the plane took her away. Molly watched him from above, alone on the runway; he was still waving as she went out of sight. He never did understand women . . . except that love was everything to them while it seemed only a part of a man's life. But as he was beginning to understand—it was a hell of a big part.

# Chapter Nineteen

## Back to the Drawing Board

Cary was back home the next evening and resting on his front porch in his favorite chair. Winter and spring had slowly passed and the hot days of August were here. He was trying to cool himself with a cold beer and ease his troubled mind. The turn of events gave him much to contemplate as he thought to himself, *Well, back to the old drawing board, guess we got to go to plan B.* Trouble was, he didn't have a plan B, but guessed it was time to come up with one. Looks like Molly's group was probably out of the picture, he was sorry to say. He really enjoyed negotiating with her; hell, he enjoyed doing anything with her.

He now thought of Thompson and Global Enterprises and wondered whether they would have the same stipulations as Molly's. It occurred to him that the auto companies would very well have the same provisions because they would want to manufacture the engine also. But then it was clear to him, Global wouldn't be so particular because they weren't going to put the engine on the market. Cary was convinced Global was only a front for the oil companies. All they cared about was getting the patent and shelving it somewhere so they wouldn't lose gas sales. Cary thought they may not be so concerned about the details of the engine—they just didn't want it on the market.

He concluded that was the preferred route to take and evidently that was Jim's thinking too. *Now I'm beginning to see the light*, Cary thought, Jim had always mentioned selling to the oil companies because he knew they would *not* put the engine on the market. If they were going to shelve it, then Jim wouldn't have to worry about any ramifications concerning how well the engine performed. *I think I'm getting it*, he thought, I may be a little slow but hell, I didn't have to back up. But if that was Jim's thinking, why didn't he tell me?

He sat on the porch late into the night and consumed two more beers as he pondered his next move. He didn't think it smart to call them outright and ask their stipulations, he didn't want to seem too anxious, or worse— desperate. He finally decided to continue his expertly designed strategy of going slow and doing nothing. It was easy for him. He finally came up with a plan and hoped the beers hadn't messed up his mind too much. He wasn't going to tell the companies he was desperate for money, but somehow he didn't care if they came to that conclusion on their own. He decided the best thing to do now was wait because he felt the oil companies would be coming back.

Cary informed Jim of his plan . . . he thought about it,

nodded in agreement and told him to continue.

Cary read the newspapers daily, and the next day's article caught his attention. Gas prices had been going up the last several months and this morning's paper read: Gas Prices up again—Ten Cents a Gallon.

Then another article under this read: The National Weather Service has announced that the third hurricane of the season, Camille, had been spotted yesterday and was tracking towards the Gulf Coast. A storm watch has been announced and everyone is alerted to be prepared. Later down in the article it warned that the off shore oil drilling rigs could be in danger if the hurricane becomes a large one, and fears are growing that gas prices could rise even further if they are put out of operation.

Cary knew hurricanes could be dangerous but he hadn't remembered a bad one hitting the States in quite a while. He hoped this one wouldn't do much damage, but news like this bothered him as he remembered his folks' concern when a kid in Florida. The next day's paper really stirred his attention. The headlines were larger this time the copy read: Since the hurricane was spotted August 14, it has grown larger and more intense and is now a category three. Hurricane warnings have been posted from New Orleans to the Florida panhandle. The National Weather Service said people in those areas should consider evacuating because the hurricane could grow to a category four or larger. The paper's date read August 16, 1969.

He turned to the business section and scanned the page until he found a short article about the off-shore oil rigs. These rigs were expected to be hit hard and evacuations of the workers were ordered. Gas prices would be affected if these were out of production for any length of time.

Two old sayings came to Cary's mind: Some good always comes from a disaster and all things come to those who wait. He figured his strategy was working perfectly because he was meeting both of those standards. He thought he would spend the rest of the day laying here, drinking beer, and thinking hard about doing nothing.

The next day no one could have expected or comprehended the devastation that was to hit them. When Cary read the paper and couldn't believe the headlines:

**Camille roars Ashore with Category Five Winds!**

Mass destruction was inevitable and they hoped everyone had heeded their warning to evacuate the Gulf coastline. Cary had never known a case where all the people had left after hearing a warning, but not doing so was ignorant or suicidal. Or maybe, some of them had nothing left to lose, and just didn't give a damn.

In the days to come more details were disclosed. The winds had reached 190 mph and the storm surge recorded an all time record of 24 feet. It was the largest ever—a record for the United States. It obliterated an enormous area of the Gulf Coast. The storm ripped through Mississippi, and when it finally reached central Virginia, the hurricane was downgraded to a tropical depression. Virginians had now lessened their concern about the storm, but that was a mistake. Something drastic was about to happen that none had comprehended. The storm had stalled and began unleashing torrential rains of up to 31 inches which caused massive flooding in the mountains—a nightmare that lasted throughout the night. 143 people were killed in Alabama, Mississippi, and Louisiana. Killed almost as many in Virginia; 113 people perished as a result of catastrophic flooding in Nelson County alone as the water cascaded down the steep mountain gorges and carried away everything in its path. He felt remorse for those affected.

Two days later Cary went to the James River at its highest flood stage. By this time the hurricane had already dumped massive amounts of rain on Nelson County and others west of Richmond. This water cascaded down the mountains and vast amounts fed into the James River. He viewed the mind-boggling event at an area where the river channel was very narrow. He had never witnessed such a phenomenon and the eeriness was pronounced as darkness began descending. The water was a roaring, violent, angry, unrelenting, smashing force like he had never seen. He saw parts of buildings, huge industrial drums and dead cows blasting down the river. An unmanned, unlighted tugboat slammed down the river sideways giving Cary a chilled feeling. The drums and boats rode high on the waves and bounced off trees on the shoreline and spun around backwards and turned end over end. The torrent drove them mercifully onwards. Incredibly, he watched two men flying by in a small boat chasing the tug and hollering to him. "Did you see a tugboat? Which way did it go?" Cary hollered "Yes, bout a minute ago" and pointed down the river, as if there was any other way. They had to be drunk, Cary thought, or crazy, the result of the most destructive hurricane Cary had ever seen. He went home and slept restlessly until he was awakened the next morning by the ringing phone.

"Hey Cary, this is Thompson from Global Enterprises, how you doing?"

"Doing good, how 'bout you? I guess the oil rigs got hit bad didn't they?"

"Yeah, looks pretty bad, there's a lot of damage, it's going to take awhile to repair them and get them back online. My old company probably hasn't had time to assess the full extent, but I'm sure they're expecting the worse. I'm afraid it will cause the gas prices to rise. But that's not my problem; I'm not with them anymore as I told you. Look, I wanted to follow up on your engine. Have you sold it yet?"

"No, but I've had offers."

"Well, we are still interested, just wanted to let you know that. Are we still in the running?"

"You are," Cary answered carefully, not wanting to sound too eager.

"Well," Thompson continued, "you mind telling me what the holdup is?"

"Well, it's just that everybody has conditions in their proposals and it's taking me time to evaluate them. Seems like they all want us to guarantee that it will make it to market."

"Well, hell, we're not going to put it on the market, sell it to us! Listen, I might as well tell you, we're just an investment group. If you sell it to us, we plan to just hold it for an investment down the road. Look—just give us all the details outlining the invention. Agree that your group will never patent a similar engine. That's not too much to ask, is it?"

Cary didn't believe a word he said, "I could live with that, but does the money still have to be paid under the table?"

"Well, that's negotiable. If you'll lower your price, we'll consider paying you above board, but we would still want you to sign a non-disclosure agreement, not to divulge the details of this transaction. We'll give you a 1099 showing the transaction, and of course the IRS will know the amount paid and our company name as the payer and your name as the receiver. Otherwise no one else would know the details as long as no one on your side divulges them.

"Is that the total of your restrictions?"

"Not exactly," Thompson said, "before we could write you a check, we would have to take the engine to our research department and tear the engine apart and prove to ourselves it's really genuine. Also, because this hurricane will have many consequences, the CEO told me we don't have two billion anymore to offer you.. It'll probably be only in the millions."

"Its getting worse all the time," said Cary.

"It's the best we can do, really."

"I could accept everything except you taking the engine before payment. We're a little paranoid of doing that simply because we don't have it patented. No disrespect to you, but that's the way it is, and we are adamant about that. And listen Thompson, we would even take *less money* if you agreed to that."

"No disrespect taken, I understand, that's just business, and I can understand where you are coming from. After all, it's a huge situation we're talking about." Thompson paused for a moment and then asked, "Did . . . did you say you would take less money if there were no stipulations beyond that?"

"Yes." Cary replied.

"Let me think about that, and I'll get back to you."

"Okay," Cary said and hung up.

Cary called Jim and told him to come over and discuss the situation. Cary brought him up to date and Jim said, "Man, things have really turned around haven't they? Well, it's in your hands now, I don't care what you do, you're free to do anything it takes—anything to get the sale. We can accept all their restrictions except the one where they want to tear down the engine and inspect it before they hand over the money. Continue your discussions, Cary, and agree to anything but that. Forget the billions; we'll be happy if we get a couple million the way I feel now. Hell, we're nearly broke."

"Okay," Cary said, "I understand what you're saying."

Cary kept wondering why Jim was so adamant about them not dissecting the engine. Was he hiding something from him? *Well, it's his engine and his ball game,* he thought, *and I'm just along for the ride*. Cary was getting fatigued, frustrated at being so close to millions yet having to watch his pennies and afraid his journey was going to end in disaster if something didn't happen soon. He decided he was going to take some drastic action to *make* something happen. Make a bold move—do something before we lose it all. His money was about gone and Jim didn't care what we got as long as it was a couple million. He sat on his porch long into the night thinking of what to do. He finally made a decision.

The next day he called his friend Jackson Boyle at *Auto World Magazine*.

"Hi, Cary, sold that invention yet?"

"Just about, I wanted to call you and thank you for that article. It's brought me a lot of offers."

"Who are you going to sell to and when? Maybe I can do a follow up article."

"That's the reason I'm calling you. The events that have taken place over the last months have been remarkable, and it might make for a good story."

"Tell me about it," asked Jackson.

"Well, I've got two serious offers pressing me for the purchase, and I'm going to decide on one of them in the next couple of weeks. One has offered more money, but they won't promise to put the engine on the market. With the gas prices being so high, I've decided to take less money and sell it to a group that will make it available to the American people."

"Ahhh," said Jackson, "that's a *great* story! Now that would make a great article for me. Listen—would you return the favor I did for you by writing that first article?

"Well sure Jackson, what can I do?

How about telling me the details now so I can publish the story in next month's issue; it would really help my career. The article would come out in just ten days if I can get it in today. It'll be on the cover and you'll get great exposure."

Cary smiled because that is just what he wanted to hear. "Okay, Jackson, for you I'll do it." Jackson was elated, and Cary laid out the story for him but did not mention any names of the possible buyers. He said for various reasons they had to stay confidential.

Ten days later the magazine hit the stands. The article was on the front cover, and it caused the phone to start ringing immediately. The bold headlines stated the decision to sell was imminent. Again the calls were mostly from the news media, and he answered them all for he wanted exposure. He told them the invention would be sold in the next week. Then he got a call he didn't want.

"Cary, it's me Molly, I've read the article. What's going on? It sounds like you may be selling to us by the story." Cary was afraid this might happen and he hoped he could get out of it without lying.

"I told them I wanted to sell to you, told them I planned selling to you, but I didn't mention your name. Your firm has not reconsidered their offer have they?"

"No, Cary, but I smell something fishy here."

"Well, I do hope to sell to you, but we've still got that problem."

"I believe you Cary, but I don't know what you're up to.

Anyhow, I hope it works out . . . we'd still like to be the buyer. But you don't fool me," she laughed, "I know you're up to something, one of your schemes probably, I know you better than you think. Cary, I've been thinking . . . and I want to make you a bet."

"Well," Cary said, "put your money where your mouth is. How much are we betting for?"

"It might be *more* than you can afford to lose!"

"Like what?" Cary asked still smiling, "What's more than I can afford to lose?"

"You think about it . . . and maybe it will dawn on you like I'm afraid other things are going to dawn on you."

"Women—I don't understand them, you're talking in riddles," he said. "Well, if you won't tell me that, tell me what we are going to bet on."

Molly came back serious as hell and Cary could feel it. "Cary . . . I found out who your partner is and probably the inventor of the engine, it's your brother Jim."

Cary was shocked that she knew and replied, "There are some things I'm not at liberty to divulge."

"That's fine," Molly said, "but before we spend one billion dollars, we did some rather intensive investigating, and that's the information we obtained. We also found out some of the materials he purchased for the invention. We think we have an understanding of how the engine works. and *it is* not without major problems. Anyhow, back to the bet, my bet is that your brother is not being truthful to you concerning the engine. I think he is hiding something from you. I think you are being naïve; no one in their right mind would turn down one billion dollars if the engine was on the level. I really don't think you know the facts. I thought you were wiser than that. *I think you have been had and I think you are being used.* And thank God, so far, I don't think you have lied to me yet. I hope, Mr. smarty-pants, that you know what you are doing and who you are messing with. Think about it! *Talk to you later, good-bye*." Cary's smile had long since vanished before he hung up the phone.

*Oh my God*, he thought, *Could Molly have hit it right on the head? Could Jim be holding out on me all this time? Has he sent me out to negotiate with these wolves with false information? Damnit, why? was this what he was telling me way back, that this could be dangerous? Is that what he meant? I trusted him . . . but am I in for another deception, another betrayal? I can't stand another one. If I confront him, will he be truthful, why would he keep it from me—if the engine was not on the level? Is he playing me for a fool? And Molly, what did she mean, she would bet me something that I couldn't afford to lose? What is it that I can't afford to lose? What is it? Oh my God—she's talking about herself! Oh Lord!* Tears came to his eyes as he thought of Molly, and that she knew him better than he thought. She knew he loved her. I think her message was—that I was putting that love into jeopardy.

Cary was sitting on his front porch the next day when a black limousine pulled in front of his house and Thompson from Global Enterprises stepped out. He walked right up to Cary with some papers in his hand, and he wasn't smiling.

"You haven't signed any contracts yet have you?" he asked.

"No, I haven't."

"Good, here's my offer in writing," he said as he handed Cary a long legal document. "Take a look and see if you're interested. Take your time, there's no hurry."

Cary paused, took his time, and read the whole document. The words were plain and simple and Cary didn't need an attorney to explain it to him. He carefully examined the agreement a second time and it was exactly what he wanted. No stipulations except the one not to disclose the details of the sale. The money was to be paid up front. The engine and specifications were to be available for them to pick up in one week. At the end, there were several phrases his lawyer had warned him to look out for. He read them all carefully, the sale was final and there were no other restrictions of any kind. Cary looked at the bottom line that said a certified check would be written and the deal would be finalized a week from today. The amount would be for eight million dollars. Cary steeled himself to think clearly and make the right decision.

He thought of Molly more than anything else, and if she were right that Jim's engine was not on the level—then he sure didn't want to sell to her group. That deception could possibly ruin their relationship. If he sold it to Global who were going to shelve the engine anyhow; maybe they wouldn't be all that upset if the invention was not perfect, and not much harm could be done. But Molly, *what would she think*; would she lose respect for him selling out to a company that was not going to manufacture the engine. Would he lose her over this? *Losing her was not worth any amount of money.* Maybe he should just walk off and let Jim do whatever he wanted to; after all, the invention was his. On the other hand, he said he didn't care what I did as long as I got a couple million. It's been a long ride and I've gotten this close . . . . Well, I can't deceive Molly by selling her company the invention that has possible flaws. I can't do that. I could turn down the money, walk away, but that doesn't make any sense, and it wouldn't be fair to Jim. He made up his mind to take the offer.

"Eight million is a long way from two billion," he slowly said.

"That's all we can do, under the circumstances," replied

Thompson.

"You've caught me at a weak moment."

"Yes or no?" asked Thompson.

"Yes," said Cary, "it's a deal."

Cary signed the agreement, and Thompson said, "We'll be here on the thirty-first. We'll meet you at your lawyer's office. You bring the engine and specs, and we'll bring your check—but don't forget—*do not disclose* this agreement or the *amount* we're going to pay you, you got it? Fair enough?"

"Fair enough," Cary answered. Thompson took the papers and said goodbye with a slight smile. As Cary watched him drive off, he took the first deep sigh in a long time and said, "Thank God, it's finally over."

The thirty-first came and Thompson and his boys picked up the engine. Cary deposited the check and gave Jim half of it. Jim was satisfied, and he showed it with a big grin that lit up his face. The lawyer's fee was very high—high enough not to divulge the details of the agreement. Two weeks went by, and Cary found it wasn't over. Thompson called, and he was angry as hell.

"*The engine was not what you said it was, damn you*!" he shouted.

"It got a hundred miles a gallon when we tested it," Cary replied.

"Yeah, maybe so, but the engine was actually propelled from electricity from those extra batteries after it was up and running. *That was the only reason it got so much mileage*! And what really galls us is what you didn't tell us—the fact that we had to stop every three hours and recharge those damn batteries, which took four more hours! Who the hell would want to go a hundred miles and then have to stop for four hours while the batteries were being recharged? When you made that test run, you must have spent hours recharging those batteries probably just minutes before making the run! And that Swirling engine was not all that great—it's going to need many more improvements. *You didn't tell us that!* You said it traveled a hundred miles from running on gas alone."

"We only stated that we could travel one hundred miles while using one gallon of gas. We didn't say anything about *only* using gas,and the Swirling engine did recharge the batteries somewhat."

"Bullshit! You've pulled a fast one on us, and we're mad as hell."

"Now hold on Thompson, if it was put on the market, the oil companies would still lose gas sales! And that was your whole idea wasn't it?"

Thompson paused. He wasn't going to admit who he was representing. "Well, we paid you that money for an investment and we still feel like you misled us. The thing is, with the current regulations in place by the government, they would never allow this engine on the market without some modifications."

"Well," Cary said, "we realize there could be problems with putting it on the road today. But in years to come and with improvements in the battery charging system coming from applying those brakes, and a change in the environmental regulations, the invention is still valuable, and if you patent it now, the oil companies will sell a lot more gas in years to come if this is kept off the road. Or, on the other hand, if you are really holding it for investment purposes, it could become very valuable as a hybrid in the near future. You would be a winner either way. Anyhow, we lowered the price, and we still think it was worth what you paid for it."

"Well I think the ten million we paid you was ten million too much!" Thompson said.

"Well, you pulled a fast one on us too; you only gave us a fraction of the two billion dollars you first offered—and what ten million—you only gave us eight!"

Thompson realized his error and covered himself, "Well . . . we had planned on offering you ten million first—but now I'm glad we didn't."

Thompson banged the phone down, and Cary said out loud, "Well, Thompson old boy, that greed will get you every time." He couldn't feel sorry for the boys who were going to shelve the engine anyhow and not allow the public the benefit. He also wasn't sorry for them because they thought they were stealing the invention for peanuts. His conscience didn't hurt him in the least. He was just glad it was Thompson screaming at him—and not Molly.

He was upset with Jim for not telling him the truth about the engine. *Maybe he had his reasons*, he thought. *I did get four million out of the deal so I suppose I shouldn't be too upset.* But he couldn't forgive Jim for jeopardizing his relationship with Molly.

And Jim was now in hog heaven, for in his mind, he had shown everyone that he was *not just* old paranoid Jim. He had got even with the world, for he had finally pulled off the big one. He would receive world wide acclaim, he thought. He had brought attention to himself. It was really all he had ever wanted, and if the truth was known, that recognition meant more to him than the money.

His feelings toward his brother were mixed between his understanding of his paranoia and his deception for not trusting him to reveal the truth about the engine. But, all in all, he felt okay and was glad it was all over.

Cary met with Jim the next day and told him the whole story of what Thompson and his group had discovered about his engine. "Why didn't you tell me the whole truth about the invention, the problems with the Swirling engine, and the thing running on batteries that had to be recharged every three hours?" Cary asked. "You knew it couldn't be put on the market as it was."

Jim gave him that knowing look that his secrets had been exposed. "Well, Cary, I thought it would be better if you didn't know the details. I was afraid if you knew, you may have let it slip somehow, and the sale wouldn't have gone through."

"Yes, but if you had told me the truth about the engine, I wouldn't have spent so much time trying to sell to Molly's group. The truth is clear now—you only wanted to sell to the oil companies because you knew the invention had flaws and knew they were going to shelve it. You put me through a lot of extra work for nothing, and we almost sold it to Molly's company, an honest group, and if we did, I would have made a fool of myself. We would have been deceiving some great people and that wouldn't have been worth a dime!" He didn't bother telling Jim his feelings about Molly because he was sure he wouldn't think it important.

"Cary, I did consider Molly's group, you remember I sent you up there to double check on them. I'm really sorry I didn't tell you all the details, but I thought you'd be a more effective salesman if you didn't know the truth. Maybe I did the wrong thing . . . but I really felt it was important to handle it like I did--and we did get it sold!"

Cary left with mixed feelings about his brother.

# Chapter Twenty

## Bankrupted Heart . . .

## And Money in the Bank

Cary came home from the bank on the thirty-first day of August with a four million dollar deposit slip in his hand. After he parked the car he was surprised to find younger brother, Lonnie, sitting on his front porch. Lonnie was seven years his junior. He was a portly guy with a quick, jovial smile. "What cha' doing here Lonnie, haven't seen you for awhile. You still driving those big rigs?"

"Naw, I'm not doing anything. The tractor-trailer business has slacked off, damn high fuel prices are killing us. I've been laid off for awhile 'til things pick up."

"Sorry to hear that, can I help you in some way?"

"Yeah, I hope so, listen, I'm kinda' short on dough right now; reckon I could stay with you awhile? Just a few weeks until I get my job back."

"Yeah sure, you can hang your hat here for a spell. I've got the place all to myself." Lonnie was the youngest of five brothers, and the older ones always tried to look out for him. He had been living in Richmond and driving long distance tractor-trailers. Now he was out of a job because of fuel prices. *Damn,* Cary thought, *the consequences of what the engine could have done have already hit home!*

"Oh man, thanks," Lonnie said, "I sure do appreciate it. I didn't know what else to do, where else to go."

"Well, don't have a heart attack; we'll always come up with something."

Cary worried about Lonnie; his reasoning had never matured into adulthood. Lonnie moved in, and Cary decided to rest up awhile before deciding what to do next. It was the first time in his life that he didn't have to worry about going to work. The next morning he was at the bank and purchased three $100,000 dollar certified checks. He then mailed them, anonymously, one each to his parents, younger sister. and his older brother.

Cary decided he needed some land and a house, a place to call home. He had always felt a deep desire to have some acreage around him, some insulation from the world. He drove to the mountains of Virginia and rambled up and down the Shenandoah Valley. He had forgotten how beautiful the surroundings were.

The area was like God's country to him. After weeks of searching, he purchased a tract of land near the scenic area of Goshen Pass, 14 miles west of Lexington. The land stretched from the top of a small mountain down to the river. There was no house, only a small cabin beside the Maury River in the valley below. He then had house plans drawn up and a contract was given out to a builder to complete a modest log home near the top of the mountain. He purchased a new Dodge four-wheel truck to better navigate the hilly terrain.

While the house was under construction he thought it was time he talked with Lonnie. Lonnie was not good at managing money and that was the reason he delayed his offer. The other siblings could take care of the funds he'd given them, but he wasn't sure about Lonnie. He was afraid the money could mess him up if he didn't handle it properly. Lonnie and Cary were finishing dinner one night when Cary brought it up.

"Lonnie, I've got something to tell you that might interest you."

"I'm all ears," he said, but his eyes were glued to the comics as he sat at the kitchen table.

"Would you like this house?" Cary asked.

"Whatcha mean? I ain't got no money to buy it."

"I didn't ask you that," he paused calmly, for he always had a problem communicating with Lonnie. "I mean I could buy this house from Mom and Dad and give it to you if you want it." .

"How you gonna do that?"

"Well, between you and me—you listening? I'm serious damn it!"

"Yeah, what?" he answered, laying down the comics.

"Between you and me, I've got a little extra money and I will buy this house and deed it over to you in a month or two if you like." Lonnie's eyes widened and a big smile crossed his face.

"Man, that would solve my problems—you mean I wouldn't have to pay no rent or nothing?"

"That's right. Is it a deal?" Cary asked.

"Yeah man, it's a deal, thanks!" Cary didn't think Lonnie would bother asking him where the money came from.

"Another thing, Lonnie, I know you are tight on money, so I'm going give you a check to hold you over. You know you will still have to pay utilities and taxes on the house." Lonnie got up smiling and shook Cary's hand as though a tremendous weight had been lifted from his shoulders.

"Oh, thank you, thank you!" he gushed. Cary got his checkbook and wrote him a check for $ 20,000 and put it face down on the kitchen table.

Cary held his hand on it and looked at Lonnie. "I'm going give you this check on one condition. I'll be building me a house in the mountains, and I don't know how long it will take, maybe several months or more. I want to stay here until I have it finished, okay?"

"Yeah, anything you say," he said staring at the check and then out of the blue said, "Jim said he had come into some money, said he had sold an invention or something. Did he give you some money too?" Cary was dumbfounded. Why would Jim tell him this? He understood the not to disclose agreement he had signed with Global.

"He's given me no money, what are you talking about?"

"Oh, meant to tell you, he called me yesterday," Lonnie said, his eyes shifting from Cary to the check. "Just said he sold that thing he'd been working on for years. That's all I know, except he said to keep it quiet."

"Well, Lonnie, you can't believe everything Jim says."

"That's for sure," he answered as Cary got up from the table. Cary told him he would catch him later, and he left the kitchen and paused on the front porch waiting for his reaction.

*"Whoooah!" Thank you Lord!"* Cary heard the floor shake as Lonnie jumped up and down and danced in a circle while staring at the check held between his hands high over his head. He never looked to see if Cary had left and didn't care where the money had come from. Cary would give him more, little by little, when the appropriate time came. Then he thought

of Jim, *already* running his mouth about selling the invention. *Is he crazy? what is he doing?*

Cary called Jim the next morning. Jim picked up the phone, and said hold on a minute. Cary heard him whistling, and there was loud music playing in the background. He was in no hurry.

"Heeeyyy Cary, how's it going?" he answered cheerfully.

"Jim, what are you doing? Lonnie just said you'd told him about the sale."

"Uhhh, yeah, I did tell him, but he's just family . . . didn't mention Globals name though."

"Don't you realize what you are doing?"

"What?"

"You're putting us in jeopardy, that's what! If the word spreads, and you know it will, Thompson and his boys will be after our heads."

"I'll be a little more careful," said Jim.

"Jim, have you reported your four million on your income taxes?"

"Nope, never got around to it, how much you reckon they'd want anyhow?"

"About a million and half dollars."

"You're kidding! You're not serious?"

"Yep, that's the cold hard facts," said Cary

Jim was quiet for awhile, "I don't know . . . I can't imagine paying them that much. That's almost half of what I got! The hell with them, how they gonna know anyhow?"

"Global was supposed to send a 1099 form to us and a copy to the IRS, but I never got mine, did you?"

"Nope, maybe they've overlooked it."

"If the IRS does receive a 1099 from Global, they'll be looking for the income on your tax return."

"Well I haven't received one yet so maybe the IRS won't know."

"Your bank would reveal your records to them one way or the other, like sending them interest income statements."

"I haven't puts any money in the bank—I'm smarter than that."

"*But Jim,* you can still get in trouble if you purchase anything—say a car for over ten thousand because the person who receives this amount is regulated by law to report you to the IRS. Then the government boys will come looking for you and asking where the money came from. If you're not using a bank, what are you doing with it then—hiding in your back yard?"

"Don't you worry about *that*—it'll be put away safe. And I know about the $ 10,000 law; that came about mostly because of illegal drug sales. *And by the way* if anything happens to me I'll leave detailed instructions where the money can be found."

"I'm just trying to warn you Jim. There are still other ways the IRS has of checking your income. "For instance, they browse the DMV files to see if anyone has bought an expensive vehicle. They can trace you down this way. If you report little or no income—you've got a problem. That's number one—now for the real problem. What do you think the Global boys will do when they hear about you disclosing the sale of the engine? You know how word travels! If this information got out to the public, that Globals bought the invention and shelved it—it could really damage their reputation. They would be looking for our heads. You're playing with fire, Jim."

"But they're not an oil company."

"Yeah, but you can be sure as hell they're connected to them, Hell, Global is probably just a front for the oil companies anyhow. I'm sure that's where the money came from, and if the truth be known, probably came from each and every oil company. And if that word gets out, you'll not just have one unhappy oil company after you—you'll have a half a dozen out to shut you up. They made it perfectly clear—*not to divulge the sale*!"

"What they gonna do? They *can't* take the money back."

"What do you think companies can do when there's millions of dollars involved? They can ruin you—they can murder you."

"*Awww,* I'm not afraid of them… I'm not afraid of

anybody."

"Okay, have it your way, gotta run—bye."

Cary was shaking as he hung up the phone realizing Jim would never change. He thought the money would help Jim's condition but he was wrong. He's still seeking recognition . . . evidently, just like when he counterfeited those $20 bills and told his friends about it hell, he might as well have told the world. Damn, $20 dollar bills were bad enough—it put him in prison, but hell—this could get us killed.

Cary tried contacting Thompson to question him about the 1099, but he couldn't locate him, and there was no Global Enterprises to be found. While Cary was worrying about Jim, he occupied his mind by staying busy trying to get a small guest house completed so he would have a place to stay while completing the main log house.

He wanted to see Molly and admit that he had sold the invention to someone else. His heart was heavy; he said a prayer, gathered his nerves, and dialed her number. They chatted amicably for awhile and, to his surprise, she quickly accepted his invitation to visit his mountain home. He thought this was a good place to lay it all out. At least she couldn't run away.

Two days later she flew to Roanoke and Cary pick her up. They left the airport and drove west towards the mountains in his new truck. They crossed over the Blue Ridge Mountains and entered the Shenandoah Valley where summer had turned to fall.

As they drove north, Molly gazed at the many mountains now covered with fall colors. “Wow, they are beautiful,” Molly said. “It’s just one mountain after another.”

“Many people have described this valley as the most magnificent in the world,” said Cary. They drove north to Lexington on I-81 and then turned west on Route 39, a two lane scenic by-way that took them to the edge of the Alleghany mountains. They passed the little village of Rockbridge Baths two miles east of the stunning area known as Goshen Pass, a breath taking gorge that the Maury River had formed as it cut its way through the Alleghenies. Cary’s mountain land was situated between two others, one by the name of Jump and another named Snow. Cary pulled his truck over at the Rockbridge Baths Post Office.

“Whatcha doing?” said Molly

“Come on, I’m going to walk you over the Maury River,” Molly climbed out the truck and went running after Cary but then abruptly stopped when she saw him standing on a swaying walk bridge over a rocky river.

“What is that?” She asked as she cautiously edged towards him.

“It’s a walk bridge. Come on, it’s safe, you can trust me.” Molly took three steps onto the bridge.

“Molly was trembling as she pondered his trusting words. “Whooo, it’s swaying. Are you sure it’s safe?”

“Trust me, come on.” Molly paused, looked down at the river far below and nervously looked at Cary.

“Don’t look down, just look at me,” Cary said. She finally summed up her nerve, gripped the railing, and crept towards Cary as her face loss its tension. She actually smiled as the wind blew and the walk bridge swayed. She finally reached Cary and held him tight as the falling sycamore leaves glided down around them.

“Wow,” she said hugging Cary, “this is wild, look at those rocks, they must be hundreds, thousands! How did you know the bridge was here?”

“I came across several when I was looking for my land.” He noticed her apprehension and walked her back to the truck. “Look up there,” he pointed to a group of mountains. “That one there is Jump Mountain and my place is right behind it.”

“How do you tell one from the other?”

“It takes awhile.” he said as they got back in the truck. They began slowly climbing upward on Cary’s mountain as Molly looked all around with interest.

“You live up here now?” she asked.

“Oh no, there’s still much work to be done. It will take a year or more before it’s completed. But there’s water, a fireplace for heat, and a roof over our head. The exterior is mostly finished, but the inside work will take a little longer. It's good enough to camp out in, but just in case you're not into camping, there's a roughed-in guest house with a Johnny."

"Where does your land start?"

"It started back about ten minutes ago, right after the bridge that crossed the Maury River."

"Really, how much land you got here?"

"This whole mountain is mine." She turned her head slowly and with wide eyes looked at the mountains that now surrounded them.

"You bought the whole mountain?"

"Yeah."

"Good God! I didn't know you could buy a whole mountain."

"Well, I do like to have some elbow room."

Molly positioned herself for a better view by taking off her seat belt, turning around, pulling up her skirt and putting her knees on the truck seat so she could view the mountains out the back window. Cary glanced at her with amusement. "What a sight?" she said.

It's fall and the colors are close to their peak. I thought it a good time to bring you here; thought it might impress you."

"Gee, it's impressive alright, seems like we've gone

around a thousand curves though."

"Well, it's kinda hard to drive straight up. If we did that, my truck might flip over backwards," Cary chuckled. She nodded with understanding as her eyes watched thousands of colorful leaves swirling behind the truck.

"We don't have mountains like this back home, gol-le-day, they're tremendous. You think you'll like living up here?"

"It's closer to God."

"You believe in God, don't you?"

"Yes, what else it left? The culture is going crazy and I have a strong desire to get far away from that maddening crowd."

"I can understand that, human nature seems to have really changed since my childhood."

"Mine too, you can't leave your doors unlocked anymore," said Cary.

"Well, I've never thought too much about God and all, it all seems a mystery to me."

"You and everybody else," answered Cary. They reached the top, and Molly scrambled out with anticipation, running around like a child. She looked at the unfinished log house and turned and surveyed the valleys far below.

"Wow . . . breathtaking, and we are so *high.* Your log home is going to be a dream and I can see why it's going to take awhile." She turned her head sideways looking at the unfinished house. “The way you’ve designed it—like it’s a part of the mountain. Just seems like . . . well, like it belongs here.” And then it hit her, how could he afford this if he hadn’t sold the invention? She said nothing, not wanting to break the spell, but her mind was racing as he escorted her around. Finally she stopped, turned and glared at him with suspicious eyes. She couldn’t hold it any longer. “You sold the invention—didn’t you?”

Cary was ready to get it over. “Yes, Molly, I did, that’s why I brought you up here . . . to tell you.” Molly took the first seat she could find and her eyes filled with tears. “Molly, I’m sorry . . . sorry we couldn’t sell to you, but I wanted to—*you know* I did.”

While Molly pouted, Cary retrieved his cooler from his truck and fixed two drinks on the tailgate of his truck. She slowly followed him to the terrace behind his house. The patio was as wide as the rear of his house and as deep as a basketball court. He motioned her to a white, concrete picnic bench that sat just outside front of four double French doors and handed her a drink. They were silent as they looked about them.

The sun filtered down through an overhead lattice that was partially covered with emerging ivy vines. The patio was paved with smooth mountain stones of mixed colors. Steps descended thirty yards down the mountain to a trail that circled the house.

"You remembered my favorite drink." She said regaining her composure.

"I haven't forgotten anything about you."

She attempted a smile but her thoughts went back to his sad demeanor when they were at the country club. "I've thought of you many times myself," she said. They chatted for awhile bringing each up to date on past events.

Cary looked at Molly whose eyes were now dry. "Let me tell you the whole story—you deserve it." She stared down and listened silently. "I wanted to sell to your group, but . . . you were right about the real inventor, it was my brother, and it was really his decision. I was only the negotiator. He just wouldn't change his mind concerning your stipulation."

"But why? Why was that such a big deal?"

"I've questioned him many times, and he always gave me the same answer. As I've told you, it was because of the patent problem. *But* you were exactly right—he was hiding something from me—the engine did have a flaw. I have thanked God I didn't sell it to your people. You were right again, I was naïve, and I didn't know the engine had problems. You had more insight than I did; I guess I was too close to the forest to see the trees."

"What was the flaw, Cary?"

"Well, the engine doesn't run on gas alone. After the gas

got the engine up and running it actually was propelled by this small Swirling engine which in turn was powered by electricity from several batteries. That's all I can tell you."

"Like a hybrid," asked Molly? "Runs partly on gas and partly on electricity? Well, that's okay, but how are you going to recharge the batteries?"

"We had an answer for that too. When the brakes were applied, they would produce some energy, and Jim learned how to harness this energy and send a charge to the batteries."

"And did that work?"

"Only to a certain extent, and that was the problem; Jim couldn't devise a good enough system to produce enough charge from the brakes. Also, the batteries manufactured today wouldn't really hold the charge long enough, and another drawback was the batteries had to be recharged after just a few hours. Jim was so afraid that if that was found out no one would buy the engine. A lot of innovation is still needed before it would be marketable. I'm glad we didn't sell the invention to your group."

"Why?"

Cary began nervously pacing and finally stopped, turned and faced her. "*Don't you see*? If I had sold it to you and your engineers found the flaw . . . then, I was afraid you'd think I had deceived you. Afraid you would lose respect for me. *Now,* I'm worried that you're angry because I didn't sell to you."

"Sure, I'm disappointed . . . I put a lot of time into it, but maybe it's best all around." Molly composed herself. "Let me congratulate you both—at least you got it sold. Hey, I'm not devastated, it doesn't affect me personally. I was just doing my job. You didn't know there was a flaw; you were on the level with me. But you know, after everything you've told me, I think your invention was really good. One day in the future, we may just see it on the market. Who knows, one day we may be hit with a hurricane worse than Camille, and the gas prices will jump so high that people will be waiting in line to buy one of these hybrids. But yes, my group might have thought it overpriced under the circumstances. So you may have done the right thing, who knows?" Cary took a deep breath and was glad it was over.

"Yes," said Cary, "but you worked so hard . . . I was so sorry it didn't come your way, but now that the truth has come out, I'm glad we didn't sell it to you. Listen, I apologize for wasting your time."

Molly looked at Cary with a smile and patted his hand, "Hey, don't be sorry, at least we got to meet each other, its okay really. Don't you worry about it—I'm fine. But I might as well ask you, can you tell me who you sold it too?" Cary opened his mouth but no words came and after a pause Molly spoke for him. "That's okay . . . you've already given me the answer." Cary lowered his head and looked away. She touched his shoulder.

"*It's* okay Cary, *forget* I asked."

"I was so afraid of telling you I had sold to someone else, so worried it would ruin this beautiful evening. Well, I'm not letting that happen. "Come on," he waved his hand toward the terrace stairs, "let's take a walk." She smiled and caught up with him as he reached the stairs that took them to the pebbled pathway that circled the house. They took a leisurely stroll around his house enjoying the autumn breeze that blew colorful leaves swaying down around their feet. They lingered at a small walk-bridge for hours and watched the leaves float beneath then as the stream carried them towards the valley below. They finally made it back to the house as the sun settled behind the mountains. He took her inside the unfinished log house where the huge, vertical rafter beams had recently been erected.

"Oh, all this wood, it's tremendous and it smells so good," she said. She walked into his great room and noticed his extensive library shoveled next to the giant stone fireplace. She glanced upwards at the enormous shelves that went from floor to ceiling containing books of varied subjects.

"These books, my goodness, you must do a lot of reading."

"There's not much else to do up here at night, and I enjoy reading. Seldom do I watch the boob tube."

Molly ran her fingers along the book titles. "You've got a

lot here—what's this one about? *Auto Accidents or Suicides on Purpose*?"

"I got that one after an incident that took place at the cemetery. A young man had died in an automobile accident, and the policeman who first arrived said there was absolutely no evidence of anything that could have caused this wreck. The policemen said they had investigated many crashes of this nature and concluded this man had wrecked the car to kill himself accidentally on purpose. That intrigued me and so I got this book to educate myself about it."

"That's enough!" She said. Her demeanor changed as though she had been attacked. She turned away and looked at the other books, took a deep breath and said, "I'd rather not discuss it!" Cary was astonished at her reaction and was sure he saw her tremble; her anger was very apparent, but he felt it best to drop the subject.

"What are these other books about?" She asked calmly as though nothing had happened. "You've got Thoreau, the Bible, a Concordance and one about DNA. This Concordance, what's it about? I've never heard of that one."

"Let me get this fireplace started. It gets cool up here in the fall. The book is something I purchased thinking it would help me understand the Bible better." He didn't elaborate, thinking she wouldn't be interested.

"I'd sure be interested in anything that would help me understand the Bible better. How does it help?"

Cary relaxed, stretched out on a blanket that partially covered the sub floors, and leaned back against the leather couch Molly was sitting in. The warmth of the fireplace reached them now, and it was dark except for the glitters of light from the fireplace that reflected off the vaulted wood ceiling. They were close to the fireplace, and their shadows cast by the flames danced on the walls behind.

"The Bible is hard to understand," said Cary "and it seems the preachers have different interpretations. They say the Bible was written originally in Hebrew, so that's why I use the Concordance. Any time I have a question concerning the true meaning of a word, I can look it up in the Concordance and get the original Hebrew definition. For instance, it cleared up something I had wondered about since childhood. In the Garden of Eden, Eve said that the Serpent beguiled her. When I looked up the Hebrew meaning of the word *beguiled,* it told me the word meant '*wholly seduced.*'"

"You're kidding me." she said.

"No, sex was the sin that Eve committed and it was no apple that gave her a tummy ache. I figured that Adam was her partner in crime and thus the father of Cain and Able. But later while reading the New Testament in the Book of John, Christ identified Satan as the father of Cain. Here, let me quote Jesus' exact words from the Bible." Cary took his Bible and quickly turned to the verse.

"Jesus was talking to the group that was calling for his crucifixion. He called them Jewish imposters. In John Chapter 8 he said, 'Why do you not understand my speech even because you cannot hear my word, *yea are of your father, the Devil* and the lust of your father yea will do. He was a *murderer from the beginning.*' Again in John, Chapter 3 vs.12 he says, 'That we should love one another not as *Cain whom was of that wicked one* and slew his brother.' End quote."

"Well, I can even understand that, but I've never heard a preacher interpret it that way," she said.

"Neither have the numerous preachers I've questioned."

"Why is that important to you?"

"Because the Bible said that Satan and his followers were thrown out of heaven down to Earth. If these Jewish imposters that Jesus was talking about were descendants of Satan, then it seems obvious that his descendants are still with us today, two thousand years later."

"Fascinating," she said, "you mean you think descendants of Satan are walking around on earth today?"

"Some preachers think Satan is here today, so why not his descendants?" said Cary.

"My, my, I've learned more today than in church, and you explain it so well. What are those other books about? I've never heard of DNA or carbon fourteen."

"DNA is something scientists are researching, and the forefront of this study is going on right here in Richmond, Virginia. It's very complicated and I don't understand it yet. What caught my attention was that knowledge is growing so fast that it's mind-boggling what the future could bring, and to add to that, the Bible prophesized that in the last days knowledge would increase greatly. As for as DNA, this study said they may be able to find something in your body tissue that is different from every other person in the world."

"Well, don't we have fingerprints?"

"Yes, but this is better. Say for instance you don't have fingerprints in the case of a murderer, you know, say he wore gloves. But just a trace of salvia off a discarded cigarette butt would give the lab enough evidence to lead them to the murderer and maybe enough to convict him. You know, that is strong stuff. It's not perfected yet, but I'm following their research closely. Carbon Fourteen is a test that can verify how old something is. Archaeologists use it in their scientific study of material remains, relics, and artifacts of past human life and activities."

Molly looked at him and tried to comprehend his thinking when she spoke. "Don't tell me you think Satan and his followers could be identified with DNA or Carbon Fourteen?"

"Who knows? It may be possible one day."

"But . . . but why?"

"Why? Because I don't know any other power that could engineer this enormous agenda to overthrow America. And this thinking does follow the Bible."

"You think what's happening to the culture is someone's agenda?" she asked.

"It sure seems that way. It's been going on for years, I've seen it continually coming on since the late fifties and it's only getting worse. Something monstrous is behind it, and I don't know any man, group, or nation that has that much power."

"Man, you've got some far out subjects to study. Now I know what people do when they don't have to work. How long you been sequestered up here in these here hills man?"

They talked on into the night and finally made their way to bed in the adjacent guesthouse.

The next morning Molly awoke to the smell of coffee. She made her way out to the terrace where Cary was sipping coffee underneath the bright morning sun.

Molly came out stretching with her arms in the air, "Good morning, oooh . . . I slept so good last night."

"Yes, this mountain air does it to you," Cary said. "You need to get out of those stuffy office buildings more often. Here, have some fresh coffee."

"A working girl has to do what she has to do, not like some millionaires I know." She sat and had her coffee and doughnuts and they talked cordially and friendly about everything except themselves. Molly was still wary of whatever was bothering Cary and thought someday she'd find the right time to find out. She had never forgotten his attitude of indifference the very moment the agreement was made to pay him one billion dollars. Anybody who couldn't smile at a moment like that *had* to have a problem.

Cary could tell that Molly was still a little disconcerted and he didn't force himself on her. She did seem to enjoy being with him, and for that he was glad. They spent the day together and Cary took her back to the airport. Some urgent business had come up, so she said, and she had to fly back to New York right away.

"I enjoyed it so much Cary. Thanks for showing me your place. It's something I'll never forget."

"It was my pleasure."

"I hope to see you soon," she smiled and kissed him on the cheek. He smiled and waved goodbye as she walked towards her plane.

"We'll see," he said but Molly didn't hear him. Cary drove back to his mountain house. He fixed a tall drink and made his way to his patio and thought about her. He could tell her demeanor had changed after he mentioned the engine sale. He felt some of her friendly ways were forced and thought it was just her Southern background that enabled her to act so graciously when she probably felt like killing him. He was afraid some of her feelings had cooled towards him, and he almost felt ashamed for the way things turned out, but then he dismissed that feeling because he knew it was not his doing. Life is not always fair, not always a fairy tale ending. He sure didn't like disappointing Molly, but he could do nothing, and hoped she hadn't lost respect for him. God, he thought, is this just *another* love I'm going to lose? He hated little hurts because he knew where they could lead. They could be a sure recipe to kill love; little hurts repetitiously thrown would surely hit their mark. A little ache here and a little pain there and guess what; your loving feelings were dissolved into oblivion. Cary knew from experience.

There were two hours of daylight left in the autumn evening when Cary left the patio and meandered around the pathway that circled his house. There were trees, flowers and shrubs on each side. The larger trees were transplanted and the shrubs and flowers he had planted. There was a mixture of holly trees, dogwoods, crepe myrtles, and English boxwoods. The crepe myrtles were still in bloom with colors of red and white. Below them were the shrubs intermingled with red geraniums and petunias outlining the length of the walkway. The landscaper had carefully graded the land from the house down the mountainside for a distance of a hundred yards and then topped it with a deep layer of dark topsoil mixed with mulch. The winter grass planted recently was just turning green and would grow to a darker color and remain that way through the winter. Cary slowed beside a small walk-bridge that crossed a little stream. Adjacent was a gazebo where he sat, lit a cigarette, and listened to rippling water as it cascaded over thousands of rocks and made its way down the mountain side.

He thought of Molly and her reaction to his book concerning auto accidents and suicides. He wondered about her unusual response when he mentioned the details of the book. Evidently the information shook her and apparently was something she didn't want to discuss. That's usually a sign of something very hurtful and entrenched. He wondered if she was beautiful and unattached because of some flaw in her character. He hoped she didn't have some deep-rooted problem that couldn't be reached. He had met some women with wounds embedded into their subconscious; so deep that they wouldn't go there and wouldn't let anyone else either. They would weep and run away when he had correctly deciphered their problem. The monster just sits within, eats away, and destroys any hopes of them living a normal, happy life. He hoped this wasn't Molly's case, but if it was, he was going to do anything necessary to help her overcome it. He would do this for her, if possible, even if he couldn't win her love. Her life was too valuable, too precious to waste.

He gazed at the hazy valleys far below that now lay in shadows as the sun was descending. It was peaceful for him here as he thought of the future and what it would bring. As for now, he didn't have to work for a living, but that presented a problem because he knew he had to stay busy unless those old hurtful memories invade him again. He was *driven* to work he knew; only this time he thought, he wouldn't be working for a living, he hoped he would be working *for* the living.

He wasn't sure how to go about it, but his priorities would become clear in the near future. He had no premonition of the phenomenal events that awaited him in the coming weeks that would turn his world upside down. He knelt and prayed, "Not my will, oh Lord, but thine be done."

# Chapter Twenty-One

## The Disappearing Girl

Cary went back to his home on Eleventh Avenue in Hopewell while the construction was being finished on his mountain house. He had an urge to do some soul searching. The money in the bank had not stopped his hurting and he couldn't shake his depression. Added to his worries were Jim's crazy actions. Damn, he thought, why couldn't he keep his mouth shut? He went to church and asked to speak privately with a pastor. He opened his soul to him and asked many questions regarding spiritual matters.

The pastor listened, brushed him off, and sent him on his way with. "You must have blind faith—you are *not* supposed to understand these complex subjects! *That's my job*, attend my church more often, *start tithing,* and maybe we can help you."

Now Cary had respect for ministers in general but this boiled his blood. He realized there were good and bad people in every profession but this conduct disgusted him. This guy was the worst kind of hypocrite, the lowest of the low. He masqueraded as a minister, pretending to serve the needy, yet turned like Judas and mocked those who were down and out only because he had not received his 90 pieces of silver. With this man of God, seeking, asking, and knocking did not result in finding or receiving, and no doors were opened. For a lesser person, this experience could have been demoralizing, but Cary's faith and strength were unwavering.

Cary didn't think much of the pastor's disparaging remarks. There was enough evidence of things unseen for Cary to retain his faith in the Almighty. Only a loving entity could grant us so many blessings. There was air to breathe that only surrounded His planet, food that grows from seeds, and water that springs from the ground. He formed a complex body with a brain and a soul that no one yet has been capable of understanding, much less able to duplicate. Who else but a Heavenly Father could have created love, something you can't see but you can't live without, at least not normally. And it made sense there must be a Satan . . . because who else could take it away? This God, this unseen force, was powerful, intelligent beyond our understanding and good. Cary had long ago, without reservation, taken the leap of faith and had decided he wanted to be on the side of this mighty entity.

But Cary was having a hard time with the problems of living. He was hurting more and laughing less. He tried hard to help himself—he studied, he read, he consumed the essence of every book he thought could help him. He had fought battles all his life, and he wasn't about to give up now. He was just a regular guy, nothing special, and he had made mistakes . . . done things he was ashamed of. He prayed for forgiveness and tried never to make the same mistake twice. He had been through the fire and had come out with holy burns. He slowly acquired a sense of a comradeship and became aware of identifying himself with others.

He had experienced a few things in life and had learned from them: A punch to the face was not the end of the world, but not getting up and fighting again was. The fear of something unknown approaching was worse than when it finally arrived. Football taught him to accept defeat, but take it only as a temporary setback. Keep your composure, never lose confidence, and be ready to fight again another day.

In this battle of life, either victory or defeat, he would fight to the death if necessary because giving up was not an option. He would walk away from petty hurts and disagreements, but when his honor was at stake, he would throw away all caution and defend himself at all costs.

Cary made his way through life by identification. He reasoned that was why people felt songs, paintings, books or any other works of art were beautiful—because they could identify with them. Truth be told, he was probably not so different from other men. He did what others had done when there was no medication available, such as the wounded soldier who bites another bullet to deaden the pain.  Sometimes pain was too much for a man. When his dentist hurt him, he squeezed the chair rails to counteract the pain. When his heart ached, it helped to hear a hurting song, and when there were no songs, it helped his suffering to read the poems of Emily Dickinson. When none of these were available, he was able to quote her poems from memory. This was a handy tool when nothing else was available. And like the oyster, he only hoped his agony could produce something of value, a pearl of great price, so his anguish would not be in vain. This identification for some reason, maybe the psychologists could explain, helped relieve his pain. A man had to find help *wherever* he could.

As the days came and went, Cary felt like some type of spiritual transformation was happening to him. He had read that your whole body could be transformed in seven years according to how you lived your life. He thought of those who committed suicide to escape their pain. He thought that was the coward's way out. He thought of those who tried to escape their torment with drugs. These things he would never do. He'd rather die on the cross than relent to such actions. He found himself helping others and began saying a repetitive prayer that he hoped would transform him for the better. Then he had the most spiritual dream ever:

*He didn't know why, but he was moving from his home to another. The house he was leaving was a nice two- story colonial with four white columns across the front. He was being taken away with nothing but the clothes on his back. He returned back to retrieve a special chair that sat on his front porch. As he reached for the chair, it crumbled in his hands, disappeared and something told him he would need none of his possessions in his new home. He drove to his new address—a prestigious neighborhood in Washington, D C. When he reached the destination there was only one white, marble mansion that took up an entire block. He circled the block several times not believing this could be his new home. Finally he stopped, exited his car, and walked towards this building of sublime beauty. He passed through elegant bronze gates into an exquisite garden while all the time thinking he may be intruding. Bubbling water flowed from a waterfall and dropped into a fountain. This was all surrounded by a garden of flowers and trees with birds singing. He checked the number of the building—it was his address! He inserted the key he was given and to his astonishment the wide double doors swung open. He walked down the wide halls listening to his footsteps reverberating from the granite floors to the marble walls as he passed one huge room after another. It was the last thing he remembered before he awoke.*

Finally, after becoming weary, he relented to prayer, the only device he hadn't utilized. One night he was sitting beside his dining room window and looking at his mother's Bible lying on his desk. It was an early, warm fall night, so he opened his dining room window and felt a cool breeze as he listened to the mesmerizing sounds of the crickets as darkness descended. He leaned back in his chair and watched the weeping willow limbs sway eerily in the night. He remembered his mother, on her knees, planting the willow tree just outside the window when he was nine. Plant trees today Cary, Mother had said, and you will be surprised at the enjoyment they will bring in years to come. Twenty years had passed and the whole side yard was filled with flowers, shrubs, and trees that left an indelible memory of Mom.

The Bible had been sitting there ever since he had moved in. He had left it there respectfully undisturbed, but finally concluded that she'd left it for him, on purpose. He opened the Bible and noticed the worn pages. Obviously, she had spent many hours intensely seeking something that evidently had been hard to find. On the other hand, maybe she had found something of great value, and was only returning for renewed strength. He noticed a hand-written note scribbled on the first page that read. "Seek and ye shall find Matt: 7. 7." Maybe she had found what she was seeking. He turned the pages with interest and read the verse: *Ask, and it shall be given you; seek, and ye shall find; knock, and it shall be opened to you*. He read the verse over twice and finally decided to take Jesus at his word—he had tried everything else and thought it only right he should attempt what Mother had admonished. Besides, he owed it to her since he had never taken her advice before.

He grinned when he remembered the bumper sticker he had read: Prayer? Don't knock it if you haven't tried it! He remembered his mother's advice: "When you need help and have found nowhere else to turn; get your Bible out, read and pray for help." Oh . . . he had prayed all his life but had never recognized any response. He had never gotten the pretty redhead and had never hit the grand-slam homer. Maybe he hadn't been praying correctly. He decided now was the time that he and God would have a go at it, give the preachers a fair hearing, and see if they were on to something. Some of them had to be on the level. All of them couldn't be wrong, *could they?*

He read the promises again that Jesus had so audaciously announced. He was acquainted with promises and good intentions and knew where they could lead. But then he guessed God did too—so maybe they had something in common. Cary decided to take Jesus up on such a bold proposal and see if Mother was right. He began praying to this God, this revered, mysterious entity that had confounded man since the beginning, praying every evening at the same time and in the same place—in front of his dining room window. He mostly prayed for his heartache to ease, and then after several weeks and having more time, he threw in some additional prayers. He prayed for a cure to his stomach ulcer and then asked God to send him a nine-pound dark-haired baby boy, someone of his own to love and cherish. Hell, everybody needs someone he reasoned. He didn't bother worrying God about the details—he left those up to Him. More weeks went by and nothing. Astutely, he presumed he must have been praying incorrectly, so before giving up on God, giving him the benefit of the doubt, he went back to the Bible to see what he had missed. Cary thought he must have been doing something wrong; after all, God doesn't make mistakes. Cary was a fair man. and he decided to give God a commensurate chance at keeping his promises. He couldn't fathom the thought that God would make promises and then not keep them. After all, a promise is a promise, and God *knows* what a broken promise can do to a tortured soul.

He scanned the verses and finally found: *You must pray with all your heart.* Okay, maybe that's it, and then thought of what the preacher's wife had said, and went back to praying, but this time with *much intensity*. He thought he might have a little inkling of what Jesus was expounding. Anyhow, it had gotten to the point where biting the bullet, listening to hurting songs, and reading Emily's poems were not doing the job. Cary resumed praying nightly for four more weeks and *still* nothing. He was getting tired and downright weary of expending so much energy in his prayers and finally explained to God that he hoped He wasn't letting him down. He also reminded Him, *very* casually . . . this thing about where good intentions could lead. About paving that road to you-know-where . . . .

Cary had challenged the Almighty concerning his promises and now after two months he had not delivered. He had given him a fair chance and had met him on a level playing field. He was thinking of his mother's advice—and *how* could she be wrong? He knew she would not lie to him—*mothers don't lie to their children*. He said a few more choice prayers to this Entity and then calmed himself and repeated a prayer that had become a weekly ritual. *"Not my will, oh Lord, but thy will be done in and through me!"* He kept in mind that patience was the highest virtue and never forgot the words of the mantra he had adopted: To run the race, fight the fight, and keep the faith. He *leaned heavily* upon these words and waited . . . patiently.

Lonnie was around the house in the daytime but most nights he was out looking for girls as young men do. During this time Cary was reading many other spiritual books including one concerning the psychic, Edgar Cayce, of Virginia Beach. He was a devout Christian, and his books seemed to go along with the

Bible, with the exception of his thoughts on reincarnation. But Cary had read that reincarnation was left out of the bible by the Catholic Church back in the fifth century. Some biblical scholars stated this was left this out so the church could better control the population, but for Cary, the jury was still out on this perception.

Cayce's books told him much about extra sensory perception, reincarnation, and about reaping what you sow. Cayce said you would reap line upon line, in the *exact* amount that you have sown. It was said that you could have a bad karma, that you could be reaping something that you couldn't remember, something you could have done in a previous life. He said this was a spiritual law that would not be broken. Cary decided that he was certainly reaping what he had sown, and if that was God's law, then he would accept it, but he kept praying for relief from his hurting.

His brother asked what he was reading all the time, and he told him about the Bible and the Cayce books. Lonnie said the bible was hard for him to understand, and he'd never heard of Edgar Cayce.

*And then it began*! A few weeks later, Lonnie came in one evening about 9 p.m. when Cary was washing dishes. He had a young woman with him who looked neat, attractive, and about the same age as Lonnie. One characteristic he noted about her appearance was her gypsy-looking nose. This feature reminded him of Jeanne Dixon, the psychic that had warned Jackie Kennedy about her husband going to Dallas. Lonnie introduced the two of them and said they had just met tonight, the first time ever, at a nearby restaurant and their conversation had turned to Cary after Lonnie had mentioned the books Cary was reading. Lonnie said she wanted to meet Cary and wanted to do something for him, so he brought her to the house. This sounded extraordinarily peculiar to Cary, but at this point, he was open to anything and nodded okay, but wondered at his statement . . . this young lady wanted to meet me? She wanted *to do something* for me? And *why*, just because Lonnie had told her I had been reading the bible and the Cayce books?

She seemed pleasant enough and radiated an elegant, angelic serenity about her as Cary examined her while his mind was swirling with thoughts. This attractive woman came with a stranger she had just met, came to a place she had never been to, and came to meet someone she didn't know, and *casually* mentioned she wanted *to do something* for *him*. Cary couldn't imagine the answers to his questions as he sat there with his eyes upon this young woman. She never said a word as they watched her in silence and waited for whatever she was going to do. He was mystified—he didn't know if she was going to strip or perform a belly-dance. She sat in a recliner at one end of the living room and Cary and his brother sat facing her at the other end about eight feet away. She looked about thirty, she was slim, neat, and of average weight and height. She wore a white turtle-neck sweater and a short blue skirt. The only detail Cary wouldn't forget was her gypsy-looking nose. He then watched and waited patiently with not a clue of who she was, why she was here, or what she was going to do.

Then, it *happened*, as he was looking at her and wondering what she was going to do—she proceeded to gradually *disappear . . . first her head went out and then piece by piece, section by section from head to foot, the rest of her body disappeared.* She was gone . . . completely, totally, *invisible*. It was as though someone took an eraser and back and forth . . . slowly erased her, clothes and all. She was totally gone, probably only out for seconds, and then *came back to normal the same way she had left—section by section*. It was as though a million miniscule increments were forming in each section at an incredible speed. One section was completed and then another started. Her body was put back together in less than ten seconds, Cary guessed. For some unknown reason, he was not frightened and Lonnie never moved a muscle. Cary figured he had gone through hell the past two years, and he wouldn't have been afraid of meeting the Devil himself. If he did, he thought, at least he would know the scriptures were true.

Cary tried to steal his nerves and thought to himself, I

don't know what this is . . . whatever I was expecting—it wasn't this. *He arose* and bravely *walked directly towards this . . . this being and sat down on the left arm of a couch that was located next to her right side. He leaned forward close to her and was staring at her right profile while she was still facing Lonnie. She seemed transfixed until Cary asked, "Do it again?" Her features started changing again and that's when she suddenly swung her head to Cary's, and there they were, only inches apart, staring into each other's eyes. Cary winced, but kept his composure as her face became hazy, translucent, and her face started moving about*. Her facial *features were being rearranged, but at the same time her eyes never left Cary's. Her appearance turned into a dozen different entities, from young to old, from smooth skin to wrinkles, from dark hair to white, her cheekbones moved down and then back up; her skin changed from a young woman's smooth, vibrant one to an elderly woman's that was dry, wrinkled, and colorless. Her lips changed from full ruby reds to older ones that were thin and shriveled. And just as quickly, the white hair and the wrinkles were changed back to faces of younger entities. Cary was staring right into these faces, watching them change before his eyes like a movie screen. One face would form and just as quickly be changed into another and then quickly they were gone,* taken away. *And then she disappeared all together for the second time*. Only then did he escape her eyes. He did think of reaching for her body to seek if she was still there physically, or whether she had departed, but he didn't have the nerve.

As he looked at the empty chair where she was sitting, he thought, does this have something to do with reincarnation? Were these many faces the faces of different bodies her soul once inhabited? Many people believe in reincarnation, some say the majority of the world's population does.

Then as he sat dazed in his wonderment, a *bright, white aura appeared . . . appeared above the chair where she had been sitting,* an aura reminiscent of the paintings of Jesus. For a *moment there was only the white aura at the end of Cary's living room above where she previously sat, hovering . . . like the moon. As she manifested back to normal, in irregular increments, like a puzzle being put back together quickly, the aura was situated around her head and down to her shoulders—a radiant, pure white aura, about two feet in diameter, and Cary was staring right into it.*

*And then she was back all together*, natural-looking, with the aura gone, and looking at Cary. He didn't know how much time had elapsed during these episodes . . . probably only minutes.

*"Don't ask me to do it again,"* she asked, *"because it takes too much energy."*

Cary didn't realize his mouth was open with astonishment, and his eyes were mesmerized with wonder. He wanted to tell her he understood (he was thinking of the tremendous energy he had expended while praying), but he thought that presumptuous of him. Steadying himself, he asked her a dozen questions, but she only answered a few. Cary felt she knew more than she revealed, and he sensed she just thought, maybe, he was not ready for any more. He earnestly wanted to understand and he managed to utter some questions.

"What *does* it feel like when you . . . vanish, disappear?" Cary asked.

"*It feels like illumination—like being filled with light*."

"Have you . . . have you done this many times before?"

*"Yes, I did it once while driving my car."*

Cary thought, *oh God, I can see* that now . . . other drivers looking at this car with no one behind the wheel.

"What's your name, where do you live, and are you married?" Cary asked, feeling like he was getting too personal.

*"My name is Laura and I live in River's Edge and I'm separated from my husband . . . he doesn't understand me."* Cary could understand her husband's dilemma because he couldn't comprehend her either . . . but he'd had that trouble with women before.

"Do you work, what do you do?"

*"I paint and I want to help children."* Then she was quiet, as though her mind was occupied with studying something of interest. Finally, her voice expressed the first sign of emotion and a slight smile of bemusement startled him with what she said next.

"*You are an old soul . . . your aura is of a blue color*," she said.

Cary winced and thought, old soul, what does that mean . . . previous lives . . . reincarnation . . . lived before? "What do you mean 'old soul'? Can you explain?" She simply did not answer, and after a long pause, Cary wanted to know more and finally asked. "What color is my brother's aura?"

She hesitated . . . and then said *"His is black."*

Cary was quiet trying to absorb everything that was happening. She really jolted him with her next words . . . .

"*I have come to your house several times before in the last two months. I came here, parked my car at the edge of your driveway, sat and gazed at that window there."* She raised her arm and pointed to Cary's window in the next room.

"*Why?*" Cary asked. "I've never seen you before."

*"I was pulled here by a light that emanated from that window."* Cary was overcome and speechless. *He could only think; she must have heard his prayers and had come to tell him so.*

She stood up, said goodbye, and asked Lonnie to take her

back. Cary watched her leave, and his body trembled as he tried to comprehend what had just taken place. Thoughts rambled through his mind. He later thought she left abruptly, presumably feeling he couldn't take any more. She was probably right. He had read that the mysteries of the unknown would not be revealed to a person until that person was ready to receive them. He thought later that her feelings were probably that this experience was all his mind could handle for now and with that he couldn't disagree.

And then he understood—she had heard his prayers! *Someone had heard my prayers. Prayers are heard! And she came to me in response to my prayer—to prove to me that she had heard it! She pointed to the window, said she was pulled here by a light from there. Then the white aura—that had to be from God. And to make herself invisible—twice—and at will!*

*Mother was right—it's all true. I prayed with much intensity, I guess I sent out vibrations . . . but even if there was some explanation for that, I know of no explanation for her making herself invisible—and at will. It's all true, and we are not alone. It didn't happen until I went back to the Bible and read where it said to pray with all your heart. I must have reached her after I increased my vibrations. I remember reading in the Bible that the Lord wanted our response to Him to be either hot or cold. Bring no actions of mediocrity before Him, no straddling the fence, He wants you hot or cold, wholeheartedly or not at all.* Cary smiled as the thoughts rolled through his mind. *God is passionate and he wants us to be passionate and—intense*. Cary's former reasoning had been reinforced—long ago he made the decision that he wanted to be on H*is* side—on his team.

Cary thought back over his life and considered the deeds that he had committed as the days had come and gone. How would his deeds measure up when his life was over? Not so good he thought. A reading from Edgar Cayce came to mind. Cayce was giving someone a life reading, as they were referred to. He was reviewing a person's past life and was summing up his total experiences. He was telling the man that in a previous life he had been a good person overall. Cary thought that was good until Cayce continued. He told the person that he had been good, but had never *done* anything with that goodness and thus lived a life that—was good—but *good-for-nothing*!

Cayce had reviewed several lives such as this one. He would explain their life span as though looking at a Dow Jones stock market graphic that depicted the ups and downs of various stocks. Cary could imagine him taking a pointer stick and pointing it towards the graph while explaining to them: "In this life you neither gained nor lost, your life was filled mostly with actions of mediocrity." Another one he would explain: "You came in here at a low point, having to reap transgressions committed in a previous life, but then by the end of this life, you had gained greatly." Still another time he would tell: "You came into this life at a high point, as your past deeds were rewarded, but then," directing his stick to the lowest point on the graph, "because of sins committed, you lost greatly."

Cary had never forgotten these incident and they remained in his memory. What *have* I done with my goodness, he thought, if I have any goodness? Would my life be one of lukewarm mediocrity? He abhorred the thought. He sensed an obligation, a duty to tell others what he had been shown. He felt a feeling of humbleness that the heavenly Father would visit an ordinary guy like him and reveal this phenomenal event. He felt this experience was shown to him for a reason and that reason, in his mind, was to share it with others.

He thought he would tell the world what he had experienced tonight; that prayers are heard, and they are responded to. He vowed to do something with his goodness, and when his life on earth was over, maybe he would not be regarded as having been good-for-nothing. He thought of what Emily had said, "If I can stop one heart from breaking, I shall not live in vain; if I can ease one life the aching, or cool one pain, I shall not live in vain."

He never saw the invisible lady after that day and couldn't remember her last name or even whether she gave him one. He did see her picture in the local newspaper weeks later though. It was a photo of her in the aisle of the Crater Shopping Center in Petersburg, Virginia. She was sitting beside one of her oil paintings for sale. He could only wonder: *was she an angel or an ordinary person—or both?* He cut the picture out and put it aside.

When Lonnie came back, Cary was finishing the dishes. He had never mentioned a word to Lonnie about what he had seen. Lonnie sat at the kitchen table and began reading the comics. Cary finally asked him, "Lonnie, what did you see while the girl was here?"

"Nothing," he replied. He asked him again, and without taking his nose out of the paper said, "I didn't see anything." Finally, after quizzing him for the third time, Lonnie became agitated and announced, "*The girl just disappeared twice and came back—that was all!*" He then returned his attention to the comics. Cary's felt that Lonnie couldn't comprehend what he'd seen and his mind had just blocked it off. Months later, Cary questioned him again and he likened the event to a fast turning fan that one could see right through it. That was his explanation, but it wasn't Cary's. He was glad that Lonnie had seen what he did, for now he had a witness to back his story, should he ever tell it.

Weeks passed, and Cary spent many hours contemplating the disappearing girl but didn't speak of the event to anyone, thinking no one would believe him or just think him crazy. This applied especially to Scarlett because she already had ideas along those lines.

Jim dropped by on his way back to Florida and they discussed his tax situation. They sat on the back screened porch and talked into the evening while it began raining. The two brothers had many talks concerning spiritual matters when they were younger and he knew Jim would be interested in his story.

After telling him every detail, Jim took a deep breath, pulled out a package of his ever-present cigars, handed Cary one and asked him to elaborate.

"Several things are worthy of note concerning this incident. Her disappearance was phenomenal, but several other incidents are just as powerful. I can't speak for anyone else, but I felt privileged to participate in an event that many people would covet. As far as I'm concerned I had just witnessed a prayer being heard and the prayer being answered. Responded to by whom, I don't know, but I believe the brilliant white aura was from above, and that was where I was directing my prayers. Thoughts are things and you should be careful what you ask for. What else could explain her coming to my house several times, and that she was pulled here from a light that emanated from that window—the very window where I had said my nightly prayers. That light she spoke of must have been the vibrations of the intensity of my prayers. Then what about Lonnie? He had no knowledge of seeing or knowing this woman previously. She said she had been here before so she knew where I lived, but how did she know my brother lived here also? How did she pick him as a vehicle to come inside my home? Can you imagine her meeting him at that restaurant? Supposedly an accidental meeting, knowing that he lived with me and making contact with him when neither one had met before?

I believe coincidences are not happenstance. There is a lot more going on here than we know—there is *intelligence* behind this, or *Godliness.* Another thing, Jim, you remember years ago when we were discussing spiritual matters, and you said you would give anything to see physical evidence that God, or the devil for that matter, really existed?"

"Yes, I remember," Jim replied, "and I'll tell you right now, I would have given my right arm to have seen and experienced what you did."

"Well, that's just it Jim. I remembered you wanting physical evidence and I thought that was wrong. I actually mentioned this in my prayers before this happened. I told the Almighty the world around me is evidence enough that He is real. I was just asking for relief from my hurting."

Jim just shook his head. "Cary, I believe . . . I just believe she was an angel."

"Well that's crossed my mind, too Jim, but *what* would an angel be doing sitting right flat in the center aisle of the Crater Shopping Center weeks after she was here? Sitting there and selling paintings? I've got a photo here somewhere that I cut out of the paper proving that she's still with us. It's possible that she is an angel and is living here in normal human form I suppose. I've been thinking about that a lot. I first thought maybe she was an angel and was able to manifest herself in a human body and then would have gone back to wherever angels come from. But now I'm wondering if she is just a normal person like you and me and maybe has just evolved herself to higher spiritual enlightenment or something. I did ask her some of these questions, but she would *never* answer. I've been wondering if she is an example of what all of us should be doing. I don't know the answer, but I have wondered; if there are people here who have done such a thing, why haven't they told us? Why haven't they showed us the way?"

Jim said this had given him plenty of thought, said goodbye and left. He had forgotten about his tax questions. Cary was left alone realizing that this woman had proved to him that prayers are heard. Then he thought of others who prayed. He supposed some prayed with complete faith that their prayers are not said in vain. But what of the others who had doubts. Would they give up? Would they lose their faith? Oh God, how he wished he could tell them of his experience? And how he wished they would believe him. Hoped they could understand how he had prayed for months and nothing, but when he prayed with intensity, sending out energy, vibrations—then it happened.

But *why me*, he thought, why should I receive such a response to my prayers when other people, greater than I and who have suffered more, have never received such? And then he wondered. There *must* have been other people that have had this experience, but he had never heard of any. Maybe they were afraid of ridicule? Maybe they were afraid of being different? *Why did this happen to me? Why?* There *has* to be a reason. Cayce had said that there is a response *to* every act; that line upon line, little by little, we reap what we sow. Many people have said their prayers were answered—*but like this?*

He also contemplated the words the girl said to him: "You are an old soul." He wished she had said wise old soul. I feel I must tell others about this experience, he thought, but I don't know how to go about it. Many might smirk or disbelieve. Many would be skeptical at first, but when they are alone with their innermost thoughts—they might give it consideration. Somehow, some way, I should broadcast this experience. If it only helped one person to not suffer as I, it would be worth all the ridicule I would receive and I would not have lived in vain.

Cary remained on the porch as rain fell heavily on the

roof above and cascaded to the ground just inches from his feet. He remained there late into the night, thinking back over the events that had brought him to this point. He had a traumatic divorce when he was 29 and had lost a dear wife that he loved with all his heart. Cary felt it was time for him to take a deeper introspection, and confess some personal truths. Admit it, face up to it, and get it over with. He finally admitted to himself that the divorce was caused by him. Too many hurts, too many disappointments, too many physical ailments, and, he reasoned, too much bad karma had driven him to hate himself. A fact Scarlett couldn't comprehend except maybe to label him as crazy. And wasn't it true that, because of this self-loathing, he had subconsciously pushed her away because he wanted to punish himself? Is that what he did? Is that what happened? Pushing away the thing that was most dear to him, sacrificing the greatest treasure that he had ever known . . . and for what reason . . . a psychological one combined with foolish pride and stubbornness. He now admitted the truth of what had happened and what an awful lesson to learn and what a high price to pay. A life-long heartache of suffering to bear, a life-long waste of potential, and God knows what damage he could do to those that cared about him in future years. And if he could pass on to others the one lesson he had learned, it would be this: *Go ahead you stubborn and prideful people do what I did, you will only receive a lifetime of torture and regret.*

Tears, like the rain, rolled down his cheeks and dropped to the floor. He only wished they were cleansing tears. As far as the disappearing girl was concerned, he knew there was a meaning to it, an understanding, but he would leave that up to others who were wiser than he. The incident was too much to comprehend for now. He only wished his old soul would communicate to him as to what the hell—or heaven—was going on, and who the hell was running this show anyway. Oh God, he thought, that does sound crazy. Cary didn't know but he had *drifted off to sleep.* His *heart* and *mind* seemed to be having a conversation, but it *sounded* more like an argument . . .

> His Heart was speaking, "*Holy* smokes, good *God* almighty—I'm tired! I'm exhausted—I don't think I can last much longer. Mind, *what* the hell has been going on? *What* has been your problem? Why haven't you written that book? I've had the information—it's all here just ready to be written. I'm about to explode with it—why the hell haven't you written it? Are you crazy or something? Or just *out* of your mind! Why haven't you written that book and told the people? Why have you kept this pent-up for all these years? You know you feel it—here inside of me! What were you thinking about?"

"*Just settle down,*" his Mind replied, "take it easy

before you have a heart attack! I figured we had to go slow! I had momentous decisions to make and I had to think them through carefully. *I had* to think clearly and slowly because a rash decision here could have wrecked this ship, and we'd all have regretted it later."

"Go slow? *Rash decisions*? It's only been forty years you feeble-minded dumb ass of a brain—forty years I've been *pounding* my heart out! I feel like pounding on your head! You muddle-headed psycho! You're lucky I didn't miss a beat—if I had, your boat would've been ship-wrecked!"

"Oh, shut up, Heart! I've had my problems too! And you were the cause of it all! I was trying to sort things out—but noooo . . . you *thought* you knew it all, and you don't *even* have a brain! You can't guide a ship with emotions—it takes a brain and you're nothing by a half-hearted emotional heartache, and you've only been a headache to me!"

"Yeah, Mind—you've got a problem alright—and it's all in your *head*! Big *deal,* all you had to do was think; I've had to pound my ass off night and day to keep you alive. If it hadn't been for me—you would've been dead long ago. Look at all the time you've *wasted!"*

"Not true!" his Mind said, "We've probably worked

harder and accomplished more than the average guy—and why? We've had to stay busy to keep your throbbing out of my *head*. You were the *cause* of all my problems!"

"You're *insane!*" said his Heart, "I tried to get you to go to a shrink, but you wouldn't pay me *nooo* mind. Well, I've *had* all I can take! I can't last much longer—my time is about up, and I'll be jumping ship!"

"Now hold on, you two!" A new voice bellowed. "You may not realize it—but I'm in command here!"

"Oh, my God," they both said in unison. "Who the hell are you?"

"I'm not from below—I am from above. I am the Soul of this entity . . . you two can ship wreck this boat if you want to, cut your life short; but me, I have my own problems—I will have to reap what I have sown in another life. I may have to find me another vessel, but I'll live right on after you two are dead and buried . . . but you must complete your project or there's going to be *hell to pay . . . .*"

The gentle rain had turned into a storm and booming thunder jolted Cary awake. Bolts of lighting lit up the skies and Cary's wide open eyes froze with fright. Cold wind-swept rain peppered his body and it was then he realized he'd been dreaming. He stumbled backwards into the shelter of his house as his mind tried to comprehend the magnitude of it all. He didn't understand any of the dream, least of all the forty years. Was the dream a premonition of the future?

He thought of Scarlett and her final words: I want to come back . . . don't worry—we've got time. The rage that still consumed him now is because, a few months later, she married another man without a word of clarification. And worse, months later, she still refused to respond after he had written her. After all this time, she didn't even have the decency to give him an explanation, and he had asked for so *little*. She didn't know the promise he'd made to himself, just to keep his sanity, to find the truth and make him free. They say that time heals but not in his case. It was so important to him *not* to think her values had been compromised. He hoped there was a plausible explanation for her actions, but if she wouldn't reply, there was only one conclusion he could reach. She must be withholding a terrible truth of moral betrayal that she couldn't bear to admit. She could be protecting the man she married for his involvement with a separated couple trying to reconcile, knowing what he might do.

He had always loved her for her weaknesses as much as for her virtues, and he could forgive her if she would just be forthcoming. He had no closure regarding the situation—a wound that wouldn't heal, a pain that visited him daily and never took a vacation. He knew of no other resources to turn for help, felt he was down to his last chance, and *was seeking help from the Almighty for that was all he knew to do.* He felt her response was the only answer, and if that didn't come, there seemed to be no getting out of it. He had witnessed people whose suffering had led to an early grave, and now he understood what Emily meant—a *piercing comfort it affords in passing Calvary.*

# Chapter Twenty-Two

## The battles fought within...

After the disappearing girl incident, Cary was clearly not himself. His mind was cut off temporarily from Molly, his log home and reality and the problem with Jim only added to his misery. His head was filled to overflowing and for awhile he seemed to lose his sense of direction. He felt a need to get out of the house where he had witnessed the girl disappearing. The log home wasn't finished yet, it would take another year to be completed because log homes are complex and construction on top of a mountain takes even more time than usual. While Cary was wondering what to do next, the phone rang.

"Cary, this is Mack, you remember me—I'm in City Point next door to Curt Flowers."

Cary had to think for a few minutes and then remembered who he was. "Yeah Mack, I remember giving you my phone number, is Curt okay?"

"That's why I'm calling—you'd better get over here quick," said Mack.

“Okay Mack, I’ll be right there,” he said wondering what had happened to Curt now. He drove up to the apartment building a few blocks away in the old section of town. Mack was waiting for him on a small front porch and looking disturbed. Mack was a retiree and looked about seventy. A tee shirt covered his rotund stomach, and his hair was about gone. “What’s going on?” Cary asked, walking towards him.

“It’s Curt, he came into some money, his mother died, and he received a seven thousand dollar life insurance check couple weeks ago. He’s been drinking steadily ever since and hasn’t been to work. I just thought he was grieving over his mother at first, but now I’m worried about him. I thought it best to call you like you asked, thought you might want to check on him. He’s in there now,” Mack said pointing to his room.

“Thanks for calling Mack, you did the right thing.” Curt heard Cary’s voice and opened his door for. With a swooping bow with one hand, he waved him in with the other. Curt was thin, lanky, balding, and needed a shave. He was disheveled—shirttail half in and half out of his oversized work pants held up with a too long belt.

“Heyyy, Cary, suh ’bout *time* you came to see me.” He ambled towards Cary and stumbled over a chair. “Whoaoo,” he hollered, taking several quick steps to keep from falling. He recovered and waved an envelope while stumbling towards Cary with eyes wide open. "My mother done died Cary, the only mother I had . . . she done went and died on me. But look what come in da mail today." He handed the envelope to Cary and staggered to keep his balance. Cary took the envelope and sat down realizing Curt was lit to the gills.

"Hi Curt, I'm sorry to hear about your mother."

"Yeahh . . . Dad went and died couple years ago, and now Mom is gone too. I'm all alone now, 'cept for my brother in Nebraska. All alone except for that check I got today." Cary opened the small envelope and took out a single personal check made out to Curt for $100,000 dollars. "My brother sent that to me, only the check . . . not 'nother word nor nuthin', whatcha think it's for?"

"It's probably an inheritance check Curt." Realizing his condition, Cary thought he'd better help him out. "Curt, listen, this is a lot of money and you ought to deposit it in the bank before something happens to it. You do have a checking account don't you?"

"Yeahh . . . somewheres round here," Curt said as he stumbled around towards his kitchen table looking through piles of paper. "Here it is," he announced grinning.

"Let me take you to the bank and you can deposit it, okay?"

"Yeah . . . I would 'preciate it, drive me down will you?

Don't have no driver's license you know." Curt found his jacket and stumbled out the door. They drove to the bank and walked to the bank teller. The bank clerk looked at Curt, then at the $100,000 check, and soon an officer of the bank came around and motioned them into his office. The officer reared back, smiling from ear to ear, lit in with a mile-a-minute spiel, and began his pitch about investments until he looked up and saw Curt, swaying back and forth, trying to focus his eyes on the banker. He soon realized Curt was in no condition for investment talk and listened as Cary explained that Curt only wanted to make a deposit for now. Cary took him home and asked what he was going to do about his job.

"I done quit," Curt said looking at the floor. "I'm done tired of buryin' dead people . . .  makes me sad." He was evidently adamant since he hadn't been to work in two weeks. Cary knew something had to be done, so he left him and drove out to the cemetery and found his supervisor roaming the grounds looking for Curt. Cary explained the situation. and the supervisor was furious.

The supervisor was furious. "Dammit to hell I've got a funeral coming up! What the hell am I going to do? I don't know anything about burying people!" Cary knew the Board of Directors had never handled a funeral and didn't have a clue. Death never took a holiday and waited for no one. "*Please* Cary," he went on, "can you help me? The funeral director called and wants the service tomorrow." Cary knew the supervisor was in a spot and had evidently never thought of a backup for Curt. Some supervisor! Even if he got the vault companies to dig the grave, they wouldn't know how to examine the records to find the proper burial site and wouldn't know how to find it if they did. He felt a twinge of guilt for recommending Curt and decided to help out. They talked awhile and the agreement was that Cary would live in the cemetery quarters and manage the cemetery, but only temporarily until they could find a replacement for Curt.

Cary took the information from the supervisor, checked the records, found the site, and was on the backhoe digging the grave twenty minutes later. It was not exactly a job for a millionaire, Cary thought, but it did keep his mind occupied, and for that he was grateful. At least for awhile, it not only took his mind off *Scarlett,* but also *Darlene* . . . and *Molly* . . . and *Jim*, and he hoped that was *all,* for a man can only take so much he thought as he furiously rammed the backhoe bucket deep into the concrete-like red clay of Virginia.

After the funeral the next day, Cary drove back to his house in Hopewell and rounded up his belongings.

"Hey, brother," Lonnie said coming to meet him at the door smiling, "I got my job back yesterday."

"That's good news," Cary said. He explained the situation

concerning Curt and told him he was moving to the cemetery. "So you'll now have this house all to yourself, and I'll be at the cemetery if you need me. I'm gonna try and find a house for Curt and have him pay cash for it, before he blows all that money."

"You're going back to work at the cemetery? Damn, I thought you and Jim had sold an invention and didn't have to work no more."

"You've been *talking* to Jim again?" Cary glared at him. Lonnie knew Jim had told him to keep his mouth shut, and he looked at Cary without saying anything further. Lonnie was sorry he had blurted that out and wanted to end the conversation and change the subject.

"The old Johnson house there," Lonnie said, pointing across the street, "it's up for sale." Cary knew the last couple that had lived there and knew they had taken good care of the house before Mr. Johnson shot and killed his wife the year before and was sent to prison. Cary took his few possessions and settled into the house at the cemetery, then drove to Curt's apartment and spent some time with him and convinced him to purchase the house. They negotiated with the real estate Agent, and two days later the papers were drawn up and Curt paid cash for the place.

Cary went to the house the next day and looked it over, and sure enough the story Bob, the funeral director, had told him was true. Bullet holes were still in the bedroom walls, and he thought it best to repair them before Curt moved in. He spent three days replacing the sheet rock, installed the trim, and repainted the room. Knowing Curt, the murder could have discouraged him from buying the house. He then made sure Curt had paid his back rent, then helped him get his utilities turned on, and then helped him settle in. Over the next few days Cary tried to reason with Curt concerning his finances and his drinking. He tried to convince him to invest his money wisely and told him he could live off the interest if he was careful with his investment.

Curt put his beer down and glared at Cary. His beer-drinking alternative personality took over. "I told you once, and I'll tell you again Cary—money don't mean *nothin'* to me." "'Member I told you it wouldn't change me a bit." When he was sober, Curt would talk sensibly and Cary could reason with him, but when he was drinking, that old know-it-all German came out, and he seemed like another person. Curt's feelings were that he didn't need help from anybody and he was smart enough to take care of his own affairs. "*Just let me be*," he cried with pleading eyes . . . *I just wants to live the way I wants to live*!" Cary finally conceded that he may have a point, and who was he to interfere with how Curt wanted to live his life, good or bad, so he decided he shouldn't be the one to play God in his decisions. Maybe it was time to cut out anyhow lest some people would think he was after his money. Curt did call one more time telling him he had received another check and would he take him to the bank again. They drove to the bank and he deposited $75,000 more from his mom's estate. Curt's inheritance now totaled a grand sum of $182,000—enough for him to live on for the rest of his life if he were careful. That worried Cary, but he thought he'd done all he could. Cary shook his hand, told him to take care of himself, and left.

Cary would go by Curt's house often when he went to see Lonnie. In the following weeks Cary noticed he had acquired many new friends. He would see rough looking men and women over there drinking beer on the porch listening to blaring music coming from the house. The foot tall grass was rarely mowed, and when it was, the one mowing usually had a beer in one hand while trying to push the mower with the other. A few weeks later he stopped and chatted with Lonnie. They sat on the front porch across from Curt's house.

"Your buddy there," Lonnie said laughing, "has an ongoing party—he even invited me over the other night."

"Oh yeah?" Cary said, "Tell me about it."

"Well, I just went there one time and that was enough for me. Those guys and girls must all be on welfare or unemployment because they rarely work. Cars are constantly coming and going and people running in at all hours. One tattooed girl was laughing as she told me she'd get twenty bucks from Curt to buy some beer, and he'd never ask for the change back, said she could almost live off that change. The neighbors are starting to complain because it seems their loud partying never stops. I haven't been back since."

"You best stay away from that crowd," said Cary. "Drugs could be involved too, you know." A few weeks later Cary learned that Curt had bought the house next door and thought he was being smart with his money. The next time he drove by he noticed some of those same friends were living there, probably rent-free.

Today he had just pulled up to see Lonnie when he heard screams coming from Curt's house. It sounded like Curt's voice so he ran towards his front door. Someone came running out, leaving the front door open and that's when Cary saw a drunken, bloody Curt lying on the floor. A huge man was beating him to a pulp and then a girl, with tears streaming, threw herself on Curt pleading with the man to stop. He never forget the woman's forlorn look as she raised her scraggly head and screamed through missing teeth, *"Stop, stop! He ain't much . . .* but he's all *I got!*" The attacker fled brushing past Cary, nearly knocking him down. Cary left the place, and the next day he called Curt's brother in Nebraska and relayed all his fears. His brother asked for his phone number and address and said he would get in touch with him. The last time Cary rode by Curt's house, weeks later, he saw an extension line running from Curt's house to the one he had purchased next door.

The next day Cary was back working at the cemetery and had just finished another interment when he noticed a young woman walking in his direction. He recognized her—she had been meandering around the cemetery the last several days looking at grave markers. She was walking straight towards him and he realized what an attractive girl she was. He guessed she was in her mid twenties, trim with medium height, light brunette hair frosted with strands of blonde. Her body tipped about an eight on Cary's scale while his eyes observed those long legs as they brought her closer. Another habit he knew he should overcome.

"Hi," she said to Cary with a pretty smile that matched the rest of her.

"Hi yourself," he answered. "Looking for somebody special?"

"No, my special-one is buried back home." She put out her hand and said, "My name is Jennie." Cary shook her hand and introduced himself as she continued. "I'm visiting next door, and I've enjoyed walking around your cemetery. Hope you don't mind—just wanted to tell you so you wouldn't think I was out stealing flowers."

"Just don't take those fresh red roses over there," Cary

pointed to the recent gravesite, "because I save them for my girlfriend. Course that's confidential," he added.

"Well, I'm sorry this job doesn't pay you enough to buy your own flowers," she said giving Cary a suspicious look. Cary didn't think his humor was going over well, so he changed his tactic.

"I'm sorry you've lost a special one. You're awfully young . . . how special was he?"

"We were about to be married . . . but he got himself killed in an automobile crash last year."

"Damn, I'm sorry to hear that," said Cary seriously. You must be suffering something terrible."

"Well, it's over he's dead and buried and there is nothing I can do about it but pull myself together and go on with my life. That's what he would have wanted." Cary thought, damn, is it really all that easy . . . wonder why I can't do that?

"Really?" said Cary. "You really feel that way?"

She looked down and quietly said, "Well . . . that's what he told me . . . he said to me, 'Jennie, if anything ever happens to me, just say a prayer for me and don't waste your life grieving over me.' "He said his troubles would be over, but I still had to live, and that's where the real problems were."

"Well, at least you have closure," Cary said. He thought about the accident and was careful with his words. "Was he alone when he wrecked and was it late at night?"

"Yes, and nobody else was involved, he ran into a telephone pole on Interstate 95."

"That's a straight divided four lane highway, isn't it?"

"Yes, it is."

"Well, if the weather wasn't bad, and he didn't have a blowout or something, what caused the accident?"

Giving Cary a quizzical look she said, "Did you hear about it?" Cary shook his head no. "Well, that's what I'd like to know—what happened? The policeman said he had no possible explanation. There were no skid marks or nothing, and they just had no idea why he wrecked."

"Late at night, huh, you reckon he could have gone to sleep?" asked Cary.

"No, it was not really late, just around midnight and he wasn't drinking, if that's what you're thinking." She looked down, brushed aside some grass with her foot, "I just could never figure out what happened, and the police couldn't either." Cary kept quiet and just shook his head.

"I'm staying next door with my uncle and aunt," she offered as she swung her purse back and forth in front of her.

They chatted for awhile and finally Cary got around to asking her out.

"Well, what about your girl?" she asked.

"You mean the one I give flowers too?"

"Yeah, you're not going steady are you?"

"No, we're not doing anything—she found out where those red roses came from."

"I see . . . well, I can understand that," she said without smiling. They started dating steadily for several weeks—he gave her flowers, but only from the florist, and they really hit it off.

But Cary's mind was still on Molly, and he wondered what she was doing. He called her but there was no answer, he left a message, but she never responded. He wrote her a letter and still there was nothing. He was afraid he'd lost her and only *God knows why*, he then did something that made him think maybe Scarlett was right about his mental condition.

After three months of dating, he and Jennie were married, and she moved right in with him at the cemetery house. He told Jennie about his desire for a Christmas present and thought she was kidding when she agreed. Nine months and fifteen days later, she gave him a dark-haired, nine-pound baby boy—the son he thought would never come but had always wanted. He loved the child with all his heart and gave him reason to carry on. Hope had returned.

He never forgot the evening when Jennie brought the baby home from the hospital on Christmas Eve. The baby was nestled down in a basket. "Here's the Christmas present I promised you," she said, and with a flourish slid the basket across the vinyl floor and it came to a stop right beneath the Christmas tree. The baby's eyes popped open in wonderment at the colorful ornaments sparkling just above his head. The biggest smile in years spread across Cary's face, and for a moment, the baby and he were dazed in happiness.

Another year passed as he doted on his son that he named Barton. He had someone to love and to love him back. It was so unreal that is was not until later that he understood that *another prayer* had been answered.

He had told Jennie about the disappearing girl incident, told her how he had prayed to God to send him a nine pound, dark-haired baby boy. His son was born perfectly, nine pounds, one ounce and had black hair when he was born. After a little over a year, Jennie seemed to change overnight, and out of the blue she told Cary she was leaving him. She gathered her things and went out the front door. She then opened the door and without coming in, paused and spoke to Cary.

"I'm leaving you now, I don't think I love you anymore Cary . . . you know . . . it's too bad you *didn't pray for a wife* when you were *praying for your son,* maybe if you had . . . *I wouldn't be leaving*. You know," she paused and thought, "you know . . . I have the distinct feeling I only came along for the lone purpose of giving you a son!" When she questioned Cary regarding the custody of the child, his glare was enough for her to realize he would never part with him. She closed the door and left. Cary thought to himself, I didn't pray for a wife because I didn't want another *one* and she will *only* get the child over my dead body. His baby was the *only* thing he had left to live for. Cary took custody of his son and raised him by himself. A few months later Jennie filed for divorce, never knowing she was divorcing a millionaire.

It was over a year since Cary had tried to contact Molly. He decided to try again—he couldn't help himself, so he dialed her number late one night. He had no idea what to expect; he hoped it wasn't a husband that would answer the phone. Molly answered the phone, and to his surprise, she did talk with him. They had a friendly conversation, but he didn't have the heart to tell her he had married and had a son. Molly profusely apologized for not returning his phone calls and letter and sincerely said she would explain it later, but couldn't elaborate at the moment. Cary didn't know whether to be relieved or perplexed about the situation. Evidently Molly also had some problems she was not ready to divulge. He hoped she had not married another as he had. They agreed to be patient with each other with an understanding they would talk again in the not-to-distance future.

Regardless of whatever events had taken place in each of their lives since they had last met, they both made it clear to each that they were still interested in staying in contact. Cary hung up the phone with a sigh and mumbled a prayer of thankfulness.

One night a few weeks after Jennie had left, Cary had put his son to bed and was up watching Perry Mason. As he did many times he was reading a book at the same time. This gave him something to do during commercials and he went back and forth depending on what was more interesting. A habit he acquired awhile back. Tonight the book was more interesting; a fascinating, supposedly true story that included spiritual and psychic events. The story about the life of Uri Geller.

It was then that Cary had the second most unusual experience of his life. He was about half way into this book when it became so disturbingly unreal to him that he was having trouble believing it. He decided to go back, look inside the front cover to see who the author was and read what credentials he had, to find out if he was on the level or some kind of a kook. It was almost midnight and dead quiet as he sat alone in his house in the middle of the cemetery. At the very instant he turned the pages back and read about the author, he heard the same words said by Perry Mason. He was awestruck as his eyes looked at words in the book and simultaneously he heard the same words on TV. As he looked at the TV screen there was the author's name on a glass door. It seemed Perry Mason had the same questions concerning the author, whether he was on the level or not.

Cary put the book aside and watched the rest of the Mason show. Part of the story was about the credibility of this author and Perry Mason and his partner were opening a door and entered the office of this author. And there was the author—in the movie—in *person.* Cary was mesmerized by the synchronism. He wondered if this strange occurrence had connections with the disappearing girl. He received his answer about the author—he *was* credible and who was better in determining that than Perry Mason himself? Cary realized he was having more and more of these coincidences and remembered reading that they may have some spiritual connotations. He had also read there are no coincidences and wondered . . . were they spiritual interventions? And were these unworldly coincidences shown to him for a reason?

A few week later the cemetery owners came to Cary and said they hadn't found a man to replace him and asked whether he would consider staying if they increased his salary. Cary declined and told them he had a solution. "I'll solve your problem," he said and only paused a moment. "I'll purchase the cemetery and give you one hundred and fifty thousand for the place in cash. My offer is good for one week, or I'm leaving." The board members called an emergency meeting, and discussed his offer. Their first topic was not whether they would sell but where in the world did this uneducated farmer's son come up with that amount of money? The money was more than the cemetery was worth and it was too much to turn down, so they accepted his offer. Cary quickly sold the cemetery, for $175,000; to a local minister he knew who had been anxious for the acquisition.

Two weeks later he and his son were heading for the mountains with their possessions in back of their new Dodge pick-up truck and quickly settled into their mountain home that was finally completed. Cary asked around for a babysitter and soon found one with good references. He hired Heidi and made arrangements for her to live in the adjoining guest house. After a few months, Barton and Heidi became acclimated to each other and Cary came and went knowing his son was in good hands. It was then, late one evening, he got a phone call regarding Jim.

"Cary, my name is Brandon Baxter from Florida. You don't know me, but Jim has worked for me here at the lumber yard for years. He's talked so much about you that I felt comfortable calling you. Have you heard from him?"

"No, I haven't—is anything wrong?"

"Well, I was afraid of that . . . that's the reason I'm calling. I was hoping he'd come to see you. He up and quit working for me a few months ago, and I haven't seen him since. I mailed his last check to him and it came back. I rode out to his place and it looked abandoned. The sheriff said somebody had torn the place up and Jim was no where to be found. Thought you should know, all his buddies haven't seen him either, they don't have a clue."

"Thanks, Brandon for calling. I don't know anything either . . . I haven't heard from Jim, but I'll check into it." Cary hung up the phone, fixed an instant cup of coffee and while watching the evening news, wondered what the hell was going on. It was then Cary almost spilled his coffee when he heard:

> "Gas prices are up again but we may have some good news; a local newspaper in Dixie County, Florida has reported from an anonymous source that a local man has sold an invention to the oil companies that will triple the gas mileage on our family cars." She smiled sweetly and said, "Now wouldn't that be great—*if* it were true, though it came from a reliable source, there's absolutely no verification of the story. In other news . . .

Cary turned the TV off and started walking the floor mumbling. "Reliable source, anonymous tip, no verification—bull. It's *going* to hit the fan now! He's going to get us killed." While he was steaming, the phone rang and he would bet ten to one who it was.

"Cary Williams, this is Thompson."

"I just heard it on the news," said Cary

"*What* are you going to do about it?"

"I've disclosed nothing. I can't control my brother."

"You can't help us?

"There's nothing I can do."

"Nothing *you* can do? If he's disclosed the *amount* of the sale—he's a dead man!" Thompson slammed the phone down.

Maybe Jim had nothing to lose, but now Cary had a son to think about—then there was Molly. He phoned Jim, wondering why Thompson was so particularly upset about the amount of the sale. He then remembered what Thompson had said about the ten million he had planned to give them, but that he'd only given them eight. Hmm . . . he wondered if Thompson had collected ten million from the oil companies but only gave them eight, pocketing the other two million for his greedy self. Jim didn't answer the phone. He hung up and the phone rang again. "It's *me* again, Thompson. Listen to me very carefully, Cary. *You* don't realize who you are messing with. We don't play games. My back is against the wall—my life is on the line."

"It's about the two million isn't it?" Cary asked.

"Well . . . there's no need beating around the bush now—the answer is *yes*! I've got to give the two million back or I'm a dead man. Let's cut to the chase—here's the bottom line. Jim may not have anything to lose, but the oil guys know *you* do—they know because I told them so. They know what you care about—*namely* your son Barton and your friend Molly. Unless they get the two million back, you'll find them both dead and your house on the mountain top blown to bits."

"Why don't you just give them the two million back?" Cary asked trying to stay calm.

"It's *too late* for that—that money is gone. I had gambling problems . . . that's another story—but it's *gone*. Listen to me good Cary Williams, your brother Jim has spilled the beans—it's all over the news. As soon as they fine out I only gave you eight million instead of ten, I'll be wiped out. Take my phone number, think it over, you've got one hour—call me back." Cary sunk into his couch, and though he couldn't understand the rationale of Thompson's thinking, he didn't doubt *one word* of his crazy intentions. Desperate men with money were not people you wanted coming after your loved ones. If this had happened before Barton was born and before he had met Molly . . . well he might have taken his chances but *now* . . . Cary dialed his number.

"Thompson here."

I can't contact Jim, sources say he disappeared days ago and his house has been ransacked. I don't know where he is, I can't get a million from him if I can't find him . . ."

"Damn it! I can't wait. I have to have the two million tomorrow. Don't you understand, the oil guys are already after him and they'll be after me if I don't hand over the two million—like tomorrow. I can save myself by telling them I saved two million dollars of their money just before our deal was made, but I'll have to turn the money over to them pronto. Listen—don't you understand? *They're mad as hell* by now hearing Jim has spilled the beans. They'll kill me if I don't give the two million back and they'll very well be after you. If you can't get any money from Jim, you best give me the two million out of your pocket"

"I don't *have* two million in cash! The IRS took almost half and I paid a million and a half from my mountain house. I don't have two million . . ."

"Isn't your house worth two million?"

"I suppose it is."

"Tell you what I'll do, sign the deed of your house over to me and I'll give it to the oil boys and explain to them you have nothing left to give them. Then they won't bother you anymore, long as you keep your mouth shut about the whole situation."

Cary thought about it while Thompson waited, he thought about his son and Molly and there was no hesitation. "I'll have the deed ready tomorrow, but I'm going to need a place to stay, so I'm keeping the cabin in the valley with the twenty acres."

"It's a deal," said Thompson, "I'll have a courier pick it up tomorrow. You can continue living there until we sell the house."

"Okay," Cary said and hung up. The next morning he drove to his lawyer's office in Lexington and officially changed the deed, leaving him with the twenty acres and the cabin. The lawyer wanted more time but Cary, with money in hand, persuaded him to do it immediately citing dire circumstances he didn't explain. He came home, instructed Heidi to give the package to the man coming tomorrow and told her he had to go away for a week or so and she agreed to take care of Barton.

He left for Florida immediately, only stopping several times trying to phone his brother and warn him, but there was no answer. Finally reaching Suwannee County ten hours later, he drove towards his brother's home but pulled over when he saw Jim's driveway packed with vehicles. He was wary and turned down a side road and then took a short cut that he and Jim once took while fishing. He parked his truck a football field away from the back of the mobile home. The brush was thick and he was able to get within hearing distance of the people there. There were several white media vans and several people standing in front of Jim's trailer. They held microphones in their hands and TV crews were aiming their cameras towards them with the trailer in the background. There were so many Cary realized they had to be from out of town and wondered what had brought them here. He heard bits and pieces of what they were saying. "Alleged man . . . Outrageous stories . . . Selling invention . . .

Oil Companies . . . Hiding out . . . Disturbed? . . . Paranoid." Cary listened for a good while and thought it odd they seemed to be repeating themselves. He left and spent the day hanging out at Jim's old haunts in the local town of Cross City, a small populated town close to the Gulf, and ten miles from Jim's mobile home. He had lunch at McDonald's and later grabbed coffee and a burger at Hardees. No one knew him and he was able to sit within hearing distance of the locals. The comments were repeat performances of what he'd heard from the media crews. He stayed at a local motel and early the next morning he was back at Hardees ordering his coffee. A group of men were gathered around a man with a morning paper spread across his table. They were talking, pointing to the paper, and laughing. He bought the small local paper, took his coffee and sat at a nearby table. An unusual, distorted, wild-looking picture of Jim was on the front page with a heading underneath:

"WHERE IS WILD-EYED JIM?"

> Rumors are flying that Jim Williams has sold a high mileage invention to the oil companies for eight million dollars, but all the oil companies are denying this claim and said there are no records substantiating this. A spokesman for the oil companies, who asked to remain anonymous, explained they've heard these claims in the past and they were always unconfirmed rumors coming from disturbed persons. The spokesman says it happens all the time and this guy probably needs professional help. Mr. Williams can't be located for

> comment. Local residents are worried as to why Jim has so suddenly disappeared.

Cary heard a roaring engine and glanced outside, but could only see a blur of a car flying past the restaurant. An excited man rushed in and hollered, "Hey guys—that looked like Jim's car!" With the door open, Cary could hear the engine revving, escalating, screaming, and whining as if it was about to burst. He knew it was Jim's car. It was then another car flew past, a big dark sedan and then police cars with sirens blaring went chasing after the cars. All the locals rushed out, scrambled into their cars and took off, following the sirens. Cary ambled out and decided to follow too. He looked back at Hardee's and thought of Jim. It was here that they had met every morning when he had visited him. They had drunk coffee, read the paper, discussed world affairs, kidded the waitresses, and debated as to who had the fastest car. He wondered why Jim wasn't here as these mornings were very special to him. He was always here each morning at daybreak, it was almost a tradition. Something had to be wrong. He slowly followed the procession until the scene in front of him caused him to pull over. He walked towards the flashing lights and past the patrolmen directing traffic. There were Jim's buddies huddled in a circle. They were stone silent as Cary made his way between them and viewed the scene. There was Jim's sixty-one Ford wrapped high around a telephone pole,

Jim was crushed between the two. He was dead. The dark sedan was nowhere to be seen.

The policeman was scratching his head, "The weather was clear, the pavement was dry, it was a straight divided highway, no tires had blown, no sign of alcohol, the traffic was light . . . he was alone, there's absolutely no reason for this to happen, there's just no explanation . . ."

"I knew he was crazy," said the auto mechanic with the John Deere hat, "all that talk about selling some great invention for millions of dollars . . . he was crazy after all."

"Yeah," another said, "always pretending to be something he was not, always bragging about his great invention that was gonna make him rich beyond his dreams."

The car was wedged high on the pole and the wrecker had arrived and was backing towards Jim's car to pull it down. The wrecker attached his winch to the rear bumper of the car and slowly pulled to dislodge it. All of a sudden the trunk lid fell open and a ton of money exploded out and fluttered down around the men's feet. A dozen mouths popped open as the men slowly took in the amount of money that drifted to the ground. They were speechless and no one moved as the wrecker stopped. The bills were in high denominations and it was easily many thousands of dollars scattered around the men's feet. The men glanced at one another with open mouths and finally one of them respectfully muttered. "Maybe . . . *maybe* old Jim wasn't so crazy after all."

*"I'll be damn,"* several mumbled.

Two days later Cary was back at the O'Brien cemetery as they lowered Jim's casket beside his sister. He knew it was where he wanted to be buried. Many of his buddies were not there; some said they were back at Hardee's, wildly debating where the remainder of the cash might be. Cary left the cemetery and was browsing around Jim's mobile home when the sheriff pulled up. "Mr. Williams, I've brought the contents found in your brother's car. Sorry, it took so long; but with this much money involved, I had to make a report." He took a box from the rear seat of his cruiser and placed it on the tailgate of Cary's truck.

Cary thought of what he said and asked, "Did you make an official record of the amount of money that was in the car?"

"Yeah . . . it's stated in the county records; the count we got was one hundred and fifty-two thousand dollars. It's a procedure we have to do when the amount of cash found is over ten thousand dollars. You know, because of drugs, it's a federal regulation." Cary nodded in understanding. "You'll be hearing from the fed's; they'll want to know where that money came from. Knowing old Jim," he said grinning, "my guess is the money came from marijuana sales, course his buddies around town are saying it came from him selling that high mileage engine invention everyone's talking about. But I think that's just talk—you know anything 'bout that?"

"No, I don't see Jim much, I'm from Virginia . . ."

"Yeah . . . that's what I heard, well, you may want to count that money before you sign this receipt. Take your time," he added. Cary looked at the items; there was Jim's Most Valuable Player award plaque and the game ball he had been given in high school. There was a crumpled up page that appeared ripped from some book. It was the poem *IF* by Rudyard Kipling. He unraveled the old stained paper and could decipher bits and pieces of the words: "If you can keep your head when all about you are losing theirs and blaming it on you." Another read: "Make one heap of all your winnings, and risk it on one turn of pitch and toss." The bank bags held cash, mostly in large denominations and Cary quickly counted it. He didn't question the amount; he figured he was lucky to get this much after the good ole boys had handled it. There was the $152 thousand, but there was no four million and he said nothing. Cary remembered Jim telling him that if anything happened to him, he would leave instructions where anything of value could be found. He knew then that Jim had stashed the balance of the money somewhere and he was sure it could be found. Cary stashed it all in the cab of his pick up and signed the receipt for the sheriff before he drove away. Cary's thoughts were on his son and Molly as he headed back to Virginia. He had found no way to help his brother.

Cary returned to his mountain home two days later and found Barton and Heidi okay and Thompson's courier had picked up the package. Cary wandered around his mountain home while considering his circumstances. Gone was his money, gone was his mountain home . . . it hurt but it meant nothing in comparison to having his son and Molly safe from harm. He explained to Heidi and his son, without going into details, that they would be moving to the cabin below sometime in the coming months. Barton grinned with anticipation but Heidi glanced at Cary with a worried look, but said nothing.

Cary spent the next weeks alone readying the cabin for occupation although it would be some time before he moved. He was tired, jaded and needed rest but he found comfort idling around the cabin environs. Sure it bothered him that he had lost his fortune that seemed so important before, but now, maybe because it wasn't his hard work, but Jim's that deserved the money, it's didn't tear at his insides. Somehow it was not nearly as hurtful as losing his company years ago. He attached a hammock to the front porch and flopped thereon with only a six pack of beer and a pack of cigarettes for companionship. He missed Molly something terrible but the love of his son sustained him The never-ending sound of the Maury River waterfalls soothed him as he listened to the ever falling water cascading over thousands of rocks, mixed with the cooing of the doves, soon lulled him into a deep asleep.

After the 'disappearing girl' incident, Cary was now more intent than ever on seeking answers concerning the spiritual world and became more interested in the works of Edgar Cayce. Cayce was a well known psychic from Virginia Beach who had a phenomenal gift. He was able to put himself into a trance-like state and then questions of any nature could be asked of him. The answers he gave were unknown to him until he awakened and they were read back to him by his secretary and later played back from a tape recorder.

When in this state and questioned as to where this information came from, he said it was from the Akashic Records from where all knowledge resides. Questions were put to him while in this state and he gave answers. His answers, in almost all cases, proved to be accurate.

At first most of the questions were medical ones. One example was a reading, as they were referred to, for a man suffering from back problems. The answers that came from his reading were that the man suffered an injury when he was four years old and had run his tricycle into a concrete step and injured his back. Cayce dictated in medical terms exactly how and where the injury affected him and what medical procedure was necessary to correct it. Everyone was amazed that he not only diagnosed the ailment of the man and what to do about it, but also what age he was and what he'd done to cause the injury. After the reading, Cayce told the man to take the reading to a medical doctor and go from there. The doctor read the readings, put the man through x-rays, determined the readings were correct and operated successfully. The doctors were amazed and this scenario was repeated many times in the coming years. It was so successful and the word spread so rapidly that Cayce was soon in much demand. He then moved his office and opened his own hospital in a large three-story building overlooking the Atlantic Ocean in Virginia Beach. His 'readings' and hospital were soon organized as the *Association for Research and Enlightenment*, better known as the A.R.E. Eventually other readings were addressed concerning other problems, including psychological ones.

In one case, Cayce diagnosed a man with a problem he identified as his karma. When asked the meaning of that, the recording from his tape recorder said it was a condition of reaping what one has sown, in this case, from conditions relating to a previous life. He said it is a spiritual law and gave information as to how one could live this life to overcome misdeeds he had committed in a previous life. Well, when Cayce came out of his trance and heard what he had said, he was dumbfounded and perplexed. He had not believed in reincarnation.

He made a statement that if any information came from him while in trance that he felt was false and was not helpful to people; he would quit doing this work altogether. He felt reincarnation was not taught in the Bible, and because he was a devout Christian and Sunday school teacher, he became perplexed. Then, in further readings, he asked for more understanding whether reincarnation was on the level or not. Finally, he must have come to the conclusion that this information was not false, was not hurting anybody, so he continued giving his 'readings'.

As Cary delved deeper into the Cayce readings, he came across details to start a group that the A.R.E. Foundation called, "A Search for God." This entailed two books that included spiritual truths for study groups to meditate upon, study and seek spiritual understanding. Cary followed their instructions and put an ad in the local mountain paper that simply said, "Edgar Cayce Study Group Forming." He was amazed at the response that came from people from around the Charlottesville to Lexington area. These people were desperately seeking understanding and help as he was. Many were like Cary, they had read the Bible and many other spiritual books including Cayce's and were still seeking further understanding. Cary received many phone calls from divergent people who were desperately seeking answers for various questions. Many of these persons related their own phenomenal, spiritual and psychic experiences and many said they had never divulged these incidences to anyone because of their fear of castigation. It was heartwarming to Cary to realize he was not alone and wondered at the significance of it. Though the stories told to him were unique, none were anything like the disappearing girl incident.

The first Saturday night of this meeting was held in his great room and so many people came that the room was almost overrun. They came from miles away, from all walks of life, and found their way to his mountain-top home. There were the young and the elderly, people with divergent educational backgrounds with various levels of achievement in their careers and many were of various social standings. One young attractive blonde was a reporter for a local radio station, others were retired, a few were disabled and many were just ordinary working people.

One lady came in pushing her paralyzed husband in a wheelchair and just shrugged her shoulders when she spoke to Cary. "He just had to come." She told him later that her husband had shot himself in an attempted suicide. Now, after surviving from a close call with death, he came across a book of Cayce's and his interest came alive when he felt maybe he had lived previous lives and still a life to come. Reading Cayce," she said, "has made the afterlife so real to him that now he's found a purpose in living."

Through experiencing the lives of these many people Cary learned something notable of worth. He felt he had come to the same conclusion concerning life as many of these people had. They all were hurting, some physically, some emotionally and some psychologically. Their beings had been terribly damaged in one way or the other and they all were seeking information as how to carry on with the situation they had found themselves in. The Cayce books told them they had lived previously and possibly would have future lives to come. More importantly Cayce told them the problems they were currently experiencing were all caused *by themselves*. He clearly stated that the *present condition you find yourself in was caused only by yourself.* For those who didn't understand the problems they had found themselves in during this lifetime, Cayce told them they may be reaping in this lifetime in exact proportion of misdeeds they may have committed in a previous life. They noted this was not different from the words of Jesus except that he didn't mention reincarnation. Many people have come to the conclusion that they must spend the rest of this lifetime atoning for the past and building a better foundation for whatever life would come next. This made Cary think of the People's Advocacy Group.

An example of one of Cayce's 'lifetime readings' for one of his patients is the following. The person was seeking to understand why he was having emotional problems of various degrees. One of his problems was concerning the cleft lip he was born with; a deformity he said had ruined his life. Cayce told him his problem was a karmic one. He was suffering from misdeeds committed in a previous life. He told him this could only be remedied by living a life so as to atone for his past mistakes.

"Why didn't Cayce give a more detailed answer as to what caused his cleft lip problem?" the blonde girl asked.

"I don't know in this case," said Cary, "but I remember a case where he did mention the details concerning a physical karma. This came about as he told a lady something that she didn't directly ask about. He said it as an afterthought to the answer he gave her concerning another matter. He told her in her past life she was a nurse and was working in a private home for a wealthy elderly man who was bedridden. She used her hands as she lovingly cleaned and bathed him for many months. This man thanked her with his foul language and verbally rebuked her with his demeaning and disparaging remarks. He treated her unmercifully but she continued without a word to care tenderly for him. Cayce then told her that is why in this life her hands were so beautiful; so beautiful in fact, that her hands were now in great demand for modeling for TV commercials." Cary looked at the attractive blonde whose mouth was now open with awe and said, "You may have done similar things in your past life."

The blonde closed her mouth, smiled and asked. "You mean to tell me that I and others—all of us," she swung her arm around the room, "are you saying that our actual physical looks could be the result of past deeds we may have committed in a past life that we can't even remember?"

"Reincarnation is a hot topic amongst many people," said Cary. "My feeling is similar to Cayce's; he was a Sunday school teacher, he didn't believe in reincarnation when his readings first mentioned it. He was very upset and said if he ever thought that his readings were not true, if they didn't follow the Bible, well, he said he would give it up altogether. But he continued having his secretary ask him questions concerning reincarnation while he was in trance and he must have been satisfied that reincarnation was a fact because he did continue this work. Where does the truth lie? I'm no authority on the subject . . . maybe that's why we're all here, we are all seeking answers. For me, it does answer a lot of questions, like, I never understood why some children were born deformed, and have cancer at an early age and many other physical defects. Some say the Bible reads that the sins of the fathers will be visited unto their children. But that doesn't seem fair; it makes more sense what Cayce said; that some laws are immutable and one of these is that you will reap exactly, line by line, what you have sown. He said there was no getting out of it. He said the exact circumstances you find yourself in today are the exact result of your own actions. For instance maybe some of these deformed children had committed vicious sins of murder in a previous life. That makes more sense to me." He turned to the blonde. "And maybe it works just the opposite too—the girl with the beautiful hands in this life had them as the result of her actions in a previous life."

After this group had settled down, they looked to Cary who had organized this meeting. Here was Cary, an introverted personality who was terrified to speak in front of a group of people. His damaged being struggled to cope and his inborn competitiveness had pushed him this far into this situation.

He was nervous and trembling but calmed himself and reached deep inside for strength. He said a silent prayer for help and brought forward courage to speak from guts alone. He relaxed himself and spoke slowly and clearly. He survived with barely a show of his discomfort. Cary realized, with God's help, he *had overcome* another giant obstacle; he had overcome his fear of addressing a group of strangers. Another prayer answered, another goal achieved, another giant obstacle overcome to reach normalcy, he thought. As he thought back he was fascinated at how events had pushed him to achieve this goal. He trembled at the beauty of it and instinctively knew he would not have a future problem with it.

This study group lasted for months and when it dwindled down, he organized a second one and the group began studying Book Two of The Search for God series. He again addressed the group of strangers successfully.

There was one man who joined the group and studied with them for several months. He was a Texan, just transferred from a civil service job in Texas to one here in Virginia. He was a likeable fellow named Van and he and Cary became friends. A few months later he brought up a lady friend, Anna, from Texas and they were married in Cary's living room. He told many stories, mostly relating to Texas. He said everything in Texas will either 'bite you, stick you, or sting you.' He was an intelligent fellow who had an airplane pilot's license and took Cary flying several times. He had two more years of work to receive his full pension.

One day he grinned and said, "You know, my job is tough, my supervisor disrupts my naps several times a week."

"Well, I can understand that," Cary said without cracking a smile, "a man named Thoreau had an answer for people with problems such as yours. He once said, after much meditation, 'He had come to the conclusion that *most men lived lives of quiet desperation.*' Van laughed so hard that he had to hold his jiggling stomach.

"Cary," he spoke between gasps of breath, "you do have a way with words."

Van had been attending a Christian Scientists group in Texas; a group he understood was relating the Bible to science. He said he had questions concerning that group when he came across a book about Cayce. He had had a tough childhood and told of many fist-fights when someone had challenged his manhood because of his small stature. He said being small in Texas was not a good thing.

Several times he described what seemed to haunt him the most. It was an automobile accident that claimed his nineteen-year old son many years ago. He said he couldn't get over it, it was his only son and it bothered him to this day. After lengthy conversations it was apparent Van was evidently holding a guilt trip concerning the accident. He later invited Cary to his house where he was drinking whiskey and began to tell him again of the incident. His discourse became maudlin as he repeated the incident many times. He kept coming to the meetings and kept seeking answers. Cary marveled at this man, a tough Texan who was consciously attempting to overcome deep personal problems and trying to find his way in his own search for God. Weeks later at a social gathering, his glass became filled more with whiskey and less with coke. He called Cary once and asked him to bring a fifth of whiskey. Cary couldn't do it, wouldn't do it and turned him down. Later, his wife said she could take no more, left him and returned to Texas.

Sometime later Cary found him dead at his home, surrounded by bottles of booze. The place looked like a war zone and Cary could only think that Van had lost his battle. A tremendous invisible battle fought within that was just as deadly as being on the front lines of war. He had good thoughts of this tough Texan, a man that wouldn't back down from a fight, regardless of the odds. Van was a man who sought after God openly and paid no attention to snide remarks made by his friends. He stood for what he thought was right and if push came to shove, he would fight you for those rights too. Van had his faults, as many men do, but Cary loved his courage as he fought his last silent battle and for that, maybe one day, he'll get credit from that 'big guy in the sky' as he would have said. Cary felt helpless and saddened that he had found no way to save his friend.

Cary helped with his funeral arrangements and following his service at the cemetery where he once worked, he wandered around the grounds looking at markers of many of the deceased he had known. As he wandered about many thoughts came to mind. The true heroes, the real martyrs in this world, are not the ones you hear about on TV, or read about in your local papers, but rather your everyday working men and women. These were his heroes, the men and women who go to work every day and come home to their families every night. They lovingly take care of their own, watch over them, worry about them today and their future tomorrow, not for one day, but everyday and every night. They never miss work even when they are sick and should be in bed. They march onward and consistently pay those bills. These people are steady, they sacrifice as many do while working at the local factories, working inside a maze of chemical conditions that some believe could be killing them. Not in one heroic moment do they act, but in many various ways they apply their devotion silently, day in and day out. Cary's hat was off to them, these men and the women, the real heroes that go unnoticed and ask for no applause.

One incident Cary never forgot happened at the end of one of their weekly meetings. They ended every meeting with each member saying a prayer out loud. Cary's baby son, Barton, had been put to bed upstairs before the meetings began and it was thought that he was fast asleep in his bedroom situated directly above the meeting room.

One night as the group was starting their ending prayers, down the stairs came his son, participating for the first time and with no invitation. He was in his pajamas and without a word from him or the group, sat himself down in a vacant chair and joined them at their round table. Cary's first impulse was to send him back to bed, but he didn't say a word and the others followed Cary's lead. The group continued saying their prayers out loud individually; taking turns from right to left, paying no attention to Bart. He sat quietly and when it was his turn to say a prayer, he put his hands together, closed his eyes and in broken words, said his nightly bedtime prayer his dad had taught him. His father walked to him, gently took his hand and led him back to bed, softly telling him he had done good. He tucked him in and kissed him on the nose, their nightly ritual that meant it was dreamtime.

The group was open-mouthed and speechless and wondered at the scene that such a small child could be able to do such a thing. It was almost surreal and they couldn't help but only imagine what influence their previous meetings must have had upon the child. Had the baby been listening unawares to any of the group? They couldn't help but think; shall we be led by children?

# Chapter Twenty-Three

## "And the truth shall set you free..."

Winter had come and gone and the first days of spring were cool but the morning sun warmed Cary as he sat on his terrace drinking his coffee. He thought of his depression that incrementally rose and fell in varying degrees, he was doing everything in his power, including prayer, to make it disappear but sometimes he felt only the intervention of some divine force could really extinguish it. He felt he had overcome some psychological problems but, it was wearisome because, physically, he had never found help for his ulcer that was flaring up once again. The ulcer had been diagnosed right after his divorce, but the doctors said there was no known cure. He decided to try for help again and spent days at the Lexington library searching the medical journals for any new cure for the problem. While researching, he did discover that the same people, who started the pharmaceutical business, were the same people who developed the first medical schools. It took no genius to figure why nothing was taught about the prevention of disease.

No drugs could be sold to healthy people and Grandmas old remedies had now been outlawed by Congress with help from the pharmaceutical lobbyists. Dare we say bribed, no, they made that legal too. He remembered a few times that doctors had made the statement, "I was not taught that in medical school."

Finally, to his excitement, he came across an article telling of a doctor in Charlottesville that had *found, amazingly, a cure for ulcers*. Two days later, appointment in hand, he began his drive to this doctor. Just before he left, a curious thing happened; or as he thought later, another coincidence. He checked the mail and opened a package; it appeared like just another advertisement for some type of entrepreneurial venture as many he had received before because of his previous business. Most of these he just tossed and started to trash it but then realized there was a tape inside. The name of the title was *Dead Doctors Don't Lie* so; since he was going to see a doctor and it was a long drive, the title intrigued him and he shoved it in his tape player. The information was fascinating and he played it a second time. The tape was by a veterinarian doctor who was previously a farmer who raised cattle. It was a fascinating, mind-boggling true story the vet had experienced while treating his own animals on his farm and later, as a vet, treating others and performing autopsies on them. After becoming a licensed physician his final conclusion was this: Physicians have no incentive to cure their patients because healthy patients don't seek them out and there is no income to be made. Only unhealthy patients would seek them out and bring their money. Farmers take care of their cattle and prevent disease for only healthy cattle can be sold at a profit. *And there it was, this animal doctor revealed the cure for his ulcer condition! Simply put, Pepto-Bismol and a shot of anti-biotic would cure his ulcer.* Cary couldn't believe it! An animal doctor had found a cure for a human condition that the physicians could not. *Oh, to be an animal he thought! Is a human not worth as much as an animal?* Evidently not to some physicians; maybe he should have gone to a veterinarian! Maybe all physicians should be required to have farms and cattle before they practice on humans. He was elated about the cure but angered to learn of such nonsense about the physicians. This enlightenment didn't cause Cary to lump all physicians in this category but it gave him much to conjecture. At the doctor's office, the physician confirmed this was indeed, the cure. In the coming weeks Cary received the treatment and in a few months the years of suffering had stopped. The ulcer had been cured. Another unusual coincidence Cary thought, or was it?

As Cary began feeling better, it caused him to reflect upon his breakup with Scarlett. He finally was able to put together the causes of his irrational behavior and understand his wife's reactions at the time of their separation. He now realized his ulcer was the pivotal point that pushed him over the line; to cause him to say and act in ways that was not himself. The never ceasing debilitating pain emanating from his stomach had finally brought him down. When his ulcer flared, his sleep was fitful, there was no rejuvenating rest, he would become irritable and after a trying day at work, his patience was exhausted and he would spout off hurtful words to his wife. To her, the pain of the ulcer wasn't visible; he was a young, tan, strong, healthy looking young man. To her, there was no seemingly excuse for his behavior. The final blow, evidently, in his wife's conclusion, was the psychiatrist's fatal prognosis that he could be wavering on the brink of schizophrenia. Later, he had realized the wrong he had wrought, but the damage could not be undone.

Cary's thoughts went back to Molly; he couldn't get her off his mind. With a deep sigh, he picked the phone up; he knew it was time to contact her and tell her about his marriage and introduce her to his son. He could only hope that she would see him, could only wish that she was still unattached. His anticipation of seeing her was almost nonexistent. He really couldn't comprehend that this beauty hadn't been snatched up by somebody. Why would she be waiting for me, he wondered? The only hope was the amicable phone conversation they had when he had called her right after Jennie had left over a year ago.

Nervously, he finally summoned up the nerve to dial her number and waited with a dire foreboding for the answer to his fate. She answered the phone and they exchanged small talk and she finally agreed, though reluctantly, to come to his mountain home. He hung up the phone with a great sigh of relief. From their conversations, both received the impression that the other had experienced some sort of turmoil in their life and both sensed the other actually wanted to meet. They made plans for Cary to pick her up at the Roanoke Airport two days later. Cary explained to Heidi that he had a guest coming and asked her to keep Barton at her adjoining house until he notified her otherwise.

Two days later he drove towards the Roanoke Airport. It was a warm spring, but overcast day, and he was to meet Molly in the early evening.

He was getting nervous and his mind was swirling with worried thoughts. It had been so long since he had seen her that he was thankful to God when she agreed to come. How would she react to my story of getting married? How would she react to the birth of my son? Would she listen to me? Would she believe me? At least I'm divorced now, but how could she trust me anymore? Is this going to be a repeat of the other loves I've lost? When, oh when Lord, will it end? Cary said a silent prayer and asked for help; help that he would not hurt another woman who had cared for him. He waited at the terminal in his white Chevy, waited and tried to control his trembling. He had the top down on his beloved car which he had recently restored. He saw her exiting from the terminal so he drove his car to the pick-up area and stopped in front of this Spanish-looking princess. God, he thought, she was as beautiful as ever.

She walked to his convertible and dropped her bag on the back seat and entered the door Cary had opened. She spoke first, "You're the first free ride that showed up, so I'll take it," she said barely smiling. She then looked at him with a mind that was brimming with questions. She was not sure she should be here.

It was the first of May and spring had sprung in the mountains, dogwood trees with while petals were just flowering amongst a backdrop of greenery. As they slowly left the city, Molly was enjoying the scenery, but she wasn't smiling as her fingers nervously tapped the top of her door and turned to Cary. "The last time I was here it was autumn and now its spring. Wonder what season it'll be next time—*if* any."

"Well," Cary replied noticing her discontentment, "you'll still have to see the winter when snow is deep on the ground."

"And all the leaves will be gone, what's pretty about that?"

"Oh, winter has its own beauty, for instance, with the leaves gone you then can see all the mountains that are now hidden by the leaves. It's a complete change in scenery; another whole new look."

"You've got an answer for everything, haven't you?"

"No, not by a long shot, wish I did."

She turned to him, laid her arm on top of the car seat and brought her knees up on her seat. "Well, I hope you have *lots of answers*... because I've got plenty of questions."

"I kinda expected that and I've got a boat-load of explanations for you."

"Really?" she asked.

"Yes."

"Like what?"

He glanced at her, "I'll tell you right off… there are significant reasons why I've been so distant with you over the last year and I will explain each and every one."

"It's been *two years* Cary!" She corrected him as she turned her head to hide her tears.

"I *have* explanations and I'm going to tell you every detail," Cary said wincing.

"If you don't to my satisfaction, I'll be leaving early!"

"Let's get to the house and I'll lay out my soul for you."

"I can't wait." She said. They drove in silence until Cary spoke.

"Molly… Jim is dead."

"Oh no! What happened?"

*What happened?* Cary thought to himself and answered her as his eyes stared at the road ahead. "It was a car accident, he was alone, the policemen said they had no idea, said there was no cause for it...."

"I'm so sorry Cary, my God that's awful."

"At least to know the worst is sweet," said Cary

Molly glanced at him, opened her mouth but didn't speak. They drove in silence the rest of the way in deference to Jim's passing.

They soon reached his home and Cary made drinks for both of them. Molly's mind returned to her anger, "Gotta have a drink, huh? It's that bad?" They walked unto his terrace now arranged with granite benches and potted plants that were filled with blooming flowers that were looking for rain. They were both too nervous to sit.

"It's only bad if you don't believe or understand what I'm going to tell you," he said. She glanced at him with a menacing look and could barely withhold her emotions that were boiling over. She would give him another minute or he was in for an onslaught.

She gave him a look of exasperation and said, "It'd *better* be good, and soon!" Cary was pacing the terrace trying to think when she said, "Keep thinking Cary, I've got a few more minutes to waste." She was getting irritated, thinking he was stalling. She took a swig of her drink and crossed her arms and waited for him to speak as a light rain began falling.

"I just . . . I don't know where to start," he said.

"I can help you!" she said.

"That's okay too," he answered.

She turned on him with hands on her hips. "Cary, you can start at the beginning, I knew *damn well* something was eating you ever since that night at the James River Club when we were discussing the one billion dollars we were going to give you. It was like your mind was on a deeper problem—you can start there!"

"Okay, okay—it was my first wife! We were divorced in sixty-seven and I haven't gotten over it!"

"Well—*finally!* Go on . . . tell it all!"

Cary told her everything—the bewilderment of losing his business, his wife asking him to seek help from a psychiatrist and then filing for a divorce with out a word.

"You mean the two of you never discussed your relationship anymore?"

"No . . . never did. I never got an answer why she said she was coming back, said we had time but then was married to another five months later."

"That was *it!*"

"You would have to understand the circumstances. The

last time I saw her I was picking up her insane cat at her apartment and was taking it to Hopewell with me. Then the doctor threw me in the hospital with what he called a staph infection. They didn't know what caused it but it was located on my arm where the crazy cat scratched me when I tried to remove her from under my car seat. I guess I was delirious for awhile and when I got well—I was thrown into a tax business that I was not prepared for. I was seeing tax clients all day, picking up their taxes and spending half the night researching information on how to file them. Tax season is one hell of a mess; it's *frantic, so much* to do—and such a short time to do it. I mean I had hourly appointments all day until seven at night and you can only imagine me, a complete stranger to Dad's clients, trying to prepare their taxes when I barely knew what I was doing. Going to strangers homes who despised paying their taxes anyhow was no fun. But I clung to the hope of what Scarlett had said, 'Don't worry, we've got time' and I prayed she meant what she'd said. I knew she was okay, she had a job, a place to live and would be okay until I could get straightened out. Anyhow, the first thing I knew she was married."

"Wow," Molly said, "she must have fallen in love at first sight."

"Yeah, she married a divorced guy with children, a ready-made family. He even threatened me by having Scarlett tell my sister that he would come after me with his Masonic Group of which he was some esteemed worshipful master. The egotistical, lucky bastard will never know how close he's come . . . I've had him in my sights more than once.

"I can't get over how desperate she was to get a husband, any husband. I guess all her chases had come up empty and she had to settle for this guy. She certainly wasn't too particular about whom she married and that's very evident by the sad sack she ended up with. I guess he's still pinching himself trying to figure out how he ended up with this prize. Little does he know he had nothing to do with it, he just happened to be in the right place at the right time for a desperate, vulnerable woman. After much soul searching, the truth finally dawned on me and it was awfully hard to comprehend. But the truth was simply that she betrayed our trust. She out and out lied to me, and worse than that, she deceived me and still can't admit to it."

Molly listened and her anger diminished as she was at long last receiving some answers of her own. "Well, I knew something was wrong with you . . . just couldn't figure out what. Your story is tragic but this isn't the only reason you've avoided me, for this long, is it? There *must* be more to your story."

"Yes, a *great* deal more" Cary said glancing to the heavens with a hopeful prayer for her understanding. He guided Molly to a cushioned chair under the protection of the ivy covered lattice as the soft rain continued to fall and the wind swirled about them. "Make yourself comfortable because the rest of the story will take a while. What I'm going to tell you next is the honest to goodness truth. But, I must warn you . . . it's a far-out story and I've worried every time I've thought of telling you this. I will tell it to you in detail and every iota of it is the God-so-help-me-truth. This event took place in my house in Hopewell, the same house where we first discussed the invention. It happened just months after you were there and I had told you about selling the invention. I have never taken drugs and I wasn't drinking." Molly looked at him with a creeping trepidation as though it was going to get worse.

"*Good God Cary*!" She said as she squirmed in her seat, leaned forward and clasped her hands tightly together. "You make it *sound* like it's something from *out of this* world!"

"*It is*—that's *just the point!"*

"*Oh my God...what...are you serious*? Molly said almost coming out of her seat; she touched her forehead and made a sign of the cross.

"I'm deadly serious and the reason it's so important is because what happened here . . . " Cary looked down trying to find the right words, "what happened here . . . will explain why I've been so distance from you the last couple of years. Following the events I just mentioned, I was in terrible shape; I was hurting and I couldn't shake my depression. I had so much pent up rage that I was about to explode. Hell, one night I went out just trying to find someone to fight with . . . probably lucky I didn't."

Cary went on and told Molly the whole scenario in detail of what had transpired between him and the disappearing girl. Told her how she made herself invisible and at will. Told her of the many faces she manifested, described the details of their conversation and mentioned the prayer for his son. It was some time before he finished and finally paused to catch his breath.

Molly's eyes scanned the heavens for understanding. "I suppose Lonnie could verify the story?" she said matter-of-factly, not knowing what else to say.

"Sure, you can ask him today and he would tell you the same."

"*Now* to the *hard* part," Cary said as he braced himself for her next reaction . . .

"*Oh Lord... what could be harder than that*?" she cried.

"A few months later, I *married* another girl--"

*"Married!"* She screamed as tears exploded.

"And nine months later she gave me a baby boy!"

*Molly was jolted and fell back on her chair as if hit by a knock-out punch.* She was speechless trying to understand everything she was hearing and her hands squeezed tight on the sides of her chair as if bracing for another onslaught. Through tears her eyes were glaring straight at him and her mind was swirling as she valiantly attempted to respond. Finally she uttered the words in a squeaky voice, "*And the baby . . . is this the one,. the one you had been . . . praying for?"*

He sighed with relief that she had caught the connection. "Yes, he's the one." Cary continued and told her about his wife leaving him a year later. Told here of Jennie's words, 'Cary, you should of prayed for a wife to go with your son… if you had, maybe I wouldn't be leaving. Perhaps in the future, you *should* be careful what you pray for.' Molly was now up and pacing in the rain, laughing and crying as tears and rain flooded down her cheeks. She flung her arms upward in a hopeless gesture as though she couldn't take any more. "*Oh. . . . my God,*" she moaned as she turned to him, "you *can't* be lying. . . c*ould* you? You *couldn't* be making this up . . . you're not *playing* with me?"

"No," Cary said quietly trying to assure her. Molly was trembling as Cary slowly came to her and gently handed her a napkin for her tears and then guided her inside the house as the rain fell in torrents.

"But what about your *mental* state?" she asked as they entered his great room. "This whole story sounds *crazy* to me. Are *you sure* you're not mentally disturbed? Are you sure you got over your condition—how did the shrink describe you—a paranoid schizophrenic?"

"Well, he said I was on the verge, I don't know if I'm normal or not; the shrink couldn't help me."

"*Why*?" She said, "didn't you ever go back to see him?"

"I couldn't—he shot himself in the head at age thirty-nine."

"*Oh, Christ*," she moaned again. Molly was down again, but recovered slowly and finally responded.

"I have to believe you . . . well, *I want to believe you* and now—you're divorced?"

"Yes."

"*Damn...* that's good to know," she said wiping her face with a tissue that Cary handed her, "that I'm not up here with a married man." Then, seemingly knowing the answer she said, "And I . . . I suppose she took the baby?"

"No," he replied.

"*No*?" she said weakly, not understanding. She looked up with bleary eyes; her mouth was open and finally the words came. "*No*?" She said unbelievingly, "Well, if she doesn't have him . . . *where is he*?" Cary walked to the kitchen phone and buzzed Heidi. A few minutes later his son, Barton, nearly two and a half years old and wet from rain, walked in the front door and ran and hugged his daddy with open arms. Molly was dazed and stepped back with wonderment at the little fellow.

"Molly, this is Barton, my son, Barton, this is my friend Molly." Molly retreated again from the little child and looked down at him. She brought both hands to her chest and managed a bewildered smile for the little boy. She saw a replica of Cary with a mop of black hair and eyelashes. Barton said 'Hi' and ran to the next room and plopped down in front of the TV, oblivious to the emotional goings on behind him.

"He . . . he's . . . a spitting image of you," she said. "Oh, hell, I—I need a drink!" Cary left and returned with two brandies and led her to the couch by the fireplace. She turned to him, locked her eyes on his and managed to speak in a choked voice, "I've *never* . . . I've *never* heard of such a story in my life! If I *find* that you're lying, I'll . . . I'll *never see you again*!" Cary waited silently. "But, for some reason, I believe you," she said, wiping her eyes, "I can't comprehend you bringing me up here to tell such a lie. What have other people thought of you after hearing your story?"

"I don't really care; the few people I've told, well, I have no idea of their comprehension, but on the other hand, no one has ever accused me of lying. They might have thought I was nuts, but it all happened just as I told you, every detail. I'm not afraid to tell the truth."

"But, *how* . . . how does this leave . . . you and me?" she asked.

"An *honest start,* a *clean* start . . . I hope?" he said with trepidation covering his face.

"You know," she said, "with *your* problems . . . most women wouldn't walk away from you—they'd *run*!"

"I know very well."

"Why do you say that?'

"Experience," he said. She sipped her drink and looked away. She understood what he was saying.

"You've lost others for the same reason haven't you?"

"Yes."

"Why will it be different this time . . . between you and me?"

"There's the difference," he said pointing to his son. "It will be different mainly because of him. I now have someone, something . . . to live for." Cary looked away in thought, "I can't run away now, I can't give up, I have an obligation, an obligation that I cherish. Before the disappearing girl incident I was . . . I was just floundering, working, struggling to get by day by day. I was dead inside, but that event changed me. So many aspects of what happened gave me a sense of purpose, a reason and the courage to continue on with hopes for the future. A prayer was said; ask and you shall receive, and a prayer was answered." Cary looked at Molly and saw a forlorn, helpless-looking being. He reached out and pulled her close to him and wrapped his arms around her, smiled and spoke. "I'm sorry I had to put you through all this, but it was important; I had to explain my actions the last two years." Molly could only nod and finally was able to speak.

"So Cary, what's your condition now, I guess you didn't hurt anybody?"

"I would never harm anybody on purpose with revenge, but when my honor is at stake; that's another matter. I'm no coward. Anyhow, the rage still burns and I'm trying to deal with it." The emotion of the moment had overtaken Cary and Molly looked at him in wonder at what she saw. He was trembling as she softly came to him and realized his eyes were overflowing with tears. She said not a word and gently embraced him, hoping to quell the shaking. Minutes passed and nothing was said until his quaking subsided and the tears had ceased. She waited in silence until he spoke, "I feel a revelation has come over me. It's hard to explain."

"I'd like to hear it if you can tell it."

"Well, you know over the years I have wondered why; why I have hurt and why I have suffered so *long*. What is the purpose? What is the *reason*? I thought surely it would have eased long ago. I think maybe I have figured it out."

"Figured out what?"

"Years ago, right before I had my car accident, I prayed to

God that if I had to keep living with this pain, this suffering, this depression, this never ceasing throbbing within, *please give me a purpose to live for*. If I was forced to live this way, at least I could *find a purpose*; a reason to make my life worthwhile; I didn't want to live my life in vain, life is too precious to waste. Then the car accident happened . . . *God knows why* I wasn't killed. After viewing how bad my mangled car was damaged and realizing I didn't have a scratch, I fell to my knees and thought of others who could find no way out; no way to cease their suffering and relented to suicide. It was then, I thanked God for my life and I made Him a promise . . . promised I would dedicate the rest of my life trying to help others such as myself. People who, outwardly seem to be fine, but inwardly, they suffer an unrelenting pain. I know I'm not much . . . I know I can't change the world . . . but I thought . . . if I could only help one person . . . it would be a good thing. After I died, I didn't want my life to read as Cayce had said of some, 'You may have been good… but *good for nothing*.'"

"So now, do you think you know what your purpose is?"

"I have a feeling that I must write a book and tell the world of my experience, but I'm afraid people won't believe me. I'm afraid they'll just think I'm another oddball and I *may just* do it all for nothing. But, I know I *must* tell of this, *for I know it's true. It's* been *proven* to me."

"But Cary," Molly said, "you just said if it only helped one person . . . it would be worth it."

"I did say that didn't I . . . kind of like being *crucified, isn't it*?" Molly was speechless; she just stared at him . . . not knowing what to say.

Cary began shaking again as tears filled his eyes and he sighed in great relief. His face then exploded with the brightest, most joyous smile Molly had ever seen. Molly watched him with apprehension, not knowing what else to expect as he turned to her with excitement. "Molly, it's just dawned on me!"

"What?"

"Pieces of the puzzle are coming together."

"What puzzle?"

"Some of the answers the churches have been seeking for eons. You remember in the New Testament as Jesus was walking on water? Then later He died, disappeared from the tomb and then reappeared. He told us that what He *could do, we could do also*. That's similar to what the girl did. She said it took much energy to become invisible. The two months I prayed before this—I prayed with much energy too, I evidently sent out vibrations and then the girl came to me."

Molly had never seen Cary so elated, joyous as though he had just recognized a pearl of great price. He was overwhelmed and Molly led him to the couch where he calmed himself as he continued. “What a revelation! What a message to relay to the millions who pray every day! To reinforce their belief that prayers are not said in vain! To help those that have doubts about their prayers; my message is to prove to them that prayers are meaningful, they are real and they are heard.” Cary then tried to smile and with a broken laugh said, “And evidently my soul is going to make me suffer until I make known to the entire world the truth that was shown to me.”

“Well Cary,” Molly smiled, “I think it’s time, time to write the book, reveal the truth... and maybe, just maybe, the truth *will* set you free.” They sat alone quietly and nothing was said as they stared out the window watching the rain as the last bit of light faded into darkness. Molly finally spoke, “But, realistically Cary, you may write the book, but how will you get the book *to* the people. It’s not that easy, you know, after all, you are not a writer and know nothing of publishing, promotion and advertising.”

Cary was undaunted; he turned to Molly with eyes twinkling and an even brighter smile. “Molly, I’ve got to tell you something. It’s something of significant importance and I hope I can explain it to you. There is a S*ecret*; *a secret so profound that applying it could dramatically change a person’s life. There is the Law of Attraction. Like begets like, visualize it and it will materialize. Think it so... and it will be. Ask and you will receive.*

*Anticipate the event and it will happen. Believe it's coming and it will arrive*." Molly looked at Cary and wondered at his words, but didn't understand. "You will see," he said, "I'll write the book, plant the seed and word of mouth will make it grow. Time will tell, you will see."

Molly looked at Cary and wondered of his sanity but was intrigued by all he was saying. "Tell me more," she said, "please try to explain what you are saying."

"It's complicated, but it's simple. I'll try to make it as clear as I can. There's no copyright on this information, it was first revealed in the New Testament and I finally understood it after reading my Mother's note, 'seek and ye shall find.' Then later that was reaffirmed in the book of Matthew where it said 'Whatsoever ye shall ask in prayer, believing, ye shall receive.' Then again in Mark it read, '*What things soever ye desire, when ye pray, believe that ye receive them, and ye shall have them*. Then after the Bible, the Cayce readings told me the same thing, Cayce said, '*Thoughts are things*' and another writer, over a hundred years ago said, 'Every thought of yours is a *real* thing—a force.' I believe that was Thoreau's thinking when he said 'if a person endeavors to live the life that he has *imagined*, he will meet with a *success* unexpected in common hours. If you have built castles in the air, your work *need not be lost*; that is *where they should be.*'"

"Molly, thoughts are real, they have frequency, the thoughts you send out will return to you in like kind. Thoughts move faster than light, did you know that? Think good thoughts and good will happen; expect the worst and it will come. Many people have dubbed this phenomenon the Secret because they have known about it and have proved to themselves that it worked, and yet, it is not widely known amongst the general public. There are many others in history that believed the same as I'm telling you. Plato, Newton, Shakespeare, Beethoven, Lincoln, Edison, Emerson and Einstein all believed the same thing. This Secret is *real* and its mind boggling what it can achieve. It can bring health, happiness and it can even bring wealth. Many of the wealthiest people believe in it. Why do you think two per- cent of the population earns over 90 percent of all the money that is earned? You want money, ask for it, you want a new car, ask for it, you want to be a success in your chosen field, ask for it, believe it is coming and it will appear."

"That's all fine and good *and* complicated, but how do you make these things work?"

"Well, maybe someday a person will describe these things in a book, make it simple and explain it in detail. I'll just tell you what I did. I couldn't believe all of these transformations could happen to me either, but what the hell, I thought, what did I have to lose?" Cary was grinning, "*Having nothing to lose* can have its benefits can it not? I began applying the rules as I understood them. I began seeking, I began asking for things, I prayed for a son and a son materialized. That's when I knew, hell—I didn't *even* have a wife at the time! I now understand the statement someone said. 'I know that I know that I know.' You've heard it said that you should be careful what you pray for? I prayed for a son and he materialized. I didn't pray for a wife and Jennie left me. You remember what she told me, she said, '*I have a distinct feeling I only came to you for the lone purpose of giving you a child. Now you have the child and I'm leaving.*'"

"You actually believe that I could understand and do what you are saying?" Molly asked.

"I'm just an average guy Molly… an everyday Joe, if I can do these things, anybody can."

"But all of these people out here that are *hurting* . . . living a heartbreak *every day*, do you think *they* could apply these rules and heal their pain? And *why* haven't you been able to overcome your own suffering?" Molly asked.

"I haven't cured my problem yet . . . this thinking is relatively new to me, but I think there is a way out for all of us, as for me, well, I haven't mastered this thing yet, but, I'm making progress. I've come to the conclusion that I'm saddled with the same problem that many people have. Many have known this secret, but knowing it and applying it are two different things.

You know *what*?" Cary brightened as if something had just dawned on him, "Now that I think back about it . . . I really think I did apply the Secret back then."

"Back when," Molly asked.

"Right before the disappearing girl came to me . . . I prayed nightly for two months asking God to ease my pain."

"But, Cary you're *still* suffering . . . what happened?"

"Things happened . . .  incidents took place, I just wasn't listening. I wasn't following my intuition and I'm afraid I didn't maintain an element that was essential . . . I had doubts . . .  I'm afraid I didn't really believe."

"What incidents took place?"

"Well for instance, just weeks later, I had a powerful dream that left me with an overwhelming feeling to write a book and reveal to the world this phenomenal event. That *must* have been the answer to my prayer along with the disappearing girl coming to me. It's though my dream was telling me if I wrote the book that somehow, that would bring me closure."

Molly was quiet as she was trying to comprehend all he was saying. "Well, you may be on to something, I don't know, but, I believe you really feel what you are saying can be done because . . . because I've *never* seen you so confident."

Cary was still smiling, "I really think a transformation is coming over me, I think I've figured out what I was doing wrong."

"But I don't understand…"

"You don't have to—that's the good part, you only have to apply the rules I'm telling you, apply the rules and have patience. One must have patience, that's probably why the Bible describes patience as the highest virtue. That's what I started doing."

He gently pushed Molly back to see her face and realized she was dazed. He felt this was enough for now and thought he should change the subject as he didn't want her to think him unstable with such talk. "Now that I've laid my soul bare to you, maybe you have some things to tell me?" She drew back and gave him a startled look as though he'd entered her sacred sanctuary.

"Like what?"

"My intuition tells me you have some demons in your background too. It's 'baring-our-souls' day, maybe it's time to lay out yours," he said.

"I don't know if I'm up to it right now... I don't know if I have the strength. I don't know if the day can stand anymore revelations! I don't think there are enough tears left. I think we've had enough for today, let's think about it tomorrow."

The two were drained and exhausted and went to their separate rooms for the night and both waited for another day.

The next day they slowly arose to a beautiful spring morning. The rain had stopped, the sun was out and the smell of fresh rain lingered in the air. After breakfast, Molly was looking at the peak of Cary's mountaintop.

"Cary, can you to take me to the highest peak on your mountain?"

"Yes I can, I've already been there, made a path up there right after I selected the house site, been there many times myself."

"Did you find yourself closer to God?" She asked.

"I don't know about that but I had that in mind when I made the trail up there. Come on, we can walk there and you can see for yourself. It only takes about half an hour." It was a fairly steep walk and Molly followed behind Cary. They trudged their way upward between and around huge rocks that jutted out from the mountainside. They finally reached the peak and found themselves on solid rock. Molly viewed the valley's far below.

"Oh Lord, what a *view*! Wow, we are high! *Cary* . . . this is special."

"I like it here myself, it was worth the climb, wasn't it?"

"Oh yes, oh my . . . I believe if I stayed here long enough . . . it *would* seem closer to God."

"I read somewhere," said Cary, "that a person, I think it was Shirley McClaine, said she went to the top of a mountain and prayed for three special things to happen in her lifetime. Years later she said all three things came to pass."

"Cary," she asked, "why do you think I have some demons in my past?"

"Because you are twenty-seven, a beautiful girl, a special girl, and yet you were not attached to anyone. I figured there *had* to be a reason."

"You were not attached to anyone either," she said. "That's why I knew something was eating at you."

"Yeah, but I'm not a beautiful girl," he said.

"Oh you'll do in a pinch; I haven't noticed any deformities yet, course I've never gotten beyond those eyes." She took a deep breath and said, "Okay, I feel good here, I feel ready to tell you of my past if you're ready to hear it. But I warn you, it's not pretty and it may take awhile. And yes, you might say, I've had some problems."

"Will your story be as rough as mine?"

"You'll be *surprised*; I guess my past has some similarities to yours and will also explain why I haven't contacted you either the last couple of years. My story also includes 'a way out' incident and I'm not crazy either so grab your hat and hold on."

"Take your time, it's early; we've got all day."

"It will take awhile because it'll have to come between

sobs," she said. "I can barely think about it without crying, much less talk about it. Don't worry if you think I'm having a breakdown . . . just don't let me fall off the mountain. You know . . . I've never told my story, my past, to anyone before, but . . . I feel okay telling it to you, I guess because I feel you know what suffering is too." Cary smiled back at her but now waited and was consumed with apprehensions of his own as she began her story. "My first experience with disaster was when my father died when I was seventeen. Daddy was just fifty-two and it came as a shock. My mother and he were so close; I wondered how she would survive without him. I later quit school, got a job and eventually received my GED. My daddy was everything to me and I was his little girl and his pride and joy. He was always showing me off when I was little and I loved him dearly. I'll never forget that awful night when the news came of his death. I *was mad* because he left me and *I beat my fist against the door until my mother dragged me away.* There were so many memories... I remember once when he let me drive his car which was a white Ford convertible. I had just got my learner's permit and we were driving down the highway, following my boyfriend in his car. I remember Daddy as usually being quiet and easy going and he always walked with his back straight and proud. I was surprised when Daddy told me to 'floor it and pass him, you've got more power than he does.' I did and he was right. I still get tickled when I remember my boyfriend's bewildered look when he saw his girl and her dad passing him by.

By this time I had met this boy who lived down the road apiece. He was really my first love and I thought he would be my last and we were happy and contented. He felt he was going to be drafted so he joined the Navy instead. Soon he was sent to Vietnam and I continued working *hard.* We planned on getting married after he came home. He came home okay and had begun working in construction at the local plant. We were saving our money and planning our marriage when he . . . he got killed . . . in an accident at work. He was taking another's place when it happened. That was the kind of guy he was, always willing to help someone else. I forget why he did it; it was the most dangerous part of their job. I never was sure of the details of what happened, but he fell a long way down inside this huge tank of some sort. I still can't view TV with a scene of someone falling.

Anyhow, after that I was devastated and lived in a daze for quite awhile. He was my true love and I felt guilty that we had waited to get married.

One year went by and I married a man who worked at the same place I did. I was hoping to have a normal life, like the people around me, and make him a good wife. It wasn't long before I caught him running around on me and I divorced him. I just couldn't live in a marriage like that. After this I just remember being kind of numb. I put it behind me, what else could I do?

I then returned home, took care of my mom, or, well, I guess we took care of each other. I continued working and eventually met a man who seemed really okay. He was kind and gentle and his name was Thomas. We had a good marriage for two years or so until I realized that something was slowly happening to him. One day he was involved in a one-car accident. A few months later he had another one that still only involved him and his car. It was on a straight road, the weather was good and the police could find no reason for the accident. They didn't know but I did; it was an accident on purpose."

Cary remembered the scene on TV in the motel room at the James River Club when they were beginning to negotiate the sale of the invention. Now it dawned on him why she reacted the way she did. "That's what upset you in the motel room isn't it? You remember that evening when I walked in and just got a glimpse of someone going off a cliff on the TV screen and you turned away with a terrified look on your face?"

"Yes, I still can't bear to watch something like that, especially if it involves suicide. Anyhow, he wasn't badly hurt but it was apparent something was going on and he finally told me. 'Molly, the voices are telling me I *have* to kill myself.'"

"What voices?" I asked him. 'Voices inside my head,

they are real and I've come close to killing myself already.' He said, 'You must leave me for your own good; I don't want anything to happen to you. I don't want these voices getting to you, and don't think they can't; I'm really scared for you.'

I wouldn't dare think of leaving him, he was my husband and I vowed to stay beside him come hell or high water and help him overcome this thing. Little did I know until later, this 'thing' was more than I could handle. Later I came home from work one evening and found him, uh, I don't know, he was 'out of it.' I talked to him and he didn't hear me, I shook him and it must of took me ten minutes to bring him to awareness. When he finally came back to his senses, he was angry at me and said he had almost stopped his heart from beating. Said he had almost done it, said he was almost gone. I was helpless and could find no one to help him; hell, no one understood what was happening, at least no one I could find. It's a long story but they soon found him unconscious in a nearby motel room. They never *knew* what he did to himself. They rushed him to a hospital where he went into a coma. After that he was taken to a Veteran's hospital where he remained in a semi-coma."

Molly paused to catch her breath and Cary wanted to comfort her but he thought it best to let her continue while she could. He knew it was difficult telling him all of this but he felt it was good for both of them. Good for Cary to know what pain she held within and good for Molly to let it all out so she continued.

"I went through hell trying to manage our affairs and work at the same time. You wouldn't believe the doctors, the lawyers and the preachers I fought with to survive. For instance, after one of his accidents, the officials impounded his car and he committed himself to a private mental hospital. The next day I went and retrieved the car and soon after that I received a notice for Thomas to appear in court. As he was in a mental hospital, I knew he couldn't do this, so I went to the county attorney's office for help. The only person I was able to see was the assistant attorney. I explained my predicament and asked if I could appear in court for my husband. He told me to have a seat on the couch in his office. It was a shock to me when I realized his intentions were not on my questions, but more my position on the couch and how close he could sit beside me. He kept sliding towards me and I kept sliding away. When my sliding took me to the end of the couch, I politely reached for the door and slid on out and fled.

"I came back the next day and peeked inside; not seeing the assistant. I waited until I was able to talk to his boss, the county attorney. I was relieved to find a very decent and helpful human being. After hearing me out, he told me, 'You have enough to worry about, just go and take care of your husband.' The case was dismissed.

"Well, he lay in that Veterans hospital for three years—

*three years* he laid there slowly curling up in a fetal state. Three years and he finally, mercifully, died. I stayed with him until the bitter end. After all that time, they still never figured out what he did to kill himself, or if he actually did kill himself. I don't really think they had any idea what had happened to him." Tears had been flowing for awhile and she was trembling.

"Didn't anyone try to help you, a minister or somebody?" Cary asked.

"Oh yes," she said, "somewhere about this time I lost my job and a minister I knew did come along, talked to me and offered me a job. It wasn't much but I was desperate. The job was helping him in ministerial duties at his home. It was only days before I discovered he had the same intentions regarding me as the assistant attorney had and I got the hell out of there; so much for God's assistants."

"Seems like we've both had misadventures with ministers, haven't we?" Cary said.

"Yes, seems so, I won't bother telling you about my doctor who displayed similar tendencies." Cary was speechless and tried to comfort her but she pushed him away.

"Let's go back a minute," she said, "let me tell you a good one of why I lost my regular job. It was very hectic during this period; my husband in the VA hospital in a coma, and me trying to work. I would get emergency phone calls every so often from the hospital as there were various immediate problems that had to be addressed concerning the state that Thomas was in. I went to the head people at my job and they were very understanding of my situation and they ordered all my supervisors to cooperate with me and give me some leeway under the circumstances. Well, they all did except one and he was my main supervisor. I realized much later that he was a sadist. More then once he wouldn't give me messages until the end of the day as I was leaving work.

"He would say, 'Oh, did you get the message from the hospital that came in this morning?' and 'Oh, did I forget to tell you?' This sort of thing went on and on. He would watch my reaction as the panic struck me. When I screamed at him for not telling me, he just stared at me with the most evil grin you ever saw. This must have gone on for months and my hatred built for this man. Talking about killing someone, yes, in my mind I wanted to do it.

"Then one day a strange thing happened. He was standing by a huge dumpster and my thoughts were that I wanted him to fall in where it would have killed him. I knew, as you do, I was no killer, I knew it was wrong and I wouldn't have done it. Well, evidently thoughts are things as Cayce said, because about this time he *did* fall in while the compactor was turned on. With horror, he watched that compactor arm pushing at him. I hit the button that turned off the electricity right before he would have been squeezed to death. Now I thought; he *knows* what it *feels like* to be pushed and squeezed. I had no choice but to quit my job. I mean, I would never have pushed him but the thought that my mind could have done such a thing scared me so much that I quit. I suppose it was just a coincidence. But on the other hand, who's to say what thoughts can do? Hell that incident could have cured him, but I was in no condition to hang around."

Molly sighed and sat down to rest on a rock ledge. "During this time, when his death was near, I went to the cemetery and purchased two grave spaces for us. After he died, I seemed to find myself at the cemetery all the time. Where else did I have to go? All my loved ones were there. They lay side by side, my Dad, my first love, my last and I've been numb ever since. I've just been trying to keep my job that I have now; it's all I can handle, much less to think about another man. That is, until you came along and somehow I *identified* with you. Somehow I sensed that you were hurting like I was and I couldn't *help* but being drawn to you. *That's* the *reason* I'm still here, that's the reason I've hung around *waiting* for you!" Molly's tears were now flowing down her cheeks.

Cary could only think to himself; all this time I've been grieving and she could tell, but I never had the insight to realize the extent to which she was suffering. A sense of shame came over Cary, he felt small and ashamed that he was so absorbed with himself that he couldn't see her suffering.

"So that's why I'm by myself," Molly continued, "looking for a man and to get married was the last thing on my mind. I felt I had done enough damage for awhile, I thought I would give humanity a rest." Cary couldn't comprehend her suffering and he was floored by all she told him. He looked at her in amazement and his voice was broken when he tried to speak.

"And... and... you're *still* standing," he said. "Damn, I had *no* idea, I knew something was wrong—but not all *this*! Oh, my God! You've been rocked four times—what God would allow it? You said you could see my suffering—I couldn't see yours! How do you cope?"

"I pray a lot… everyday."

"But how could you keep your faith, my God, your father dying when you're seventeen, your fiancé dying when you're twenty, then your first husband betraying you and then of all things, your last husband killing himself a few years later. You make me feel ashamed of my suffering; it was nothing compared to yours. It's a wonder you're not in a mental hospital. How do you keep your composure?"

*"I've been holding back the scream!* For years . . . I held back the scream, but finally I relented and *just let it out and* . . . and you know . . . it helped me."

"*Jesus*," said Cary. He caressed her softly and stroked her hair and held her for a long time and finally said, "Molly, I want to help you."

"I want to help you too," she answered and returned his embrace. She looked up at Cary with eyes still wet. "Cary, do you really think… do you *really* think you could help me overcome this pain, these terrible memories? Do you think I could transform myself as you were telling me with the Secret? Do you *really think it's possible*?

"What I was telling you about the Secret is no pipe dream, no pie in the sky."

"But I can't imagine me doing it, I can't imagine anyway possible to erase my suffering."

"Well, Molly, I'm on the verge of doing it myself. All you have to do is see if it works on me. If it does, I'll be living proof," he said with a smile.

Molly was shaking her head. "It just all seems too complicated…I just don't understand how it can work."

"You ask for what you want and then cling to the highest virtue, patience, then incidents will appear out of the blue and these events can change your life in ways you can't now imagine. Don't worry, I'll lay it all out for you, and as I said, you don't have to understand it to make it work. I'll give you one example that's simple to do, so simple that you may think I'm kidding—

but I'm dead serious. You remember the tale about Aladdin and the lamp. Aladdin holds his lamp, brushes it off and out pops the Genie. The Genie always makes one statement, "Your wish is my command." The story goes on to say there are only three wishes she will deliver, but the truth of the matter is there are no limits. Ask, believe, and it will happen. We'll start you on that one, but you will *have to believe*. That's the hard part."

"Is that what you were telling me about applying yourself?

"Yeah, well, that's one way, but there are other ways. For instance, I've typed a list of affirmations and placed them on the door of my refrigerator. The list contains things I've asked for and I read them out loud every morning. I believe . . . I expect to receive what I've asked for. There is something else I think is important to do, I repeat these words with great intensity, which is what I did before the disappearing girl came to me."

"Oh . . . my . . ." Molly murmured as Cary put his arms around her. They held each other close and their tears intermingled as they stood high on the mountaintop. They were silent for a time and many silent prayers were said. Shadows from clouds were forming below but the sun shone brightly on their faces as they dropped to their knees in unison with hands clasped tightly. They lifted their eyes towards the heavens and intensely sent their vibrations to the forces above. Cary's journey had already begun and today Molly was taking her first step in learning the Secret and Cary's dream of helping her had just begun. They were there for hours and eventually made their way down as daylight was fading.

They went into the house and Cary watched Molly play with Barton as he tended the fireplace as it was still cool in the mountains in early spring. Molly and Barton took easily to each other as if they were old acquaintances. They later put him to bed and Cary watched as Molly carefully tucked him in and tenderly kissed him on the forehead. She looked down at the little boy and said, "It's strange but I feel like we know one another, maybe the forces above have sent me the little boy I've always wanted."

"You've never had a child?" Cary asked.

"No, it was just one of the things I'd never gotten around to, but I've always wanted one."

Cary guided her back to the great room and they sat on the leather couch facing the warm fireplace. "You know the Lord works in mysterious ways." Cary said.

Molly crossed her legs and grabbed a pillow for comfort, grinned and said, "You mean maybe I should pray for a child?"

"You could, but my advice is to pray for a husband first, you know they generally come before the children. That was the mistake I made, you know."

Molly knew that Cary was referring to his prayer for a son

while not praying for a wife. "Okay, but I will pray for the husband I *want* and God won't have to find one for me." Then smiling she said, "Aren't we a couple of characters?"

"How so?"

"Here we are; two people with devastating pasts and as strange as it seems, I feel we have been drawn together for some reason."

"Maybe the forces above are playing with us," he said.

"You mean, you think there is something spiritual going on? Something spiritual involved in bringing us together?"

"Maybe God wanted us to realize that we were not alone in our suffering," he said. "Maybe He wanted us to realize there were other lives more devastated than ours."

"And maybe God brought us together to help each other," she said.

"You mean, you think it's possible for one damaged being to help another?"

"Maybe that's the answer . . . yes, maybe that's the answer . . . ."

"What do you mean?" he asked. Molly was now up and pacing back and forth in front of the now-blazing fireplace. She seemed to be in deep thought; her fingers were pressed to her forehead as she turned to Cary as though something had just dawned on her.

"Well," she said, "maybe . . . maybe—it just might be that helping others is the answer for both of us. It sure seemed *helpful* to me to *want* to help you! Somehow, it seems that was the *reason* I kept coming *back* to you, kept waiting for you. It seems I needed to *help you* so as *to help myself.* Cary . . . I'm trying to reach closure over my hurt; I know I have to put it behind me. I know if I don't, I will only be hurting myself in the long run. *Now* you've got to do the same thing!"

"No disrespect Molly, but your loved ones are dead and buried while mine is still alive and in bed each and every night with another."

As Molly listened to Cary, it became clear that he had not received closure and was still living in pain. She knew that to save him, something had to be done. She turned to him in a confrontational manner and said, "She's married Cary, would you take her back now if she was available?"

"Of course not! This is about closure—not reconciliation."

"You've got to find closure *now*...or it's no good between us!" Molly said. Now it was Cary who was up and pacing beside Molly. The two narrowly missed brushing each other as they walked in deep thought back and forth in front of the fireplace. "Have you ever thought of hypnosis?" Molly asked. "You know, having those memories of her erased from your brain."

"Sure, I looked into it, but all in all, it didn't seem the right thing to do. I gave it serious consideration but then decided against it." Cary said absent-mindedly as his mind was deeply troubled at Molly's words of "no good between us."

Molly continued looking for answers as she thought to herself; *I'd like to stomp her out of your brain.* "Cary, has it ever crossed your mind to *forgive* both of them?" She asked.

He thought of what she said for a minute and answered, "You know, I did that once and it worked. Oh it was not concerning her, but it was something that my parents accused me of when I was in my teens. It's insignificant now but back then I was very depressed over it and couldn't find a way to release my anger. I remember praying to God to let me forgive them. I'll never forget it; in a matter of weeks the anger had completely disappeared and you know... the prayer really worked."

"Maybe it wouldn't hurt if you tried that again—concerning them?"

"I don't know, maybe I can, it will be very hard... but yes, I'll try," he said.

"You'll try, huh, well... what else did you have in mind—you plan on kicking their asses?"

You wouldn't believe how close I've come to doing just that."

"And where would that get you?" she asked.

"It'd *sure* make me feel better . . ,"

"Yeah, and you'd end up in jail sure as *hell*!"

"I think it would be *worth* it."

"See—you shouldn't even let those thoughts enter your head; remember what mine almost accomplished. Cary, how many loves have you lost because of this? Do you want to lose *another*?"

Cary thought back to the bet Molly was going to make, "Molly, you remember what you told me, that you had something for me to bet on, that I *couldn't* afford to lose?"

"Yes."

"Well, after you hung up... it only took me a minute to know what you were going to bet."

"What was that?" she asked.

"It dawned on me, as you said it would, the only thing I could think of 'not affording to lose'—was *you*."

Molly stared at him for a moment and finally said, "I thought it might come to you . . . sooner or later, but my dear man, the bet has not been decided yet! Not until you find a solution, a healing to your problem." Molly was quiet, trying to think and then turned on Cary, "Cary, you're not psychotic, you may be suffering from unresolved psychological problems and I think you know that, but—why haven't you driven to her home and confronted her and her husband and hashed it all out?"

"You don't understand Molly, no one understands! I'll *tell you why*! If I did that, I . . . I'm afraid of what I would do . . . I'm really afraid I couldn't control myself . . . I'm terrified I would do something *horrible*. Seeing another man with my wife—*I'm afraid I'd . . . I'd . . . awww, hell—don't* you see? Whatever I'd do . . . I'd make an ass out of myself, then everyone would think I'm nuts for sure." Cary was walking in circles, hands flailing, "*Hell,* because of the shrink's diagnosis, *some* people may already think I'm unstable, and *if* I did that—they would really be sure. I *couldn't* live with that."

"No one thinks you're unstable— "

"Maybe not, but some would *perceive* me to be and that's *just* as bad! It's the stigma attached, you know? *Don't* you see," Cary said pleadingly, "I'm stuck . . . I'm in a quandary."

Molly's tears were falling but she wouldn't give up. They now were revolving around the leather couch like two boxers, "Cary . . . *sometimes . . . you have to take a chance,* sometimes you have to live life with a little reckless abandonment . . . *you can't hold it all inside . . .* or you may *miss living* altogether! I *love you . . .* you've *got* to do *something . . . .*"

"*Well, hell's bells*! I've been *trying* to do something, there's *got* to be something—it's *not* right what they did to me. It goes against every grain of decency. Her husband is lucky old-fashioned duels were outlawed, because if they hadn't, one of us would've been dead long ago. I *have* to do something . . . don't you *see*, *don't* you *understand* what Gary Cooper felt in the movie *High Noon?* It was a *matter of honor* for him to face up to those who were trying to kill him. He *had* to *do* what he had to do *even* if it would mean *losing* the woman he loved!"

Molly turned her face from Cary and started giggling, but soon she was overcome and exploded in laughter. Cary just looked at her with a blank expression and said, "Well, I can see you're just like Gary Cooper's wife—she couldn't understand *either*!" This caused another eruption of laughter as Molly held her jiggling stomach and tears came to her eyes. She finally recuperated enough to speak.

"But . . . but . . . this isn't a movie Cary, *this is reality*!" She said still laughing as she plopped down on the couch resting between rounds.

"I liked the movie better," he replied. She shrieked again and doubled over with laughter and Cary couldn't help but smile as she came forward and embraced him. For a moment his body trembled and his only hope was that he could hold her forever.

Molly's eyes lit up, "Cary, *I think the answer to your closure has come to me. Yes—I think I've got it*! When you were telling me all about the incident concerning the disappearing girl; you mentioned you had a strange dream that very same night. Are you sure it wasn't something more, maybe a foretelling of the future, *maybe* a message that you brushed off as a nightmare? Didn't you tell me the next morning, after the dream that you felt a strong spiritual obligation to tell the story of the disappearing girl in a book?"

"Yes, I did and still do, *more* than ever! What are you getting at?"

"Maybe that dream was a spiritual one, maybe the Almighty was trying to tell you something" Molly said.

"After the dream I did have a tremendous urge to write the book and tell about the disappearing girl."

"I agree . . . but think a minute—were you going to explain in the book *why* you were praying?"

"Because I was hurting."

"And *why* were you hurting?"

"Because of Scarlett—"

"*That's it! That's it*!" Molly shouted.

"That's what?"

"You *would* also be telling about Scarlett, and *don't* you see, you would be releasing all that pent up rage, all that poison your body is consumed with. *Don't* you see? *Don't you* understand?"

Cary was silent for a while trying to comprehend everything she was saying and finally grinned. "Why would the man upstairs pick me for such a project?"

*"He was answering your prayer! He was answering your prayer!"* Molly was jumping up and down, happy that *she* understood and praying that he would. "You see, I can't speak for the Almighty, but I believe He knew if He sent the disappearing girl, you would tell the story about her, but he also knew to tell the story, *you would have to explain about Scarlett* and the Lord *knew* that would release your pent-up rage and it could bring you closure." Molly was staring at Cary as she spoke. "As you said, God works in mysterious ways. Why did He pick you to tell the disappearing girl story? He didn't just pick you; He was answering your prayer! On the other hand He may also have *picked you to tell the story of the 'girl'* because *you're* a *non-conformist* and would speak the truth *no matter* what the cost! No matter what other people would say, no matter what the consequences! *You picked your God… you* prayed to Him, now—are *you man enough* to speak *for Him*? You would *only* be telling the truth . . . and if the truth hurts—*so be it*! There is nothing wrong with anger, hell, Jesus got mad. And now it's *about time* you do; release your anger and frustration in a book and maybe, just *maybe*, it will solve your problem. Scarlett is part of the story any way you look at it. She did love you… and you her… I don't think she was a bad person, I just believe things happened for a reason, and in your case, maybe *only God* knows why. The Lord above knew you couldn't tell the *whole* story

without including her, so you might as well tell it all, but—you must be truthful, *for only the truth... will set you free*. You've been holding these hurtful feelings in your mind concerning Scarlett and until you release them, you'll *never be free* and *whole* . . . and *we* will *never happen!* Don't you understand there are people, who knows how many, that are walking around daily harboring similar hurtful feelings and living in misery. Unfortunately no one explained to them or you how to get help. I learned one thing . . . there is some way, *some how,* that you have to purge yourself from these demons. Until you do you'll never be *whole* . . . you'll never be able to give love and consequently, you'll never be able to receive love. I'm telling you Cary, it *can* be done."

"Easy to say but hard to do," said Cary.

"Well, it's your choice you stubborn ass if you want to help yourself. Otherwise you'll remain just like many others, just wasting the rest of your days walking in a dazed trance. People have tried many things to overcome what you're trying to do. Me—I screamed my way out.

"Some used punching bags to release their anger and unfortunately some of these punching bags turned out to be their loved ones. Some did realize the need for a psychologist and the ones that could afford it made the attempt.

"But psychologists can't cure everyone, some people

they just can't reach. Others gave up, turned to drink, and wasted their lives away. Many times I would enter a closet and scream at the top of my lungs. Don't laugh; in my case it helped, I would just scream my problems away. In your case, I think your best hope is to release it *all* in that book you're going to write, tell the *whole* story, including Scarlett, for she was involved, right or wrong. After all, she was the cause of your suffering and that was the reason you were doing all that praying and the praying is what brought the disappearing girl to you. You must t*ell it* all, *release* your rage, *tell it like it was,* let the chips fall where they may and— *get it out of your system and cleanse yourself! Expend your pent-up rage in a book and it just might cure you and bring you closure*."

They both collapsed on the couch, exhausted, and finally Cary *knew* it was time to tell her about the house and the money. He dreaded telling her and it showed on his face. "Molly, I can't wait any longer, there's something else I have to tell you."

"Something else? Like what?"

"All the invention money is gone."

*"Do what! Gone? You're kidding*! What happened?"

"The buyers of the invention found the flaw and well, they demanded the money back . . . and I gave it to them."

"Not this beautiful mountain home too?"

"Yes, it too, I'm a millionaire no more."

"*Just like that*! You gave the money back—and after *all* you've been through. You knew you didn't have to, *didn't you*?" Molly looked him over, mouth open . . . analyzing him from top to bottom, wondering if he'd lost it, and wondering if she *really knew* this man sitting next to her. "What could've *made* you do such a thing?" she asked. "I'm afraid you've really lost it this time Cary? I'm sorry . . . but I *really* think you've lost it—I really do."

Cary was studying the floor when he spoke. "It just wasn't worth the hassle . . . it's a long story."

"Damn . . . I'm sorry . . . oh *hell!* I don't know *wha*t to *think*!" Molly was back walking the floor again but abruptly stopped and turned on him. She threw up her hands in disgust. "I'm really sorry Cary . . ." she mumbled. "A long story, *huh?* Well . . . *maybe* sometime you can tell me the long story, but for now—it's all *too much!*" *And another thing, it appears that* all this talk about you *really* writing your book is just that—*talk, and talk just won't cut it."* She put her hand up in a defensive gesture and backed away trembling. "*I've got to think about it* . . . I've got to think *about us* . . . I think its best I go . . . please . . . please take me to the airport, *now*."

They drove in silence to the airport and Cary left her there with her thoughts. They were all talked out and the last thing she said was, "Good luck Cary."

Cary's house had finally been sold and he and his son evacuated the mountain home and moved into their cabin beside the Maury River in the valley below. He thought of everything Molly had said and knew it was time to overcome his stubbornness. While he was thinking, he spent his summer days taking care of his son, cutting wood for his fireplace, fishing in the Maury River and finally started writing his book. He started slow but soon with a passion, he began writing continuously for hours, then for days and the days turned into weeks. He wrote until he was exhausted, but soon realized he was releasing his pent up rage concerning Scarlett, and as the weeks went by, he began telling of the disappearing girl, and it was then he noticed a phenomenal feeling. It happened one morning when he awoke, the hurting was easing, it was actually going away, he was amazed, it was the first time he had ever felt a descending release from his burden, as though a heavy weigh was lifting from his heart. He wanted to scream in happiness, in thankfulness to the Almighty. Molly was right he thought as he smiled; the more he wrote the better he felt, and was amazed at the occurrence. Maybe with Molly's help, he had found the pearl of great price, an answer to his long time suffering that seemed would never end.

Each evening he would idle his time away sitting on his front porch swing formulating the material for his next chapter.

His front porch overlooked the quarter mile lane that led to the hard surface road. He would sit there every evening until after dark while enjoying every aspect of Mother Nature's parade of life. There were the soothing cooing of the mourning doves and the sighing of the whippoorwills. The mountain hollows and valleys were alive with every type of wildlife, there were deer, squirrels, rabbits, foxes, woodpeckers, groundhogs, owls and various other creatures that kept him company. Cary thought of the Almighty, He took care of these creatures; each and every one were ordained in all of God's glory and didn't the scriptures say that we were of *more value* than any of these, and didn't He say that He knew the very number of the hairs upon our head. God was taking care of them he thought and he hoped He would take care of him.

Cary took a deep breath and thanked God for the things he did have, he had his son, Molly was safe, the Almighty had revealed a miracle to him with the disappearing girl, his ulcer had been healed, there were a few dollars in the bank, Jim's money was hidden somewhere, the book was started, and for the first time in years, his hurting had subsided. He had been at his cabin for three months, three weeks and four days when he glimpsed a movement at the far end of his lane. Was it another animal? By the size he thought it probably a deer as no human had entered his lane since he'd moved here. The evening valley mist was lingering close to the ground as he tried to make out the form. This animal was walking upright, taking small steps towards his home. It was then the wind blew, the mist cleared, and he could make out the form. It was another one of God's glorious creatures. *It was Molly.*

## *Author's Note*

Chapter twenty-one, The Disappearing Girl, is true in every detail.

**What people Are Saying About This Book, Based On A True Story!**

"The character, Cary, was awesome!! I was *so* into the story and what a beautiful ending. I started reading the book on Saturday morning, couldn't put it down and finished it on Sunday."— Sharon Hargrave

"*I couldn't put it down*! Finished it in two days. I wished there was more, didn't want it to end... waiting for his next book." — Della Harrison

"Watching Cary making decisions from a broken marriage kept me going from an adventure to a *new* future." —M. J. Roeder

"The story goes from one exceptional experience to another with breathless speed. I was reluctant to finish reading the book because the stories are so perfectly crafted it was hard to "*put a stop*" to it."------------
—Jerrell Sober

"I started it on Friday and finished it on Sunday. *I couldn't put it down*! It was the *most inspiring* novel I've ever read! The book portrays a great lesson to all of us. To always get back up after falling and push forward." —Christina Wolfe

## The Story

Various circumstances have caused Cary to teeter on the ragged edge of schizophrenia. His childhood was one, losing his business because of his embezzling partner was another, and finally his wife files for divorce after asking him to seek help from a psychiatrist.

His suffering was becoming unbearable and just when he was close to losing it, as the last resort, and after trying everything else, he turns to prayer.

And then it happened! A young unknown girl *comes to him and commences to disappear in front of his eyes.* "*You are an old soul,*" she says as she reappears with a white aura surrounding her head, "*I've come to your house several times before, sat outside and gazed at your house. I was pulled here by a light that emanated from your dining room window.*" This window was where Cary had said his nightly prayers for the last two months.

"*What does it feel like when you make yourself invisible?*"
"*Illumination, like being filled with light,*" she answered.

**This is the first time this true phenomenal event has ever been published, and will surely be treasured by all who have wondered of the effects of prayer, and perplexed at the responses they may have received, or not received, to their own prayers.**